P9-BHR-310

Malibu

ALSO BY PAT BOOTH

Sparklers
Big Apple
Master Photographers
Palm Beach
The Sisters
Beverly Hills

PAT BOOTH

Malibu

CROWN PUBLISHERS INC., NEW YORK

Published by Crown Publishers, Inc., 201 East 50th Street, New York, New York 10022

CROWN is a trademark of Crown Publishers, Inc.

Manufactured in the United States of America

Quality Printing and Binding by:
Berryville Graphics
P.O. Box 272
Berryville, VA 22611 U.S.A.

To Ansel Adams, Robert Mapplethorpe, and Man Ray—
thanks for the memories.

Malibu

PROLOGUE

The headlights of the Porsche probed the winding road, and the hot wind moaned through Malibu Canyon. There were other sounds in the still night and the purr of the engine didn't drown them—the howl of a coyote, the throbbing staccato of a fire department helicopter patrolling the Santa Monica Mountains, the roar of the faraway surf. The driver wore gloves of soft red leather, and the wheel twisted and turned as the car powered higher into the hills, leaving Pacific Coast Highway below, a neon ribbon of traffic along the moonlit beach.

A hand reached for the Blaupunkt and the creamy voice of Gladys Knight sang of a man who was leaving L.A. for a simpler place in time, leaving on the midnight train, never to return. Now the driver laughed—a cruel laugh, far from humor. The song was an omen. Because tonight there would be leaving; tonight there would be heartbreak; tonight there would be fear, loathing, and a terrible destruction in Los Angeles County.

The driver looked up and watched the eagle swoop across the moon, its wings magnified in silhouette against the silver backdrop. Then the wicked eyes turned back to the road. A shuddering sigh merged with the music. It was an adrenaline sound, full of excitement and tension, and a foot pressed down on the accelerator as driver, car, and its murderous cargo hurried toward their destination.

On Mulholland Highway the Porsche slowed. A graveled view site platformed from the roadside. The sleek car nosed onto it, tires crunching, and the headlights played across the gorge below. The gloved hand killed the engine, and the sound of silence was broken only by heavy breathing. Next, the hands reached for the empty gasoline can. It flew from the car, clattering against the rocks, before coming to rest in a crevice where tomorrow it would be discovered. The moonbeams caught it, and again the maniacal chuckle erupted from the throat of the driver. It was only a can of fuel, but it was also a death warrant. And it was the path to power, billions, and a horrible revenge.

Now the driver moved fast. The hands reached for the garden hose that lay against the red leather of the backseat. The door opened and closed. The pipe was thrust into the gas tank of the Porsche, and soon its other end was snaking down the precipice. The pungent smell of high-octane fuel merged with the scent of sage and eucalyptus on the night air, and the trickling sound was as innocent as genocide as the gas ran in rivulets among the tinder-dry brush of the canyon. There had been no rain. The earth was parched. The chaparral was dying of thirst at this, the dangerous end of the Malibu summer when the desert winds roared through the canyons to the sea.

The driver returned to the car, flicked the ignition switch, and the eyes watched the fuel gauge as the gas siphoned in a slippery stream down the hillside. When the tank was nearly empty the flow was stopped and the hose was gathered up and stowed in the trunk of the car. The driver walked to the brink of the canyon and scanned the valley for the house. There it was, tucked down low among the rocks, adobe calm, its stucco draped with climbing jasmine. The victim was asleep in there, and the Santa Ana wind was gusting, searching for the flames it longed to carry.

A simple Bic lighter, cupped in the gloved hands against the hot breeze, flared unsteadily in the phosphorescent moonlight. Down it went, toward the ground already wet and dark with the gasoline. The flame burst into life and the wind fastened on to it and made it its own.

The driver stood back from the heat, and then the door of the Porsche was opening, closing, and the engine was gunning, the tires screeching as they spewed gravel into the already flaming canyon. In seconds the car was gone, speeding down toward the safety of the coast, leaving behind the holocaust its driver had unleashed.

The orange ball rolled down the hillside and the sky was alive with marmalade flames. Smoke curled around the football moon, and the brush evaporated, its burning cinders floating on the crazed breeze. The roar of the flames and the searing heat were the only warning of the firestorm as it raced at seventy miles an hour toward the unprotected home, and the person inside.

The flames engulfed the house. They reached into the open windows and probed the courtyards. They consumed the creepers, and they feasted from the beams that projected from the stucco. They exploded the plate glass of the picture windows, and rushed up the wide wooden stairs to the bedroom. The victim was awake now in the short seconds before the longest sleep—back to the wall, eyes wide with the vision of infinity, hands raised in horror to prevent the unpreventable. There was no time for prayers to God, for mother, for mercy from the fire. Instead there was death by murder in Malibu, the heaven that was so suddenly burning in the flames of hell.

ONE

Pat Parker crept through the state-of-the-trend New Yorkers, well aware that she was the only person in the pulsating auditorium who was permitted to carry a camera. Crouching low at the edge of the stage, she knew that her black jersey Alaïa microdress was sliding up her long legs to the point where sculpted thigh became jutting buttocks, but she didn't care. She only cared about getting the shot. It was moving fast, as it always did. The magic moment wouldn't wait. There was no time for dress adjustment, slow focusing, or meter confirmation of the fast-changing light. Here, on the cutting edge of photoreportage, she was flying by the seat of her pure silk bikini-brief panties, guided only by long experience and endless practice. The battered Nikon twirled in her fingers as if attached to them by flesh, blood, and nerve fibers, and the glorious image filled the ground-glass screen as she eased her forefinger onto the shutter release.

At the Brooklyn Academy of Music's "Don't Bungle the Jungle" fundraiser, Madonna and Sandra Bernhard were acting as if they were coming out of the closet in public, and the Olympus Pearlcorder on Pat Parker's hip, and the Pan-X film in the bowels of the black Nikon were capturing it for posterity. She could feel her heart pounding in her chest, and, beneath the wool dress, her taut breasts were sticky with sweat and excitement. As she always did at such moments, she prayed that the image would find its way onto the celluloid, and that no mistake would ruin the picture.

Inside her head, behind the aquamarine eyes, behind the perfect nose with its flared nostrils, behind the full slash of the edible mouth, Pat Parker was computer cool as she made her calculations. She had thirty-six exposures. A fast reload would take thirty seconds. How far were the two girls on stage from a climactic moment? To motor drive or not to motor drive—that was the question. Should she rattle out the film now, and risk missing a hot shot later as she juggled the reload—or should she stay on single snaps like a sniper in the grass, making every bullet count as it banged into the target?

"Sit the fuck down," hissed a five-hundred-dollar ticket holder in the front seats.

She didn't turn around. She didn't even *think* of obeying. Nothing could come between her and her objective, the picture in the can. Nothing ever had. Nothing ever would. She waited, her luscious body draped over the sharp edge of the stage, as she stared up the endless Sandra Bernhard legs to where her bottom bumped and ground against Madonna's.

"I got you . . . . *babe*," they sang to her tape recorder and to the vibrating audience, and many who heard them thought they knew *exactly* what they meant.

Pat Parker caught her breath. The stage was exploding. The steam was rising. She hadn't seen anything so hot since Mick Jagger and Tina Turner at Live Aid. The surprise duet hadn't been announced and the more impatient of the fashionable New York art/design/model-world crowd had already left for Indo- and Undochine, where dinner was to be. But Pat Parker had heard the rumors. She always did. So she had hung around to the bitter end, and it was turning into the sweetest media event she had ever experienced. Madonna and Sandra had been provocative on the Letterman show, and in an *Interview* interview the megastar had hinted that she had entered a new stage in her sexual development.

In the banter before the rip-roaring performance of the Sonny and Cher song they had introduced themselves as a couple of dy . . . big, pregnant pause . . . namos. And while Madonna, smiling broadly, had told the audience not to believe the rumors about their relationship, Sandra had capped it with a heartfelt, "*Believe* them."

Now, before the all-seeing Nikkor 105mm telephoto, the audiovisual event peaked.

The two girls changed the lyrics of the song.

"Although we may not have a cock . . .

At least we're sure exactly what we've got . . ."

In unison they clamped their right hands to the crotches of their identical cut-off floral jeans, and as they did so, hips thrusting, heads flung back in glorious defiance of convention, Pat Parker's waiting finger pounced on the button of the motor drive.

The sophisticated downtown art-scene audience erupted behind her. The save-the-rain-forest benefit at the newly trendy Brooklyn Academy of Music was a million miles from the traditional Big Apple charity bash, and the Suzy crowd—the nouvelle-society Trump types, the Euro-trash, and the patrician Astor/Buckley set—were safely tucked away at the Tiffany Feather ball at the Plaza. Here were long-legged models like Iman, black and hot as the May night; Elle MacPherson parading the best body in the world bar none, way above 10; and the spellbinding Christie Brinkley melting down minds with the brilliance of her smile. These people, the ones who gave the famous energy to New York, cared that every second the world was losing a football-field-size area of trees. Madonna herself had told them about the fatal carbon dioxide that only plants could remove, and explained how it was creating a greenhouse over the world that would one day warm the globe, melt the ice caps, and burn up their grandchildren.

But right now Clementes, Harings, Lichtensteins and Schnabels, Oldenburgs, Mardens, and Ruschas were thinking about something else. They were cheering, whooping, and waving their hands above their heads in delight at the gutsy irreverence and brave honesty of the once virginal, once prayerful, once material girl.

Pat Parker hugged the camera, crushing it against her breast as she looked quickly at her watch. It was past eleven. It had happened later than expected. Damn! This would miss the early morning papers. That meant the story would break in the news no-man's-land of the later editions. But that was just thinking New York—the *News* and the *Post*. Nationwide, *USA Today* would run it big on Thursday morning, and there was always TV. "Entertainment Tonight" could show stills to back up a news item, and of course the tabloid shows like "A Current Affair" would be fascinated. As a backstop there were always the more happening magazines like *US* and *Details*. Right now she had to get the film into the developer to see if the image was safe. No photographer, however great, however professional, took that for granted.

The crowd was surging toward an exit crammed with paparazzi, a colorful sea of psychedelic T-shirts, rap fatigues, baggy pants, and rainbow string ties that were the trendies' interpretation of the invitation's "casual evening attire." Now the faces ran the gauntlet of the Sony cameras and the phallic directional microphones as they muttered platitudes for the sound bites. Nobody would get more than seven seconds. Network research had shown that to be the average attention span of the TV audience. Pat Parker, however, skirted the photographers, and as she hurried down the steps she was looking out for Jed, her driver, and for the Range Rover parked out there somewhere in the oily black sea of limousines. She saw him and shouted out Jed's name, which was when she bumped right into Kenny Scharf.

The graffiti artist was tall and good-looking, with short cropped hair, and he seemed nervous as hell. The jungle bungle evening was his production. He had badgered Madonna into doing it, and everyone else had fallen into place—Bob Weir from the legendary Grateful Dead, the B-52's, and, of course, the sharp-tongued temptress Sandra Bernhard, whose duet with Madonna had elevated the evening from the memorable to the legendary. On stage Scharf had given a rambling speech. His hand had shaken, and it had been clear that the strain of it all was beginning to tell. Now he had something else to worry about. Who the hell had given the Parker girl photographic privileges? It hadn't been him, and Madonna had insisted on "no cameras." The signs were up all over the auditorium.

Scharf looked at Pat's excited face. His eyes fell toward the Nikon clutched in her hand.

"You didn't . . . take pictures of Madonna's duet . . . did you . . . ?" he mumbled hopelessly.

"I sort of did, Kenny," said Pat simply.

Kenny looked desperate. Pat Parker stood her ground. He was far too gentle to make a grab for the camera. If he had she'd have fought for it, and probably won.

"Pat, please don't do this to me. Don't publish those pictures. I mean, I promised Madonna, and she did it all for the conservation thing, and . . . and . . ."

Pat Parker took a deep breath. Kenny's approach was the only way to play her. All her life she'd been tough as nails. She'd had to be. She'd had to survive her childhood, her adolescence, and growing up in the hard city. And she'd had to get where she was today, the up-and-coming photographer to watch, the beautiful one, who looked so much better than all the hard chargers who sat for her portraits. Macho men she ate for breakfast. The sensitive ones at least had a chance.

"I don't know, Kenny. I mean, I didn't gate crash. Medina gave me the okay to shoot. He even put it in writing."

Kenny desperate metamorphosed into Kenny destroyed.

"He had no right to do that. It was agreed 'no photographs.' It was part of the deal."

"Yeah . . ."

Pat Parker shook her head and her blond hair swirled in the warm air of the New York evening. She knew all about show business ambivalence, the love/hate relationship with publicity. You had to do it, or the flame of fame might flicker and die in the fight for success. But you resented the invasion of privacy, the endless hassles, the uneasy symbiosis with a press you despised but needed if you were to keep reality in your dreams. Why had Madonna done that duet? As a secret revelation to a roomful of friends on a "not beyond these walls" understanding? Hell, no! She was a dedicated professional who changed her image with the calculation and split-second timing of a symphony conductor. Was this the unveiling of a new Madonna, a surreptitious trial run of a brand-new persona to see how it might play? It was highly possible. And yet . . . and yet . . . Madonna *had* made mistakes, and they had been emotional ones. Perhaps the film in the belly of the Nikon had recorded one of those—an outpouring of genuine affection that had been totally spontaneous and that would be later regretted.

Pat Parker sighed. "Kenny, she wanted everyone to know."

Kenny ran a hand through his hair. "It was a joke, Pat. She was teasing."

The Parker eyebrows arched and her lips relaxed into a wide-open smile. "Oh, Kenny!"

"I'm asking you, Pat, as a friend. If you don't make it happen, it'll sink. You know New Yorkers. They're so wrapped up in themselves the outside world hardly exists for them. They wouldn't know a story if it sued them."

Pat laughed a bittersweet laugh. It was true. The audience had been so frightened of committing the cardinal Big Apple crime of being the last to leave, that many had missed the climactic duet. Those who had stayed were already wondering where they would be seated at dinner. Upstairs at Indochine, or tucked away in the basement? At the A table with the Joels, the Wenners, and the

Kleins, or languishing in outer Siberia at the back of the restaurant, far from the warmth of Brian McNally's smile? They had limo problems, and how the hell did you get out of this place called Brooklyn, and did they have the staying power for the late-night/early-morning appearance at Rudolf's Mars? None of the city papers would have bothered to assign a reporter to cover the show. They relied on their syndicated columnists for that. The whole shebang wouldn't rate the column inches of the Plaza party. At best the gossip writers would pull a few names off the press release and say they'd been there. So Middle America would be starved of the juicy tidbit, and quite suddenly Pat Parker found herself thinking that might be no bad thing.

She shrugged her broad shoulders. The hell with it. Who cared?

"Okay, Kenny," she said at last with a weary smile. "You win. I'll bury it."

"You're a sweetheart," he said, relief all over his face. He hugged her quickly and disappeared into the people graffiti of the milling crowd.

Pat Parker slowed down as the adrenaline fountain faltered. Wow! It had been a biggie, but she had let it go. What did that *mean?* Last year she would have had to have been ripped from the story by saber-toothed hound dogs. Yet she had just surrendered it, because a nice guy had asked nicely. Was she losing it? Getting weak? She bit her lip, chewing at it gently in the middle of the frantic crowd. But already she knew the answer. She was bored with her life. In the early days of deadlines and graft, and dangerous streets, there had been something to prove as she had run the gauntlet of male sarcasm and disbelief that a woman—a beautiful woman—could do the job better than they. Back then, she'd had no time and less inclination to question the worthiness of what she did, because until she succeeded there was a sense in which it had not yet been done. Now it was. She wasn't the most celebrated photographer in New York, but she'd already had a one-woman show at the Staley-Wise, Crown was talking a book, and her network of contacts among the glitterati and the night fungus was something everyone envied. She knew the city and New York knew her, and she had reached the stage of technical expertise where she could forget about the science of photography and concentrate only on its art. Art. That was it. That was the place she wanted to be. She had surrendered her scoop so easily because winning was no longer enough. What she wanted to do now was to *create* beauty.

Jed leaned over and opened the door of the Range Rover. Adoration shone from his eyes.

"How did it go?"

Pat Parker clambered in like a trucker into the cab of an eighteen-wheeler. Thigh, underpants, garter belt, everything hung out. She flung the Nikon with its once-precious film onto the backseat as if she had gotten it as a gift in a McDonald's Happy Meal. She let out a deep sigh of regret/satisfaction and she shook her head from side to side to let the air at her overheated scalp.

"Only brilliant, and I blew it."

"Bob Weir was that good? The crowd was stiff with Deadheads."

"No, silly rabbit. Madonna just about did it with Sandra on the stage. I got it." She jerked her thumb over her shoulder at the Nikon as Jed eased the car out into the limo soup.

"That's great, Pat. You want we go to the lab an' do the prints right away? Where will they go? The *Post?*"

Pat shrugged.

"The filing cabinet. The wall of the john. Under your pillow, I guess, red-blooded male."

She turned her smile on her assistant, lighting him up in the street glow. Poor Jed looked his usual dear, sweet mess—the wire-mesh glasses, the wire brush hair, the jungle rap, jungle brother clothes—but he smiled back at her, pleased that the boss he loved was pleased with him.

"Whaddya mean we're not going to *use* them?"

"I just promised not to. Guess I'm going soft in the head."

"They *leaned* on you?"

Jed's tone was incredulous, prepared to be indignant. Nobody pushed Pat Parker around. Not while five-foot-nothing of uncoordinated nerd look-alike was rooting on her team.

"In the nicest possible way. Kenny's friendship with Madonna was on the line. He'd promised no pix. Somebody screwed up giving me the okay."

"Jeez!" Jed said it all. Was this the Pat Parker who'd pay in blood for a hot picture if that was its price?

She reached up and stretched, like some sleek, sleepy cat in one of the jungles about to be saved.

"Oh, Jed, I don't know. I just think I'm at some sort of career crossroads. I can feel it coming on. Like, who *cares* about reportage anymore? There has to be more to life than illustrating gossip. Maybe if I'd taken some shots of the disappearing rain forest *that* might have made a difference, but Madonna and Sandra rubbing butts . . . I mean . . . I mean . . . it's hardly *crucial*, is it?"

"Maybe not *crucial*, but I guess it is sort of interesting."

"Yeah, men like that, don't they? Women, too, maybe."

Pat Parker's bright eyes went dreamy, but she wasn't really thinking about the bi-girl duet anymore. She was thinking about her future. Was New York over for her? Had she cracked it open? Was there nothing left to find, nothing more to prove? And if she had scooped the meat from the claws of the world's most complex city, what the hell else was left for an encore? One thing was certain. The challenge would have to come from a different direction. She scratched absentmindedly at her crotch, oblivious to the leaping Adam's apple of her boy Friday.

"Indochine?" he managed in a squeezed voice.

"I suppose."

"You've got a ticket. You get to eat. Table twenty-nine," said Jed. He was her secretary, too, and his information was important. She needed to know where she stood in the dangerous forest of the New York night. Was she just the photographer? Or was she a guest? If the latter, then the famous would relax around her. It would be easier. Brian and Anne McNally, inventors of Odeon, Indochine, and the Canal Bar, were Pat's good friends, but they had to walk the thin line between guarding the privacy of their star-spangled clientele and providing them with the publicity outlets that were so vital to their careers.

Jed snaked through the deserted downtown streets like the native he was. Not many people could do Brooklyn to Indochine without running directions on the cellular phone.

"I'll be outside. No hurry. You want a thirty-five an' a wide angle for the inside stuff? The 400 ASA should be fast enough without flash. I seem to remember there's light in there, upstairs anyways."

"Yeah. Thanks, Jed. Tomorrow's yours. Come in on Friday. You're fabulous." She leaned over and kissed him quickly on the cheek, scooped up the couple of Nikons he pulled from the glove compartment, and opened the door as the car came to a stop outside the restaurant.

She pushed through the knot of photographers, waving to a couple she knew, ignoring the scowls of the many who knew her. Most of them didn't like her. The Big Apple chauvinists had perfected their art. They were jealous of the contacts they hadn't the charm or the brains to make, and they excused their career failure and Pat Parker's fame by attributing it all to her beauty. The broad got in by putting out, they whined. Was there any other way for a woman? In the early days, in the war zone between a job and a union card, some bright spark had once filled her car with grass cuttings to pay her back for getting a picture published. Finding that much grass in the inner city had probably been the most creative thing he'd ever done. For a while, the meaner and more jealous of her colleagues had taken to calling her "the lawn." They didn't do it anymore because even the most myopic could see that the towering beauty was now a towering success.

Pat waved her ticket at the door police, and soon she was inside, her practiced eye sliding around the long thin restaurant, sizing up the scene, sorting it out.

The hot table was stretched out along the wall and the heavy hitters were already there. Billy Joel and the luminescent Christie were sitting with Mick Jones of Foreigner, and Pat knew that Jones was producing the new Joel L.P. *Rolling Stone* publisher Jann Wenner formed dangerous liaisons with crop-haired Glenn Close, and the seriously attractive and footloose Lori Singer. Sweet Kelly Klein wore the 1.2-million-buck duchess of Windsor's ring, and Calvin, the man who had bought it for her, sat neat and tidy in an immaculate suit of old-fashioned cut, one that looked like it might have belonged to the duke. The art scene was represented by stayer Brice Marden, currently showing in the Whitney's biennial. Model, musician, publisher, couturier, movie star. It was an interesting meritocrat mix. The aristocrats were all at the dull Plaza party, and they were the only thing missing. Apart from Lee Radziwill and Tatum O'Neal, most of the BAM "faces" had come on to the restaurant.

People bounced off Pat Parker like Ping-Pong balls in a wind tunnel. They didn't stick. Half a sentence was heavy-duty social intercourse to a professional party player in this town. Maybe it was the coke. Maybe it was the propulsion pressure in the cooker of the city. There seemed to be so little time, so much to say. Or was it so much time, so little to say? Whatever the reason, the fervor of the game-show-host greetings unfailingly failed to follow through as the hungry eyes searched the room over Pat's padded shoulders for fresh social prey.

"Shoulder pads, darling? I know it's difficult to go cold turkey and give them up, but we've all got to try . . . I was just saying to . . . Oh, hi, sweetheart, are you renting Bridgehampton this . . ."

The wife of the arbitrageur charged on, blowing a soundless kiss at Pat to cover her retreat as she fastened onto Di Cummin, a fabulous-looking girl in a Rifat Ozbek multicolored top, whose houses in the Hamptons, Sun Valley, Fifth Avenue, and the Virgin Islands were *Architectural Digest* regulars.

"Pat Parker! Working? In Alaïa? It's not allowed."

Jacqueline Schnabel, fabulous ex-wife of the painter Julian (canvas), had left her husband for another type of painter (houses, the town). The ebullient boss of the Alaïa shop looked ravishing in a leopard-spotted low-cut dress, again by Ozbek, hot designer of the millisecond. In answer, Pat ducked down and took her friend's picture.

"There, now I made money out of you." She laughed. "Come on, Jacqueline, let's go eat. Come and sit at my table, wherever it is."

Number 29 was a good one, making an L with the A table. Pat squeezed herself onto the banquette from where she could shoot right down the corridor of celebrities as they picked at the prawn balls and sucked at the iced Chablis. It was funny. On the East Coast the famous drank. On the West Coast they didn't. But then of course they didn't eat much here, whereas on the other side of America they were always jamming in the fuel for their endless aerobics sessions. She peered around her table, giving Jacqueline a little squeeze to tell her that she loved her. Hmmmm. Mainly queens. In the old days the homosexuals had dressed like women. Not anymore. The macho heteros were dolled out in the frock equivalents. The gays wore wall-to-wall Wall Street. Above their boxlike British-style suits, their pink faces were scrubbed till they shone, not a hair out of place, not a kind sentiment allowed past flossed, bleached, water-picked teeth. At first the tailored brigade affected a lofty disdain for the two great-looking chicks who had invaded their table. They melted a bit when Kelly Klein waved at them, a bit more when Brian McNally came by and cracked a few jokes, and then they rolled over, legs in the air, when Lauren Hutton blew heavy kisses. The Indochinese food that had been embargoed at the far end of the table began filtering through. The repartee began to flow. The New York evening was loosening up.

Pat Parker fired off a roll of Kodak at the laughing faces, called for an outsize can of Sapporo, the hot cold Japanese beer, and wondered why it was okay for the famous to enjoy themselves in the Big Apple but uncool for them to do so in L.A. Somebody should write a dissertation on it. Undoubtedly, in Ph.D.-rich America, several already had. Suddenly, she was having a good time as the existential career doubts of the earlier evening began to fade. Iman and Bond Girl Talisa Soto, trailing a string of black-clothed liquid lovelies, their impossibly long legs draped by implausibly short skirts, dropped by to kiss "hello." So did chic Anna Wintour, editor of the new and more "now" *Vogue*, allowing her glacial façade to drop just an inch or two for the photographer she admired. Jean Pagliuso, fashion photography's Pat Parker and hot from the altar at the Bel-Air Hotel, stopped at the table. She was followed by Peter Beard, the Kenyan conservationist cult figure whose "I-was-discovered-by-Iman" badge hinted at his sense of humor. In a few significant moments, the social center of gravity began to shift imperceptibly toward the Pat Parker table to such an extent that Ian Schrager, Steve Rubell's partner, whose whole life was an exercise in the recognition of such things, actually felt the need to comment on it.

Then, quite suddenly, she saw him. The fingers of alarm ran with Jerry Lee Lewis abandon up and down her back. She caught her breath. She looked again as her stomach tightened. Across the room, partially hidden behind a column, a man watched her. His pallor was not the legacy of the long Manhattan winter. It was the haggard paleness of the terminally ill, and his devastated good looks, his crumpled, listless skin, mocked the memory of the man he had once been. But he was dead. She had been at his funeral in March. She had wept bitter tears for her lost friend. What was he doing, this ghost at the feast? She stood up. Her shaking fingers reached for the edge of the table, to push it back, to squeeze out of the cramped space. Her eyes never left the eyes of the man who watched her. A glass of wine toppled onto the white tablecloth, but Pat Parker didn't stop. Her body was moving but her whole being was on hold. Her essence was frozen over with the ice of dread. Around her, the party chatter was wrapped in a fog of unreality as the faces became Magritte faces, surreal symbols, stereotypes, the flesh and blood of individuals no more. She felt a hand on her arm, but she brushed it away. She had to go to him. She had been sucked from her seat by a supernatural force that terrified her, and she was a free agent no more. How had he escaped from the cold grave? What was he doing at Indochine among the bourgeoisie he loved to hate? Why was he watching her, his hands gripping the arms of his wheelchair, his dear head held high as he questioned her soul across the sea of frivolous laughter, his expression troubled, quizzical . . . mocking? She pushed across the waves of table hoppers, and the vision disappeared from view.

He was behind the column. She was nearly there. She steeled herself. She went around it.

"Robert!" she gasped.

But it wasn't Robert. It was someone else, of course. Someone who looked so very like him.

The mists blew away from her eyes, as common sense came back to banish emotion. The man was Robert's double, and in a wheelchair, and clearly so very ill. She stood foolishly before him, looking down at him, and he up at her as she tried to put her experience into words.

"I'm sorry . . ." she blurted out. "I . . ." Her hands splayed apart to say this couldn't be said. For an age the sick man stared into her face, and she into his as the differences multiplied and she saw that he was not Mapplethorpe, was not really him, was not nearly him. She had invented the similarity. In the midst of the frivolity, her unconscious mind had spoken to her. It had taken her back to the last time she had seen him, wrecked and so near to death.

"Pat," he had whispered as he had held out his frail hand to her.

"Oh, Robert, are you all right?" She had asked her hopeless question as she had dropped down beside his chair, and she had held his hand as her eyes had filled with tears at the sight of his suffering beauty.

"There have been better days," he had replied with a watery, rueful smile. And then he had asked her if she remembered Bond Street.

How could she ever forget it?

It had been five long years ago, and she had been down and out in the big city. She had had no direction, no skills, no money, just the power of her personality, her beauty, and the iceberg of her talent. It seemed like yesterday—a bar downtown, a black guy who'd made her laugh, the accepted invitation to go see some photographer who lived nearby. She had crammed into the rickety elevator and it had been like traveling in a mobile prison as she had headed upward, the uncertain light streaming through the grille of her cage. At seventeen she had known she was not being wise, but she had learned from her childhood that wisdom was a luxury that only the rich and secure could afford. Her new friend, who'd said he was a dancer, had knocked on the door, and the leather guy who'd opened it had seemed so small, yet so perfect, and he'd been pleased to see them in a laid-back kind of way. Pat had flopped down on the black leather sofa and slung her feet onto the fifties glass table with the arrogance of the very young and the very beautiful and she'd looked around the small studio, taking in the oak chest of drawers, the crucifixes, the single lily in the slim vase.

"Christ, it's like a church in here," she had said irreverently, and the guy in the leather pants had laughed and agreed.

"I make altars all the time. It's my Catholic past."

It had started there. She'd admired the flower prints all over the walls and the frames he'd made and designed himself, and he'd watched her carefully with the professional detachment of a man who desired only men. She hadn't been shocked when he'd pulled out the beautiful pictures he'd insisted on describing as pornography, despite their obvious status as supreme art, and she hadn't minded, although she hadn't joined in, when he'd smoked a joint and told hair-raising tales of how the pictures had come to be taken, and about how vitally important it had been for him to be a participant, not merely a voyeur, in the wild S&M world in which he lived. It had been her very first lecture on the value of artistic integrity, and despite the bizarre nature of the subject matter, she had learned the lesson. To record it you had to become it, to be it. You had to be involved, to have a point of view. Otherwise you were just another tourist in town, there to milk the moment of a fast buck, and to live vicariously from the experiences of others. They had talked into the night, and he had liked her, and the very next morning, he had offered her a job as his assistant, and in a moment of inspiration she had accepted. It had been the time and place that her life had begun. At their last meeting, dying of AIDS, he had needed oxygen to help him breathe, but he had fought to talk to her.

"I see your stuff all the time. It's good, Patti. It's very good," he had whispered.

He called her Patti, and Pat had often wondered if that was why he had been drawn to her in the first place. Patti Smith had been the wind beneath his sixties wings.

"It's shit, Robert. You know it. It's meaningless shit."

She had been surprised by the vehemence of her own self-denunciation. It was as if she had realized it for the first time. The clouds of hypocrisy had been blown away, as they were around Robert, and she had been left with nothing but the rude truth of her artistic inadequacy.

"It's a transition," he had said softly. There had been a calm in his words, and they had been full of the wisdom of the end of life. There had been the sad feeling he was talking about them both, voyagers on a journey to the greater beauty, speaking of all the unfinished business and the joy and the angst of all the unfinished business to come. You had only to keep the faith. You had only to struggle and not give up, and out of the weakness would come strength and out of lies would come truth.

Pat had felt her eyes fill with tears. He was a reproach to her, this dying friend from long ago. She had drifted from his world to find her own as he had encouraged her to do. She had thrown herself into the demimonde of the New York night, and she had taken his advice and submerged herself in its creative frivolity, in the dark brilliance of its social satire. This soft underbelly of the great American Empire was as real and as vital as Astroturf, and she had chronicled it faithfully, lending it the eye of her mind, and pulling beauty from the shallows, and plucking art from the lush thickness of the drug- and sweat-scented air. At one time it had seemed to her the most important work in the world. At her last meeting with Robert she had realized she had been wasting her life.

"What should I do, Robert?" she had asked.

He had laughed, the sound affectionate, not humorous.

"Oh, Patti, if there was ever a way to answer that."

She smiled now as she remembered. Robert of all people had offered no easy answers. He had known about the agony and the ecstasy that he had refused to separate from his art. The artist had to find his own way. It was a vital part of what he did, perhaps the most important part of all.

"Are you still able to work, Robert?" she had asked.

"In my mind."

He had smiled at the girl he had always loved and admired. Then he had asked her for a favor.

"Patti," he said, "do something for me, will ya? For the old days."

Pat Parker had felt the tear roll right down her cheek. For the old days. For the wonderful mind-bending old days when she had learned the slippery feel of film in her hands, the snap of the lens as it attached to the camera, the sensual touch of the shutter beneath her fingers. She had bathed then in the soft glow of tungsten and caught images against the hard edge of strobe, and she had wandered deliciously in the gloom of the darkroom cooking the chemicals until the magic moment that the image was born. They had lived at night and slept briefly by day, and the man the world would one day remember as perhaps its most original photographic artist had taught her all the secrets that were possible to impart. For the old days . . . ? Anything.

She had leaned in closer to find out what she was being asked to do.

"Go to California," he had whispered. "Go to Malibu, Patti. Go see Alabama. Do it for me."

Pat Parker's face crumpled at the memory. The sob exploded from her heart. Beneath the bright lights of the big city, she was crying for her dead friend and for all that he had meant to her. She stood there wracked with sorrow, dimly aware that the man who had conjured it all up was looking at her in amazement, a worried expression creasing his parchment skin.

She backed away from the stranger as the tears came from the tap of regret, and she pushed through the party people toward the door. As she did so, she recognized the turning point within her. At Indochine she had discovered her own road to Damascus. Her old life was over. Her new one was about to begin. She would go to see Ben Alabama. She would look for her future in Malibu.

TWO

The notes from the blue piano hung in the heat of the New Orleans evening, sitting sweet on the sticky wind. Across from the building, the L&N tracks still rumbled with the memory of the streetcar, and Stanley, dirty with sweat, scratched at the stubble of his beard. He was a caged animal, all wrapped up in the heat and the boredom, and he looked across the room at the woman he loathed, at the woman he so suddenly wanted.

The ambivalence shone from him, like the moon over the muddy river. He wanted to hurt. He wanted to love. And he wanted revenge for all the insults and the airs and graces, revenge for all the high-blown lies. In the sex dance he would be as powerful as the muscled arms that sprang from his tank top; as strong as the lean, hungry legs that lived in his grease-stained pants; as triumphant as the taut, tense buttocks that would punish this vain woman who stood before him.

The faded Southern belle tried not to look at him, but she couldn't avoid his eyes. It wasn't decent, yet she had to watch him because she could sense his want, and it merged with hers. God, she could smell his sex. It dripped from him, the sensual drops burning in her brain as the summer night breeze plucked at her damp clothes and the blue piano lied that it was all just fine. She wanted to go to him and rub herself against his barbarian body. She wanted to hear his foul mouth yell the coarse things it would find to say. Her pretty yellow frock stained with his sweat, that was what she wanted. But she couldn't tell him. He mustn't know those things. He must never be allowed that triumph, never suspect that anything as common and uncouth as he could light the light of a lady.

So she turned away from his smoldering eyes, and she dabbed at her brow with the cologne-soaked handkerchief and tried to escape from desire in the comforting world of make-believe.

In the front row of the Juilliard Drama Theater, Emma Guinness shared Blanche DuBois's dilemma. She sat on the edge of her seat, and a smile of outrageous joy played across her pert features. God, he was *fantastic!* The moody boy was a dream. His black lank hair was messed up all around his face, and his grimy skin glistened beneath the hot stage lighting. It was the face of a fallen angel. It was long, aquiline, far from the Brando prototype, and the straight nose flared down deliciously from a high brow into the fullest lips that Emma had ever seen. He looked so dangerous. Physically and emotionally, this boy could wreck hearts, bodies, peace of mind. Around him there would be no relaxation, only love and fear, passion and pleading, only the fierce excitement of undreamed-of pleasure and pain.

She half turned to the flame-haired woman on her right.

"Who *is* he, Dawn?" she hissed.

Dawn Steel, one-time toilet paper designer and now in turnaround as the most powerful woman in Hollywood, the studio boss of Columbia, didn't know. But she was going to find out. She leaned back in her chair and asked the minion in the seat behind her.

"He's apparently called Tony Valentino. Not only great-looking, but the name hints at a sense of humor," she said to Emma with a laugh.

Emma Guinness allowed herself a small, tight smile. Goodness, she'd expected to be bored out of her pants by this Juilliard play for the agents and casting people. Instead, someone was setting them on fire. The nobody student actor had his fingers on her sexual rheostat and, boy, was he twisting it in the right direction. She turned to her other side. The girl sitting next to her jumped to attention.

"He'd be wonderful for our 'Stars of Tomorrow' section, wouldn't he," Emma stated. It was not a question. Although Guinness was not her real name, Emma tried to act as autocratic as she thought a British brewery heiress might. Disagreement with the editor of about-to-be-relaunched *New Celebrity* magazine, was simply not an option. Samantha du Pont, who headed up Features, hurried to admit that Tony Valentino would be just perfect for any role that Emma might suggest.

"Shall I talk to him about it at the reception afterward?" asked the subservient Samantha.

"No," said Emma Guinness, quite loudly in the hushed theater. "I will."

As she spoke she tingled inside. God, the body! They didn't have things like that in England. He was tall, about six foot, and he must have spent an age with chest expanders or whatever they called them over here. But it wasn't just the muscles and the face, it was the total package. There was an insolence, a brooding, screw-you James Dean vibration about him that just had to extend beyond the role he was playing and into his private life. That meant Tony Valentino was a Tennessee Williams man, full of contradictions and fascinating dead ends, the aggressive surface masculinity, the primal colors, the overt sexuality masking delicious layers of subtle complexity.

Emma wanted to possess him. She wanted to tame him. She wanted to break him like one might a wild and dangerous mustang, and then to show him off in some safe corral, walk him about, tell everyone casually, "Oh, he's mine."

She looked around to see if the audience were seeing what she was seeing. Yes, they were. And this was the toughest crowd in the world. Every May the fourth-year drama students at the prestigious Juilliard School put on a play in the 206-seat drama theater for Broadway's and Hollywood's finest. The tickets were two hundred bucks apiece, and were strictly invitation-only so that the hottest talent spotters in the business could have a chance to preview the raw material. Now, the agents and casting people sat entranced by the stage presence of the novice genius as he played the part of Stanley in *A Streetcar Named Desire*, the role that had launched Brando's career.

For a second or two, Emma Guinness was sorry that her own impressions were so dramatically confirmed by the knowing audience. She would rather have discovered him all by herself. She didn't fancy having to barge through a checkbook-toting crowd of industry and theatrical hustlers to reach the boy wonder at the reception. But immediately she relaxed. This was the theater. There were no jobs for unknowns. Certainly there was no money for them. The hard-nosed players might be enjoying themselves right now, but they would not go out on a limb for a nonpro when ninety percent of the track-record actors were out of work. She smiled. There was no doubt in her mind. She could have him. The latter-day Valentino would crawl all over her like a hot rash in summer when she told him who she was, and what, if cards were well played, she just *might* do for him. Mmmmmmm! It was a delicious thought.

Tony was lost in the world of his character, but he was detached enough to realize his performance was a triumph. He had it. It was working for him in the way he had always known it would, on this, the most important night of his life. The adrenaline stew was just right, simmering, spiced, bubbling up to the rim but not boiling over. In the superreality he could feel the emotions of Stanley Kowalski, but up there, layered above them where they should be, were his own. He knew exactly what he felt about uptown Allison Vanderbilt/Blanche DuBois so pretty and demure in her yellow dress, because in real life he had taken time out to experience her firsthand. He had seduced the patrician millionaire's daughter simply because he had known that they would be playing this scene together, and for no other reason. He had wanted the chemistry to be right. He had wanted her to want him so that it showed on the stage, the only place it mattered. It was his version of Method acting. While the rest of the twenty students who made up his "year" had gone to bed early, and tossed and turned in discomfort through the steamy New York night, he had taken Allison Vanderbilt, a Vanderbilt whose lineage predated the Commodore, as Stanley would have taken Blanche—cruelly, greedily, mouthing lewd curses and leaving the marks of his fingers as bruises on the smooth white skin of her butt.

Now was the payoff. He could see her tremble as he swaggered toward her. He could see the naked need in her frightened eyes. His body was taut like the strings of an instrument and for a brief moment his own desire threatened to derail his precision. So he reined it in and allowed himself to see not the beautiful, reserved Allison Vanderbilt but the defeated Allison/Blanche of the previous night, her long legs thrashing in the liquid aftermath of his crude invasion. She had wept in the lull after the storm of bodies, and she had tried to communicate with the Tony who had, unbeknown to her, become the Stanley of the drama. But he had cut short her string of words, as Stanley would have done. He had nothing against the upper-class innocent who had tried to talk of love. It wasn't personal. It was strictly business. Because Tony Valentino was off and running to the place he had to be. To the spotlight. To the pinnacle. To the fame that only movie stardom could give him.

Dawn Steel leaned in toward Emma Guinness.

"Good chemistry, no?" she said.

Emma Guinness growled her assent because, unbelievably, she was jealous. Valentino had made love to the girl who played Blanche. There was no doubt about it. Emma felt less certain that the sun would rise tomorrow. Yes, they were lovers—real ones, and tonight while Emma Guinness slept alone between the Pratesi sheets in the triplex on Fifth she would dream of the young stranger in the pale girl's arms. She could hardly believe what was happening to her. Could it be anything to do with jet lag? Had the power and prestige of her new position in the New World unhinged her? Sex had always been something she used. Now here it was popping up, out of the blue, for no apparent reason. It was deeply, deliciously unsettling.

Tony reached out for Allison, and she leaned against his chest as if all her life had been a long journey to this destination. She could feel his heat. She could hear the beating of his heart as it thumped against hers. The acrid smell of him was alive in her nostrils, as the warmth of his cruel, beautiful body lived in her memory. She tried to think about what she was supposed to be feeling, but the counterfeit emotions warred with the real ones. Blanche was drawn to this lowlife as a flirt to the flame of masculinity. Blanche didn't know about love and caring and commitment. Blanche was too caught up in hysterical illusion to have time for such meaningful emotions. Now she was supposed to swoon Southern style in the arms of the macho hero. But Allison Vanderbilt didn't feel like swooning. She felt like crying. All her life she'd been protected. That was what Daddy and the trust funds had been for. Here, in the middle of the raging drama called love, she was beginning to lose the plot. Tony's hands were so rough and uncaring on her shoulders, just as they had been on her naked body the last terrible, wonderful night. For four long years she had harbored her secret crush on the unresponsive Tony. They all had. It was the students' private joke. None of the girls had managed to break through the wall of icy politeness that surrounded him. In the safe distance from him, the feelings had grown until every girl in the class was ripe fruit on the tree of lust. But Tony, single-mindedly relentless in his pursuit of artistic excellence, had noticed none of them. Then three weeks ago he had noticed Allison Vanderbilt. When he had beckoned, she had come running, and in the madness that followed she had fallen in love with him. Last night, however, in the fury of bodies, it had seemed not so much the end of the blissful beginning as the beginning of a horrible end. So now she clung to him like a limpet, aware that this might be the last chance she ever got to hold him. The adoration shone from her eyes. The devil-may-care indifference lasered back from his. His voice rasped into the magic of the brilliant theatrical moment.

"We've had this date with each other from the beginning!" he whispered as the weeping Allison sank to her knees before him. The curtain swept in from the wings, and the audience dissolved into a massive wave of applause.

Tony Valentino stood next to the bust of Dvořák in the reception hall of the Juilliard, and the crowd clustered around him. He knew what had happened. He had triumphed. The play had passed in the blur that to performers was an infallible pointer to success. The audience had hummed in tune to his acting like a high wire in a brisk wind, and then there were his own feelings—the lightness that was lifting his feet from the floor, the almost sexual sensation below his waist, the tingling at the tips of his fingers. He had been brilliant and everyone had recognized his brilliance. From this precious moment on, the world would give him the things he must have. He peered at the smiling faces. Which packet of human skin and bone would give him the first gift? Who would offer him work? Should he stay "pure" for a little longer and stay with the theater, perfecting his art for the silver screen that was his real target? Or should he take the plunge now and sign with a Hollywood agent? He could tell which were the Hollywood players. They had the suntans. They held back at the edge of the crowd, happy to bask in the gravitational field of the man of the moment, but biding their time. The Broadway people had no such scruples. They leaned in hard, not above hustling, happy to point a shoulder to clear the way. Tony got the message. In the Big Apple, his home for the last four years, life didn't wait for you. In the Big Orange, it did little else.

Then he realized that someone was missing. He turned to Allison, standing beside him in the packed crowd.

"Allison, have you seen my mother? She wasn't there when the curtain went up."

Allison shook her head. It would be weird for Maria to miss the performance. Tony's mother, Maria Valentino, was a regular at all the plays. She had herself been an actress of sorts, and the young actors were drawn to her fierce independence, her jaunty humor, and the touching way she handled her prickly son. Allison had often wished her own mother, a patrician emotional prune who wandered through life as if it were a purgatory sent personally to plague her, had been more of a free spirit like Tony's mother.

Tony's eyes searched the crowd. If there was room among all the excitement, he was a little worried. It was his big night. His mother wouldn't have wanted to miss it. She had intended to come. She'd said so. Yet punctuality was not his mother's strongest suit. Nor predictability, for that matter. It infuriated him sometimes, but it was also a part of her he loved. All their lives together they had wandered across the slippery surface of America, coming to rest briefly in rented apartments as the schools and the jobs came and went. The only continuity had been the perpetual motion. A flower-power child of the sixties, his mother had believed with Donne that change was the nursery of music, joy, life, and eternity, and so home had been the open road and the tacky rooms with their tattered metaphysical books and torn Beatles posters, a cockroach-and-grime soup that was always too hot, always too cold, always a billion miles from the security Tony craved. His father hadn't bothered to hang around for his birth. "Not good enough to marry," his mother would say bravely with a dismissive wave of her hand and a vivacious smile, but Tony would not smile, and his hands would clench in anger as he thought about his father's betrayal. It was so difficult to understand. His mother had been so beautiful. The photographs of her proved it. More important, she had charm, that indefinable quality that intelligence tests didn't measure, but which was as vital as it was rare in the sparky war that went by the name of life. How the hell could anybody ever leave her?

Tony turned toward the first-year student who was hovering nearby, the girl who had acted as his dresser. "Tina, would you be really kind and see if you can find my mother? Tell her where I am. Thanks a lot."

The girl hurried off, pleased to be asked a favor by the man she secretly worshiped, as the crowd jostled closer to Tony Valentino.

Across the room Emma Guinness watched him, and her eyes

shone as she waited for her moment. It was almost time. The lover boy was preening himself as if the admirers of the nanosecond would be around forever. How deliciously, wonderfully, predictable. He had strutted his brief moment on the stage and the first whiff of success had gone to his head like hard liquor to a teenage brain. Goodness gracious, why didn't people realize that the struggle was forever, and that the higher you got the more important it was to try harder, to appear more humble, to ignore the increasingly gushing PR? Surely some cheap doctor must have written a book about it. They had about everything else. She took a deep breath. Short and squat, she pumped up her chest, and cut into the edge of the crowd, trailing her retinue behind her.

Dawn Steel hung back. She wasn't a follower, and although she liked the sword-tongued Englishwoman, her sixth sense told her that something unexpected was about to happen. You didn't get to run a studio without at least six senses. The three *New Celebrity* employees, however, clung to their peripatetic boss like Saran Wrap. Already they had learned that the Guinness court made that of the Borgias look like a nunnery. Daggers and gift horses were distributed with a Machiavellian cunning that made it difficult to distinguish one from the other. It was important to stay close to the boss. Over her shoulder Emma Guinness said, "I'll do the talking." The comment was unnecessary. She always did.

Tony Valentino saw the crowd around him do a passable imitation of the Red Sea as the woman stalked through. She was coming on strong and her whole persona screamed "power," but what Tony couldn't take his eyes off were her extraordinary clothes. She was a fashion tragedy of enormous proportions. She was a complex joke, an aesthetic affront, a dreadful, appalling terrorist act of taste. Whoever she was had succeeded in looking like a cross between Little Bo Peep and the Sugar Plum Fairy. Her great bosom heaved out of the tulle, her waist strained against a yellow satin belt that was covered in bows, a tutuesque frock surrounded short, thick legs like the frill on a ham bone. Tony felt the wind whistle from his lungs. Clothes were things he noticed. In all his life he had never seen anything so dreadful. Laughter and tears, tears of laughter, fought for possession of his eyes. He had no idea who she was. He couldn't know that clothes had always been Emma Guinness's problem. He couldn't have dreamed up the paradox that had put the ultimate fashion victim at the head of a magazine dedicated to the single-minded pursuit of style. But he could recognize a disaster when it was aiming at his face.

"Hello, Tony. I'm Emma Guinness," she said, thrusting out her hand at him and smiling lasciviously. Tony took the hand carefully, with minimal enthusiasm. His expression said the touch of a wet fish would have been more welcome.

For a second, her smile dimmed. The Guinness name had scored no points. Drat. That was the problem with nobodies. They were no one. And they didn't know anybody. It would all have to be spelled out.

"I'm the editor of *New Celebrity* magazine." She waved a dismissive hand at the three minions that flanked her. "These people work for me." The "for now" hovered in the air.

Tony couldn't think of anything appropriate to say. The dress filled his vision. Had it been intentional? Was it kitsch? Was it *good* kitsch? He looked at her face. She wasn't ugly, wasn't even plain, but neither was she good-looking. The owllike eyes were round and brown, the nose big and straight, the chin far more than determined, absolutely certain. Her mouth, however, was small and mean, and two pointed ears stuck straight out from the side of her head, giving the unsettling impression of some distant Spockian relative, the other-worldly genes diluted by a few earthly generations. Her breasts were the main event. They were huge and rather fine and, strapped into the Patrick Kelly party frock horror in *Dangerous Liaisons* style, it remained a distinct possibility that they might pop out like twin rabbits from a conjuror's hat.

"You've heard of my magazine," she barked.

Tony splayed open his hands and laughed. His gesture said he didn't know where to begin. The stranger was over the top in every direction. What did you say to thunderbolts, tornadoes, and other high-energy natural disasters?

The woman was smiling again. Her eyes bored into him. First his face, then his chest and torso, and then, unbelievably, the rest of him. She was looking him up and down. The whole thing was surreal.

"You can act," said Emma Guinness. Her tone was patronizing, and at the same time vaguely indecent. Tony was left with the distinct impression that she had wanted to ask, "What else can you do?"

"Thank you," he said coolly. For some reason he sensed that his crowd was listening to the dialogue. Did they know the girl from the top of the Christmas tree? Were they subscribers to her boring magazine? *New Celebrity? New Celebrity?* Wait a minute. Wasn't that the one that Dick Latham was about to relaunch in a media blitz? *New York* magazine had done an article on it. This must be the Brit he had imported to run it. Okay. It was an important, mainline magazine. She could probably do him some good. He tried to calm the screw-you vibes that were running through him.

"We might be able to do something with you." Emma Guinness's laugh was that of a coquette as she dangled the bait before the loser. She peered into what would be his upwardly mobile heart through the limpid pools of the Valentino eyes. Valentino! Really! What had he been christened? Fellatio, probably. I thought Fellatio was an Italian footballer until I discovered Smirnoff. Ha. Ha. Ha. Emma was enjoying herself. This was what it was all about. *This* made all the insults, all the bottom licking, all the social climbing worthwhile. Here she was, using the power of her position to score the most beautiful piece of trade she had ever set eyes on. And there was an audience, and not just any audience. Dawn Steel, her brand-new best friend, was behind somewhere. Then there were the various *New Celebrity* office girls whom she allowed, as a magnanimous gesture, to use meaningless titles like fashion editor and art director. On either side were people who had whole suites at CAA, ICM, and Morris. She was making an impression, and it wasn't on horseshit. Tomorrow quality tongues would be wagging. And tonight it was baked in the cake that the Valentino tongue would be putting in time and a half.

Tony Valentino didn't like it. He was not someone that people did something "with" or "to." He did the doing. He always had. He always would. Once again, he was being underestimated. Yet once again, the underestimater would have to be reeducated. It was a wearying process, but it had to be done. Now he felt that for once it could turn into a pleasure. The puffed-up would-be temptress in the catastrophic frock was an accident waiting to happen.

He swayed back, and an insolent hand found the bone of an insolent hip.

"Just what did you have in mind?" he drawled.

They leaned forward to catch it. The casting couch? What was the New York magazine world's equivalent? Surely not cash?

Emma Guinness knew exactly what she had in mind. The problem was how to get it into words in front of all these people. What she basically wanted was to take this thing home. She didn't even mind if the greasepaint stayed on, as long as the dirty clothes came off. Then she wanted to play with his body, and even more than that she wanted him to play with hers. Of course, before she could get to that she would have to endure a wordy foreplay during which, basically, she would promise to make him a star in return for services rendered. It wasn't such an old transaction, or such an unusual one. The gender reversal was the only topspin.

"A gentleman should never ask what is in a lady's mind," she said and turned the force of her full frontal smile upon him, pushing out her breasts, standing up a bit for badly needed extra height, and letting her tongue play over her scarlet lips in a gesture of unmistakable suggestion. All the time her eyes stripped him. They lingered lovingly on the sallow, grime-streaked skin, on the delicious beads of sweat that stood out on his upper lip, on the mouth that had been made with pleasure in mind. By her side the *New Celebrity* cohorts shuffled in acute discomfort. The boss was excelling herself on the downside. They recognized the potential for disaster, and they exchanged glances among themselves as they dared to hope for a social tragedy.

"You want to put me in your magazine?" said Tony. His tone was still mocking, but he had injected into it a hint of interest, the veiled insinuation that, despite his self-confident pride, appearing in her magazine might be a clever career move.

Emma Guinness smiled an indulgent smile. My, was he pleased with himself! But then this was America and he was an actor, albeit an unknown. In England to be an actor was irredeemably common. It was what the gays did. And the incompetents. Here, of course, actors were aristocracy in the society whose bones, muscles, and joints were constructed of celluloid film stock. She must never forget the difference.

"Yes, we have a section called 'Stars of Tomorrow.' I pride myself on the fact that it is a self-fulfilling prophecy." She wondered if she should have spelled it out for the thick simpleton. "Fuck me for fame" would have gotten through the neuron mess all right, but it wouldn't have played so well with the agents, the staff, and dear old Dawn.

"So you put me in your magazine, and you make me a star," he said, as if he had followed her reasoning with some difficulty, but had managed to reach the bottom line all by himself. He was leading her on. Somehow he couldn't help it. Curiosity was too strong.

Emma gave the laugh she would have described as tinkling, the one that came out like tearing tin foil. She had him. He'd wear briefs, wouldn't he? Not boxer shorts. Perhaps those hideous French-style ones that all the greasy studs wore on the beach in the South of France. Yes, it would definitely be Club Méditerranée in the underwear department. Would they be colored? Red! God! Surely not black! The crowd began to recede. She moved closer. Yes, she could smell him now. No-nonsense masculine. The sweat of work. A million miles from the acrid underarm sweat of fear and excitement. She wanted to reach out and touch his arm. That might be a cool move. Seeing is believing, but touching is the truth. She laid her fingers on his arm, feeling the merchandise. It didn't withdraw from her. It was warm, and grubby, and very, very firm.

"And what would I have to do in return?"

He let the flirtation in among the words like a butterfly loosed in a tense stomach. The slow smile started at the outside of his lips, lit up his eyes, creased the greased skin of his forehead. Was his arm pressing out against her fingers?

Emma Guinness opened up like a flower in sunlight. Boy, for a second there, she'd been worried. Confronted directly by his presence, she had wondered briefly if she was trying to put the bite on more than she could chew. The guy had an aura about him, a distance, the sweet but daunting whiff of charisma. Now, however, she was inclined to think that the whole package might be nothing more nor less than a cunningly disguised stupidity. Good. Great! The thicker they were, the harder they came. Anyway, the contract was all drawn up. It only needed to be signed.

She breathed out, her sigh suggestive, and she lit the fires in what she imagined were her smoldering eyes. She gripped the skin of his forearm, hoping that it wasn't a pinch, and she drew him toward her as she swayed, or was it tottered, toward him.

"What would you say to a candlelit dinner for two?" She laughed to show that she knew it was a cliché. She laughed to say that they were grownups and that beating around the bush was for lesser mortals, not for the gods and goddesses of desire. She laughed to show the world that she could joke, and to cover, with the thin cloak of decency, her naked invitation to fuck.

Tony could hardly believe his ears, but he knew she was serious. He had played her along to see just how far she would go, but he had never expected this. Now he was irritated, but he was not the first to react. Allison was. She had been beside him all the time.

When she spoke her voice was shaking with ice-cold anger. "Tony will be a star without your magazine, or your 'candlelit dinner for two,' " she said. The rebuke was in the words, but it was also in the accent, in the haughty tones, in the body language of the upper-class girl. Two hundred years of history and ancient money peered down the Vanderbilt nose at the parvenue who had dared make her moves on the man Allison loved. The patrician eyes bored into Emma's soul, effortlessly seeing through her social pretense and recognizing her for the class impostor she was. High on the alabaster cheeks of Allison Vanderbilt twin spots glowed red.

Emma turned on her rival. Her eyes narrowed. Her mouth tightened. "Listen, sweetheart, get a transfusion before you mess with the grownups. You look like you've given your last pint of blood. If you could act your way out of a paper bag I'd say you were playing a corpse."

Tony Valentino took a step forward. "Don't you *dare* speak to Allison like that," he exploded. "Who the *hell* do you think you are? You prance in here, like some Christmas decoration come to life, and you make the most disgusting and unprofessional suggestion I have ever heard. Are you on something? If you are, for God's sake go get some help."

Emma Guinness took one short, fast step backward. Her head rolled on her shoulders, her face was wiped clean of expression, and for a second or two it just hung there, pancake flat, as it prepared for various depictions of shock. A hand flew to her open mouth. Breath rushed into her lungs. "Oh!" she heard herself say. "Whoooooooh," agreed the listening crowd. The adrenaline sluice gates had opened inside her. She was sinking. She was falling. Her insides were an elevator on the move. The words were still whacking into the target, but they hadn't yet acquired the meaning that would cause the pain. It was numbness time, but already it was ceasing to be. *Unprofessional!* In America, the ultimate abuse. *A Christmas decoration!* He was being rude about her frock. He had sussed her Achilles heel. He had realized that she was the trendsetter who didn't know how to *dress*. He was suggesting that she took drugs, that she needed a psychiatrist. The thoughts tumbled over themselves and they added up to one word. *Humiliation*. She had been publicly humiliated in front of an audience who would not forget. Tomorrow, tonight, there would not be an employee of *New Celebrity* who hadn't heard the story. In Hollywood, she would be the joke of the week. In speedier New York, the joke of the day. It was the worst moment by far in a life that had not been short of them, and as Emma Guinness tried not to cry, she was already beginning to hate.

In front of her was the boy who had done it. There was no answer to his insults. There was a time for words, and a time for retreat. She was aware that her face was on fire. She knew that they could all see the thick film of tears in her eyes. She realized that her shoulders were sagging. But she still had to get away. Eyes downcast, her heart thumping, her mind already obsessed with vengeance, she turned her back on her tormentor and pushed through the crowd toward the exit. As she did so, she muttered her promise. It was low, inaudible, but to her the words she spoke were the most important she had ever uttered.

"I will destroy you, Tony Valentino, for what you have just done to me. I will destroy you . . . destroy you . . . destroy you . . ."

She was dimly aware of a girl pushing past her in the opposite direction, but she was so taken up with the vehemence of her promise, with the solemnity of her dreadful threat, that she didn't notice that this girl was also on the verge of tears, also shrouded with the aura of misery and defeat, also consumed by vast sorrow.

Tony's smile of triumph died as he watched Tina's path cross the line of Emma Guinness's retreat. He could recognize the body language of emotion as easily as he could portray it, and both the back of the departing girl and the front of the advancing one said the same thing. Anguish.

"What is it, Tina?" he called out to her across the few feet that separated them. But already he knew. Tina had gone to find his mother.

And his mother was dead.

Tony Valentino could do every emotion in the book, but he had never been able to cry. Now he was learning. The tears rolled down the proud cheeks, and his chest heaved with the sounds of his sorrow. He sat, his head buried in his hands, and he swayed backward and forward, and then from side to side as if somehow he could shake the misery from him. The boards of the stage were hard beneath his harder bottom, but the outside world had ceased to exist. It was all inside, where the memories were, the memories of the only person he had ever loved.

"Don't. Tony, please don't . . ." said Allison. She reached out to touch his shoulder, to tell him she was with him, to let him know she cared. And she did. Love made the loved one you. More than you. Through crying eyes she watched his grief, and she prayed for something to say that would make it better. But all she could think of was what she had seen outside the theater. Tina had brought the news of the accident and Allison and Tony had rushed to the sidewalk beneath the underpass. Maria Valentino had seemed so frail, her white frock stained with blood, a rag doll of a former person crushed to death as she had hurried across the road, hopelessly late as usual, to catch her son's triumph. Allison had stood there, bathed in shock and swathed in sympathy for the boy she loved, as he had held his dead mother tight in his arms, kissing her, washing her with his tears, and murmuring helplessly all the things he had longed to say to her but had never said. Eventually she had led him away from the tragedy, and she had taken him back to the deserted theater. He had walked beside her in a daze. Now, Tony's rich voice was small as he spoke through the sobs.

"We were together," he said. "It was us against the world, always. She was on my side. Whatever happened. When I was bad, when I was good, when I was cruel . . . whatever . . ."

He gulped in great lungfuls of air, and he let them out in shuddering gasps, his whole body, so strong and powerful, given over to the emotion the world considered weakness.

"I know . . . I know . . ." said Allison Vanderbilt, who could never know. When she had been bad as a child she had been punished, or rather banished to the wings where nannies ruled. Her parents had smiled distantly and said, "I think Allison is tired . . . perhaps a little bed . . ." and the next day they would be gone, to Kentucky for the horses, to Virginia for the fishing, to Palm Beach.

"She was wild and she was free . . . and she wanted what *I* wanted, not what she wanted for me. She used to say if I killed, she'd hide me, and if I wanted to be a fucking *accountant* she'd be proud of me, because she loved me. She loved me . . ."

Again the wave of sorrow shook him. He had been poor. He'd never had a real home. The high-school diploma from Tennessee actually contained spelling mistakes. His father had abandoned them. Yet he had never been emotionally deprived. His mother had been the foundation on which he had built the mighty edifice of his ambition, and in the tempests of life, she had held firm for him. Always.

"She wanted to be an actress, too . . . she'd talk to me about that and about how all the assholes tried to score her, and how she'd laugh in their faces and she never played the game . . . never. She was better than everyone. She was so good . . . and she was the only one who could make me fucking *laugh*."

Tony slammed his hand against the dusty boards of the empty

stage. Somehow the memory of the laughter made the sorrow worse. Was fun gone forever now? Would the struggle for greatness take place against a gray backdrop, the scenery always drab in the darkened auditoriums in which he would be doomed to seek his dream? He didn't resist as Allison hugged him in the solidarity of sadness. She had known his mother, too. She was a link. She knew a tiny part of the things he was saying.

"I took her for granted. I never told her how much I loved her, how much I needed her. She gave her whole life to me. To me, some bastard son by a bastard who walked out on her, when she could have thrown me away with the garbage and made something of her own life . . ."

"No. No." Allison couldn't take that, and she couldn't allow Tony to take it. Maria Valentino had created him, and he was the most wonderful thing Allison had met in her sheltered life. He was her hero. His arrogance, his focus, his ambition were what she aspired to, born as she was in the will desert of the rich. She had floated through the best schools, through Smith, through the chummy, plummy Anglophile world of WASP America on a cloud of cash and carelessness. When she'd discovered her talent for acting, the family had clucked, and smiled patronizing smiles, and gone out of the way to hide the fact that they were impressed when she'd been among the two percent accepted annually by the Juilliard drama school. But Tony wanted. Tony *was* his desire, and his ambition was a laser so concentrated that it melted anything that stood in his way as it had melted Allison Vanderbilt's tender heart.

"You are her memorial, Tony," she sobbed through her own tears. "She was so wonderful and all she wanted was to make you wonderful, too. I loved her. I wish she had been my mother. I wish . . . I *wish!*"

Tony melted against the body he had used so cruelly. His triumph was empty. The movers and shakers might have watched it, but one had not. His mother had not seen his greatness. And it hurt like *hell* in places he never knew he had, in his heart, in his soul, in his essence.

"I can't believe it . . . There's no point in going on . . ."

But Allison wouldn't permit the self-pity. Not from Tony. Not ever. He was strong. He was brutal. He was cruel, and she loved those characteristics, because they were worn on his sleeve for the world to see. Take me as I am. Leave me alone. Don't mess with me, if you can't stand the heat of my fire. There was an honesty about him that made everything else unimportant. What were the mere feelings of mere mortals in the white-hot crucible of purpose? In the glory land that was his destination there would be rewards that eclipsed the mundane longings for peace, quiet, and comfort, for security, self-respect, and a normal life. The sly nastiness of her own family was another matter altogether. Around her, words were liars. "I love you" had been used so much it was the cheapest currency, and it bought no satisfaction when it was the substitute for the loving actions that alone would have given it meaning.

"Tony, don't ever say that. You'll go on and on and on, because you're you, you're the 'you' your mother made, and she made the most beautiful person in the world."

She hugged him tight, and for these peak moments of sorrow, he was the little boy he had never really been. He tried to see the future through the black clouds, but there was nothing out there.

"I don't know what to do," he said.

It was a question. For the first time in his life he needed help. Allison Vanderbilt took a deep breath. Did she dare to say what she had been dreaming? It was May. Their final term was over. Juilliard was finished forever.

"Tony, let's go away together. Let's go far away, while you feel like this. Maybe I can help. I want to . . . so much . . ."

He looked up at her then, his face stricken, the tears tracing great rivers of grime and grease down his cheeks. It was as if he was seeing her for the very first time, her beauty, the blueness of her eyes, the determined cut of her chin. He said nothing, and his silence encouraged her to carry on.

"We could go to California," she said. "My family has a beach house there that nobody ever uses. We could go to Malibu."

THREE

The bright Malibu sunlight poured in through the French doors from the beach. Power-bleach strong, it played over the already faded Sheraton furniture, sucking the brown from the wood. It ate voraciously at the Clarence House chintzes that covered the sofas and chairs, hungry for their still sharp color. It even threatened the vibrant shades of the Mirós, the Kandinskys, and a lingering Egon Schiele whose misfortune it was to have been hung too close to sand. Mostly, however, the sun shone on the face of Richard Latham and he inclined his head toward it, basking in its rays as if recharging a solar-powered battery.

He shifted easily on the golden chair and fingered the only tie in the room. He hadn't gotten used to Malibu informality yet. But then, in this life, he didn't have to get used to things. Other people did. He looked around his vast John Stefanidis–designed drawing room at the small crowd of celebrities who were his guests. There were maybe fifty named faces, and nearly all would have been asked for an autograph on a street in Peoria. It was flattering that they were there. But soon they would realize it was *they* who should be flattered.

The chairs had been arranged in a semicircle around a lectern to avoid the problems of precedence that could upset sensitive show-business egos. Martin Sheen, brand-new honorary mayor of Malibu, was giving the speech and everyone was wishing that his predecessor, Ali McGraw, hadn't decided to swap Malibu Cove Colony for Pacific Palisades. The speech was a rambling, sixties time-warp affair, full of pseudolove, flower-power idealism, and slack intellectual associations. The good news was that it was nearly over.

"And so I now declare Malibu to be a nuclear-free zone, a sanctuary for aliens and the homeless, and a protected environment for all life, wild and tame."

He smiled around the room aggressively, well aware that his hippie seeds were falling on stony ground, and not caring a bit. The muted, polite applause had stopped by the time he had returned to his seat. Latham stood up. He ambled toward the vacant lectern, his movements slow and unhurried as he let everyone know he was totally unfazed by his "power" audience.

"Thank you, Martin," said Richard Latham. His smile was unconvincing, but his whole demeanor insisted that nothing disturb the outward harmony of the meeting. "I'm sure that none of us in Malibu wants to be blown up, and luckily there are no plans that I know of for a missile base on the Pepperdine campus . . . everything else certainly, but I'm assured nothing nuclear . . ."

He paused to accept the relieved laughter. The actor/activist was getting his from the billionaire, but in a way that couldn't cause offense. They liked the Pepperdine crack. Malibu was always fighting with its university. The seat of learning wanted to expand while the Malibuites wanted everything to remain the same. In the most recent skirmish the Pepperdine growth plan had been given the go-ahead despite the vociferous complaints of the homeowners, who objected to the flowering of the groves of academe in the intellectual desert of the beachland. He peered around the immaculate drawing room. Would the fireplace wall take the Hockney? Would it be happy so close to the Bauhaus painters? He'd have to give it a try.

"And I know we all feel for the plight of the homeless, and, perhaps to a lesser extent, for the predicament of the aliens . . ."

Again he hesitated. This was tricky ground. There were Republicans in Malibu like himself, but not many, and the celebrity activists who crammed the drawing room of his Broad Beach home had voted solidly Democrat. They cared about the homeless all right, but they didn't want them cluttering up the beach, causing accidents on the already life-threatening highway, or cooling the steam heat of the property boom. And the aliens, of course, were the Mexicans. These were irritating when they came from East L.A., brandished stilettos on the beach, and got sick on Corona and Tecate while they swayed to ghetto blaster salsa rhythms.

However, there was the garden to be done and the kitchen to be cleaned and the high-end cars to be washed. Somebody was required to hose down the roof when the brushfires started in the late summer; to house-sit and lug sandbags in the winter storms when the sea threatened; and to cook and serve the quesadillas at the Ali McGraw–designed Malibu Adobe restaurant, which was the slick place to lunch.

"But I think we'd all agree that this is a national problem, not to be solved by Malibu alone. I don't think any of us would like the media to encourage a massive exodus of the homeless and the aliens to our little neck of the woods. Unless, that is, Martin and Charlie and Emilio can find room for them all up at Point Dume . . ."

Charlie Sheen laughed loudly at that. He loved and respected his father, but didn't fully share his ideals. Emilio Estevez, not a loud laugher, permitted himself an enigmatic smile. Perhaps the hardest worker in Hollywood was wondering how he'd found time to attend this meeting.

"But we can certainly all applaud Martin's last sentiment. All life must be sacred here, wild or tame, including the life of the coyote who just ate your dog."

Now Dick Latham laughed, and it was a deeply wonderful sight. His sunburned face dissolved into a liquid of charismatic charm. His blue eyes sparkled like the ocean the audience could see over his left shoulder, and the gull-white teeth, a dental dream, shone in the sunlight that beamed across the dunes. His hair, Brylcreemed in a patent-leather patina, was flecked with the gray of his fifty years, and the weathered mahogany of his skin, firm and tight, was wrinkled only by the exuberant warmth of his smile. Even the sound he made was a turn-on. His laugh hugged you. It was intimate, soft, yet masculine, the laugh of the co-conspirator, of the man who secretly wanted to steal your heart. ,The women just loved it, and the men really liked it, and the special feelings he gave out came winging back, amplified, in the bonhomie soup that was now the room's atmosphere. Even Martin Sheen, chastened by the gentle chastisement, could hold no animosity.

Of course, Dick Latham was far more than his handsome exterior. He was not merely the immaculately cut cashmere blue blazer with the bright burnished Marine Corps buttons; the gray worsted pants with the Wilkinson sword creases; the spit and polish of the Bass Weejun tasseled loafers. He was the richest, randiest man in America. He was the Rhett Butler robber baron who had had the balls to build an inherited fortune into megabucks. And he was single. That, too, was a factor to be taken into consideration as the room shared his little joke with California enthusiasm, the bleached, bonded teeth baring in the money mirth of the early Malibu summer.

Dick Latham flicked into "seriously, though" mode, cutting off the laughter as if turning a spigot.

"Well, what I really wanted to do, apart from responding to Martin's generous and undoubtedly heartfelt sentiments, was to thank you all for coming to my home today. Many of you I don't know personally, but of course your fame and your talent, and your warm hearts have made you public property to some extent, and so, on one level, I know you all."

Flatter them. Go over the top. Beyond. The famous could never get enough of it. To succeed in the movie industry you had to believe in yourself through all the failure years when nobody else did. If you didn't have an ego, you didn't have a prayer.

"Nobody ever accused J.R. of having a 'warm heart' before," laughed Larry Hagman from the back of the room. Hagman had lived in the Colony forever, and there was no Malibu resident who gave more to the community or laughed louder at the cantankerous pomposity of some of his fellow citizens.

"Well, *j'accuse.*" Latham laughed. "I saw you working your guts out for the emergency-room benefit a little while back, and I don't believe it was because you were worried about cold heart failure."

The clapping drowned his words. Malibu's twenty-four-hour emergency room was always in danger of closing down. Residents Johnny Carson, Dyan Cannon, Olivia Newton-John, and Michael Landon had all helped Hagman raise money for the Nighttime Medic charity.

Latham held up his hand shyly, the little boy diffidence quite clearly nothing but a charming act. He had them. All of them. They were on his side.

"I'm a newcomer to Malibu, but already I love it, and I share your concerns about its future. I wanted to meet you today to let you know that my . . . resources . . . such as they are . . . and any expertise I may have, are at your disposal in the fight to get Malibu incorporated as a town and in the battle to preserve it from those who want only to make money for themselves while they destroy one of the most beautiful places on earth."

It was a tour de force of understatement. The Latham assets, the "resources such as they are," were estimated by Forbes at around ten billion bucks. The Latham lawyers, arm in arm, could have spanned the borders of Malibu from Sunset Boulevard to the Ventura County line. The Latham media empire, newspapers, magazines, books, TV, and radio stations, peddled influence that presidents envied. Here, before their eyes, the money mountain was pledging himself to fight on their side in the war that now they would win. It was a magic moment, but it was about to get better.

"And I wanted to tell you, as evidence of my commitment to Malibu, that apart from this little house"—he paused while the property-wise audience appraised it at around six and a half million —"I am negotiating to buy a thousand acres, in various parcels in the Santa Monica Mountains, most of it in what will soon, I promise, be the town of Malibu. It goes without saying that this land will be used in the spirit of preservation, conservation, and total environmental respect. We must look after the land with the same dedication with which we look after our own bodies."

They undressed him with their eyes. What did *his* body look like, this plutocrat from heaven who would help preserve their precious privacy from the hoi polloi? It was why they were all here, difficult miles from where they worked, safe from the prying eyes of the tourists who had wrecked Beverly Hills and Bel Air. In Malibu there were no maps to the stars' homes, no buses full of gawping gapers, no riffraff to disturb the gilded privacy. The nine million visitors who came each year thronged Zuma, and Topanga, and Leo Carrillo, and were far too busy contracting skin cancer to bother the Shirley MacLaines, the Benatars and the Van Halens, the Stings and the Rob Lowes, who made Malibu the star capital of the Western Hemisphere.

The group X-ray vision liked what it saw. If Dick Latham looked after the Malibu hills with the same loving care he expended on himself, then they were home free. His shoulders were square and broad and they indented, via a triangular torso, to a flat, hard stomach. He was tall, and he stood well, with the posture of an athlete, the gorgeous brown skin of his expressive hands merging happily with neat, expertly manicured nails. Were the rumors correct? Was it true that he was in love with all the women in the world, but that he wanted only to break their hearts? Was there an ounce of truth in the stories of his hard, cruel lovemaking, of the callousness of his subsequent rejection, of the suicides and the nervous breakdowns of the girls who had dared to fly too close to the Latham flame? The delicious speculation rolled around the room. Goldie Hawn and Kurt Russell wondered about it, and so did Robert Redford, all Broad Beach neighbors of the billionaire.

Over in the corner, nursing the James Dean loner talent, Sean Penn bothered to think about it, while Steven Spielberg and Kate Capshaw, who had walked across the dunes from their rented house, speculated on what Latham would be like to love.

But Latham hadn't finished. With the flair of the natural showman, he had saved the best till last. "One other thing before I let you get on to the champagne and the Calistoga. I have made one other little investment in the Southland, and I wanted you to be the first to know about it, because I hope that many of you will be working with me at some time in the future."

Working with him? *For* him? And nearly everyone in the room a movie person. It couldn't be. It was.

"Two days ago, I bought Cosmos Studios. As you know, times have been hard there. Somewhere down the line, with your help, I know I can make it once again the very best studio in Hollywood. Thank you very much."

He opened his hands in a gesture that said the formalities were now over. On cue, red-jacketed waiters bearing trays of champagne and mineral water erupted through the French doors from the terrace, whose terra-cotta stone merged with the white sand of the beach.

All around the room his guests stood up. If the heavens had opened and he had ascended publicly to the right hand of God the Father Almighty, Dick Latham could not have produced a more impressive finale to his speech. The redeemer of Malibu, and now, at least potentially a career doctor, too. In L.A. County there was more than enough of all but one thing. There was more than enough sun, sushi, sin, and sexual fantasy. There was far too much money, and material goods, and men with genes as perfect as their jeans. The whole place was awash with a plethora of wine, and wishes, and wall-to-wall women with the wild wind in their perfect blond hair. What there was *not* enough of was work. For every "go" project there were hundreds of thousands of insubstantial dreams. The deals were so seldom "done" deals. The lights were hardly ever green, and the favorite word was *no*. And without the work, where was the fame, the success, the power? Cosmos had been making bombs for the Air Force for the last ten years, and there was no sign of a turnaround. It was rumored that the studio was on the verge of bankruptcy, and if it went under, a vital source of "work" would be removed. Now, with Latham as the billionaire owner, Cosmos would arise phoenixlike from the flames of failure. The collective imagination had been well and truly fired. The moment they got home they would call their agents. Cosmos was back in the game. Overnight, Latham had become numero uno of the two hundred or so "players" in town. Despite the reputed dangers, a couple of the braver women decided then and there that they would risk playing with him.

Dick Latham scooped up a Baccarat glass of '81 Cristal from a silver salver offered reverently by a great-looking actor/waiter. He didn't usually drink, but the room was screaming "celebration." He didn't like to disappoint them. Oddly, at the very moment everyone wanted to engage him in conversation, there was a disinclination to do so. The famous Malibu cool demanded it. These people were genuine stars. The starlets who wouldn't have hesitated to make their pitch hadn't achieved Malibu yet. They were still pigging it in the Hollywood Hills. And the prestarlet beach girls, who hung around the public Malibu, the most beautiful girls in the world bar none, hadn't been invited to this particular Latham party. So the heavy hitters talked among themselves, waiting in sophisticated mode for the billionaire studio owner to approach them first.

The great-looking woman who *did* walk up to Latham was difficult to recognize as one of the world's greatest rock and rollers.

"Hi," she said easily. "Malibu's lucky to have you. I'm Pat Giraldo." She put out her hand.

Latham took it as if it were her heart, holding it for a millisecond longer than was necessary with the delicacy of someone who feared it might break.

"No, you're not," he said. "You're Pat Benatar."

"Only on tour and in the studio. Here I'm Giraldo and I'm Mom."

"When you're as beautiful as you, it doesn't matter what you're called." He laughed to show that he knew it was just an L.A. compliment, but that he couldn't resist it anyway.

Pat Benatar was drawn to him. He seemed totally relaxed. There was no tension anywhere near him. He was apparently devoid of the vaguest hint of neurosis. So few people were totally without anxiety around the famous. Still, as a no-nonsense person of considerable morality despite the raunchiness of her stage image, she couldn't help feeling that there were parts of Richard Latham that were vaguely disreputable. His eyes were too intimate, the touch of his hand too light, too strangely insistent. She was well and truly married, but he was coming on to her. No question.

"I hear you're building on a plot above Zuma." His eyes said that he knew most of the things he needed to know—about her, about everything. At fifty he was too old to be a fan, but he would know that her *Heartbreaker* album had done five million, that she was married to her lead guitarist, that on stage she was the leather lady.

"Yeah, we move in by Christmas, hopefully. Building in Malibu is a nightmare. Seems like you have to get permission from ten different organizations. It took a couple of years to get zoning on the plans. Still"—and she paused and cocked her pretty face to one side, her expression quizzical—"that won't be a problem for you on your thousand acres if you're not going to build on it. What'll you do, pitch a tent and watch the sun set?"

Dick Latham laughed. The supersuccessful were shrewd. When you could work a stage and take home millions, you had to know a thing or two about human nature. Was she on to him? No. She was just firing on instinct. That was cool. *She* was cool in her dressed-down, washed-out, trendily ripped blue jeans, steel-tipped black cowboy boots, and long pink sweatshirt. He took in the tiptop ass, and the tranquil, knowing eyes, and decided there and then that he liked the Benatar/Giraldo split personality, and the hard rock body that contained it.

"I thought I might allow myself *one* house." His voice was mock pleading and his eyes smiled soothingly at her, as he seemed to sway just a little bit closer to the edge of her space, so that she, involuntarily, found herself swinging back away from him.

He reached out for her and took hold of the brass key chain that hung around the rock star's neck, squinting up the eyes that were too vain for glasses as he read the inscription.

" 'Heartbreaker,' " he read. "Do you break hearts, Pat Giraldo?" His voice was creamy, like a low ballad, but it was urgent, probing, asking for some less than neutral response.

"Only the hearts of fantasists, *Mr.* Latham. If you've just bought a movie studio, you're going to have to learn about illusion."

There was a rebuke in the words, in the subtly emphasized *Mr.* But there was admiration, too, for the superb execution of the pitch.

For a second she glimpsed the steel behind the smiling charm of the billionaire. She had patronized him on purpose. He wasn't used to that. But at once the chink in the smooth armor closed.

"It's a pity you're in the wrong line of work, and I can't offer you a job," he said. *It's a pity I can't own you, use you, break you,* said the eyes that watched her. The thought occurred to him suddenly.

"But I could offer you an in-depth profile in my magazine *New Celebrity* when you next have an album to plug. I think schizophrenic mom/rocker caught between male groupies and the PTA would be great copy. I'll have a word with the editor. Get your PR people to get in touch with her."

It was Pat Benatar, not Pat Giraldo, who laughed. She had seen him want her, seen him look for the angle, the way to control her. That was what you did on a gig. You had to find out what they needed, and then you gave it to them, and then they loved you. But she didn't want Dick Latham, didn't need his magazine, wasn't interested in the things his eyes offered. He was too cocky by half. He underestimated people. He needed to be put in his place.

"I heard *Celebrity* was a bit of a disappointment, after all that money you spent on the launch."

The arrow quivered in the center of Dick Latham's psyche. His eyes narrowed, his heart speeded, his fists clenched. Suddenly the attempted flirtation had turned sour. There was only one thing that Dick Latham cared about more than beautiful women, and that was business and winning at business. His father had done that to him. Every day of his childhood he had been told how weak he was, how stupid, how incapable of measuring up to the crude old meritocrat property millionaire. There had been two alternatives in the shadow of the oak. Perish, or grow into the sunlight with a greater vigor and determination than the parent until the young plant was a taller and bigger tree than the one that had fathered it. Latham had chosen the second course. As a result he was *seriously* rich, and his father's "fortune," the one that had always been rammed down his throat, was now barely the income on the income on the income. That was reality, but what mattered in life was how you felt inside. The hungry and the poor never forgot their hunger and their poverty despite any riches the world might shower on them. So Latham could never forget those early days when he had been made to feel a failure by the only person he had ever wanted to think him a success. As a result every business reversal, however inconsequential, cut him to the quick. In his wounded heart he saw every loss as the beginning of the end, the day when the triumphant ride up the mountain became, overnight, the slippery descent down the other side. *Celebrity* had been his baby. He had conceived it. He had watched it grow. He had borne it. Others had expressed their doubts. Did America need another *People*, another *US*, another *Interview?* Yes, he had said as he had put his reputation on the line. No, had said the subscribers, the advertisers, and anybody else whose opinion was remotely of value. *Celebrity* had bombed. It was moribund. It needed the kiss of life. He had given it everything, plowing money into PR, into cover price reduction, and even, in desperation, into give-aways. But money had not changed *Celebrity*'s terminally ill status, and the world in its wisdom knew it. They didn't even want it for free. Okay, so Benatar didn't know about his plans to relaunch a revitalized magazine under the leadership of Emma Guinness, the new and brilliant editor he had just hired from England. But that made no difference. The beautiful rock star had reminded him of what was still, right now, a personal tragedy, and it made him madder than hell.

"Magazines take time," he whispered between suddenly clenched teeth. It was true, but who cared? In Malibu everyone recognized the whiff of failure. It could clear a room. Quite suddenly, Dick Latham turned away from her and plunged into the relieved crowd, leaving the singer wondering just what particular chord she had struck deep in the personality of the strange billionaire.

The Malibu that now surrounded Dick Latham was an impressive group. Sartorially they were a million miles from Beverly Hills, aggressively underdressed, ostentatiously casual. Jewelry was minimal, Adolfo and Galanos conspicuous by their absence, not an Armani suit in sight. Instead there were tennis clothes, Ralph Lauren shorts, Levi's, Top-siders, and Cole-Haan loafers worn Palm Beach style with no socks. The women were exercised, the younger ones happy to show the results in Lycra, Day-Glo, and supercasual stuff from Agnès B. and Katharine Hamnett, body-conscious gear, often of faded denim, that looked its best on the edge of a beach. Those who had dressed up had done so in the clothes of cutting-edge designers, light-years from the safety of Valentino, Bill Blass, and Oscar de la Renta. There were a couple of Rifat Ozbek shirts, three great girls in Gaultier, and a long-legged model in a heart-stopping Isaïa sex skirt, which singlehandedly restored Dick Latham's good mood. He gravitated toward her, through the Paul Young men and the unscented women, noticing the sobriety, the cold sense of purpose, and the almost tangible self-control of the group. Boy, he thought, if California is first and Malibu leads the way, watch out, America. In a year or two the fun and games will be over.

A hand at his elbow deflected him from his tawny-haired target. Its owner was *not* cool. No way. He was small and fat and bearded, and it seemed like he was on blow or booze or both. He thrust his sweaty hand into Latham's and massaged the Latham elbow with his other, as he leered up into the billionaire's face.

"I'm Fairhaven," he barked, "the agent at CPA. Phil Struthers. Grace Harcourt. Fritz Silverberg." He rolled off the second-string clients he represented as if they were a potted curriculum vitae. "I live down the beach. We're neighbors. And I want to congratulate you on the Cosmos thing, and on all your success, and your *beautiful* home." He released the Latham hand and waved an arm around the drawing room, encapsulating the yellow "Benin" fabric-covered walls, the Bessarabian rugs, the Solia carving and the exaggerated swirls of the Grinling Gibbons looking-glass that the David Hockney would soon replace.

"It's just a beach house," said Latham dismissively, hoping his cold water would wash off the creepy crawling thing that clung to him. Across the room, the girl with the micro-mini was watching.

"Listen, beach house, schmeech house. Who's gonna head up that broken-down studio you bought? I got some scripts he'd like. Maybe I could run 'em by you first. You want breakfast tomorrow? I could walk down the beach."

Fairhaven grabbed a passing glass of champagne as if it were a life jacket in a rough sea. His nose was beginning to run. The Latham stomach was beginning to turn.

"We're here to discuss the incorporation issue, not the movie business," he said sharply. Jesus. The girl with the skirt had just cocked her leg forward and Latham could have sworn he had seen a patch of white panties flash against a sun-browned leg.

Fairhaven's skin was not quite thick enough to miss the rebuke.

"Listen, Latham," he said with a surly smile of what he hoped was patronization. "You listen to me. You're the new kid on the block down here. I been here a lifetime. I moved to the beach five years ago, so I know the score. In Malibu you're rich, an' you got a studio, an' you live in a real classy, real expensive home, but when it comes to things like incorporation an' preservation an' all that bullshit, you're blowing in the wind. When people wanna talk all that crap they talk to Alabama." He peered ostentatiously around the room before delivering his coup de grâce. "An' Alabama ain't fuckin' here." He leered pugnaciously at Latham to see how his words had landed. He didn't care. He felt good. He had a mill of equity in the house, business was "mustn't complain," and the Maserati was almost as much fun as the chick he kept in West Hollywood to sit on his face.

For the second time in ten minutes Dick Latham froze. It wasn't the crudeness of the industry bit player. During the long march to the crock of gold, Latham had lunched off nastier specimens. It was what he had said about Alabama. That had hit home, because it was the truth. Ben Alabama, biker, art genius, archconservationist—the most respected and acclaimed photographer in America. Nobody in the know used the "Ben," of course. Alabama was bigger by far than first names. He was monumental, an institution, mightier than the mountains in which he lived, loved, and protected. Alabama had taken over the Sierra Club when his friend Ansel Adams had died. He was president of the Santa Monica Mountains Preservation Society, and when he wasn't brawling with the bikers he loved up at the Rock House in Seminole Hot Springs, he was lunching at the White House, being fêted by every Democrat congressman and senator on Capitol Hill, and selling his landscape prints for a hundred thousand bucks a pop, and his rarer portraits for more. Alabama wore a red bandanna and a ponytail, and Willie Nelson looked like him, only Alabama was tougher, and despite his sixty years, Alabama had muscles where they had no right to be. But all that meant nothing beside the central point. Alabama was not there. He had been invited, of course, but he hadn't showed, and without him Dick Latham's attempt to hijack the Malibu preservation movement for his personal, private use was nothing more nor less than a pathetic failure.

Failure. Once again the word did the scenic ride of the Latham mind. Once more the music began to play as the adrenaline squirted. A second time he turned around and walked away from an unwelcome Aladdin who had unleashed the failure genie to plague him. First, *Celebrity*. Now, the absence of Alabama. For chrissakes. An environmental party without him was Malibu without the goddamn beach. Why hadn't he come? Latham knew the answer. Because of Paris, twenty-five years ago, and the thing that had happened there. Apparently Alabama hadn't forgotten. Already it looked as if the enemy of old was destined to become the enemy of the future.

Suddenly Dick Latham had had enough of his party. Any gossip columnist would have sworn on his mother's life that it was the best roomful that Malibu had seen in years. George Christy from the *Reporter* looked as if he'd died and gone to heaven. It was stellar fusion, no question. Yet Latham wanted out. Ignoring the ripe parted lips and come-on California smile of the simmering model, he headed straight for the sand. He kicked off his loafers and the silk Saks socks, and threw the thousand-buck blazer on the grass of the dunes as if it were a girl's broken heart. He strode across the beach in the vertical midday sunlight and he kicked aggressively at the surf, not bothering to turn up the bottoms of his once immaculate pants. Pat Benatar had told him that *Celebrity*, his pride, his would-be joy, was a washed-up rag. And some disgusting nobody from nowhere had gotten it right. His party had been blowing in the wind. Alabama was somewhere else.

Alabama sat bolt upright, his hands held high on the bars of the Heritage Harley, and he leaned into the turns so that the burning chrome pipes of his bike were millimeters from the melting tarmac. His fearsome goatee and the trademark red bandanna streaming out in the canyon wind emphasized his role of easy-riding ruler of the road, and now, ponytail flying free from his helmetless head, he turned to shout over his shoulder at his passenger.

"We coulda been sipping champagne and nibbling canapés right this minute, King. I delivered us from the fate worse than death."

The guy who sat behind Alabama was impressive too. His high concept could be summed up in one word. *Muscle*. There was very little else on his body, less than six percent fat, khaki shorts and a tank top, the minimalistic clothes straining desperately to contain sleek bundles of actin and myosin that looked as if they had come straight from a Leonardo da Vinci anatomical drawing. At medical school they could have taught off him. There would have been no need for corpses. Every bundle of fibers stood out in sharp relief from its fellows, and King could name them all.

He leaned over Alabama's broad shoulders. "What's Latham like, Alabam?" Alabama's assistant, friend, and brilliant printer of his photographs was the only person alive who was allowed to pronounce his name with only three a's.

"He's an asshole."

"A rich asshole."

"Yeah, rich and smooth. Let's just say his mother knew a thing or two when she decided to call him Dick."

The two friends lapsed into silence, both tacitly agreeing that conversation was too difficult against the background of the throbbing engine and the hot wind. As he threw the bike into the chicanes, Alabama thought back to the time he had last seen Dick

Latham. It had been Paris, in the mid-sixties, and Alabama had been staying with his friends Juliette and Man Ray in their tiny apartment in Montparnasse. Alabama had just branched out into portraits, on a brief holiday from the brooding landscapes that had made him famous, and Dick Latham, heir to a large fortune, had made an interesting subject as the traditional American playboy in Paris who kissed the girls and made them cry. Alabama's photograph of Latham had caught all that—the haughty pseudopride of the little boy lost as he tried to be the ultimate sophisticate; the surface arrogance; the almost feminine good looks. They had hated each other on sight, of course, and the crackling bad vibes had produced a great portrait, as they so often did. Latham had loathed the print and had refused to pay for it. In the normal way that would merely have been intensely irritating, but Paris had been a difficult time financially for Alabama. He had laid out francs on the Latham shoot, and it was cash he could ill afford. In the normal way his prickly pride would have prevented him from asking for money, but he already owed his friend Man a few hundred dollars, and so, biting the bullet, he had gone to Dick Latham and told him that he needed to be repaid for his film and processing costs. The haughty playboy had turned down the perfectly reasonable request and had laughed in his face. Even after all these years the memory of the humiliation was more than enough to send the bile bubbling into the back of Alabama's throat. To have his precious work scorned was infuriating. To be forced to beg, and then to be rudely refused was worse. It was behavior that could never be forgotten or forgiven. For three days Alabama had actually gone short of food and booze. Hunger had been a minor inconvenience, but forced abstinence had been as intolerable to him then as it would be now.

There had been revenge of sorts. Latham had been going out with one of Alabama's favorite models, the speedy, lovely, and incredibly beautiful Eva Ventura, and the playboy had met his match in the sparky girl. He had fallen in love with her, and the alien emotion had threatened to turn his spoiled-brat life-style upside down. Eva had heard about Latham's appalling treatment of her friend Alabama, and had apparently hurried to his apartment to give him the hardest of hard times, only to catch him in flagrante with an old girlfriend. The strong-willed Eva hadn't hesitated. She might have been able to forgive his faithlessness alone, but on top of the character flaw revealed by his behavior toward Alabama, it was too much. She had walked out on the playboy who was supposed to do the leaving, and she had never returned. Latham had searched everywhere for her, hiring detectives, taking ads in the papers, even daring to badger a hostile Alabama, but she had disappeared without trace. Finally, Latham had given up and returned, heartbroken and devastated, to America.

Alabama had not seen him from that day to this, but he had heard about him. Everyone had. In twenty-five go-go years the playboy had metamorphosed into the hard-nosed entrepreneur and the inherited loot had been transformed into media megabucks. Now he was in Malibu, apparently trying to buy huge hunks of Alabama's beloved mountains and to muscle in on Alabama's unquestioned role as top friend of the environment and chief scourge of all developers. For the last two weeks Alabama's house had been under telephone siege as Latham tried to get him to come to his party. Well, screw him! Paris was not forgotten, and Alabama chuckled to himself as he thought of one investment the financial shrewdini had blown. He had refused to pay Alabama a hundred bucks for his portrait. Today it was worth a hundred and fifty thousand and change.

"I need a six-pack of Mexican," shouted Alabama.

"You always need a six-pack of Mexican, and you always drink a twelve-pack, man," screamed King into the wind as Alabama nodded. "An' I get the Sprite so's I can drive you home."

"Mexican don't agree with your muscles, King," roared Alabama. He was having a good time. He was sixty and at last life was getting simpler. It was bikes, beer, and the mountains now, and nothing else. He hadn't shot a photograph for ten years. Not that anybody knew, of course. It was a carefully kept secret. For thirty years he had taken photographs of the nature that he loved, and he had sold only a tiny fraction of his stockpiled prints. It had been more than enough to establish his reputation. So now, when he needed money to finance the environmental wars he ceaselessly fought, he merely pulled a few fifties or sixties negatives from the vault and had King print them up. The sun rising over the mountain in 1955 looked much as it had this morning, and the 1989, together with the scrawled Alabama signature, was good for a hundred thousand minimum any day of the week. When the critics traced the stages of the development of his work in prestigious magazines like *Artforum*, Alabama would laugh like a drain.

He could remember the actual day the thought had occurred to him. He had read somewhere that there were more photographs in the world than bricks. The idea had zapped him right between the eyes. All he was doing was recording beauty, drawing people's attention to it in an interesting and novel way. But all around, nature, the ultimate raw material of that beauty, was being destroyed by greedy, unthinking people in the name of profit, progress, or profligacy. Surely the true artist, the person who really cared about beauty as he did, should make it his mission to preserve that beauty rather than merely recording its disappearance. From that moment on he hadn't taken a photograph. Instead, he had become the champion of every leaf, every branch, of every animal and insect that existed in the beloved hills in which he had always lived.

But if that was the main part of his life, this was another. It was the weekend, and L.A. County was a hundred degrees hot rather than the usual seventy-eight that Neil Simon maintained was the same number as the interesting people that lived there. So today he was doing what he always did on a Saturday. He was going to the Rock House in Seminole Hot Springs to hang out with the bikers, drink cold beer, and eat glutinous chili in the sun-drenched canyons.

As the Harley turned the corner in the road, the shining vision unfolded. There were maybe two hundred bikes parked in line abreast along one side of the highway, a hundred more on the other —two long, luscious ribbons of chrome and paint, gleaming and glistening in the bright sunlight. Over to the right, set back from the road, were a couple of nondescript wooden buildings, one approached by high steps. A sprawling courtyard joined them, in the middle of which stood a magnificent sycamore tree. All around this central tree swirled a black river of leather. The bikers were everywhere, swarming like flies over the picnic tables, arguing, roaring, shouting, swearing, and each man, each biker girl, held in his or her hand a can of beer. Strangely for such a gathering, the floor of the courtyard was clean. No human detritus marred it. There were no cigarette butts, no beer cans, no napkins stained with ketchup, no nastier items. All these unwanted objects were stowed in the two or three vast bins that were strategically placed throughout the eating and drinking area.

As Alabama rode into view, the crowd acclaimed him.

"Hi, man. Hi, Alabama," roared the bikers in raucous unison.

He raised a gnarled hand to acknowledge them, and, riding right up to the door of the restaurant, he parked next door to the sign that read NO PARKING. It was his slot. Somewhere in Detroit the chairman of General Motors had one. Well, so did Alabama.

"Okay, King, my man. I'm drinking Dos Equis. What are you eating? Biker burger, like forever?"

He barged into the Rock House restaurant as King set off to the next-door Rock Store where they sold the cold beer.

Inside, the filthy cubicles quieted briefly as he walked in, and then erupted again with a muted howl of universal welcome. They didn't throng him, they just let him know that they knew he was there, and were glad, and then they were back to the boasting and the baiting and the banter that bikers loved. Alabama noticed Mickey Rourke at one table, surrounded by the nobodies who were his equals for this one day. Gary Busey, Leif Garrett, and Justine Bateman leaned over to wave "hi" from the upper level of the diner. It was like that, this place, and it was older than most of the restaurants within thirty miles of the center of L.A., the city that wasn't supposed to have one. They shot movies at the Rock House from time to time, and celebrities like Jon Peters who loved bikes dropped in and acted ordinary, but mostly everybody hung out in the sun and enjoyed being around people who were just like them.

A guy sidled up to Alabama as he put in his food order. He palmed a Nikon onto the counter.

"Hey, Alabama, you shoot good pictures. What's my best lens for this, man?"

"Throw it away," growled Alabama pleasantly. "It gets in the way of your eyes."

"No, I'm serious, man."

"So am I, man. Take too many photographs and you forget to see. The Japanese are totally blind. Near as they get to nature is photo albums."

The greasy bacon/cheeseburger they called "biker" hit the counter. The bowl of chili—cheese, onions, and green peppers added—came next. Alabama scooped it all up.

"But I want to make some serious art, Alabama," said the Rock House regular. What he meant was some serious bucks like Alabama.

"Art, fart," said Alabama, smiling. "God's the only artist around, man. I never met a human could compete with him. Look around you. Relax. Sit back and enjoy it. Trade in the Nikon and send the money to me. I'll try and make sure there's some nature left for you to enjoy."

He slapped the embryonic photographer hard on the shoulder to show that there were no bad feelings, and he wandered out into the sunshine to get started on the beer.

King beckoned him from Alabama's favorite vantage point, a scuffed, brown plastic-covered banquette at the back of the garden where the bikers were gathered. He mumbled some greetings as he pushed through the crowd, but he didn't stop. He was thirsty.

He flopped down and took the beer that King handed him, nipping the neck of the Dos Equis between thumb and forefinger where the lime was wedged.

"Nice day, King," he mumbled, burping his satisfaction at the brightness of the sunshine and the hazy heat blanket that had settled over the canyon. He scratched the lobe of his ear, and then at the T-shirt where it clung to his full stomach, and he thanked the Lord he wasn't having to endure the industrial-strength bullshit that right now was being ladled out at Richard Latham's "Hello, Malibu" party.

"Jeez, Alabam, take a look at that," said King suddenly.

Alabama squinted into the sunlight.

A vast man stood in the middle of the courtyard over by the central sycamore tree, and he was not a sight for weak stomachs. He was a great beast of a person with a mountainous ass, powerful legs, and glistening, bulbous muscles. The tattoos that ran along his arms were Nazi in origin, swastikas in red and black, crosses, eagles, skulls, crossbones, and other skeletal objects. He was naked above the waist and in large letters across his broad, sweaty back was tattooed the slogan FEAR THIS WHITE SUPREMACIST. He wore a peaked cap and black pebble sunglasses. A pair of handcuffs dangled from the back pocket of his leather jeans and an enormous "Crocodile" Dundee knife swung from his belt. On his scuffed black boots were silver spurs. He gripped a can of Budweiser in his right hand. In his left was an outsize polystyrene cup. By his side stood a thin bleached blonde. On the edges of good-looking, she wore a denim jacket over tough, braless tits, and a pair of cutoffs. It was clear that she belonged to the white supremacist who was to be feared. It was also clear that the incredible hulk wanted to emphasize this fact.

"Fill me up, slag," he boomed.

The local bikers exchanged glances, and some sort of silence descended on the previously rowdy crowd. The man mountain was in trouble mode. They could recognize the symptoms. He was cruising for a bruising and in any fight he looked to be a likely winner. One or two of the regulars looked across uncertainly at Alabama.

The girl took the Budweiser from his right hand and the cup from his left, and poured the one into the other in a gesture of total and unconditional subservience. Please and thank you were not in the stranger's vocabulary. He took the cup and the empty can, and he tossed the latter into the air. It arced through the sunlight and landed, clattering on the ground, a few feet from Alabama. Next he lifted the cup to his mouth and he downed the beer in one gurgling swallow.

Alabama stood up. He stepped forward, bent down, and picked up the empty Bud. Saying nothing at all, he dropped it into a nearby bin. He returned to his seat. The silence was now complete. The Rock House regulars were quiet as the grave. Only strangers and masochists dropped litter around Alabama.

The stranger seemed to sense the unease. He looked around and followed the direction of the eyes until he was staring straight at Alabama. He smiled, a hideous, leering smile because he had worked out what was going down. The old buzzard on the bench was the guy who had picked up his discarded Bud. Obviously he was some environmentalist freak, and clearly, too, he was some sort of respected figure around here. That was why the milksop bikers were eyeballing the old crone. He let out a rumbling guffaw. Shit, the guy was *old!* Late fifties, maybe even sixty. Who *were* these chicken noodle California bikers? The sun had clearly burned the balls off them. They took their orders from the Geritol Kid. Well, he'd give them a lesson in the eating of humble pie. He dropped the empty cup. Then, carefully, his eyes never leaving Alabama's, he ground his heel on it, laughing defiantly as he did so.

"Pick it up," said Alabama. He spoke softly, but he didn't need to shout. In the pregnant silence his words lanced across the space that separated him from the white supremacist.

In response, the stranger smiled a loathsome smile. He reached down and he pulled out the knife, and he turned it around in the sunlight as if he were roasting it on a spit. "I would, old man," he rasped, "but I'm saving energy to carve my initials on that tree."

He ambled toward the sycamore.

Alabama stood up once again. He put down the Dos Equis on the seat. He breathed in deeply, inflating his barrel chest, and he pushed out both his arms to the powder-blue sky, stretching them, flexing the ropelike muscles. Now he exhaled, his sigh weary, resigned to the *que sera*. He moved slowly, like a sunburned snake on a hot highway.

Out of the corner of his eye, the stranger watched Alabama's approach, sizing him up. He was old, but he was big, and he was cool and there was something about the confident way he walked. There was no fear near him. None at all.

The stranger held the knife up to the tree, and he ripped at a poster pinned to it—one about fighting the new helmet law.

"Don't touch my tree," said Alabama.

They were close now, and the stranger could see the glint in the old man's eyes, saw the flexing of his sinewy muscles, but again he laughed because, of course, he had the knife.

"I don't take no orders from no grandfathers," he sneered.

Alabama spoke slowly as if to a lesser form of life, and his voice was arctic cold in the midday heat.

"Listen, shithead," he drawled. "You touch my tree an' I'll carve my name in miniature on your needle dick."

The stranger's mouth dropped open as the words began to wander around his brain. He was only halfway to realizing that he had been insulted, about a quarter of the way to realizing exactly what had been *said*. But already he knew that he would have to cut the old boy open. The knife jerked up from his side, as his mind fought for the appropriate response.

Twenty paces behind Alabama, King wondered if his friend and employer had bitten off more than he could chew. But long experience told him not to worry. All around, the others felt the same. In the quiet, the expectation shone from their faces. How could the stranger know about Alabama and trees? It had taken them a while to learn.

"You fucking corpse . . ." started the stranger, but he never finished. Alabama's cowboy-booted leg had liftoff. The instep, dusty and nail hard, met the would-be sculptor's crotch at the point of its maximum upward momentum. As the irresistible force of the Alabama boot collided with the immovable object of the stranger's pelvic bone, the unfortunate bits of flesh between them were crushed to pulp. The biker sank to his knees as the sky danced around in the heavens and the pain promised to come later. He dropped the knife. "Aw shit," he said on the tide of air that rushed from his lungs.

Alabama took his leg back. He stooped down and he picked up

the knife. He leaned forward and he placed the tip against the distended jugular vein of the white supremacist who was to be feared.

"You dropped your Styrofoam cup on the ground," hissed Alabama. "An' it ain't biodegradable."

"Aaaaaaah," screamed the stranger. The pain had arrived, elbowing out the numb void that had gripped his crotch. His head shook from side to side, his eyes swam, and in his ears was a word he'd never heard before.

Alabama ignored his scream as his own would have been ignored if he'd lost the millisecond fight.

He whispered into the ear of the wounded psychopath. "The plastic is made of these long-chain hydrocarbons, man. Don't nothin' break 'em down. I'll show you. Eat it."

It took a bit of getting used to, but he managed it. In many ways eating the remains of the plastic cup was the most impressive thing he'd managed in his miserable life so far.

Alabama stood up and he tossed the knife into the trash as he went back to his seat. But he didn't feel like drinking anymore, and somebody else could pick up the pieces. He signaled to King, and in a minute or two the Heritage was gunning, and the old street fighter, the biker, the beer guzzler, the environmentalist, and the most famous photographer in the world was going home.

FOUR

Pat Parker roared past Sunset Boulevard in the open Jeep Islander, and her blond hair streamed behind her California-style as it was supposed to. The late afternoon sun burned hot on her face, and to her left, along the beach, the surf was up, and the wetsuited teenagers were still riding the waves. She held on to the wheel tightly as she played the dangerous video game called Pacific Coast Highway, where the prize was a safe arrival, and the penalty was the fire department chopper ride to the hospital in Santa Monica. Boy, was it a long way from New York! She had been out of the Big Apple for seven hours, and it felt like a lifetime.

She flicked the switch of the radio, found a surfing station playing vintage Beach Boys, and wondered if she dared attempt the death-defying application of total block to her exposed nose. No way. Of the various life-threatening options, melanoma looked deeply attractive. So she shook her head, exhilarated by the sun and the warm wind, and the new mood that flowed through her. This was what she had needed. A fresh beginning. A challenge. A change of direction. She felt like singing, and she laughed into the breeze as she ran over in her mind the events that had brought her here.

It was three months since the dying Mapplethorpe had made his enigmatic suggestion that she go see Alabama in Malibu. At first she had dismissed it. What would the grand old man of American photography want with the trendy chronicler of the "vitally important" New York night scene? Alabama was a legend. He was landscapes and portraits and one-man retrospectives at the Whitney and the Met. She was prancing poseurs and posturing pansies in hellholes that rejoiced in the inventiveness of their ugliness. He was medals in the Rose Garden, groveling reviews in the *Times*, sleek Fifty-seventh Street galleries, and megabuck collectors. She was five hundred dollars a throw if she was lucky, spreads in *On the Avenue* and *Details*, Amaretto di Pat, loose talk of a cooperative effort with the ubiquitous Tama. They couldn't be further apart . . . and yet . . . and yet. Wasn't that what she needed? A total turnaround. Had Picasso shrunk from the journey from blue to cubes? Had Goya allowed himself to be stuck at naked duchesses, and forsworn the new frontiers of madness and black Satans? Had Gauguin slaved on in the Paris stock exchange, Michelangelo balked at the roof of the Sistine Chapel? The list was endless of artists who'd risked change, but it was longer of those who hadn't. Pat Parker didn't want to be in the last category, and the weird experience at Indochine, when she had seemed to see the ghost of her dead friend, had helped make up her mind.

Over the next weeks she had gone through the entire body of her work and had selected six prints. With her heart in her boots, and the prospect of ridicule hanging over her head, she packed them up and Fed-Exed them, with a short note, to Alabama.

> Dear Alabama,
>
> Robert Mapplethorpe suggested that I do this. I think these six prints are my best work, and I'm not sure that I even like them. I'm at a sort of crisis—photography-wise. Would you see me? I could come to Malibu.

She hadn't expected an answer. At the very most she supposed there might have been a short, polite note from some patronizing administrative assistant. But the Western Union telegram had not minced its words. It had said simply, "Come. Alabama." And she had obeyed.

Now she was in Malibu, and soon she would meet the mythical figure who had issued the incredibly cryptic invitation. Her heart speeded. Would it be a disaster? On paper, almost certainly. But what did paper know? One thing was going for her. Alabama was known to be an eccentric, and, of all the people in life, Pat Parker got on with those best of all. She looked out to the beach. God, the sea was blue. And so was the sky, dotted with gulls and swooping brown pelicans fishing lazily in the stiff breeze. To her right the cliffs rose roughly, their face scarred by countless landslides that would have closed the road she now traveled. A sign saying GETTY told her where the richest and dullest art was, and soon she was cruising into the heart of old Malibu past the pier of Alice's Restaurant, where Arlo Guthrie maintained you could get anything you wanted; past the gates to the Colony where the movie stars had once lived; past the Hughes Market, its architecture brand-new ancient Spanish mission; past the bleak neatness of Pepperdine University, whose hilarious mission impossible was to push mind stuff in Malibu, where the only thing that anyone cared about was bodies.

She knew only vaguely where she was going. Someone at Alabama's called King had told her where to turn right off PCH. Then she was to head straight up into the mountains. She could see them now, stretched out against the skyline, battleship gray in the sunlight, massive, mighty, majestic. He lived somewhere up there in the heart of the hills that some called Malibu and others called Santa Monica, and it was rumored that he acted as if they belonged to him. Pat took a deep breath. Everyone she had spoken to had agreed on one thing. Alabama either liked you, or he didn't. You were his friend, or his enemy. Toward nothing and nobody was he neutral. So she hadn't packed much in the way of clothes. If things went badly, she would just walk away. In the pocket of her faded Levi's the ticket was round trip.

Malibu was changing. The speeding highway now whizzed past small shops whose neat neon said serious beach and body—pastel T-shirts, Day-Glo swimsuits, tone for the copper people. There were sexy-looking restaurants with names like Something Fishy, Zooma Sushi, and the Coral Beach Cantina, and there were designer gyms and adobe mini-malls, their lots well stocked with Samurais, Wranglers, and Porsches, those potent icons of the Southland dream. On either side of her, fellow death dancers on the freeway, were the product of the fabulous California gene pool. The impossibly pretty girls tossed their American hair in time to the thundering basses of their Blaupunkts, while blond surf supermen posed, pouted, and powered their cars into nonexistent spaces in the teeth of the oncoming traffic like kamikazes in search of an honorable end. Bearded agents in black Beamers looked suitably serious, as they creamed past wetbacks in bangers from East L.A. Creepy, crawling families of Hertz tourists rubbernecked the roadside as they searched for the elusive spirit that went by the name of Malibu, while bearded bikers, their sunglassed eyes set in time warp on some vision of a Peter Fonda past, rode proudly, heads and handlebars held high, on their endless journey to nowhere.

Pat Parker eased the Jeep into the right-hand lane as the horns of her fellow travelers blared in universal irritation. Some of the beautiful people even found the energy to shout indistinct abuse into the ozone as they rushed past her on Narcissus errands to the star-studded futures that they knew would be theirs.

Pat hung the right and laughed at the angst so surprisingly revealed. In New York being pissed off was a way of life, an intelligent response to the crime, the temperature, and the noise. What was the excuse here? The souring of dreams? The blandness of perfection? The predictability of yet another wonderful day in Paradise? Maybe she'd find out. She climbed the winding road, and each S bend delivered its visual feast as she snaked higher and higher into the hills. Above her, hawks rode the thermal currents of the canyon, searching the scrub of the chapparal for mice, while on either side patches of brilliant color lit up the brush. There were tall white-plumed yucca plants, blazing red patches of wild fuchsia, and clumps of creamy yellow bush poppies. Mustard, wild tobacco, and castor beans grew along the roadside, while the air was heavy with the scent of purple and black sage. It was a beautiful wilderness, dotted with outsize sandstone rocks, and all the time life erupted around her; the flash of a blue jay, its harsh cry preceding its brief appearance; quarrelsome groups of jet-black crows disputing the ownership of telephone poles; the sudden disturbance of the vegetation by an unseen animal—a coyote, a deer, a rare bobcat?

All around her was naked beauty, and Pat Parker, who understood such things, vibrated in tune to it. It was what she had been looking for. Here in Alabama's mountains she would make the photographs that would matter. She knew it with absolute certainty. Everything that had gone before was dress rehearsal. In a thousand sweaty stink boxes of the night she had perfected the technique of photography. Now, she could afford to forget about the skills she had acquired. The only thing that mattered was the vision, and God had given her the eye to see the wonder of the nature he had created. On an impulse, she slowed down. She steered the Jeep off the road, and, at the edge of the cliff, she stopped, turning off the ignition and basking in the warm wonder of the silence. She got out and reached into the back for the Nikon, clipping on a 28mm wide-angle lens. Way below her was the dark blue carpet of the ocean, the specks of the surfers tiny against the white peaks of the waves. The canyon framed it, dark gray and rusty brown, and the birds soared on the hot wind against the ceiling of a cloudless sky. On remote control, she flicked the f-stop to 11, the speed to 125, the distance to infinity. The light reading was in her head, the lightness of being was in her heart. This would be the first photograph of her new life.

Then she saw the movement. Below her, in the thick bushes beneath the shade of a giant oak, something was stirring. It was big, threateningly big on the lonely roadside, and Pat Parker caught her breath as the beauty of the moment receded to be replaced by sudden fear. At once she was aware that she was a stranger in these rugged mountains. Mean streets, with their well-known dangers, were her natural habitat. Here she was a foreigner. She lowered the camera. She looked over her shoulder toward the Jeep. She looked down at the continuing disturbance, and her legs were already asking that they be allowed to run. What animals lived here? What kind of *people?* Red-necked mountain men, dangerously unpredictable in their interbred remoteness? The sort of person who might enjoy frightening a long-legged New York photographer halfway to her grave?

The voice that wafted up from below, however, was not scary. Instead, it was scathingly cynical.

"Good idea. Good idea for a chocolate box," it boomed. "Or one of those postcards to send the folks back home."

The face poked out from the bush. It was pugnacious, its leathery lines cracked up in a patronizing smile, and the small goatee jutted up at Pat like an exclamation mark. In answer, Pat Parker's Nikon flashed up like a mugger's Saturday night special, and her finger darted down on the shutter.

"There," she exclaimed, her voice heavy with sarcasm, "now I've got myself a garden gnome."

Alabama had never, ever before been described as a garden gnome. Of all the things he didn't want to be, a garden gnome had to be high on the list. In the Rock House unwise bikers had called him ostensibly ruder things, and facial rearrangement had followed to the satisfaction of all. But this insulter was a woman. A very good-looking, very feisty, very quick-witted woman, and it was with a frisson of surprise that Alabama realized that he wasn't angry at all.

He continued his act of physical revelation, and, as his massive bulk exploded from the plant that had hidden him, Pat Parker realized that a garden gnome was not what she had "got." What she *had* got was the side of a house, a land whale, a menacing mountain man whose T-shirt, dirty and torn, read unequivocally, I SHOOT PHOTOGRAPHERS.

She took a step back. He took a step forward. Her supercilious smile faded from her face, as one of genuine amusement crept over his.

"A garden gnome?" he said, his voice thick with incredulous humor.

"It was just the way your head poked out of the greenery, I mean . . . I mean . . . I didn't mean . . ."

But already she could see the laughter in his intelligent eyes, and her pseudoapology petered out. It wasn't every day that Pat Parker was accused of taking a boring photograph, especially by some ignorant, superannuated biker in the Santa Monica Mountains, who should have bothered to take time out to grow up.

"Well, I guess I deserved it, but from here your photograph did look major-league dull," said Alabama.

"From there isn't from here. It's lesson one in photography," said Pat evenly. It was. Millimeters made the difference. Washington Square only looked good if you were Kertész looking down on it.

"Oh, it *is*, is it?" chuckled Alabama. He continued to advance upon her. She held her ground, chin stuck out in defiance. "And what," boomed the greatest photographer in the world, "is lesson two?"

"Don't criticize someone else's work unless you have *some* idea of what it is you are talking about," said Pat.

Alabama's smile broadened. She was getting angry again. Her eyes were sparkling. The indignation was heavy in the words. Lord, she was a looker, and her anger made her more beautiful. He just had to wind her up one more turn. A garden gnome, indeed!

"Work!" he guffawed. "*Work!* Jeez! If that's work, so is jerking off."

"Don't," said Pat with all the coldness she could muster, "be so disgusting."

A disgusting garden gnome. It was a first. At Alabama's stage of life, not many things were.

He had reached her now, clambering up onto the edge of the road, puffing slightly from the exertion of the climb. Up close she was better than from down below. Her eyes were wide with righteous indignation, and huge blue irises swam in a white sea beneath no-nonsense bushy eyebrows. Her voluptuous mouth was peeled back in a snarl over perfect teeth, and her whole body, from the top of her lustrous hair to the toes of her scuffed cowboy boots, leaned toward him as if it longed to become an offensive weapon. Her blue denim top was open to show the cleavage of clearly braless breasts, and her ballet dancer's butt strained against the indigo of faded 501's at the top of rainbow legs. To Alabama, it was definitely time to make up, if not to kiss. She was old enough to be his grandchild, but there had been younger.

"Listen, I'm sorry. I'm teasing. Are you a photographer?"

He pushed out his hand at her. She didn't take it.

"Yes," she barked at him.

"In which case it may be that you have heard of me," he drawled. "They call me Alabama."

"They do?" said Pat Parker in a voice that seemed to come from at least another mountain range.

This would be an excellent moment for the earthquake, she thought. The earth could open now. She could swallowtail in, and then it could close again, and that would be that. Alabama. Alabama, the disgusting garden gnome. Alabama, to whom she had just taught lessons one and two in photography. She recognized him now, of course, from the photographs. But it was a tad too late. That she hadn't expected to meet him erupting from the canyon bushes would hardly do for extenuating circumstances.

There was a rushing noise in her head.

"Listen, I'm most terribly . . ."

He waved away her apology as if swatting a fly.

"And you are?"

"I'm the Pat Parker who was coming to see you." Her voice was strangled. The past tense seemed absolutely inescapable.

For a second he paused. Then his massive hand pumped up and landed on his broad thigh with a resounding *thwack*. The peal of delighted laughter exploded from the depths of his bull neck.

"Well, that's wonderful, Pat Parker," he boomed. "For a moment there I thought I was going to miss out on lesson three."

Dick Latham slid into the New York boardroom of Cosmos Pictues like a little boy late for assembly. His shy smile said he was so sorry for hanging everyone up, for the rudeness, for the personal inefficiency. He shrugged his shoulders in apology, and he sidled toward the Hepplewhite chairman's chair, motioning for everyone to continue as if he weren't there. The man who leaped up to pull back his seat was nodded down again by the Latham eyes. Oh no, he didn't want to put anybody out. He'd just sit down and shut up and let the boys get right on with it.

The CEO of Cosmos, however, had acquired a speech impediment. His formerly smooth delivery was now a spurting, staccato affair full of half-finished sentences, cul-de-sacs, and mysterious nonsequiturs. He fished around with his finger in the collar of his Sea Island cotton shirt and the words of the TV bite went round and round in his mind. "Never let them see you sweat." Well, he'd blown it. Here in the boardroom, beneath the heavy-duty art, the cunning John Saladino lighting, before the eyes of the superboss, the moisture was dripping from him like dew on a Smoky Mountain morning.

"Like I was saying . . . I mean . . . oftentimes . . . oftentimes . . . when a studio changes hands the slate is looked at . . . is gone through with a view to . . . I mean, so that the new management might want to change direction . . . ."

He stared in desperation down the mahogany table as if the gleaming wood could help him escape from his verbal mess. *Oftentimes* was a word he had never used before. Now it filled up his mind like a football. The dictionary had just been boiled down. There was nothing left but "oftentimes . . . oftentimes . . ." And what did he mean "the new management"? He was the *old* management. The whole table was the old management. That there might one day *be* a new management was why the gardenia-scented air was tinged with the unmistakable smell of fear.

Dick Latham smiled. He sat way back in his chair and his immaculately manicured nails drummed on the shining table. He looked up at the Titian, over at the Rembrandt; his laughing eyes scanned the stricken faces of the Cosmos management. They tried to smile back. God, how they tried. Mouths were ripped back over bonded teeth, eyes tried to scrumple up in some pale imitation of warmth. It was as if the executioner, on a whim, had decided to spare the victim who managed the best smile on the edge of eternity. Hearts were simply not in it. Latham reached forward and pulled the Limoges coffee cup toward him, as the waiter materialized at his side.

"What is it?" said Dick Latham.

The Cosmos CEO stopped. At last someone had said something

interesting. For brief seconds he could relax. Mr. Latham was inquiring about the brand of coffee.

"Kenyan, sir. From the Rift Valley, Mr. Kent says. Will that do?"

Latham nodded, as the stream poured sedately into the porcelain from the Georgian silver pot.

He waved a hand in the air, the hand that lied "Don't let me interrupt." He looked carefully at the two-bit agent, one-time lawyer, and general Hollywood hanger-on whom he had inherited as his studio boss. God, he was disgusting. Small and fat, built for a foul-smelling cigar and for the game of musical chairs that was job hunting in Tinsel Town. What deals had he struck with the devil to reach his moment of mini-fame? From the series of box-office bombs he had presided over, talent was clearly not one of his attributes. Nor, apparently, was public speaking.

"So, as oftentimes we do this . . . sort of review . . . oftentimes we should do it now."

He sat down suddenly as if he had been sandbagged, and he nodded to the bearded, bespectacled man at his side.

This man now stood up, adjusted his glasses, coughed, and began to speak in a small, thin voice. His eyes were fixed on the open manila folder on the table in front of him.

"In the usual way I have divided the projects into those currently in production; the definite done deals that are presently green lighted; and the preproduction development deals that have either reached step status or in which we have significant upfront exposure. I won't deal with projects in turnaround." He paused. The roomful of eyes were on Latham. The billionaire was magazines and publishing. Would he understand the movie jive? Would it matter? The head of production droned on.

"But I should just start by saying that CinemaScope test marketing of *Home Fires* is extremely encouraging. They're getting sixty-five percent A's from the preview audiences, which is blockbuster bullish. We're hoping for a huge opening on Memorial Day."

"How many screens?" said Latham suddenly. His smile had gone. The laughing eyes were narrow.

They all sat up straight. It was the right question.

The studio boss discovered an enormous interest in the intricate plasterwork of the ceiling, then in the state of his nails, finally in the design of the Chinese silk rug.

"A thousand, I think," said the production guy unhappily. "We're going for a slow, steady build," he added in desperation, aware that this did not exactly gel with the hoped-for "huge opening" on Memorial Day.

"Budget?" snapped Latham with killer speed.

Oh, dear! He'd gotten there. He knew. He was on top of it.

The production head was beginning to fall apart.

"Over the line or under the line?" he tried, in a forlorn attempt to stave off disaster.

"Both," said Latham with asplike deadliness.

"Thirty-five/forty," admitted the broken man.

It was no good. A forty-million-dollar picture, whose stars alone had cost five million, could not afford to open on as few as a thousand screens. Two thousand plus and the marketing surveys might be meaningful. A mere thousand and the picture was doomed.

In the silence they all thought first of their careers. Where would they go when the music stopped? Where would they find the seats for their asses that would enable the game to continue, the platinum cards to remain in play, the people who now loved them to love them still?

"So *Home Fires* is burning," said Dick Latham in summary. "It would appear that Cosmos has not yet ended its losing streak," he added.

They didn't move. Would it be quick? Would it hurt? Would he do them all at once? Here. Now. Or would he leave a few of them around to keep the offices clean, to hang out the welcome mats for their replacements.

"But it just so happens, this is no big deal," said Latham, "because, as from this minute, Cosmos Pictures is no longer in the movie business."

What! They were history, but so was the studio? That wasn't how it happened. Studios, like cans of bad sardines, were for trading, not opening and closing. The cast of characters changed, but the studios remained the same. They were owned by conglomerates, or soft drink companies, or by superrich individuals who fancied movie star ass. Currently, the Japanese were sniffing around. Tomorrow maybe it would be Martians. You could do anything to a studio—you could rape it, ransack it, polish it, cherish it—but you couldn't close it down. It was an un-American activity, like burning the flag or sandblasting Mount Rushmore. Dick Latham, apparently so smooth, suave, and well informed, had clearly gone off his rocker.

The CEO, from the relative safety of unemployment, actually found the balls to say it. "You can't do that," he blurted out.

"Well," drawled Latham, "I think you'll find that I can. Cosmos is sitting on around a billion dollars' worth of prime L.A. real estate. If I were to sell it off, close it down, and put the billion with the Treasury, I'd be seeing close on a hundred million a year . . . against a retrospective five-year average profit of . . . well, you tell me."

His eye found the Cosmos finance man, the only one in the room apart from Latham with a gleam in his eye.

"Twenty million, tops, depending on how you account for—"

"Precisely," agreed Latham, cutting off the accountant in mid-sentence. "And what I say is, 'Why bother to make bad movies when you can be making good money?' "

There was no answer to that, or rather the right answer could not publicly be admitted. The truth of the matter was that it was far more *fun* to make bad movies than good money. A billion in Treasuries was no fun at all. A billion financing your fantasies was fascinatingly fantastic. This was the bottom line that Hollywood always denied, as it preached instead the propaganda of business efficiency. None of the has-beens in the room was about to articulate it now.

"So, gentlemen, I am afraid it only remains for me to ask you all for resignations, and of course to say that which goes without saying, that all contracts will be scrupulously adhered to."

He stood up. He smoothed down the nonexistent creases in the jacket of his immaculate suit, and he smiled once more as he cast them into the outer darkness.

"Good luck," he said, as he walked quickly to the door.

He closed the oak doors behind him and stalked briskly through the anteroom. The secretary, nearly pretty, smiled hard as he passed.

"Mr. Havers is waiting in your office, as you asked," she said breathlessly. "And then you have a one o'clock luncheon appointment with Emma Guinness at the Four Seasons."

"Good," snapped Latham. He ignored the elevator, and instead took the stairs to his penthouse office. He moved fast. That had been fun. Twenty-six executives all executed at one sitting. Must be some sort of a record for face-to-face firing. Lord, how he hated incompetents. God, how he loved the Guinness tits.

He burst into his office. Havers jumped up from the sofa.

"How did it go?"

"Great! They tried to give me some bullshit about *Home Fires* turning Cosmos around. Can you believe it?"

"Yeah," drawled Havers. "I imagine there'll be a few people out there who'll prefer to go see Indiana III."

Latham laughed. He liked Havers. He liked the fact that he was ruthless and dispassionate in his sincere pursuit of profit. It was why he had elevated him to the number-two slot at Latham Communications.

"So shall I go ahead and hit the wire services with this?"

"Give Liz Smith an hour or two first. I owe her one. Okay?"

"Who gets the real estate? Fred Sands? Douglas?"

"No, give it to Steven Shapiro at Stan Herman. Give him a two-month exclusive, then you can open it up to the others."

Latham walked over to the partners' desk, to the picture window with its view over Central Park.

"Tell Steve that he should come and see me at Broad Beach over the weekend. I'm going down to Malibu tonight."

"I'll have the 727 stand by."

"No, don't bother with it. Let's economize. I'll do an MGM. I want to check it out. Never done it before. Book me a private room. Guinness will be coming with me."

He didn't mind treating Havers like a gofer. In the Latham world they were all gofers, whatever the fancy titles on their doors.

"When do we go to the second phase of the Cosmos deal?"

Latham sat down, shooting the cuffs of his blue poplin Bonwit-Teller shirt. He swung to the right in the swivel chair. He swung to the left. He checked himself out in the Chinese Chippendale mirror. Yeah, he looked good. The New and Lingwood neckties were so White's. The tan was beginning to fade, though. He'd have to work on it over the weekend.

"Yes, phase two, Cosmos. The hornet's nest," he mused over his long, sensitive fingers. He breathed in deeply. He wasn't sure about the Calvin Klein Obsession. It wasn't at all subtle, was in fact rather sickly. He'd throw it out. Go back to Royal Yacht. It wasn't so sensual, but it was effortlessly correct.

"We're close to closing on the Canyon tract. It was peanuts. Five million bucks, six hundred acres. The old fart wanted a nondevelopment clause in the contract. He got an extra five hundred thousand instead." Havers sneered visibly at the weakness of humanity, as he smiled at the awesome power of cash.

"And it runs next to Alabama's land," said Latham to himself, a faraway expression on his face.

"Yeah," said Havers. "I wonder what he'll do when he finds out you're going to build a movie studio next to him."

Latham chuckled as he contemplated the enormity of what he was planning. He was going to build a brand-spanking-new Cosmos studio slap bang in the middle of Alabama's Malibu hills. The famous Cosmos trademark, the spinning globe against the star-spangled universe, would live on. The name of the legendary studio would not die. He would build it for nickels and dimes on the Malibu land he had just bought for small change. And most of the billion dollars he realized from the prime real estate on which the studio now sat would sit safely on loan to the United States government. It was a deal created in heaven, a dream deal that made the juices bubble and flow inside him.

But one thing was quite certain.

When he discovered that Dick Latham, posing as an ecological savior, was in fact an environmental rapist, Alabama was going to go stark, staring, raving mad.

"She didn't!"

"She *did!*"

"In front of *everybody?*"

"Of everybody. I was standing right there. So was Jennifer. Like *ask* her."

"Omigod . . . I can hardly believe it really happened. It's just so deeply . . . crucial."

"And he said . . . I can't remember the exact words. But he told her she was disgusting and unprofessional and that her clothes were a complete *mess.*"

"What was she wearing?"

"A dreadful tulle thing—like a ballet dancer, with this humungous yellow belt and Alice in Wonderland shoes. She looked like Doris Day dressed for Halloween, or one of Cinderella's sisters. I can't *tell* you what she looked like. You know the kinda thing she wears."

"What did she *say?*"

"Nothing. I mean, she was blown away. She was totally destroyed, and this great-looking guy had pissed all over her. It was unreal. Totally and completely *unreal.*"

"I'd just die. I'd have to hide. How can she come in and like . . . carry on, when she knows we all *know?*"

"Amanda says that's what used to happen in England when she was working at *Class* magazine. She was unfazed. They were real mean to her, you know how the English can be with all those words they use. Apparently she came from the North, which is like coming from 'Joisey,' and she changed her name from Doreen something-or-other to Emma Guinness, which is like being called Whitney or Cabot Lodge, and she took all these lessons to get her accent straight. Amanda says they were merciless with her. They found out she'd screwed her way to the top job at some out-of-town magazine, and they used to call her the British Open, after a *golf* competition."

Samantha du Pont and Mary Polk, the fashion editor, dissolved into laughter, scattering the colored pencils, the layouts, the transparencies, and the empty coffee cups across their desks. In the lunch break at *New Celebrity* the atmosphere of manic delight was building fast. Samantha, who headed up features, had actually been *there* on the infamous Juilliard evening when their hated boss had been so gloriously humiliated, and she was milking the fact for every last drop of its dramatic potential.

"Anyway, for years Emma just took it all. Never said a thing. Never laughed, never cried, just hung in there and swallowed it. Amanda says Victoria Brougham, the editor, used to ask her about the working classes. You know, like 'How will the working classes react to this, Emma, you're the expert, how will they feel about that?' They used to put bottles of Guinness, which is some kind of beer, on her desk and laugh about her 'cousins,' and they were so cruel because she was so gross and pushy and brash, exactly like she is here.

"And then one day, the magazine changed hands and before anyone knew it, they made Emma editor."

The manic buzz of excitement quieted. The sun of the collective pleasure was suddenly obscured by cloud.

"Amanda says Emma tape recorded Victoria bad-mouthing the new owner. Apparently he'd made all his own money, which is not at all the thing to have done in England. Emma played the tape back to him. Victoria had mimicked his accent or something. That's what Amanda says, anyway. She says they're real sensitive about that kind of thing over there."

"And then they all got fired."

"They sure did."

An uneasy silence descended. It had been three weeks since Emma Guinness had been imported by Richard Latham to take over his rapidly fading *Celebrity* magazine, and so far Samantha and Mary were still there.

They were not, however, including pensions in their long-range financial planning. They were working on the last edition of the old-style *Celebrity* magazine. *New Celebrity* had been conceived, but was in embryo and no one in the magazine's offices could cross their hearts and say they truly believed they would be present at its birth.

The two friends tried to stay "up." There had to be some more mileage in the Juilliard debacle somewhere.

"What was the guy's name?"

"Tony Valentino. Forget Rudolph. This was the real thing. I mean, he was adorable. It's the only time I've ever seen Emma show any taste. It was incredible hunk time, and I don't even *like* muscles."

"God, we ought to do something for him. I wonder how he'd feel about . . . he'd feel about . . . marriage!"

The laughter was back. Not for long.

"Who is marrying whom?" said Emma Guinness from the door. Somehow the pompous accuracy of her grammar was more sinister than the snarl of her voice. She stood there, her owllike eyes scanning the room for treachery, heresy, for lèse-majesté.

Mary Polk, whose life was fashion, did a double wince. Once for the unwelcome presence of the boss at the moment they were ridiculing her. Twice, for the clothes she wore, a gruesome magenta matching coat and skirt and an identically colored cloche hat.

"Oh, I was joking about someone Samantha met," she managed at last.

"Yes, I'm sure Samantha's friends are an unfailing source of humor," agreed Emma Guinness, advancing into the office. "Her articles are pretty funny, too . . . funny peculiar, rather than funny ha-ha, I should say."

"You didn't like spa burnout?" said Samantha.

"One doesn't like or dislike spa burnout any more than one likes or dislikes antiwrinkle cream, plastic surgeons, and how-to-be-happy books," barked Emma Guinness. "It is merely that one is transcendentally *bored* by them. They are part of the reason *Celebrity* went down the loo, they and the 'brilliant' people who write about them."

Emma leaned into the insult, wrapping the word *brilliant* in a patchwork quilt of sarcasm, cynicism, and irony. She knew these girls. She had their number. They were the transatlantic cousins of the bitches who had made her life hell at *Class* magazine. In the battle for upward mobility, she had swallowed about every insult the daughters of the British aristocracy could dream up. And social cruelty was their blood sport. Hundreds of years of training in the defeat and repulsion of social climbers had been distilled into their genes. They knew with surgical accuracy how to inflict the worst possible pain with the smallest word, the most economical gesture, the apparently careless smile. Compared to Victoria Brougham and her army of class fellow travelers, these Americans were amateurs in the art of the putdown, but despite that, and their position as her employees, they still tried. And when they did, like now, they were punished, as their English predecessors had been. She had repaid *their* social violence with her own medal, the grand order of the sack, and now the New World snobs were in line for a similar investiture.

Emma sat down at the desk, flicking with her fingers through the trash that littered it. She picked up a transparency between thumb and forefinger as if it were a dead roach, and she held it up to the lamp.

"Lord Almighty, I didn't know we were using *Penthouse* photographers these days, Mary. And the girl looks like a hooker. Am I missing some deeply meaningful social trend here, or is it just the tit-and-bum it appears to be?"

Mary Polk's mouth dropped open. They hadn't talked to her like that during hazing when she was a sorority pledge at Brown. Damn it, the *judge* hadn't even talked to her in that tone of voice after the little lapse from grace with cocaine in the early days at Area. The trust funds existed to protect you from experiences like this. So did Uncle Willie's law firm, and all the cousins, and the appalling mandibular discomfort of the Boston Brahmin accent. Now some jumped-up Brit was as good as telling her she had no taste. No taste! Mary Polk. Her ancestors were so grand they hadn't come over on the *Mayflower*, they'd met the boat. Jesus, her family had the import monopoly on class. She stuck out the family chin, and flashed the family eyes, as she prepared to do battle.

"Those photographs were taken by Claude Deare, and the girl is Sam Acrefield." She intoned the names of the star photographer and the supermodel as if they were the death sentence on Emma Guinness's artistic judgment.

"Exactly right," said Emma with a wicked smile, throwing the trannie back on the desk. "A pornographer and a hooker. The question is what are they doing in the magazine?"

"Listen, Emma, everyone uses Claude, and Claude uses Sam. You must know that." Samantha's adrenaline was on the move. She had to stand by her friend.

" 'Everyone uses Claude,' 'Everyone uses Claude' . . ." mimicked Emma cruelly but accurately, setting her jaw in concrete to catch Samantha's accent. "Of *course* I know that. Anyone in the Western Hemisphere not already dead from déjà vu knows that. That's the problem. Listen, love, it's impossible to tell one *Celebrity* fashion layout from another, or the *Celebrity* layouts from those of any of the other drossy magazines, and why? Because 'Everyone uses Claude,' and because the blinkered fools who tinker around pretending to work in this industry are too lazy or too blind to see that Claude Deare is a superannuated, impotent old lecher and Sam Acrefield is a high-class call girl."

"I don't see what their sexual behavior has to do with it," intoned Mary haughtily. For all sorts of reasons Boston liberals liked to leave sex out of things.

"Then I'll *tell* you, fashion guru," hissed Emma Guinness. "Obvious sex," she intoned, "is last year, and so, I fear, are you."

She threw down the gauntlet. It was High Noon. Emma, gun drawn, was about to fire. If the Bostonian moved a muscle in retaliation, she would be dead.

"Who would *you* use, Emma?" Samantha rushed in with her diversion.

"Pat Parker." Emma shot out the name without a second's hesitation.

"Pat Parker?" both girls intoned in unison.

"She's reportage," said Mary dismissively.

"She's trendy," said Samantha, giving the word pejorative topspin. "I mean she's underground, not mainstream, hardly *Celebrity*."

"Boy, are you right! Hardly *Celebrity*, but very, *very New Celebrity*." Emma Guinness's voice was triumphant. "Pat Parker is 'now.' She's 'happening.' She's where it's at. I don't give a damn if her lighting's off, or she hires the 'wrong' hairdresser, or if she hasn't worked for the correct magazines. You don't get excitement in this world without exciting people. That's what it's all about. Safe is dull. Let's get the hell out there on the cutting edge and dare the readers to catch up. They will, but we've got to wake them up first. Wean them off the visual Halcion."

"Visual Halcion? Thank you, Emma. Thank you very much," said Mary, wilting under the criticism and well aware that sarcasm was the lowest form of wit.

"Maybe we could get her to shoot the 'Stars of Tomorrow' section. Perhaps she could persuade that Tony Valentino to change his mind about doing the slot."

Samantha smiled as she unleashed the verbal missile with the nuclear head. Almost certainly she herself would perish in the blast, but it would be worth it to let the dreaded Emma know that everyone in the office knew the smallest details of her humiliation.

Emma's world stopped in its tracks. Once again her antennae had been right. She could have sworn that they were discussing her when she had walked into the room. Here was confirmation. The blush exploded up from her neck and expanded from the center of her cheeks, like ripples from the splash of a stone in a pond. She clenched her fists, and her heart speeded. In her mind she could see all the amused, astounded faces, feel the scornful words dripping like acid into her psyche. The fire of embarrassment burned in her anew as she remembered the face of the boy god, so full of scorn, so utterly sure of himself, as he demolished her publicly before all the people that mattered. It was the story of her life. The battle to reach the position in which no one could touch her. The hard work, the sacrifice, the scheming, and the eventual victory. Then what? There was always another person to plague her. First an army of the socially powerful, and now, at the height of her success, a nobody from nowheresville called . . . *Valentino?* The rage was sucked into the vacuum of shock that had opened within her. Her eyes narrowed, and the malice lasered out at the girl who had dared to mock her.

"Do you two know . . . can you have any idea, why I kept you in your jobs? Well, I'll tell you. I wanted you to produce one last issue of your moribund magazine, an issue more dreadfully dull and cunningly complacent than any you had ever produced before. Why? Because it will show back to back with my first edition of *New Celebrity*. Everyone will get to compare the sublime with the ridiculous. That's why I left it all to you. I could never have produced anything so startlingly mediocre. You two have the rarest talent. You bore for the galaxy. You invented banality. When the Lord created lack of creativity, he was dreaming of you. Now I'm just off to the Four Seasons to have lunch with Dick Latham, and I'm going down to Malibu with him for the weekend. And I'm going to tell him that I'm going to sack the lot of you. Every sodding one, do you hear?" Her voice rose in both decibels and pitch.

The tears of terminal irritation glistened in her eyes. The boot was too good for them. These girls would never starve. They would never be too hot, never too cold. They'd go to the Hamptons for the summer, or to England where some grand WASP publisher would have them head up his PR department when the weather turned nasty in the fall. They'd never go away. Instead they'd truck on and on, telling and retelling the saga of how Emma Guinness, despite her position and her fame, got hers, in public, at the Juilliard Theater from the beautiful actor whom nobody had ever heard of.

She walked to the door. When she reached it, she turned, and her face was twisted with a terrible rage. "I hate you," she hissed. "I hate you all. And one day I'll show you just how far and how high I'm going to go."

Tony Valentino lay back in the bubbles, shielded his eyes against the sun, and tried desperately to have a bad time. He scowled, he flicked his head from side to side in irritation, he ran through his repertoire of miserable, fed-up expressions and gestures. Usually that was enough. Make the body do it, and the mind followed. Not this time. No way. Malibu was too powerful. It had crept inside his brain and was rotting it with the alien sensation called pleasure.

He twisted around in the Jacuzzi, and the water jets followed him, plucking deliciously at his hard body. Through the low glass barrier that bordered the compound he watched the surf barely fifty feet away across the beach. The Southern California waves came in lazily, as mellow and unhurried as the citizens of the dreamland who wandered by the side of the sea. Pelicans and gulls practiced their nosedives in the hazy heat. Sandpipers cavorted on the caramel sand. He reached for the glass of iced San Pellegrino, and as he crushed the fresh lime into the mineral water, he sang along to the Milli Vanilli song that wafted from the poolside speakers of the Sony sound system.

"Glad you came?"

She hovered above him, her graceful body silhouetted against the sun, and he squinted up at her, both his arms stretched out around the rim of the Jacuzzi. He smiled to say yes, that despite everything, he *was* glad, even though he knew it was an interlude, an opiate for pain that had been dulled but would never go away. Malibu was numbing his feelings in the way he had intended, but reality wouldn't hide forever. Nor did he want it to.

Allison took the smile gratefully. For the poor little rich girl, who had lived forever beneath the emotional poverty line, it was a precious gift.

"What do you want to do about lunch? I got some stuff from Hughes earlier. You want to help me do a barbecue? It's the California thing."

Again he didn't answer. He scooped up the Oliver Peoples horn-rimmed sunglasses from the wooden deck that surrounded the Jacuzzi and slipped them on, masking the eyes that could give away his feelings.

"Only 'healthful' food, I hope. No salt. No cholesterol. At least no low-density lipoproteins." He laughed, surprised that he still could.

"What do you think I am, a murderer? Listen, in the land of wheatgrass juice polyunsaturated fat is poison. We've got asparagus, and then chicken breasts and spinach salad. Strawberries and blueberries afterward, if you like."

The laughter danced in her words. She was so happy, thought Tony. And so very good. She had spirited him away from misery, and now every move she made, every word she spoke was designed to make him feel better and to encourage him to forget. She was in love with him, of course, but why, that was the question. Why would an angel, rich, beautiful, talented, born with a whole canteen of platinum cutlery cascading from her mouth, fall in love with a cold, uncouth psychopath in whose veins iced ambition had replaced warm blood? He had been cruel to her. He had used her. He was using her still, and she had repaid him with kindness, generosity, and good humor. The strange feeling inside him just had to be guilt, but already it was merging with something else.

She stood over him, straight and proud, like an actress should, and the patrician cut of her genes showed at each curve of her body, every contour of her face. The one-piece Donna Karan thong she wore was, however, the class enemy. It gave the lie to her aristocratic Ralph Lauren/Calvin Klein model looks, the haughty height of her brow, the thick bushiness of her eyebrows, the pencil straightness of her nose. Black as night, it bisected her full bottom and spoke eloquently of her longing for the low life. Wrapped tight around her hour-glass waist and the nipples of small, firm breasts, the sheer black Lycra, slinky sexy in the bright sunlight, told the truth about Allison Vanderbilt and the things she wanted when she crawled at bedtime between the faded cotton of ten-year-old Pratesi sheets. The girl needed love, but she had never been loved, and somehow, over the years, she had concluded that she wasn't lovable. So now she no longer looked for admiration and respect, for warmth and consideration and tenderness. Those things, unlike the houses, the horses, the jewelry, and the servants, had never been part of her birthright. Instead she saw it as her role to dispense pleasure, not to receive it, and gradually, as time passed, lust had filled the vacuum where love should have been, and subservient desire had become the fuel for her nocturnal fantasies.

"Get in, Allison," said Tony Valentino. His voice was husky, urgent. He took off his sunglasses and laid them on the weathered wood.

For a second she paused, but then the smile of satisfaction crinkled up the corners of her mouth. Her eyes sparkled, and she tossed her hair in the beach breeze like a young pony. She stepped toward the edge of the Jacuzzi and slid quickly into the foaming water. Across from him, she watched him and he made no move toward her, as their eyes met. She swallowed hard. He could see her throat bob beneath the skin of her long neck, see the perspiration standing out on her upper lip, and her eyes snaked away to the safe sky as his lasered into her mind, reading her passion like the big-print storybook of a child. He knew! Oh, God, he knew her secrets, and her whole body shuddered beneath the warm currents as it prepared itself for the delicious insults that would be the making of their love. Over his shoulder a surfer strode down the beach, his board slung beneath his arm. He was barely ten yards from them. The Colony beach was private to the high water mark, but in a fierce democracy there was no enforcing of that mobile boundary. Whatever happened now would take place in public, and Allison Vanderbilt's heart hammered against her chest in delightful panic at the thought. Once again she dared to look at him. Both his hands were below the surface of the water, and his eyes were hooded, his head to one side, his expression hungry. As she watched, he straightened his back, and he wriggled down and then his swimming trunks were bubbling on the surface of the Jacuzzi.

Again Allison swallowed. Her eyes widened. Her stomach tightened. The breath trembled in her flared nostrils, and her lungs shook as the currents of air rushed in and out in long, unmeasured gusts. The blanket of unreality descended, and the day receded from her, here at the edge of total passion where the desert met the sea. Her mouth was dry as the canyon wind. The thong of her swimsuit bit into the part of her that was now commanding her body and ruling her soul. In the wetness, she was melting, wetter somehow than the water that surrounded her. She was slippery inside, as her ass pushed against the rough seat of the Jacuzzi and her breasts tingled as the bone-hard jet current caught them, tensing her already taut nipples. Across from her he was naked now, naked and stiff with the longing it would be her privilege to satisfy. But still she didn't move. He would tell her what to do. He would know, and whatever he wanted would be right. She reached for her breast. Her fingers fumbled at the edge of the material, scurrying inside to feel the blood force itself into the throbbing cone of her nipple. She squeezed tight, as it thrust back at her thumb and forefinger, and all the time the pleasure fountain played within her, lighting up her mind, soaking the velvet walls of her secrecy, mixing with the waters that cocooned the soon-to-be lovers. Her butt tightened. Her back arched. Her pelvis contracted and relaxed, opening and closing in anticipation of the pleasure to come. Now with her left hand she felt for her other nipple, and she watched him, proud and defiant as she played with herself, lewd and abandoned, as she tuned her body for him. She crushed her ripe breasts beneath the flat of her hand, and she rubbed from side to side, pulling them from the black material so that they floated on the surface of the Jacuzzi—lost, revealed, then lost again—in the froth of the steamy water. Strawberry pink and vanilla they pointed at him, their pure white in contrast to the delicate rose of her sun-teased torso. She cupped them, pushing them up so he could see his gift. She pinched the rock-hard nipples, thrusting the blood into them until they swelled to bursting point, oblivious to the sharp pain, wanting only to inflame him to the point where there could be no turning back. She was burning. The flames of lust were alive inside her. And now her right hand dipped down, drawn to the core of her by a force far stronger than her will. Her legs splayed out and her forefinger hooked beneath the narrow strip of fabric. She moaned gently as she found the pleasure source, and she abandoned her humanity as she became the animal she longed to be.

"Yes, Allison," he whispered gently. "Do it. Play with yourself. Do it to yourself."

His words opened the floodgates of passion. She bucked out at her hand, desperate for the surrogate satisfaction. She reared against herself, thrusting, pushing, crushing, as she ground against stiff fingers. Her mouth fell open. The breath rushed past perfect teeth. Her head lolled to one side on the frothy sea of abandonment. Her hands raced up, down, back behind to the dark, trembling skin of her buttocks. Now her fingers moved forward again, chasing the ecstasy, milking the cream from each spine-chilling moment of joy. She felt so crude. She was rude and without shame as she masturbated for the man she worshiped. The expression on his face was her reward.

She was inside herself now, her hand sucked into the dripping smoothness, and the silken walls clamped down on the tearing fingers. Slowly her greedy, inaccurate movements acquired a rhythm and she arched her back as the music built within her to the awesome crescendo of release. Her eyes were hazy with the closeness of the orgasm and her hand moved cleverly, in and out, up and down, in the piston purpose of desire. All the time she watched him. This was for him. Everything was for him.

He launched himself across the watery space that separated them, and she was surrounded by the steel ring of his arms. His face was against her face, and his breath was hot on her sweat-soaked cheeks. His body was plastered tight against her, and she wrapped her legs around him, her hand still buried in her own core. Then, against the flatness of her lower stomach, she felt the part of him she longed for. Impossibly large, harder than mountain rock, he reared against her skin, and she smiled in triumph at what she had created, and she dared to imagine what it would do.

But first he wanted to drink from the moisture of her lips. His mouth found hers, and the stubble of his beard rubbed wonderfully against her smooth skin. There was no delicacy in his kiss. It was the kiss of the barbarian conqueror who had fought long and hard for the spoils he now claimed. Trembling, she surrendered to him, striving to divide herself into two separate parts, the better to savor the two distinct areas of ecstasy that were now her body. In the clash of teeth, in the merger of mouths, in the bruised battery of lips, she lived at the pinnacle of joy. But against her stomach, against the back of her hand still clasped against her throbbing mound of love, she could feel the source of his power. It stabbed at her like a dagger; it was heavy, angry, like a club; it thrust at her, the spear that must impale her in the thousand deaths in which alone she would be reborn.

His hands were lost in the luxuriance of her hair, twisting, pulling, forcing her mouth against his. His tongue twined with hers, and their liquid merged to lubricate the slam dance of slippery love.

He drew back from her, and his wild eyes bored into her. They signed the pact then. He didn't love her, but he needed her so badly that he would take her now, whether or not she wanted it. He made no promises to her, except to fill her body to overflowing with his pent-up lust. There could be no consideration for her, no tenderness, no commitment. She would have to take what she could find on the bleak steppes of his emotions, and he would not be held responsible if she starved in the emotional wilderness. She understood that. She loved him. Her body would be her gift to him. In the giving of it she would find her ultimate pleasure. She had wanted more, but it would do for now, because bodies had unfinished business, and because reason was the poor relation of almighty emotion.

He reached down roughly, and he plucked her hand from between her legs. He bent at the knee, and she felt faint as he positioned himself to take her. There at her opening, he waited. She could feel his sharpness nestling dangerously in the slippery hair, throbbing tight against the supreme softness of her quivering lips of love. Her hands floated to the surface and she gripped the surround of the Jacuzzi to steady herself for the wonderful, vicious assault that he was about to unleash. She wanted to touch it, to marvel at its hugeness, but more than that she wanted it to own her. She wanted to ride it. She wanted it thrust up inside her. She wanted it buried so deep in her body that it could never, never escape.

Her legs trembled beneath her, and she forced them farther apart until the whole of her lower body was an abyss demanding to be filled. In all her life she had never been so wide open, and the juice of her love ran like a river over the pulsing walls of her heartland.

"Please, please," she moaned.

It was enough. He thrust forward at her, and his vastness slid inside her. She cried out in joy as he filled her. She shook as he rammed into the roof of her, lifting her whole body with the crude, cruel force of his invasion. She gasped in awe at the wild feeling, and her eyes widened in wonder at the size of the intruder. On the borders where pleasure met pain she hung on to him, pinned to the wall of the hot tub, her whole body a mere envelope to the power of his desire. Now he stood up straight, his legs straining beneath the weight of her, and dripping, the thong of her swimsuit rudely displaced from the midline, she emerged from the foaming water impaled on the still expanding point of him. Her breasts thrust out from the top of the Lycra swimsuit, and he buried his head between them, his strong hands cupped beneath her buttocks, as he manipulated her whole body around the fulcrum that was now the center of her universe. She clasped her legs around his waist and hooked her ankles over each other, clamping herself down over the pleasure source, and as she did so she knew that she couldn't stop the orgasm.

The breath rasped from her lungs, and her muscles lost their coordination. She cried a short sharp cry of painful satisfaction, and the world turned on its axis, the blue sky kaleidoscoping into the battleship gray of the mountains, merging with the aquamarine of the sea. She was a surfer, her firm body writhing and twisting on the cresting wave. She was a bird, soaring, swooping on the thermal currents of the canyons.

Twitching, convulsing, her body shuddered with the spasms of her climax and her legs untwined, jerking in a crazed rhythm of release amid the fine spray of her sexuality. The air was thick with the musk of her. Her love was heavy on the warm breeze. The longing cascaded down her thighs as it soaked his stomach and conjured up the look of wonder in his faraway eyes.

"Ooooooooooh!" she howled at the heavens as she danced the threshing dance of the dying, her legs the legs of a hanged man windmilling frantically as they sought the platform they would never find. He didn't free her. He paid no attenton to her little death. He moved through it and beyond it as if it had never been. And so, inexorably, did she. The source of her crazed delight reverberated still, but on the other side of the hill Allison Vanderbilt wanted only to climb it once more.

He twisted around, spinning her on the tip of him, lifting up her leg and pushing it past his muscular chest. Then he was behind her, yet still inside her, and she could see him no more. Now she was supported only by the stick of hot flesh that joined them. He arched his torso away from her back until she was balanced on the point of him, hanging in midair, steadied only by the tips of his fingers at her narrow waist. She could feel only the place where he surged into her and her body hurtled upward at each powerful thrust of his hips, before crashing down with its own weight as he relaxed. For long minutes of eternal bliss he rode her. He was anonymous, invisible, known to her only by the baton of his lust, and once again the music inside her was building to a crescendo as her whole body howled for release. This time he seemed to hear it.

Once again he spun her around until she faced him, her eyes thick with tears of longing, her lips bared, her chin thrust out in helpless defiance. Her hair, wet with sweat, was plastered across her forehead and the breath rushed in angry torrents across her parted teeth. She had melted down. She had become liquid. She flowed toward him on a sensuous sea of sexuality, and he could drink her, do with her as he wished, as long as she could watch his eyes at the very moment he flowed into her. That was all she wanted now. She wanted to feel the truth of him, soaking her own fountain, drowning her own waterfall, submerging the ocean she was with the one he was about to become. In the lust land, he responded. It was time. He stopped. He was still. Her rocked and rearing body was motionless. There was only the fullness, the enormous presence, joining him to her in the bondage from which she wished never to be freed. She tried to conjure up the vision of it, buried in her warm depths, to capture in the eye of her mind the beautiful thing it was about to do. In the heart of her there was the tiniest movement, the vibration of a hummingbird at the face of a wide-open flower. Then, once, twice, three times, she felt it, a spurt, a silken caress, three delicious discrete splashes of molten love that signaled the moment of union. It was the lull before the storm. He exploded, rushing forward, his hands clutching frantically at her thighs, as he followed through into the heart of his orgasm. As he did so she clamped down over him, strangling him with the soft noose of her love lips, and her own climax collided with the exuberant force of his. On and on it went, fearful in its intensity, and his rumbling groan of pleasure merged with her sharp cry of release, as the gulls swooped overhead, and the majestic mountains stared down at the lovers.

"I don't know how to take a great photograph. I don't even know how to recognize a great subject, but I do know where beauty is an' it's here. The thing to do is to hang around and sooner or later something good happens."

"You're saying it's luck, Alabama?"

"No such thing, sweetheart. Just hard work. Just being ready for the moment whenever it comes. You have to master the technical side until you can do it in your sleep. The most important thing then is to forget it, and let the mind see. The moment you start to think, you're lost. First develop the instinct, then trust it. There's not much else."

"You don't think it can be taught?"

"Only to the person who has it already. It can be developed, refined, polished, but it has to *be* there. The talent can be raw, but without it there's no art. Just another boring photograph."

Pat Parker winced in pain, not at Alabama's optimistic/pessimistic analysis of what made a photographic artist, but because the inseams of her jeans were now two tight balls of material chafing the skin of her inner thighs. For the umpteenth time that afternoon she attempted to smooth them flat, knowing that in a minute or two they would ride up and the agony would start all over again.

She debated whether to tell him. No. She didn't want to be a city girl whining in the great outdoors. Alabama, up ahead of her, looked absolutely monumental, indestructible like the vast rock formations they were riding past. To complain about something as essentially trivial as pain was out of the question.

"Now I understand why people wear those riding pants. I always thought it was to turn everyone on."

He didn't look back. He wasn't interested. And his blue jeans, for some reason she didn't understand, hugged the ankles of his battered brown cowboy boots. Apparently, like taking photographs, riding was an art you mastered and then forgot. She gripped the reins and thought of the prized Japanese trait of "gamay"—perseverance. If it had projected the yen into the stratosphere it might be useful on a horseback photographic field trip in the Santa Monica Mountains.

"You know there's only one enemy in these mountains," said Alabama over his shoulder, his face shielded from the overhead sun by the brim of his snakeskin-rimmed, black leather Trilby hat. "An' that's human. They light the fires that burn them, an' they build the tract trash that litters them. Never met a developer I didn't want to shoot."

His hand lingered longingly on the pearl handle of the Smith & Wesson .45 that dangled from an intricately tooled holster at his hip. Pat was glad she wasn't a builder. She breathed in deeply, and the scent of the sage and the pine on the superheated breeze hurried into her head. She adjusted the wide-brimmed hat that Alabama had lent her, and felt the sweat trickle down between her breasts, beneath the already saturated white camisole top. Jeez, this was worse than the World, Mars, and M.K. rolled into one. It seldom got to be a hundred degrees in the slime pits of New York City. At least there were no cigarettes here. In the Alabama world of the high chaparral, smokers probably rated right next to developers in the popularity stakes.

"Is that why Malibu wants to become a town?"

"It's the main reason. If we incoroporate, then the people who live here can decide what the place gets to look like. Not a bad little idea. It's called democracy. Used to be quite popular."

"But not with the developers."

"Yeah. Right now, for the most part, the people who make the zoning decisions aren't residents. An' they can be 'influenced.' Development means more tax dollars, and more tax dollars equals bigger bureaus for the bureaucrats. They don't have to live in the mess they permit, so what happens to Malibu doesn't affect them."

"The local papers seem to talk about nothing but sewers. That's hardly the Malibu image."

"Sewers are shorthand for development. Right now every house in Malibu has a septic tank, and I'll tell you when the sea comes in, those fancy beach houses in the Colony are knee deep in it. But the residents are happy to put up with the inconvenience because without central sewers nobody can build hotels and restaurants and convention centers. So the homeowners want to kibosh the sewers, and the county politicians and the developers want to put them in. The whole thing comes down to what to do with the shit."

He laughed, his great belly wobbling in the sunlight, at the thought of all the movie stars and the millionaires, the rock stars and the writers, the painters and the piss artists fighting for the God-given right to dispose of their own waste.

"Who's going to win?" asked Pat.

"I am," said Alabama simply, and he laughed again and dug his heels into the flanks of his horse, sending the animal scurrying up a steep slope beneath an overhanging rock.

Pat smiled as she attempted to follow her leader. It figured. Alabama was as far from losing as he was from grace. Already she was beginning to love him as the father she had never had, and his prickly impossibility, his drinking bouts, and his eccentricity were charming idiosyncracies that enabled her to relate to him as some sort of an equal.There had been no formal lessons, but each time he spoke she learned something about photography, and more important, about art. Beneath the banter and the baiting, Ben Alabama was a Zen soldier. Everything was intertwined. All was related. The way you lived your life, the values you held were every bit as vital as the direction you pointed your camera. "Every man has a photograph in him," he was fond of saying. "And it's the best place for it to remain." Even his apparent weaknesses, he sold as strengths. Drinking beer was to mock the seriousness of life. Fighting was good clean fun, and part of an American tradition the sweeping away of which had led to a weaker, more dependent society, one that suffered from a soul-sapping deficiency in self-respect. His social abrasiveness was really only self-assertion, and that was the duty of anyone who lived by a moral code and was proud of it.

They had reached a peak that looked down on all the others, and Alabama reined in his horse and turned in his western saddle to savor the extraordinary view. Pat did the same, the wild beauty of the hundred-mile vista taking away her breath. To one side stretched the San Fernando Valley, the houses and the "civilization" dwarfed by the majesty of the mountains. To the other, the Malibu hills were bordered by the sea and in the crystal clarity she could see Catalina, the south side of Santa Monica Bay, and north way into Ventura County. The sun played across the colors, shading rock and shrub, the hills and the valleys in subtle grays, browns, and sage greens, while over it all, separating earth from sky, hung a hazy layer of purple and magenta, of lilac and burnished orange, mixed in the magic of the constantly changing light.

"Knocking on heaven's door," said Alabama, in awe of the beauty.

Pat slung her legs gratefully over the saddle as she dismounted. She reached for the crumpled Mark Cross canvas tote bag that contained everything in the world she cared about. She fished out a Leica and an 85mm telephoto lens, which she clipped to the battered body of the camera. Her eyes searched the distant horizon, computing the light. Next she thumbed open a pack of Ilford HP3, and without looking she loaded it, snapped the camera back closed, and ran off three exposures with the lens pointed at the dusty scrub.

"You need a five-by-seven view camera," said Alabama. "You'll get nothing with a Leica. An' it's a color photograph. You want Kodachrome, an' maybe a red filter to bring out the shadows. Sun's overhead. Vertical light's no good for landscape. You wanna go wider than eight-five millimeter. Way wider for a halfway decent picture."

He leaned pugnaciously from the saddle toward his protégé. She was disappointing him. She was going for the obvious, and in a not very well thought-out way. He didn't mind telling her so. He didn't mind telling anybody anything about photography.

She whirled around on him, and the long lens zeroed in on the jutting point of his aggressive chin. Her fingers twirled on the serrated edge of the viewfinder. His irritated eyes swam into focus as his tree-on-a-blasted-heath saddle stance melded perfectly with the rocky backdrop in silhouette against the harsh overhead light of the sky. *Click* went the shutter.

"Oh," said Alabama.

"I think you'll find that *that* is the photograph," mocked Pat Parker.

"I think that maybe I will," agreed Alabama, laughing at himself and his presumption. He should have known. The girl was a genius. From the moment her six prints had cascaded onto the pine of his kitchen table, he had known that she had the X factor. It had been years since he'd seen such good photographs, and the alien subject matter hadn't made an iota of difference to the excitement that had gripped him. The girl could visualize, and she could seize the moment. She could compose, she could cut, and she could print. In short, she had the knack, and he had immediately invited her to Malibu. He wasn't sorry. The photographs she had taken while staying as his guest had confirmed her brilliance. On two occasions only had he doubted her, and for the second time she had turned the tables on him. The garden gnome picture, as he now referred to it, had made a superb print. Elliott Erwitt funny, it defined elves, pixies, and little people in the forest and the fact that hard-as-nails Alabama was its subject merely added to the joke. Now, she had duplicated Karsh's Churchill trick. The Canadian photographer had deliberately made the statesman angry to capture his definitive belligerence. The resulting portrait had been one of the greatest ever taken. There was no doubt in Alabama's mind that this picture, too, would be a revelation. He turned to check the background, the light, the sky, and his mind's eye conceptualized the angle he'd have made with the horse, the expression that must have been playing on his face, the one that the telephoto lens would have captured perfectly. He could actually "see" the print, in the way that Mozart could "hear" the music he wrote, and it was superb.

He swung himself out of the saddle.

He walked over to Pat, and he put his arm around her shoulders.

"I'm sorry," he said. "I've got to stop doing that."

She laughed. "You don't have to stop doing anything. You're a legend."

"I used to be." The strange feeling welled up in Alabama. Good God, he was going to tell her the secret that only King and he knew.

"What do you mean, 'used to be'? I went to your Metropolitan show last year. I saw your recent photographs, Alabama. They're as beautiful as anything you've ever done. I mean they're the *same*."

He had surprised her. The humility, the self-doubt were totally out of character. Surely he hadn't been fishing for anything so mundane as a compliment. He *must* have had enough of those by now.

"I'll tell you why they're the same, Pat Parker. They're the same because I haven't taken a photograph for ten years, and I don't intend to take another. I just print up the old negatives and stick on today's date. What do you think of that, my friend?"

Pat knew she was being tested. Shock/horror/reproach was not the correct reaction. Either it was some complex joke, or there were perfectly good reasons that would explain the unthinkable. She was being asked to believe that Bacon had given up painting, that Carson had stopped cracking jokes, that Reagan had refused to appear on television. It was bizarre, but then the truth often was.

"If it's true, why are you telling me?"

Alabama looked puzzled, *was* puzzled.

"I'm not quite sure," he said at last. "I think it's because I like you. I think it's because I think that in time you'll understand."

Somehow the subject had closed itself off. It was on the back burner, to be investigated and discussed as part of the ongoing process of friendship development. He did like this girl, but more than that, he trusted and admired her. She was his own speed. In Los Angeles County, precious few were.

"Anyway, talented girl, we should be getting back if we're going to make that Latham lunch. How do you feel about billionaires? They do anything for you?"

"Not yet, not yet," Pat Parker laughed.

FIVE

The butler, his whole life a complicated training in unflappability, had lost the plot. He stood in the open door and wondered whether to shout for help, to call the police, or to stand back and welcome the extraordinary duo into his house.

"Alabama and friend for Dick Latham," growled Alabama in threatening tones. The beer smell and the beer belly preceded him, and behind the tree trunks of his Levied legs the pipes of the Harley still crackled and creaked from the heat of the furious descent from the mountains. The English majordomo had heard about bikers, remembered Brando in *The Wild One*, but he had never expected to see one this close.

"Mr. Alabama?" he managed, his question mark vast. A Mr. Alabama had been on the guest list for lunch.

"Yeah," grunted Alabama, not bothering to put the butler straight on the small print of his nomenclature. He pushed past the gate guardian, and Pat, smiling at the confusion, followed in his wake.

Fait accompli and *savoir faire* were about the only French that Englishmen understood. If the house was to be raped and pillaged, then the surrender should be handled with decorum.

"May I take your 'hat,' sir?" said the butler, allowing himself a liberal measure of sarcasm to cover the defeat he had just suffered.

"No," said Alabama. "It's grown onto my head." That looked to be true. It was battered enough to have been slept in for several years, and where brim met forehead there were nutrients that would have supported growth of sorts. The Englishman winced. In America it was the limeys who were supposed to have the monopoly on dirt. Lack of cleanliness and their legendary meanness were far better known national characteristics on this side of the Atlantic than the phlegm and sophistication that the British liked to think they were famous for.

Pat Parker looked around at the serious money. It was everywhere—in the museum-quality furniture, in the serious art, in the superb architecture—and her aesthetic vision lasered in on it, melding it in her journalistic mind with the bits and pieces she already knew about Richard Latham. He lived most of the time in New York, and he owned magazines for which she had occasionally worked. She had seen him around at the grander parties she had covered, but mostly they had lived in parallel but distinctly separate worlds, and she had never actually met him. She knew he had a reputation as a ladykiller, and he was very good-looking for an older man. That, and the megabucks, made him interesting, even to a girl whose heroes and heroines were photographers, painters, and writers, not superrich robber barons with Don Juan complexes. Alabama had told her the Paris story, and that had added depth to the one-dimensional character of the press clippings. Latham might have behaved badly all those years ago, but at least he had had the balls to stand up to Alabama, and the heart to break when the girl he loved had walked out on him. Many of the men she knew possessed neither.

The Mexican-tiled foyer in which they found themselves was full of flowers. Geraniums cascaded from terra-cotta pots, pink and mauve impatiens sprouted from hanging baskets, bougainvillea climbed around stucco columns. In the center a fountain, tiled in ancient Spanish tiles, tinkled pleasantly, and eyes were drawn past it to a courtyard in which a forty-foot pool sparkled in the midday sun. The walls were heavy with paintings—Dutch seventeenth-century still lifes, Van Dycks of serious soldiers, what looked suspiciously like a genuine Franz Hals. Mozart's Violin Concerto in E minor, soft and harrowing, warbled from hidden speakers.

"Can I offer you a drink, madam?" tried the chastened butler as he attempted some kind of recovery from social shock.

"I'd love a Coke," said Pat.

"Classic . . . or . . . otherwise?"

"Oh, Classic, I guess."

"Diet . . . or otherwise."

"Diet."

"Caffeine free . . . or . . ."

"Otherwise," said Pat sharply.

"Sir?" said the butler.

"Beer. Dos Equis, Corona, or Tecate, in order of preference. Bottled. Slice of lime. Cold. Quickly," said Alabama.

He leered pugnaciously at the hired help, as he covered the options.

"Welcome, welcome," said Dick Latham, leaking the oil of affability onto the troubled waters. "Alabama, at last. And the beautiful and talented Pat Parker."

He creamed forward, his over-the-top smile happy on his sunburnished face, his teeth flashing and shining in the bright light. He was Polo casual, pink on blue, the Guess? watch a gentle joke on his muscular forearm. His shoes shone and his pants cut, and, as he reached for Alabama's hand, he devoured Pat with amused, solicitous eyes.

"You owe me a hundred bucks," grumbled Alabama, shaking the hand that Latham offered with minimal enthusiasm.

"How clever of you to remember," Latham laughed without missing a beat. "Paris, wasn't it? A lifetime ago. Youth is wasted on the young, don't you think so, Alabama?"

He smiled at her as he spoke, aware of his social smoothness, of his formidable self-confidence, as he deflected the aggression with his so-subtle apology. Despite herself, she smiled back. The articles in *Time* and *Forbes* hadn't captured the charisma, hadn't mentioned the lean, hard body, the Anglicized accent. He was fifty going on forty, and the charm juice sprayed from him like scent from an atomizer in the perfume department at Bloomingdale's.

Alabama's belligerent eyes narrowed. Latham might have gotten his act together, but the boy was the father of the man. Inside he wouldn't have changed that much. People didn't. And he wasn't going to get away with making his slimy moves on Pat Parker.

"Oh, I never thought youth was wasted on Eva Ventura. Do you remember that beautiful girl? I wonder whatever happened to her."

The sexy smile vanished from Dick Latham's lips. They were tight now, and devoid of blood, drawn in a pencil line across his jawbone. His eyes shut down and he froze as his shoulders stiffened and the breath whistled into his flared nostrils. He hadn't heard that name in twenty years, but scarcely a twenty-minute period passed during which he didn't think about her. Eva Ventura, who had floodlit his heart and given new meaning to his jaded life. She had been all the fun and the gaiety and the spontaneous energy that had been absent from his dark childhood, and he had loved her more than he had known it was possible to love. All the disparate chords had merged in a secret harmony of beautiful music as, in Eva Ventura, his future had made sense at last. But his devils had never been completely exorcised. When an old girlfriend had made her play for him, he had gone through the sexual motions more out of habit than anything else, and because he had forgotten how to refuse. Eva had found them together. She had laughed in his face at his fickle faithlessness, and she had vanished into thin air. The nausea welled up in his stomach as he remembered the dreadful loss, and he gritted his teeth in rage at the wrong that could never be made right. Now, his feelings extroverted once again, he turned in ice-cold fury toward Alabama. It was clear that the old biker had brought up Eva's name to irritate him. He could tell from the jaunty way the weather-beaten head was tucked to one side, its eyes fascinated by the effect of its tongue's action, the half smile of revenge puckering up the corners of the chapped lips. Alabama hadn't forgotten Paris, Latham's rejection of his work, and the millionaire's callous refusal to pay him the money he was morally owed.

In Latham's mind the potential insults queued up up for consideration. Then the training of the last twenty-five years reasserted itself. In the rarefied money maze he inhabited there was no room for petty emotion. Tit for cheap tat was for losers. It was a revelation of weakness. The need for retaliation pinpointed the precise location of your Achilles heel, and where you had been hurt once you could be hurt again. So the trick was to disguise the pain but never, ever to forget it. Revenge was a dish better served cold, but Dick Latham had acquired a taste for it deep frozen. He didn't merely get even, or marginally ahead. Instead he leap-frogged into other worlds as he put distance between himself and his enemies. Then, when they were eaten away with jealousy at his success, he lobbed clever bombs at them from outer galaxies, wrecking their lives and humiliating them, while making sure they were well aware of their destroyer's identity.

But with Alabama there was another angle. He needed him. He had to have him on his side during this crucial period. Alabama ran the Santa Monica Mountains Preservation trust singlehanded from his abysslike pockets. He was the money source, and he had the ears of the politicians, the public, and the vital media. He was the thrust behind Malibu's antideveloper cityhood application. He would be a difficult friend, but an intolerable enemy. Without Alabama, Dick Latham's land purchase, the site of his secretly projected Cosmos studio, would be derailed. If for one second he thought Latham would be an ecologically unreliable neighbor, Alabama could use his influence with the landowner to block the sale, or to write antidevelopment clauses into the contract even at this late stage of escrow. He might persuade the government to buy the land. He might even mobilize the money to buy it himself. Now was not the time to antagonize him, whatever he said, however he behaved. Latham took a deep breath. "Yes, she was a wonderful girl, wasn't she? Sometimes I think I should have married her."

He bit on his lip as he forced the banality through it. He stuffed the jauntiness back into his step, and he dragged on the debonair mantle once again, reloading his charm gun, as he fought to camouflage the wound he had suffered. He turned toward Pat. "Pat Parker, I've got someone here who's dying to meet you. She's my secret weapon. I've brought her over from England to revamp my magazine *Celebrity*. You'll love her. She's full of ideas. Name's Emma Guinness."

He laid a hand on Pat's shoulder, and she was aware of his touch as he steered her across the pool patio to the double doors of the main house.

"Of course, Alabama's far too grand for magazines anymore, I'm afraid. Too frivolous, I expect, after MOMA, the Whitney, and the Met. By the way, Alabama, I love your recent work. So fresh. *So* original. Not that you have any reason to respect my judgment after my sad little performance in Paris. Have you still got that portrait? I'd swap it for a quarter of a million to the Sierra Club."

He turned over his shoulder to watch the effect as he dangled the cash carrot. It was way over double the rate for an Alabama portrait, even an early one. And the Sierra Club wasn't as rich as it had been in Ansel's day. Yosemite could do with the bucks, and it was a subtle hint that he, Latham, was an environmental friend. But his stomach tightened. He could do without a physical reminder of that time. Maybe, he'd be spared it. Alabama had probably used the print as a dart board.

Pat turned also to see the effect of the windfall on her friend, as the Latham hand, exerting an intriguing pressure, continued to linger on her arm. She knew Alabama disliked and mistrusted the billionaire. How would he deal with the dilemma? Would the Sierra Club's gift horse be looked in the mouth to satisfy his prickly ego? It would be a close call.

Not for Alabama.

"Half a million," he said.

"A million," countered Latham perversely, "on condition that Pat Parker keeps my portrait on the table beside her bed."

He laughed as he spoke, and they all stopped in their tracks. But the Latham hand was still on the Parker arm.

"You're joking." She smiled as the red exploded high on her cheeks.

"I've never been more serious in my life." His smile was changing. His eyes bored into her. He was telling her something she wasn't quite ready to hear. Inside, she felt the drums begin to beat, as she realized he did mean it. He wanted to see her in bed. He wanted to see her curled up and sleepy, catlike and vulnerable in the early morning, see her rubbing the dust from her eyes, hear her yawn, smell the earthy scent of her as she tumbled beneath the cheap sheets after the too-late nights in the too-loud clubs. For a mere million his picture could see all that, and she could see him, and she wouldn't forget him because she was the sort who would keep a promise, however frivolous, however bizarre.

"It's up to you, Pat Parker," growled Alabama. "A lifetime of nightmares in exchange for a million for the mountains." He had forgotten how rich Latham was, how capricious, how consumed by the need to conquer beauty. The chase was on. He had seen it start. His brand-new friend was the quarry and she had better watch out.

"Listen, a bedside Alabama of Mr. Latham would be no hardship at all. Certainly more appetizing than one of my folks."

They both heard the cheerful banter of her first sentence tail off into the pathos of her second. For a brief moment the pain was visible, almost tangible, and she paused, seeming to hear hidden voices, to see invisible demons.

But there was a distraction. The doors before them were flung open. A small bundle of humanity was all wrapped up in a frilly bikini, the upper portion of which struggled to contain vast breasts, while the lower bit served both as wrapper to a broad-beamed butt, and launching pad for short, stocky legs. The brilliant white of the swimsuit offset the lobster pink of her skin. Whoever she was had economized on the sunscreen.

"Emma!" said Latham, wincing at the visual. "Come and meet the famous Alabama, and the beautiful Pat Parker. I've just bought a portrait Alabama did of me in Paris when I was young. I'm hoping it's going to perform the same function for me as a similar one did for Dorian Gray."

"On my bedside table? Thanks a lot!" Pat laughed. She held out a hand to Emma Guinness. "Hi, I'm Pat Parker," she said.

Alabama waved a halfhearted greeting, his hand firmly by his side.

"I know you are. I'm a fan. I love your work," said Emma. "If they'd used people like you, *Celebrity* wouldn't need to be turned around."

"Thanks," said Pat. A compliment was a good way to start. Already she liked the girl in the dreadful swimsuit. There had been no pretense that the ghastly *Celebrity* had been a success. The truthfulness added weight to the Englishwoman's flattery.

Latham smiled in satisfaction at the promising beginning. Both Emma and he had different plans for Pat Parker. Emma's would dovetail neatly with his. His would certainly not harmonize with Emma's. He turned to Alabama.

"Alabama, let me spirit you away for a few minutes. I want to show you some plans I have for building a house on that land I'm buying near you in the mountains. I want it to merge with its surroundings. I thought maybe you'd have a few ideas. You two girls get to know each other, and we'll meet later for lunch."

Alabama grunted his acquiescence. He hadn't looked forward to this lunch, but he had accepted out of curiosity and because any knowledge of a potential enemy was better than none. Now he had already scored a million dollars for the high Sierras and was about to get a preview of the monstrosity that the high roller was trying to build in his mountains. Great! It would be ammunition for the Coastal Commission hearing on the zoning when he later objected to the Latham plans. He grabbed at the cold Corona that had just materialized on the butler's Georgian silver salver, and he shuffled off with the billionaire.

Emma Guinness flopped onto the slubbed-silk sofa, and Pat Parker into an armchair.

"So, Pat, why Malibu?" She watched the photographer, taking in the good looks and the powerful fashion statement. The T-shirt she recognized. It was by hot new English designer of the moment, John Richmond. The tattoo motif—God, America, Mom, Elvis—was very "now," Harley biker chic, as the trendsetters tired of Chanel and conspicuous consumption and began to look for their fashion statements among the lowlife of the wild side. She must remember that for *New Celebrity*. Earthiness was coming back.

Roots, the working class, dressing down were coming up in a modified sixties rehash after the rampant materialism of the fifties-style Reagan years. The Parker boots, battered, comfy, would run and run like the endless Parker legs, and the jeans, baggy, faded, would make sitting down a pleasure rather than an ordeal.

"I'm here because Alabama's here. I'm working with him. Developing a new perspective. I was stuck. He's helping me."

"You didn't look stuck to me. I loved your work."

"Yeah, well, it's what you feel inside, isn't it? I wanted to move on."

"To what?" Emma wasn't discouraged. The new Pat Parker might be more exciting than the old. Brand-new photographs for her brand-new magazine. She prayed it wasn't watered-down Alabama nature shots, though. More or less anything would play but those.

"Oh, I don't know, really. That's why I'm here. To find out. People still, I guess. I can't get away from them. They fascinate me. But not frothy people. I want to shoot deep people, dangerous people. You know, people who *care*."

"Yes, I know what you mean. More than Warhol died with Andy. 'Wows' and 'goshes' aren't enough as conversation. Frivolous is passé. But will you find those sorts of people in Malibu? I've only been here since yesterday and I'm on the verge of coma. I can't stay awake. There's this mellow yellow poison gas drifting in from the sea that bleaches out all the dark, brooding, productive thoughts into pretty, pale pastels. A week or two of this and I'll be the Day-Glo girl."

Pat laughed, not least because the Day-Glo girl would be a dramatic improvement on the frilly lobster. But she liked the rapid-fire conversation of the English girl, liked her unashamed trendiness, her analytical mind.

"Listen, color's a relief after all that New York black. And sleeping at night is a weird experience. I'm trying to get used to the noise of the quiet."

"Yes, but the sea makes such a racket. I keep thinking it's coming in the bedroom window. Apparently it's only a matter of time before it does." Emma laughed, and then she seemed to make a decision. She leaned forward, her arms on her knees. "Listen, Pat, I want you to work for *New Celebrity*. How would you feel about doing that on an exclusive basis? You'd get a retainer, a big one, and total artistic freedom to produce anything you liked. That might be just what you need right now. Cash, but no deadlines.

An outlet, but no directions. I'd be buying your judgment and your vision, because I trust them."

Pat sat back in the chair. Despite Andy's death she wanted to say "wow." But she was enough of a New Yorker not to let her enthusiasm show.

"The trouble is, I'm sort of blocked right now. You say 'no deadlines,' but you'd have to see something for your money. And how much money were you thinking, anyway?"

She laid her head in her hand and smiled to disguise the hard-nosed negotiating position.

"Say one hundred thousand for two big spreads a year."

"Wow!" said Pat Parker, despite herself.

Now Emma smiled. She had cleared the deal with Latham, and he had suggested adding twenty-five thousand to the retainer. Pat Parker would never have been offered a contract like it. But Emma had learned that in life you had to pay over the top for excellence. If you had the guts to do it, it always looked cheap later.

Emma Guinness leaned forward. "Are you on?" she asked.

"I'm not off. I'm not off." Pat laughed, playing for time. There was probably extra juice to be squeezed from the deal, but she couldn't think where. Ritts, Weber, and Newton didn't get offered contracts like this. Now, out of the blue, and at the very point where she was considering throwing in the towel on photojournalism, she had been offered the moon and the stars. How like life. Already she was wondering just what the hell she would choose as a subject for a *New Celebrity* photo essay. Her mind was blank. Writers weren't the only artists who got blocked.

"And I could choose whatever I did? I mean, you're not hoping for New York nighttime reportage and all the stuff I've concentrated on so far."

"It's up to you. If you want to do more of that, fine. If not, that's fine, too."

"You say two spreads a year, but you say 'no deadlines.' How would that work?"

"It'd be loose. Of course, I'd really like something yesterday, for my first issue, but if you haven't got anything in the can, I'll live with that. What I mean is that you won't be pinned down too tight. I just know we can work together. I can work with anyone I admire. The trouble is there aren't many who fit that bill."

"I accept," said Pat. There was a time for chatter and a time for action. She had a dream job. She was artistically underwritten. "Scorpions of the Santa Monica Mountains" would get a five-page spread and earn fifty thousand, at least in theory, at least in the contract. Okay, she wouldn't do that to Emma and Latham, but in a pinch she could. It was major-league freedom and it meant she could stay on in Malibu with Alabama. She could be a humble assistant, a gofer to the guru, and yet retain an outlet for her work and a magnificent income. All she had to do was what she did best. She had only to take photographs.

Emma jumped up.

"Great. Terrific. That's wonderful." She rushed over to Pat and hugged her tight. Inside she was bubbling, too. Her success had been built on the backs of the brilliant people she employed. Recognizing greatness in unlikely places and then hiring it was her chief talent—perhaps her only one. Now she was on the road and running. Michael Flaubert, the trendsetting black fashion journalist, had already agreed to take the vital fashion portfolio, and Kit Jacosta, the young, hip novelist, had been bribed to step down from his intellectual ivory tower to head up features. The Parker-Flaubert-Jacosta triumvirate was the stuff of magazine legend, and the adrenaline sang in the Guinness arteries as she contemplated her magnificent future.

"Come on, Pat, let's have some champagne to celebrate. I'm *so* excited."

"I'll stick with the Coke. I don't drink." Pat laughed, infected by Emma's enthusiasm and still trying to acclimate to the amazing thing that had happened to her.

"You don't? God, I do, and I feel like getting absolutely plastered." Actually, in all her life Emma had never once been drunk. She was a control freak, and that included self-control. But she had learned that people were not naturally drawn to those who were fearful of letting go. So she cultivated the appearance of looseness and pretended to enjoy the pointless business of having a good time. "Come on, let's go for a walk on the beach, then. I'm your boss, you've got to humor me," she said breathlessly, jumping up.

Pat stood up too, and, laughing, the two brand-new friends walked out through the French doors onto the sand of the private volleyball court that bordered the terrace of the Latham home. The sun scorched down on them, angling in sharply across the tranquil ocean. The smog-free air was fresh in their nostrils.

"Jesus, I could do with a surfer," said Emma suddenly.

"What!"

"A surfer to play with. Wouldn't that be nice? All slippery muscles and speechless, blond hair, brain dead, and tasting salty.

Stamina of a horse, called Ricky, with parents my age. Ever since I've been in Malibu I haven't thought of anything else." Emma laughed to show she was serious.

"Oh, Emma, you're joking. He'd bore you rigid. 'Ricky' would be the kind of guy who thought a double entendre was a strong drink. How about Dick Latham? More your speed, I'd have thought," she added shrewdly.

"That's the alternative," agreed Emma with a smile. She sat down on the corner of a windsurfer that lay across the dunes.

"But he *is* a little too good to be true, isn't he?" Emma's voice went reflective as Pat sat down beside her. What she meant was that Latham liked girls who were ten times more beautiful than she—girls like Pat Parker, from whose face and body the Latham eyes had not strayed during the brief moments since they'd met; girls like Pat, whose salary he had suggested increasing by twenty-five percent; girls like Parker, whose photographic career had seemed so very well known to the satyrical billionaire.

"Listen, once in a blue moon they're allowed to be good."

"Mmmmmm. I don't think Dick's really very 'good,' do you? I mean, it's good that he's rich, and he's not gay, and it's good that he's interesting and bright and it's good that he's good-looking and knows how to make a woman feel incredibly good, but I'm afraid, really, he's very, very bad."

"Are you having an affair with him?"

Pat had never met such a wide-open English person. She must have died the death in her emotionally constipated homeland, have found nirvana in the mood incontinence of America. She was getting to know her at breakneck speed.

"Not unless you call a mile-high fuck in the loo on MGM Air an affair."

"Emma, you didn't!" Pat sat down on the serrated platform of the windsurfer. The incredulous amusement was thick in her voice.

"Oh, yes, we did."

"Why, I mean, how . . ."

"With very great difficulty and a certain amount of perseverance," said Emma, her voice mock serious. "He said he'd always wanted to try it, and as an employee, I felt it was my duty to accommodate him. Joy was minimal, but afterward there was a certain sense of achievement. He seemed chiefly concerned with the fact that it gave him the right to wear some sort of club tie. Oh, and he said it was good for the calf muscles on a long flight. You're supposed to exercise on aeroplanes nowadays. But then, being an American you know all about that. Health is something that hasn't caught on in Europe, you know."

"God, Emma, that's just unbelievable. I always imagined Latham to be so cool. I can't imagine him . . ."

Pat Parker tried to imagine what she couldn't, and as she did so she wondered what she felt about it. Clearly Latham had a problem. He had to have women, had to humiliate them, wasn't *that* fussy what they looked like. Emma Guinness's sharp mind and quick tongue were attractive, but she was very far from the drop-dead beautiful girls that hung on the Latham arm in the glossy magazines. Then there was the venue for the assignation. Original? Daring? Tacky? Bad manners? It was difficult to say. When she had first met him she had been flattered by the attention he had paid her, despite the subterranean feeling that he was not entirely wholesome. What should she make of that in light of what she had just learned? One thing was certain. With Dick Latham what you saw was not necessarily what you got. Emma's revelation had added surprise to his list of attributes/defects.

"Anyway," laughed Emma, "surfers permitting, I am hoping for a rematch in slightly more salubrious surroundings. Afterward, I am hoping for an exchange of sentiments more meaningful than remarks about aerobics and club ties. What are you after, Pat Parker, surely not Alabama? He looks like the proverbial old man of the woods, and I'd be *very* nervous about the state of his underwear."

"Oh, God, no, I mean not like that. He's my hero, that's all. And he's kind beneath all the bluster, and he's the most honest man I've ever met in my life."

"How awful." Emma shuddered. "Honest people are so brutal."

"Well, he *is* a little brutal, but only to those he doesn't trust."

"He doesn't trust Dick, does he?"

"No, I don't think he does. He hates businessmen, and then there was some fight they had in Paris a long time ago."

"Well, all I know is that Dick wants to buy up all this land in the mountains, God knows why, and he needs Alabama to okay it. Alabama's the godfather around here, apparently . . . and Dick reckons *he's* the godfather everywhere else. They're probably up there now, each making offers the other can't refuse. There shouldn't be any trouble finding horses' heads to stick in each other's beds. Malibu's stiff with them. More nags than beach boys . . . unfortunately."

She looked transcendentally saddened by the deficiency of human flesh, the oversupply of the equine variety, and Pat had to laugh, despite the less than flattering press Emma had given Alabama.

"How did you get to meet Dick Latham, Emma?"

"Anglophilia is one of his perversions. He has a house in Chester Square, which is where all the grand Americans live. Member of White's, debentures at Wimbledon, fittings at Anderson and Sheppard, the whole nine yards as you'd say, whatever that means. He was looking for someone to pull *Celebrity* out of the shit, and I'd just done that with a rag called *Class*, so he offered me a million a year and the use of his brownstone on Fifth, and I said yes, of course. I'd been dying to get out of England."

"What can you possibly mean? England sounds wonderful. I'm longing to go there."

"The tourists enjoy it. The English are quite nice to them, and they don't have time to get fed up with the food and the weather. It's the English that the English don't like. The whole place is in a state of constant undeclared civil war. The accents are the uniforms of the rival armies, and the different classes rape and pillage and take no prisoners. The 'workers' steal, the aristocrats drink, and the bourgeois suffer. It's vicious stuff, believe me. For you Americans class warfare is an ethnic affair. You know . . . black hardhats playing rap music on building sites to irritate redneck foremen who are playing country music to infuriate the blacks, and they're both cranking up the volume to madden the Jewish doctor across the street who's trying to listen to Strindberg. It's child's play compared to England, where everyone really *cares* about the class struggle. People work for peanuts all their lives to score a knighthood that the real aristocrats giggle at."

"But hasn't Thatcher changed all that?"

"God, she's tried, but they'll change her first. Until they get rid of the royals, it'll be business as usual."

The bitterness was beginning to show, and from the ashes of the amusing, irreverent, self-confident Emma Guinness a new animal was emerging. It was a wounded one, a hound at bay, dangerous, frightened, angry, hurt. Her lips curled over her words and her eyes were narrow, her lips tight and mean. She clenched her fists, and her knuckles were white against the red of her skin, as she relived the pain and the cruelty of the words that had clearly hurt more than the proverbial sticks and stones. Pat saw it all, and filed it away in her memory. As with Dick Latham, first impressions of

Emma Guinness were misleading. The girl she saw now was one who had to be handled with caution. The hatred was alive in her. Pat could almost touch it.

"You're not allowed to feel like that in Malibu," said Pat gently. "It's against the law."

Emma started, as if emerging from a nightmare sleep.

"What? Oh yes, England." She laughed unconvincingly. "I was on my hobby horse. It's a bad subject for me."

"You should hear me on parents." Pat felt the need to show solidarity. There was no pain that she couldn't cap with the pain of her childhood.

"Bad parents?"

"Only the worst." Pat bit her lip as she dared to remember.

But Emma Guinness, not even a sounding board, was certainly no wailing wall. Other people's lives were deeply uninteresting to her. To that extent she was thoroughly British.

Her eyes went dreamy. "I *suppose* I had parents," she said at last. "I could never get very interested in them."

She stood up. "Come on, I'm hungry, and I ought to change for lunch. Let's go and join the others before they bore themselves to death."

Pat stood up. A new job. Dick Latham, member of White's, the Forbes 400, and the Mile High Club, his laughing eyes probing her. Alabama, a bomb on a short fuse in the billionaire's lair. Emma Guinness, Pat's new boss, a witty, vicious trendsetter who talked of surfer's bodies and schemed secretly to become the Latham wife. One thing was certain. It was going to be one hell of a lunch.

"Watch out for the salsa," said Pat. "It's red hot."

"Good," boomed Alabama, scooping a mound onto a tortilla chip. "If you can't insult your stomach, what the hell can you insult around here?"

"Oh, I'm sure that finding something to insult isn't a problem for you, Mr. Alabama," said Emma Guinness pertly, sipping gently on the white Napa Valley chardonnay from the Jordan Vineyard.

"We must all call Alabama Alabama," said Dick Latham pleasantly. "It's like Sting . . . or Cher . . . only different, of course." He allowed himself the gentle jab. His earlier meeting with Alabama had gone far better than expected. The mock plans for the house he never intended to build had been impressive, and expensive. He'd hired Richard Martin to design a low-slung contemporary that had melted into the mountain landscape. There had been detailed plans for solar heating, underground power lines, and rich landscaping so that the whole modest ten-thousand-square-foot compound would be all but invisible, and yet at the same time would make a low-key artistic statement destined to appeal to an aesthete like Alabama. The old boy had grunted and groaned but, reading between the lines of his token protests, Latham had known that he'd been impressed.

"If you must, I suppose you must," the prickly environmentalist had concluded, and Latham had known that all objections to his buying the land would now be withdrawn.

He smiled gently around his lunch table as he dreamed of the real-estate coup he had pulled off. Cosmos Studios in all its ancient glory would be reborn in the mountains that looked down on Malibu, and Alabama would go ballistic. There was no fool like an old fool. There was nothing sweeter than revenge on a long-time enemy, especially if you were enriched by the process.

"What do you think of Mr. Latham's house, Alabama?" asked Pat. He was glowering at Latham, his brow darkening at being mentioned in the same breath as a pop star and an anorectic actress whose proudest possessions appeared to be her belly button and her butt.

"Not bad for a gin palace. You know, a cross between ancient Rome and 2001. Press a button and the swimming pool turns into a think tank."

"Surely not that bad," laughed Latham easily in the tones reserved for an unruly and overindulged child. "You had to admit that it was environment-friendly, Alabama. It *is* rather modern, but I think Martin's going to win a prize with it, and after all, we are living in the present, aren't we? I can't stand the idea of trying to build something old."

"Yeah, that was the problem with *Celebrity*," said Emma, demonstrating that she was not afraid to irritate her boss.

Latham frowned. With great deliberation he eased a small piece of butter onto a tiny sliver of melba toast.

"Well, let's just hope that the trendsetter from across the water doesn't repeat the old mistakes . . . and that she doesn't replace them with new ones."

The temperature sank a couple of points. Alabama looked up,

encouraged. Pat watched Emma, saw the two red spots high on her cheekbones. The English girl was living dangerously. Intimacy at thirty thousand feet clearly provided no easement into the billionaire's good books. The prenuptial agreement looked light-years away. Latham's sense of humor did not extend into his business dealings.

"I hope *I'm* not going to prove a mistake," said Pat suddenly. "But I want to say that I'm really looking forward to working with Emma."

"What?" The question shot from Alabama.

"Emma offered me a job working exclusively for *New Celebrity*. I'm on a generous retainer, and I do two spreads a year of my own choosing. Isn't it wonderful? It means I can stay on with you without being a burden, and have an outlet for my work at the same time."

"Why on earth do you need an outlet for your work?" said Alabama.

He was thoroughly put out. Pat had expected it. She wasn't frightened of him, but she knew this would take some handling. Across the table she sensed Latham's eyes upon her. He wanted to see how she handled pressure. Why did she feel that he wanted her to fall apart beneath it?

"An artist needs an outlet. You know that, Alabama. How many exhibitions have you had over the years, how many print sales, how many books?" She looked straight into his angry eyes. She knew what was coming.

"No pretty pictures in silly, glossy magazines," he barked.

"When you were my age you were selling wedding photographs in Kentucky." Pat Parker's jaw was set. Her bright eyes flashed. She would have to use her temper. She could do that, because in all her life so far she had never lost it. It was a survival trick she had learned during the bloody battles of the war that had been family life.

"Lucky you," crowed Emma Guinness. "Weddings are almost as much fun as funerals. People make such glorious fools of themselves."

Alabama ignored her. The Kentucky crack was up under his ribs like the blade of a blunt knife.

Dick Latham's eyes were in Wimbledon mode. This was turning into serious spectator sport. Rows were *such* fun to watch. But which way to bet? Alabama, the sore-headed bear veteran of a billion such encounters, or the spunky girl with the breasts and the legs and the thoroughbred personality? He shook his head. It was no good. It was too close to call. He reached for the wine and settled back in the Chippendale carver to catch the fun.

"I'm not ashamed of that. Why should I be? It was honest work and I did it well and I made people happy . . ." Alabama stopped, suddenly aware that he had been forced onto the defensive. Now he had left himself open to an unanswerable counterattack. Nor was Pat Parker ashamed of the job she had taken; it, too, was honest work that made people happy. His eyes flashed. He would cut her off at the pass. "*Celebrity* magazine is a trivial pursuit run by parasites and poseurs that panders to the worst instincts of the neurotic and idle rich," he spluttered.

"I *hope*," said Emma Guinness with a brittle laugh. "If it doesn't, it won't be through want of trying."

Latham, despite the insult to his baby, laughed too. The ball was deep against the Parker baseline.

It was to be effortlessly returned.

"That," she said dismissively, "is both patronizing and elitist. In a free society the people decide what gives them pleasure. They are more likely to be right than a group of hypocrites with egos too big for their hatbands. Living life isn't so easy that you can do it for others. Intellectuals always make that mistake."

Alabama went red. He went redder. He went reddest. He began to pulsate. Latham swore he could hear him hum, see him throb, feel the heat that burned from him.

"I'm not a fucking intellectual," he boomed. The word infuriated him. It was the ultimate insult.

"I know you're not, but you should try to avoid sounding like one."

"Don't patronize me," he howled at her.

"Don't patronize the public," she shot back.

"I don't have to listen to this," screamed Alabama. "You charge into my life uninvited, unwanted, because you needed my help and here you are telling me what to say and think, like the mind quacks in the godforsaken magazine that's hired you. Maybe you deserve each other. Maybe you should go back to the stink zone and scurry about taking snaps of the roaches. And maybe you should get the hell out of my life, and not come back."

He stood up, pushing out his butt at the chair. His gesture was so sudden, so precipitous, that he caught the butler as he moved forward with the tray of iced gazpacho Andaluz. The glutinous soup had liftoff. It left the silver tureen and it flew like red-wine vomit, rich in bits and pieces of vegetable, tomato cubes, onion, croutons, red pimientos, straight at Emma Guinness. She took the direct hit in the cleavage of a sequined Beverly Hillbilly bolero top, across the front of which was the legend NEW CELEBRITY. The gritty first course surged down between her tits, dyeing the ghastly garment blood red, and saving it instantly from sartorial disaster. She who had looked fashion tragic, now looked fashion bright.

"Oh *fuck!*" she screamed.

They all looked at her in horror. The butler darted in, shrunk back from the enormity of the task that confronted him, summoned up the courage to approach once more. He dabbed delicately at the mammary mountain with a damask napkin, well aware that the only appropriate response would be with a fire hose.

"I'm sorry," lied Alabama.

"Oh, *Emma!*" gasped Pat.

"Oh *shit!*" added the soup target.

The silence that followed was broken by two sounds. The first was the gentle drip, drip, drip of gazpacho onto the priceless Kirman Persian carpet. The second was the gentle tones of Dick Latham's laughter.

They were soft at first, but they strengthened, and slowly his whole body began to rock with the emotion. He put both hands onto the soup-splattered tablecloth and his eyes creased up as he beheld the angst and confusion of his lunch party. Emma Guinness, so full of herself, so quick and sharp, was now a clawed lobster swimming in her own bisque. Alabama, the Rock House and White House regular, was the clumsy klutz who had dropped the food. And there, floating above them all in the star slot, was the girl whose body he suddenly wanted more than his next breath. So what if there was soup on the John Singer Sargent, gazpacho on the four hundred-knot-to-the-inch silk rug. They could be replaced if they couldn't be cleaned. But the high-noon drama of his luncheon could never be repeated. In mellow Malibu such an event could not have been staged. It was brilliant. It was beautiful. And it was breaking him up.

Alabama was the second to chuckle. Pat Parker wasn't far behind. It took Emma Guinness longest to get to the joke of which she was the punch line, but get there she did. The butler alone, appalled by the *Valdez*-size spill and the cleanup it entailed, remained isolated from the gales of laughter that now roared around the room.

"There's a girl in my soup," tried Alabama.

"Don't let on. They'll all want one," Pat giggled.

"The soup's deep in me," Emma laughed.

"Pass the girl," howled Dick Latham.

"Don't be a Dick, " they all roared at him in unison, quoting the T-shirt.

"Oh, my . . . God . . ." Latham laughed through his tears. "What a fabulous bloody lunch."

SIX

Pat Parker walked slowly across the dunes, the Nikon dangling loosely from her arm. She was full of Mexican food, and she felt at one with the beauty, her whole life in tune with nature, with the beach, the mountains, with the pale blue of the sky. Beneath her feet the sand was warm but not burning, and the Malibu sea breeze ruffled her hair and cooled her skin. The salty air licked at her. The heat haze wrapped her. The bright brilliance of the colors floodlit the inside of her mind. It was one of those moments of transcendence when life fitted into place. The jigsaw was no longer a pile of unconnected woodwork on the floor, promising only frustration and hard work in return for some unspecified later reward. Instead everything had merged in a visual feast of total satisfaction. It all made sense. The doubts and fears had melted in the burning kaleidoscope of the heatscape.

She stopped at the crest of the dunes and looked down Broad Beach, all the way to Zuma, a sun-bronzed crescent of oiled humanity. There it was breast-to-face intimate. Here, where the plutocrats hung out, it was as crowded as Central Park in the wilding dusk. She smiled as she remembered lunch, and how the harmony had replaced the discord. It was a metaphor for how she felt right now, the good coming out of the bad, the struggle and the strife metamorphosing for no apparent reason into the pleasure of peace. Her fight with Alabama had strengthened their relationship, not harmed it. The bully in him had tried to cow her, and she had not allowed it. She had seen the respect grow in his eyes, the admiration for her artistic talents merging with admiration for the strength of her personality. And Latham's interest in her was deepening. It was flattering, and nicely disturbing, because there was a sense in which now she was his employee. The billionaire media king would be looking out for her and her work. He had begged her to stay for the afternoon, and when Alabama had left after lunch, she had remained. But her trigger finger was itchy. Out there on the sands of Malibu pictures were waiting, photographs that might one day form part of a spread in the Latham/Guinness magazine.

Now, she looked around her. The surfers were busy in the waves, and the girls who watched them were lost in Walkman sound as they basted their bodies with Coppertone and revolved spitlike in the ultraviolet rays. A windsurfer knifed through the water. A girl-watching chopper pilot droned overhead. Joggers jogged, lovers lingered, and the only sounds were the waves, the gulls, and the *plop-plop* of bat against ball as the eternal beach tennis battles raged in the dreamland. There was nothing there that would look better on film than in reality. It was almost too perfect, and not for the first time in her life Pat speculated that the photo opportunities in heaven would pale beside the ones in hell.

Which was the moment she saw him. He stood like a god against the crest of the dunes, a foot thrown forward, his head held back, Viking proud, and the sun lit him from the side, casting his long shadow like an omen across the sand. He wore baggy jeans of faded blue, and a washed-out shirt of a deeper color, beneath which a brilliant white sweatshirt ringed a long, powerful neck. He was totally preoccupied, staring into space and yet seeing nothing, lost in the scary, wonderful world that Pat knew instinctively would be his dreams. His body seemed taut, poised for perpetual motion, some action of single-minded purpose that he was scared to commit to. Pat's Nikon rose from her side like the stealthy rifle of the hunter, unwilling to disturb the prey, yet hungry for the kill.

In the lens she had him, a proud and dangerous animal in her sights. The ball of her forefinger twirled the focus. She gasped in excitement as his profile clarified. God, he was extraordinary. He was an eagle, and a lion, the strong brow racing down the proud aquiline nose to a sensuous, knowing mouth. His chin poked out at the world like an exclamation mark, his broad shoulders supported the head where the violent will would live, and his muscular chest, triangular beneath the navy-blue cotton of his shirt, parceled the heart that wouldn't know how to love. His image was sharp now, and Pat could see the honey brown of his lightly tanned flesh, see the lustrous glow of his midnight hair. Although she was forty feet from him, she had the mad sensation that she could actually smell the masculine musk of him, the scent of his liquid charisma borne like a love potion on the erratic breeze. Deep in her soul the molecules rearranged themselves.

Her finger strengthened on the shutter and it hovered at the point of release. And then he moved. His head swiveled around suddenly, and, through the telephoto lens of her camera, he was staring deep into her eyes. They lanced into her, searing in the majesty of their total disapproval, and her finger froze at the point of fire as she was numbed by the weird intensity of his gaze. The camera was the glass through which she saw him, but she did not see darkly. This was face to face. It amplified him. He had become his eyes and his whole body poured into the scorn that lasered out at her. Pat was stuck at the edge of her picture. The viewfinder was still jammed tight against her cheek, and yet she couldn't move. She couldn't shoot him. She couldn't fail to do so. The thoughts rushed through her mind—desire, confusion, excitement, and yes, shame. In Africa they believed that photographs robbed you of your soul. That was what the magnificent eyes were accusing her of. And she was guilty—of impoliteness, of voyeurism, and of lust in the first degree. She lowered the camera. She lowered her gaze and, full of the most wonderful foreboding, she walked slowly toward him. He didn't move as she approached, but he watched her carefully. Pat Parker had never thought much about her beauty. Usually she took it for granted. Not now. For the first time in her life she was grateful for it. It would be the shield that would protect her. And it would be the open sesame to the closed book with the gorgeous cover that she had found on the sands of Malibu.

She smiled shyly as she got closer, and she splayed out her hands in what she hoped was a disarming gesture.

"I'm sorry," she said. "I should have asked your permission. It was rude of me."

He didn't answer. He didn't smile. He stared through her, haughty, cold, clearly unmoved by her apology. She was near to him now, standing on the brink of his aura, and the aggression and the pride, the insolent self-righteousness were so real she felt she could reach out and touch them.

"May I take your photograph . . . *sir!*" she added with a laugh.

"No!"

"Why not?"

"I don't have to explain myself to you." His head notched back. He seemed to be watching her from a distant planet.

Pat's heart quickened. She hadn't expected that, and why was her stomach so suddenly without a bottom, and her mouth dry as the low desert, and where was the reflex anger that at any other time would be bubbling through her body?

"You don't like having your photograph taken?" she said simply. It was halfway between a question and a statement of a fact.

He looked away from her, back toward the houses, as if her remark didn't deserve an answer.

"Why do you suppose they all live here?" he said suddenly. "I mean the actors."

"Because it's the most expensive beach in Malibu. Why Malibu? Because there's peace here? I don't know. Are you an actor?"

He waved away her question as if *he* was not the point, in a gesture that somehow emphasized that he was the only point.

"I think it has to do with revenge," he said.

"Revenge? As in 'living-well-is-the-best . . .' "

"Yeah." He turned toward her, and the sun behind him paled to a yellow irrelevance in comparison to the warmth of his totally unexpected smile. His whole face launched into it like a swallow diver from a high board, and Pat Parker was sucked up into its liquid intimacy, thrilled beyond any reason that she had found the right answer to the mini-riddle he had posed.

"You see, nobody believed in them till it was too late," he said. "Not too late for success, but too late for it to matter."

"Do people believe in you?"

She wanted to get away from "them." She wanted to get to "him."

"*I* do."

"Is that enough?"

"For now." Again he smiled. Or rather the intensity of the original one strengthened.

"I still want to take your picture."

"If you let me take yours."

He laughed as he spoke, aware that she wouldn't want that. Already he seemed to know her.

"I'm a photographer. Nobody shoots the photographer."

"Okay, so now you know how I feel."

Pat gave up. On the photograph. Suddenly it didn't seem so important. Other things did.

"Are you from here?" she asked.

"Nobody's from here. I live in New York. And I *am* an actor. I just finished at the Juilliard. I'm Tony Valentino." He held out his hand to her.

She took it, and his firm grip closed on her, tightened, and then left her. There was no flirtation in his touch or in the eyes that watched her. His whole demeanor said he was above and beyond such mundane things. But Pat remembered the feel of his flesh, the first fleeting brush of bodies, and there was a tingling at the base of her spine, and a lightness in her heart.

"I'm from New York, too. Isn't it weird we're not friends," she joked.

"Yes, it's a big place," he said. His answer was strangely literal, and it was with a shock that Pat realized that he possessed no sense of humor. People were supposed to have that. It was something the world considered important. Not that she had ever rated it. Those who laughed at themselves were usually a joke. It was the people who took themselves seriously who ended up getting things together. Revolving bow ties and whoopee cushions were the mortal enemies of houses on Broad Beach.

"Do you want to walk along the beach a bit? Big Apple refugees should stick together in Wonderland. We can keep each other nervous."

"Sure," he said.

"You want Zuma and real people or Broad Beach and vengeful fantasy ones?"

"If I'm talking to you I won't need to worry about the other people," said Tony Valentino.

She cocked her head to one side to show that she hadn't quite fathomed what he meant. It sounded suspiciously like a compliment from lips that were obviously a stranger to them. On the other hand it might have been a remark about his concentration, as in "When I'm talking to someone, whoever it is, I focus exclusively on them."

"Let's do Zuma. Beach Boys, Gidget, and Frankie Avalon. My mom would have died to be here." She winced as she thought of her. Perhaps the most valuable thing she'd done for Pat in her entire life was to lend herself to this conversation. She looked up at Tony, and she started in amazement at what had happened to him.

He had fallen apart. His square shoulders were slumped, his high head was low, and his fine features, so proud and glorious, were stricken with a terrible sorrow. The change of mood was devastating in its suddenness and in its totality.

"What's the matter?" said Pat quickly, as the alarm bells sounded within her.

"My mother died last Friday," he said, his voice shaking. His face was pointed at the sand. She couldn't see it. But she knew it. Mist would shroud the arrogant eyes. The sensual lips would be trembling. She reached out. She had to touch him. Her hand found his forearm.

"I'm terribly sorry," she said. And she was. It was extraordinary. This stranger had moved her with his beauty, and now he was moving her with his sorrow. She had been wrong about his unfeeling heart. Before her eyes, it was breaking.

He looked up at her, haggard, haunted, unashamed of his weakness as before he had been oblivious to his strength. The tears filled his eyes, hovering at the brim, at the base of his long lashes. He took a deep breath, forcing himself together through a stupendous act of will.

"I'm not used to it. I never will be."

"Time helps." Pat mouthed the platitudes that were all language offered at moments of supreme importance. She linked her arm through his, surprised and pleased that he allowed it.

"I guess." His laugh was bitter, as he acknowledged her attempt at comfort, recognizing the inadequacy of words, and yet their necessity. "The trouble is that I was too busy wanting things to tell her I loved her."

"I think she knew." Pat would have known. She had never seen anything so expressive as this man who stood before her. His feelings were on his forearm, beneath her fingers where his sleeve would have been. They exploded from his forever eyes. They beamed out in the charisma that clothed him. His feelings might not be nice, or kind or comfortable, but they would always be impossible to ignore. And the target of his love would be illuminated in a light so bright it would melt the heavens.

"Thank you," he said.

And as he said it, Pat Parker knew just exactly what was happening.

She was falling in love.

Pat Parker sat all alone in the crowded restaurant, and once more she looked at her watch. It was seven thirty. He was half an hour late. She sipped at the Calistoga mineral water, but the ice had melted and it was losing its fizz. So was she. The clientele of Zooma Sushi didn't help her mood. They were young and hip and great-looking, and they were having the good time she wasn't. They laughed, and they giggled, their lustrous brown skins vibrant against predominantly white clothes, and it was perfectly clear that they all stood close to the movies. Outside in the lot the Jeeps and the open Corvettes, the Mondiale Ferraris and the convertible Jaguars confirmed it. There was money to burn here in this Malibu hot spot, networks to be set up, parts to be gotten, deals to be done.

Pat sighed. Jeez! Could she have been so wrong? It was the oldest mistake in the book. A good-looking boy on a beach. In *Malibu!* A short conversation. High-speed getting to know you. Emotions emoted. He had even admitted to being an actor. They had walked hand in hand on the sand and they had stopped for a cold Coke at the food stall on Zuma, and she had listened spellbound to the history of his life, but mostly she had watched him, bowled over by his beauty, and the extraordinary expressiveness of his face and gestures. His personality had been so real. There had been no hint of a line being shot, no whiff of a come-on. Pat had not hesitated to become a believer. Now she wasn't so sure. Distanced from the power of him, there was a place for doubt. The clock said he was half an hour late. That was fact. It was entirely possible that this was the first half hour of life without Tony Valentino. She held up her hand and grabbed the sleeve of the passing waiter. He stopped, and smiled, his blond hair, male-model good looks, and his ponytail giving away his Thespian dreams.

"I think I'll eat," she said. "I guess I've been stood up."

"No, you haven't," said Tony Valentino.

He stood over the table like Heathcliff on a blasted moor, brooding, moody, black as a thundercloud against the pastel colors of the restaurant and its diners. He wore a leather jacket, faded but totally clean, and beneath it a simple legendless T-shirt, crisp and white against the olive skin of his neck. A buckled cavalry belt held up standard-issue faded 501's. Black cowboy boots peeped from their bottoms, on one of which was a matte-black spur. He lowered a battered crash helmet onto the small table, and outside, through the picture windows of the restaurant, Pat could see the red-and-white striped Kawasaki Ninja bike that had clearly been his transport. The light was above and behind him, as it had been earlier at the beach, and his features were obscure, as if he specialized in mystery, his whole being a complicated essay in disguise, camouflage, and the delicious excitement of the unknown.

"Hi," said Pat, her tone neutral, waiting for the apology. But already she was losing it. The nasty half an hour was already a memory. The exotic now had wonderful promises for the future. It was the way he held the weapon of his body. It was a spear, hovering above her, ready to strike at her heart. It was so strangely dangerous. The threat was not overt, but it was everywhere. It hung in the air, it steamed from the corners of his broad shoulders, it hammered its jungle rhythms in the pit of her stomach.

"I'm sorry I'm late," he said. There was no excuse offered, just the bare apology. He reached for the chair opposite her, and he sat down. As he did so, his face was fully visible. He didn't look very sorry. He looked deeply wonderful.

"Is lateness a problem for you? I imagine it must be complicated to be unpunctual—as an actor."

"No, it's not a problem for me." He smiled at her irritation. His eyes dared her to keep the subject alive. The "for me" was almost, but not quite, a taunt.

Pat felt the anger fuse begin its slow burn inside her. Her head told her to cool it. She didn't know this guy well enough to quarrel with him. If all she wanted to do was fight with him, she should walk right out of the restaurant. They had started like that, with some sort of confrontation. Now it was happening again. But he was so damned pleased with himself. It wasn't fair that anyone could be so cocky and so beautiful. Okay, so she fancied him, but it wasn't enough. She wanted to control him, and the place to establish that was square one.

"Well, it's a problem for me. I've been waiting here for thirty goddamn minutes. The least you can do is make up some excuse. It's called manners."

"Do lies make you feel better?"

Again he smiled the marvelous, infuriating smile. Lies were for little people, it said. They were for cowards; for those who were not proud of themselves and their behavior; for the weak, who cared what the world thought. His eyes bored into her. He wanted an answer. She was on the defensive, and yet *he* was in the wrong. Or was he?

Did lies make her feel better? Yes, they did, but it wasn't the sort of thing she could admit. Yet to deny it would be to hand him victory on a plate. In an attempt to conceal her Catch-22 predicament, Pat said nothing.

She swept up the menu, furious and yet at the same time weirdly elated. Never in her life had the two paradoxical emotions existed side by side.

"I'm going to have salmon, tuna, and yellowtail, and a California roll wrapped in cucumber rather than seaweed," she said. "What are you going to have?"

"I don't know," he said. "I've never had sushi. You'll have to help me."

Pat smiled her surprise. He had done yet another 180-degree turn. Total vulnerability had replaced the screw-you macho almost-insolence of the previous moment. But then Pat realized that was merely on the surface. Actually, his behavior was in character, and the salient features of that character were honesty and fearlessness. He had been late, had no excuse, and had apologized for it. He wasn't ashamed of that, and he didn't need to lie about it. He'd never had sushi before. That was merely a fact. He didn't care that it might imply a lack of sophistication. He could have come up with another restaurant when Pat had suggested they meet at Zooma Sushi, but he hadn't wanted to. He wasn't afraid of his own ignorance, nor of asking for help even from a person to whom he had just given both the motive and the ammunition for an attempt at a mini-humiliation.

"Oh, well, it's raw fish," said Pat. A part of her hoped he would recoil from that, the godlike face crumpling in the disgust of the mere mortal.

"Yeah, I know. I've been waiting for an aficionado to show me the way."

"Why do I get the feeling that not many people show you the way?" Pat laughed to show that he was forgiven and that they were friends again, friends on a journey to something else.

"Because I know where I'm going."

"And where is that?"

"To the top."

"Of?"

"Acting. Movies. The world."

He leaned in toward her, daring her to laugh at his presumption. But she didn't want to. Maybe it was a laughable ambition, but not when it tumbled from those lips, not when it was allied to the fire of those eyes. Certainly there was no doubt in her mind that it could be achieved. Pat knew about the will and what it could do. It was the faith that blew away the opposition, and atomized the obstacles. It was the fuel that kept you going when the tank was on empty. It was the motive force that loved nothing more than the word *impossible* because of the opportunity it provided for proving the silly world wrong.

"Do you have a game plan?" Pat dared to ask the question. This boy was no run-of-the-mill Hollywood and Vine dreamer, a hapless soldier in the army of the hopelessly hopeful who would end as cannon fodder in the Tinsel Town wars. But there should be substance in his powerful dreams. Laser purpose could not be pointed merely at the stars. It must have earthly targets, too.

"I'm going back to New York. I've got a small part in an off-Broadway stage adaptation of *East of Eden*. I need more experience. It's too soon for out here."

It was the right answer. The determination to win and the belief in himself had not interfered with his judgment. Hollywood didn't want you if it knew that you wanted it. It preferred to imagine it did the discovering, because it was the most insecure, paranoid, and aggressive place on earth.

"And after that you'll get an agent, look for more parts in the theater?"

"Yeah."

"Do you need photographs, for when you're job hunting?"

"Yes, I do." He watched her.

"Can I take them?"

"Are you expensive?" His smile was enigmatic. "I haven't got much money."

"I'm free. For you. And I'm very, very good. As good a photographer as you are an actor. Maybe even better."

She smiled to show she meant it, and that it was a challenge. She was daring him to take something for nothing, this proud man who wouldn't usually do that sort of thing. But already she was thinking of the photographs she could take of him. If she could capture one-quarter of his essence on celluloid she would have made a masterpiece. Already she was laying him out in her mind, choosing the backdrop, arranging the lighting. He was tungsten, no question . . . and he was naked. God, yes he was, naked as the dreamy day he was born, his skin glistening with sweat, hot beneath the lights, the juice of him staining the white background paper, his steam rising like mist from the floor of her studio. Would he be shy then, at last, as she moved with the precision of the surgeon around him? Would he avert his eyes from hers as they plundered his defenseless body, raiding it, pillaging it for its visual splendor without shame or mercy. Dispassionate, she would capture him; the cool professional, she would use him; untouched by his beauty, she would order him about, move this way, turn that, and "Oh, what a pity your legs are a little too short for your torso, your feet a tad too large for your legs."

The sushi hit the table, flattening Pat Parker's fantasy. In confusion, she picked up the chopsticks, poured some low-sodium soy sauce into the bowl, and transferred a small mound of green horseradish from the plate to the soy.

"Watch out for this stuff. It can tear the top off your head. What you do is dunk the fish in the sauce, add a sliver of spiced ginger, and a touch of horseradish, then go for it. Here, like this."

She reached forward for the glistening salmon, the wedge of raw fish nestling on a small tight mound of white rice. She rolled it in the soy allowing the rice to blot up the sauce, dressed it with horseradish and ginger, and held it out across the table to him.

He leaned toward her and allowed her to feed him, but his eyes never left hers, and the moment was not about food. It was about taking, and being given, and about tenderness and looking after people, and, unmistakably, it was also about eating and being eaten.

"Mmmmm, it's good," he murmured. "Like smoked salmon. Thanks."

Pat felt the feeling explode in the middle of her. It was too strong. He was too much. She was jealous of the fish. She wanted to be it, deep in the recesses of his mouth, all mixed up with his saliva, about to be swallowed into the delicious darkness of his body. She knew that she was just staring at him, her mouth half-open in a smile of serious longing. She knew he would notice that, and probably he would think it her weakness, but there was nothing to be done about it. It just was. Mr. Honesty would have to deal with it.

"What kind of pictures do you take?"

Pictures? What did he mean, pictures? Oh, yes. Reality, not the steamy jungles of lust.

"Reportage mainly. Portraits, too. I've just made a deal with *New Celebrity* magazine in New York."

"The billionaire's magazine that the English girl edits?"

"That's the one."

"Do you know her?" he asked.

"Emma Guinness. Yes. She was lunching at that house on Broad Beach where we met."

"She *was?*"

"Yes. Why?"

"I met her the other day. She was at the end-of-term production at the Juilliard. She came on to me, with an 'I'm-going-to-make-you-a-star' pitch."

"Emma Guinness? She didn't!"

"Oh, yes, she did."

"And?" God! Surely it was too early for jealousy.

"I was a little hard on her." He smiled the understatement.

"What did you say?"

"Whatever. Rough stuff. She'll be an enemy now."

"Quite a powerful one, no? I mean career-wise. Was it a real casting-couch thing?" All sorts of ideas were streaming through Pat's mind. Emma and her surfer fantasies. Short, squat Emma with her designs on the Latham empire. Big-titted Emma who would have squawked while she came a mile high over America. But mostly she was trying to visualize Emma putting the moves on Tony Valentino. It was not an exercise for a squeamish stomach.

"Yeah, it was for real. I didn't imagine it, if that's what you mean."

"Well, I'm glad you rained on her parade," said Pat with a conviction that came easily to her.

"I wouldn't like to have to work for her."

"I hope it's easier for a woman." Pat laughed. "Actually, she's quite funny, and she's very bright. Latham thinks she can turn the magazine around. She's hiring some pretty impressive people. Myself included."

"What's Latham like?" said Tony suddenly.

Pat paused. She had to think about that.

"Sort of sleek, dangerous, rather charming." She paused. "A bit like you, really."

"Older. Richer. More powerful."

"For now," agreed Pat.

Their eyes were gridlocked. Emma and Tony had unnerved her. Was it possible that Latham and Pat were unnerving him?

"I heard he's a bastard."

Pat smiled in triumph. It was definite. There was a spark of jealousy.

"Only if he's allowed to be."

For a minute or two they ate in silence.

"Did you know he just bought Cosmos Studios?" Pat floated the bait. If money was the flame that attracted the mothlike women to the Latham persona, a movie studio might well be the sticky paper to the Tony Valentino fly.

"I didn't know that," said Tony slowly.

"Would you like to meet him?" She knew she was playing with fire.

"In what capacity?" So did he.

"Oh, as my friend. As an actor. What else?"

"On the off chance he'd stick me in a Cosmos movie?" The sarcasm was up there on the surface. There was accusation in his voice. He was hinting that Pat's suggestion was not a million miles from Emma Guinness's. The expression on his face said he was disappointed by her.

She retreated fast. Aggression was her reaction of choice when she was caught playing unworthy games.

"Oh, come on, Tony. You know that's not how things happen. Studio owners don't handle casting. He might be a lot of things, but I hardly think Dick Latham's unprofessional."

Would he be humbled by the putdown? Would he ever!

"Then why the hell would 'your friend, the actor' want to meet the old fart?" His lip curled on the question.

"Lighten up, Tony. It was only an idea. I thought he might be a useful contact, that's all. This *is* California. We're in Malibu, for God's sake. It's how things *work*."

"It's not how I work, Pat Parker," said Tony simply. There was no anger in his voice, only a patient desire that she should understand. "I'm good at what I do, and I'm going to be the best at it. Sooner or later everyone will recognize that. It's just a matter of time. I don't have to push and pull, and hustle and lick butt. All I have to do is what I do. Don't you feel that way about your photographs?"

"No, I *don't*," said Pat, her voice raised with the vehemence of her emotion. "Listen, the world is littered with undiscovered talent. People squash it on the road. There are photographers out there who make me look like a blind woman. But they're unknowns, nobodies, and they'll stay like that if they subscribe to your philosophy. You've got to sell yourself in this life in this land, otherwise for sure nobody's buying. You've got to have charm. You've got to catch them with honey, not vinegar. It's not enough to be brilliant. They've got to be persuaded to look, to see, to *understand*. And if an artist can't handle the self-promotion shit, then for sure he'd better latch onto someone who can."

She leaned across the table to emphasize her point.

"If you *really* believed in yourself, you wouldn't feel like that," he said. "You push because you're insecure about your talent, and because you don't trust the public to recognize it. That's a mistake. They're always right. They always know. Every ounce of energy has to go into the work. There should be none left for the bullshit."

Pat took a deep breath. There was something so magnificent about his naïveté. The world hadn't touched him. Perhaps it couldn't touch him. There was something awesome about that. A blinkered vision made you narrow, but it made you single-minded. The Valentino will was aimed directly at the eye of the bull. Not many people's were.

"Tony. Tony," she pleaded. "Listen to me. If you were producing your art simply for its own sake, for your personal satisfaction alone, then maybe you'd be right. You could paint your pictures or act your dramas in secret and then, of course, nothing would matter but how good you thought you were. But you want more than that. You need the world to recognize you. You want fame. Hell, you want to be a movie star. To *want* that is artistically impure. It's like wanting money. I'm not saying it's bad. I'm just saying that you want to compete in the marketplace, and if that's what you want, then you've got to roll up your sleeves and start to peddle the dreams and shovel the shit. Otherwise, however great you are, you're going to lose out to a slicker salesman with better PR. Can't you see that?"

"You don't believe faith can move mountains."

"I'd rather put my trust in nitroglycerine."

"Faith and high explosive. That's a good combination."

"Yeah, we could be a good combination, Tony Valentino," said Pat Parker, and her hand snaked out across the table to touch his arm.

In Alabama's studio the chaotic confusion was skin deep. The polished wood of the floor was littered with the foil and discarded cardboard of dead Polaroid packs. Background paper, pink, white, and russet brown, hung drunkenly from poles, from the backs of chairs, from drawing pins on the black-painted walls. Through the skylight streamed the sun, and hard rock, Tom Petty and the Heartbreakers' "Full Moon Fever," amplified the excitement in the shaking, vibrating air. The trolleys of film were piled high with lenses, and Hasselblad backs, jars of vaseline for soft-focus effects, lens brushes, cans of Diet Coke. And through it all, like a gunslinger on a lead-soaked street, Pat Parker ducked and dived, as she picked off the photographs, her camera swiveling as it fired, a twelve-shot six-gun that never missed her man.

He was totally unself-conscious, and she hadn't expected that. It was yet another surprise in the magical process of getting to know him, and as Pat positioned herself to find a new angle on him, only part of her was a photographer. The rest was already a lover.

He was naked to the waist, and his skin glistened beneath the heat of the photofloods, the thin wisps of hair that formed a T from his chest to his navel damp with his sweat. He lay back against the black leather of the chair, his hand to his chin, his blue-jeaned legs stretched out straight, and he stared away in the distance just as he had done at the moment she had first seen him.

High on the balcony that ran around the top of the studio, Alabama watched them. His girl was as good as he had known she would be as she conducted the complicated orchestra of the shoot. Every nuance of light, every contrast, every motion had to be recognized and used. What was not there had to be created, what was not wanted had to be abolished. Film speed, shutter speed, focus, depth of field had to be fed into the mind computer, and all the time the subject had to be relaxed, excited, directed, manipulated as the moment was milked of its artistic possibility and greatness was coaxed onto the film. She had the knowledge, but she had more than that. She was involved. She was not merely a voyeur. She was engaged in the process. A part of her performed the technical tricks, but the more important part was allowing herself to feel. Photographer and subject had merged in the magic whole that allowed each to transcend himself. Their souls had gone from their bodies and hung in the air between them, melted together in a throbbing harmony of feeling. And it was as clear as the daylight that streamed through the skylight that they were falling in love.

He chuckled to himself. Once he had lived there at the cutting edge of feeling when the world had been alive, and full of the intense meaning that went by the global name of "youth." At that precise moment she looked up at him, aware of his presence in the heightened sensitivity of the creative process. He put his thumb into the air, and he nodded once, twice, smiling down at her, as she smiled back at him in thanks for the confirmation of what already she knew.

"Stand up, Tony," she said. "Look away, chin up, right arm forward a bit, left arm back—as if you're walking but don't move. That's great. That's wonderful. You look terrific. Oh, God, you look just great."

The stream of talk was a caress that pulled him closer to her, and his body responded to her commands automatically. He was a natural, accepting direction intuitively, his movement anticipating her desires as he struck the poses that would conjure up the dreams. No model could do this. No weak person could. This boy was in harmony with his body, and the gravitas that dripped from him gave weight and depth to attitudes that would otherwise have been narcissistic, almost effeminate. Here was male beauty—raw, undiluted, blatantly masculine, and devoid of any hint of softness or subterfuge. The honesty would be in the print, and all who saw it would know that Tony Valentino was as hard and as real as the steel in his eyes.

Damn! She was firing on empty. She tore the back from the Hasselblad, reached for another, and clipped it on. She looked up at Alabama, but he had gone. She looked back at Tony. He smiled at her, angling his body in the light as if moving it beneath a waterfall. Good. He was deep into it. He was with her. The magic moment hadn't gone. And now they were alone.

She peered down into the viewfinder, allowing the lens to roam over his body. Where next? She swallowed. Suddenly she knew. She paused, and once again she looked up at him. Could she ask him that? Would he understand? Would he get it wrong? The question was in her eyes, but she knew it would never reach her lips. It didn't have to. On some secret wavelength he heard her, and on another he answered. Slowly, deliberately, with all the time in the world, Tony Valentino reached for the buckle of his belt.

Dick Latham clapped his hands and leaned back against the wall of his office. The scale model took up most of the room. It sprawled across a vast metal table, and it was detail perfect to the tufts of sagebrush, the model cars in the lot, the miniature security house at the gates. Dick Latham's Cosmos Pictures studio was a functional scar across five hundred acres of the most beautiful mountains in the world, and his heart leaped for joy in his chest as he beheld it.

Across the room Havers smiled at him. "Good, no?" he said.

Dick Latham didn't have to answer. His expression said it all. He was following in the footsteps of the legends. When had anybody built a brand-new studio from scratch? People traded them. Nobody built them. It took a Goldwyn, a Mayer, or a Warner to do that. Or a Latham. His father would be turning in his grave with jealousy. *His* vision had begun and ended with shopping malls. Now his son, the one he had always despised, was boldly treading where no latter-day celluloid visionary had trod before. The Latham media empire was about to expand into the areas from which it had so far held back—feature film and television production, and the icing on the cake was a property deal richer by far than his dead father had ever dreamed of being.

"So where do we stand, Tommy?"

Havers preened himself. "Tommy" was a Latham departure. It meant an unusually good Latham mood.

"It's going well. We closed on the land. No antidevelopment clauses in the contract. Alabama gave the nod to the landowner. It seems like you turned him around at lunch the other day. Your intervention made all the difference. So now we're moving as fast as we can on the zoning. As you know, it's a business. We'll need environmental impact reports, have to deal with landowners' groups, the California Coastal Commission, the cityhood people."

"Does the development fall within the boundaries of the proposed Malibu city limits?"

"At least eighty percent of it."

"So we want cityhood delayed as long as possible?"

"You bet, and obviously we want the sewers. You can't run a studio on septic tanks."

"How does it look for planning permission?"

"It'll be tough, but we're winning. Our attorneys are getting together a powerful case. The moment we go public with this they'll be off and running. In the meantime they're planning all sorts of lawsuits to delay the incorporation thing until we can ram the zoning through. We're spreading money around like muck and the politicians are feeding fine. Political contributions. Freebies. Favorite charities. Every which ways."

"Don't underestimate the land lovers, Havers. They're zealots.

And Alabama's a leader if ever I met one. I don't like him, but hell, I respect him. He'll want our balls when he hears what we're up to."

"Yeah, we're not overconfident. If it was a country club, we wouldn't have a prayer. But a studio. In Malibu! It has to have a good chance. I mean, it's a movie colony. Always was, always will be. The guys that pull the strings here have to be at least ambivalent about it. It'll be work for them, for chrissakes, and no commuting. The studio/Malibu round trip can be four hours on a bad day, worse if PCH is blocked in the slides. They'll pretend to be anti, but they'll be busy when it comes to the fund raising and they won't call in their IOU's on this one. My gut says we're home free, but I could be wrong."

"The plans are on the money," drawled Latham, drooling over the Cosmos model. "And Grossman knows what he's doing on the nuts and bolts?"

"Yes, he's good. We've cross-checked him with the industry pros. The sound stages, the studios, the back lots are all state of the art. The recording stuff alone is twenty-five million. It's Swahili to me, but the technical boys are on top of it. Grossman can put it together all right. No way he can run it, of course. Making the right movies will be the toughest part."

"Jesus, I'm going to go from vandal to savior to environmental rapist faster than a roller coaster," said Latham, far from displeased at the thought. "When I closed the old Cosmos and turned their land into bucks, I was a philistine moneymaker with no sense of history. Now half the world will see me as a soulful Cecil B. DeMille, and the other half as an ecological barbarian."

"Well, you know what Ricky Nelson said—you can't please everyone, so you'd better please yourself."

"Who *are* we going to get to run it?" said Latham suddenly. Since the death of the last mogul it had been the question to ask in Hollywood. "I never saw a sorrier crew than the old Cosmos management. Firing them was one of the better moments."

"It's tricky," said Havers. "The Peter Principle applies. You know, people rise to the level of their own incompetence. However slick the show business attorney or agent, however brilliant the producer or director, they all screw up on the main job. You go business, you go creative, and the bottom line *still* makes itself up independent of the boss-man and his team. I don't know whether random walk applies to Wall Street, but it seems that you can only pick hit movies with a pin."

Dick Latham moved toward the model and ran a finger over the gleaming roof of an outbuilding.

"Don't worry, we'll find a winner. I always do. And I'll give Cosmos some personal input. I know traditionally that's supposed to be a disaster, but I don't buy that bullshit. When you put together a ten-billion-buck media business, you've got to have some idea of what the public wants."

He smiled lazily. It wasn't often he said things like that. Ten billion bucks, give or take a few hundred thousand million. If you knew exactly how rich you were, you weren't.

"Listen, Mr. Latham, you could do it in your sleep," lied Havers, who was of the opinion that nobody could. "The only question is how much time you want to put into what will only represent ten percent of the company."

"A bit, a bit." Latham laughed. "Cosmos is my new toy. I want to put it together. Make it run. You'd be surprised how often ten percent of a business becomes fifty or more. There are a whole load of people I want to bring back into the spotlight. Puttnam could make some heart art movies after we've stitched his tongue. *Miss Saigon* sounds interesting, and *Aspects of Love* is a must. Wouldn't you just love to see Whitney Houston in anything? And what about that Melissa Wayne? She's dynamite. She lights up the screen. She'd have to sign a contract. I'd want her long-term."

"I heard she was big trouble."

"She's big sex appeal. That's always trouble. It can be handled." Latham spoke softly. Melissa Wayne was a target. She was his own size.

"Do you know her?" Havers's question was cautious. He had gotten where he was today by tuning his antennae to the subtle vibrations that emanated from Richard Latham. Powerful men didn't like to spell things out. They preferred everything to be cloaked in the reassuring cloud of ambiguity. That way you could preserve mystique while insinuating your wants and needs, desires that if spelled out in black and white might demean you, or return to haunt you. Watergate burglars, arms-for-hostage conspirators, the murderous knights in Becket's cathedral had all made a business of interpreting the whims of the masters they served.

"No," said Latham slowly.

"If she's going to work for Cosmos, perhaps we should meet with her . . . maybe in a social situation."

Latham admired the "we," the way the suggestion had come from his lieutenant. It was why Havers was his number two.

"I was thinking of taking the yacht over to the islands on the weekend. That might be a good opportunity. You come too, Tommy. You could fly back to New York tonight, then come back on Friday. Take the helicopter out to us on Saturday morning. We'll anchor off Catalina. Oh, and Tommy, invite that photographer, Pat Parker. I want to keep tabs on her, now we've got her under contract."

"Fine. I'll do what I can. Can I dangle a career carrot at the Wayne girl?"

"Dangle what you like," said Latham shortly, flicking his hand in a gesture that said he didn't need to be bothered by the procedural niceties. "What did you think of the ten million that conglomerate paid for *Interview?*"

"It was brave money. I don't reckon Andy's ghost will hang around for long."

"Yeah, I agree. It makes the two Condé Nast paid for *Details* look cheap. The four American Express shelled out for *L.A. Style* was about right. We looked at it, didn't we? I remember speed reading a boring memo."

"It was too small."

Latham nodded.

"You're off, then?"

"I've got the plane standing by at LAX."

"Okay, let's do a quick lunch at La Scala, then you can take the Rolls on to the airport. I want to go over the Cosmos financing, and I want to talk to you about getting David Mlinaric to redo the Chester Square house. We'll use two cars. I'll take the Porsche. That suit you?"

Havers's head bobbed up and down. Suicide suited him if Dick Latham suggested it.

"Oh, what was the name of the photographer again?" said Havers as he walked toward the door.

"Pat Parker," said Latham quickly. But it wasn't quite enough. It seemed to require emphasis. "Yes, Pat Parker," he said.

There was silence in the semidarkness. The red light shone dully in the gloom. Pat leaned forward and reached into the water, taking the print by the corner. She turned it over and peered down into the basin.

"How does it look?" growled Alabama. He leaned over her

shoulder, and he couldn't hold back his enthusiasm. It was years since he had felt like this. He had seen her take the photograph and he had sensed the excitement of the shoot. The lighting had been inspired, the subject had been inspiring. The angles, poses, the nuances of expression had been picture perfect. If the focus was right, the camera hand steady, the exposure congruent with the speed, the print would be a masterpiece. It had stood out on the contact sheet, a priceless gem among fine jewels, and now he couldn't wait to see it washed, dried, and mounted.

"It looks good. Very good," murmured Pat almost to herself.

She fished it from the bath and stuck it, dripping, on the wall where it hung by capillary action. Tony Valentino stared back at them in the dim, religious light. She felt the breath seep from her body. The print was magic, and it was only the first roll of the ten she had taken. If it was a harbinger of things to come, she had had the shoot of a lifetime. And there was always that last roll—the one she had marked with the big red cross. If this was brilliant, there was better by far in the can, and the goosebumps stood out on Pat Parker's arm as she dared to remember the pagan beauty of Valentino's naked body. Her finger had trembled on the viewfinder as she had fought to focus in the emotional noose that had gripped her. Somehow she had managed it, she'd never know how, and at the end, when something had badly needed to be said, there had been nothing at all to say. He had pulled up his pants as if lowering them had been the most natural thing in the world. He had buckled his belt, and flopped down on the sofa, and asked her how she thought the session had gone as if making a comment on the weather. She had gulped and muttered "real good" and fought to clear her mind of the steamy vision as, at the same time, she had battled to fix it forever in memory. And there, on the bench, undeveloped, were the results, and up on the wall was the charismatic face of the man who obsessed her.

"It's not bad," said Alabama. The guilt welled up in him. "I mean, it's good. It's excellent." He was pleased, thrilled even, by the portrait she had made. But he was also envious. It had been so long since the creative juices had flowed, and now, watching the image emerge, he dared to remember the intense pleasure of the darkroom.

"*Why* is it so good, Alabama?"

"Ah, the great American question. The 'why' question." He laughed. "We always assume there's an answer to it. It's our optimism. The Europeans who deal in pessimism say there seldom is.

Let's see. Well, it's technically good. That's maybe a quarter of it. The sharpness, the light illuminating one side of the face, casting the other side into shadow. That gives starkness, and that harshness matches the expression. Mostly it's in his eyes, isn't it? You've captured the longing, the desperation, the loneliness, and even the cruelty. Valentino is dangerous. He could hurt you. He'd rather enjoy it."

"You mean hypothetically?" Pat was anxious that Alabama not read too much into her relationship with her subject. His last bit had sounded suspiciously like a warning.

"Whatever."

"He does look terribly unhappy, doesn't he? His mother just died. He was real fond of her."

"What's he doing out here? Hustling the movies?"

"No!" Pat's denial was far too partisan, too emphatic. "I mean, he's just finished at the Juilliard in New York. He was a drama student there. He's staying with a friend in a house in the Colony."

"Girl-friend?"

"A friend who happens to be a girl," said Pat, not at all happy at the way the conversation was turning out. The sex of the Valentino host rankled. "She was at the Juilliard too. She asked him out here to help him get over his mother."

"Must be rich if the family has a house they don't use in the Colony. What's her name?" said Alabama. He knew most of the longer-term residents in Malibu.

"Vanderbilt. Allison Vanderbilt. I think she's big money."

"Yep, she is. Genuine American aristocracy. Not many of them around here. 'Specially not on the beach. A few scattered landside in the hills in places they can keep their horses. Jews on the sand, gentiles in the mountains is the rule in Malibu."

"I don't think that Tony is very into money." She looked at the eyes on the wall. What *were* they into? The career success he craved? Or was that just a line thrown out to catch the fish he really wanted. A golden fish like Allison Vanderbilt, perhaps, with her millions, her pedigree, and her WASP-ish Lily Pulitzer wraparounds wrapped around her waspish waist.

"Maybe. Maybe," said Alabama. "But take a tip from an old one, Pat Parker. Don't listen to what they say. Watch what they do."

"He's not a beach bum, Alabama. He's not on the make."

"You met him on the beach. He's living with a rich girl on the beach. He's an actor. He's ambitious. Jesus, this is Malibu, not Lourdes."

"You don't understand," she said coldly.

"Listen, honey, you can handle it. Have fun. What's life without a little angst? I'm just reserving the right to say 'I told you so.' It's one of the few advantages of being my age. You get to say it quite a lot."

He scratched himself, suddenly bored with the role of solicitous uncle.

"Anyways," he added, "however it turns out, you got some great pictures. You used him first. Should make a wild spread in that magazine of yours."

"I'm not going to publish these. They're for Tony's portfolio. They're for him." For us. Damn it, for *me*.

"Oh, I see, said Alabama with a chuckle.

"Anyway, he's already tangled with Emma Guinness. She wouldn't publish his photographs even if I submitted them." The Valentino face stared accusingly from the wall, dramatic in its uncompromising beauty. Yes, she would. Anybody would. Whatever her personal feelings, Emma Guinness would override them when she saw the material. She was an editor first and foremost, and *New Celebrity* was what mattered to her. Pat had thought about it. Now she was thinking about it again. Her conclusion was the same. The stumbling block to a Tony Valentino photo spread in *New Celebrity* would be Tony Valentino, and nobody else.

"I thought your famous contract gave you the right to submit your own material and insist that it be published."

Pat said nothing. He was right. It did.

Soon she would have to confront this. The dilemma was building inside her. All her life, work had been her fuel. She had lived for it, and it had been her crutch in all the times of her trouble. And it was so seldom that the work was "right." Sometimes it was passable, sometimes good, but so very rarely great before the unforgiving jury of artistic self-judgment. But here, now, in front of her, was perhaps the very best photograph she had ever taken, and there on the bench were the others . . . and the roll of film marked *X*. They couldn't be held back. They had to be published. Sounds in the forest unheard were for the Alabamas of this world. He might be big enough, confident enough, to create masterpieces for his eyes only. She wasn't. The photographs should be forced into *New Celebrity*, if necessary by invoking her contract. Her art demanded it. All resistance would have to be swept away. Emma's resistance. Tony's resistance. She took a deep breath as the immobile mountain felt the touch of the immovable object. Could she possibly publish Tony's photographs without his consent? He hadn't signed a release, yet he had agreed to the shoot. He wasn't the kind of guy who'd know about attorneys, but their relationship in embryo would be aborted with night-follows-day certainty. She would lose him before she had won him, and for what? For the glory she craved, perhaps more than the uncertain love he could provide. But maybe he could be persuaded to say yes to publication. After all, he, too, was powered by his dreams. The photo spread would do wonders for him. If the world shared half her enthusiasm for the pictures, he would become that rare-as-a-mockingbird's-teeth phenomenon, an overnight star. There would be deaths in the stampede of agents and casting people. Then he would thank her, because she would have been good for him. They would have used each other, and love and ambition could merge in the potent synergy that would fuse them together, body, soul, and mind . . . forever and ever.

She turned toward Alabama, and he smiled at her in the twilight of the darkroom. He knew what was in her mind. In the early days he had wrestled with problems like that before the god of fame had touched his shoulder with the sword of success and elevated him to the mountain from which he could laugh at the preoccupations of the lesser mortals. It was the age-old photographer's dilemma. When did you betray the trust of a subject? When did art matter more than keeping the faith? Did the ends justify the means in the name of supreme beauty?

"Of course, maybe this print is the only good one," said Alabama slowly. "Then the whole thing's academic. Anything else in this lot? What about the one marked *X?* What's that for? Hidden treasure?"

She blushed in the darkness. Alabama's instincts were phenomenal.

"Oh . . . he . . . took his clothes off for that one," she said, looking away.

She shouldn't be embarrassed. She hadn't asked him to. It had been a million miles from a come-on for either of them. But Alabama hadn't been there. He couldn't know how "right" it had been in the context of the shoot. Now it sounded tacky. Why had she told him? It had slipped out, as the truth did around Alabama. She prayed he wouldn't take a cheap shot at her.

He didn't.

"That would be the logical conclusion of this one," he said simply. "I suspect the chronology of the pictures would be the sequence of the layout." He paused, lost in thought. "It *will* be dynamite," he added.

"But Tony wouldn't want them published," she said.

"Yeah," agreed Alabama. "But he'd be wrong. Maybe not with just any pictures, but with these he'd be wrong."

Pat leaped at the chance, thrilled that Alabama agreed with her.

"Alabama, could you talk to him? I mean, when you've seen the other prints. He knows I've got an interest in this. He'd know you were objective."

Alabama shook his head. "I'll tell him I like the photographs. I do. I won't tell him how to run his own life. I don't do that."

"You tell me all the time," said Pat ruefully.

"You ask all the time, and anyways, you came to learn, and you're a photographer. I actually know a little about that."

She laughed. "You're right. I'm sorry. It *is* my problem, and it comes with the territory. A month ago I couldn't take a photograph I liked. Now I've got an outlet, and a wonderful print, and I'm blocked by conscience and/or a guy whose feelings I care about."

"It's happened before, Pat Parker. It's called a moral dilemma."

"What do you do about those?"

"I wait and see what I do. It's quite interesting. You argue the case for and against, and then you sit back and wait for the verdict. It seems to come from somewhere else, and it's impossible to predict."

"Oh, great. Thanks, Alabama. I'm a spectator, not a player."

"Relax, honey, and try a little gentle persuasion. Take him away for the weekend. Work on him. Show him the prints. Tell him he'll be a star. Plead. Beg. Blackmail."

"Latham's CEO called, a guy called Havers, and asked me on Latham's yacht for the weekend. They're going to Catalina. I said a definite 'maybe.' Do you think I could take Tony along?"

Alabama paused. Latham made him nervous. He was a neighbor now, largely because Alabama had withdrawn his objection to the huge land purchase. But he didn't like him and he didn't trust him, and he was suspicious of the interest he was showing in his protégée. Still, the presence of the uncompromising Valentino on the Latham yacht would for sure spike the billionaire's guns. The prickly Tony, young, virile, and fiercely proud, would be the author of some supremely unsettling on-board moments.

"Yeah," drawled Alabama. "You do that. Moon on the water, salt spray in the hair, beluga in the belly. You should have a magic time. An' I feel sure that Dick Latham and Tony Valentino are going to be the hottest item since Batman and Robin."

"Holy bat-boats," laughed Pat Parker.

SEVEN

Pat sat close behind him, closer than she needed to, and her arms wrapped tight around his waist as he leaned into the sharp turn. It felt like Alabama's bike, but they were miles from a road, and a thousand yards from land. On either side of her bare legs, the water funneled up as the wave runner forged through the crystal clear waters of the Pacific off the deserted western side of Santa Catalina Island. She laid her head against his back to hide it from the wind and to smell the scent of him, and she looked up at the barren cliffs that pointed ruggedly at the royal-blue sky. She couldn't remember when she had been so happy, but with the greed of the lover she wanted to be happier.

"Let's go explore one of the coves," she shouted into the stiff breeze above the buzz of the engine. The sun beat down on her shoulders, tickling the skin beneath the brand-new tan, and she shook her salt-stained hair behind her, as she scanned the coastline for a sandy strip of beach.

He slowed down as he heard her, and raised his hand to shield his eyes from the glare. He turned the vessel toward the harsh coastline, his eyes searching the shore for a landing place. He half turned and pointed to where the canyon cut into the mountain. She nodded, and the wave runner nosed toward the pocket beach, as a bald eagle swooped from the jagged rock face and painted its shadow on the shimmering water of the ocean. A few yards from the sand she swung her legs across the red saddle and prepared to guide the craft through the six-inch swell. He cut the engine. The silence crowded in on them. He jumped into the sea and steered the Yamaha up onto the sand.

For a minute or two they pushed it, using the tiny waves as rollers, until the wave runner was wedged safely on solid ground. Then, exhausted by the effort and drained by the heat, they collapsed onto the sand.

"No people," said Tony. He laughed at his understatement. They were miles from anywhere, as they had intended to be, and they were deliciously trapped. On either side the 165-million-year-old metamorphic rocks reached for the sky. Ahead of them lay a wall of stone, maybe a hundred feet high, jagged and unclimbable. Behind them stretched the vast ocean. The beach on which they lay was barely thirty feet wide, fifteen feet deep, and the sun covered it with a hot blanket, the warm air isolated from the ocean breeze by sheer cliffs.

"Not a good place for engine failure," said Pat, looking at the red-and-white striped wave runner with apprehension.

"Oh, I don't know," said Tony. He said it quietly, and Pat felt the thrill she was meant to feel. She turned to him, squinting in the brightness to see if his expression was adding to, or subtracting from, his words. But he lay flat in the sand, the ocean playing around his feet, and his arms were stretched out like Christ's on the cross, as he buried himself in the beauty of the moment. She saw the wisps of black hair beneath his arms, damp with the sea and his sweat, and she watched his muscular chest heave as he breathed. His eyes were closed. His face was a mask of peace. His feelings were an enigma.

Pat felt the stab of disappointment. "I hope the others aren't worried about us," she said, forcing reality into the Treasure Island illusion. In her mind she could see them. It was nearly lunchtime. They would be spaced out decoratively on the aft deck of *The Hedonist*, as smooth stewards dispensed the canapés and the Taittinger Rosé, and Beethoven did his bit on the Technics sound system. Dick Latham, formidably casual in L.A. Gear sneakers, white cotton slacks, and a plain white T-shirt, would have his battered Top-siders up on the Jon Bannenberg–designed banquettes that surrounded the vast deck. He would be effortlessly maintaining his outer calm, but inside the irritation would be growing. He was an obsessive beneath the cool veneer. Pat had picked that up. Lunch was at one. And two of his party were missing.

"Who cares about them? They're in another world," said Tony lazily.

"You don't care about Allison?" Pat bit her lip. She hadn't meant to say that, yet she hadn't been able to resist it. Allison Vanderbilt would be sitting across from Dick Latham, and already she would have turned down the champagne in favor of something more aristocratic, like Coke. She would be uncomfortable among all the conspicuous consumption, and she would be eying Latham with all the suspicion that the very old money reserved for the relatively new. Mostly, however, she would be sick with worry because Tony Valentino was missing . . . and because he had taken Pat Parker with him.

He didn't answer her, and there was a rebuke in his silence. Pat looked down. She picked up a handful of sand and let it slip through her fingers. Allison Vanderbilt was a problem. Havers hadn't been enthusiastic when she had made Tony Valentino a condition of her presence on the Latham yacht. She had hardly been wild with joy when Tony had made Allison Vanderbilt a condition of his.

"I'm staying with her," he'd said simply. "I can't take off without her." The implication had been that she was a friend and a kind one, nothing more nor less. There had been no amplification on that theme, nor would there be. Pat had not needed to be an amateur psychologist to get the picture. Allison Vanderbilt, her fawnlike eyes wide with vulnerable wonder, was head over heels in love with Tony Valentino. He was not in love with her. But there was a courtesy in his treatment of her, a kind of solicitous care, that Pat found alarming. He was always wondering if Allison was too hot or cold, whether she was comfortable, and he asked her from time to time if she was "all right." That last was an understandable question. Allison Vanderbilt looked stricken, brave, permanently at the edge of tears, and only her patrician genes and stainless-steel upper lip prevented her from dissolving into a sea of liquid misery. But if it was quite certain that Tony and Allison were not lovers, it was far from definite that they had not, somewhere along the line, made love. Now Pat Parker's stomach formed a tight knot as a wave of panic passed through her.

"Latham wants you," said Tony suddenly, his voice piercing Pat's thoughts like a spear.

"You're crazy!" He'd surprised her. Yes, Latham *was* interested in her. Of course he was. Why the hell hadn't she admitted it? It wasn't the biggest deal in the world. Latham fancied everyone.

"I'm not crazy. He wants you." Tony Valentino sat up. He looked at her. He was serious. He took everything so seriously.

"No, he's just interested because he's employed me. I'm the new kid on his block. The new toy. He flirts with everyone. It's his style. He does it with Allison. He *certainly* does it with Melissa Wayne. *She's* the target of the weekend."

"No, you are."

"To*ny!*" She emphasized the last syllable in mock reproach, and she threw the sand at him halfheartedly to lie that this was embarrassing. Why was he going on? Was he jealous? Could such an emotion possibly exist behind the disinterested eyes?

"What do you think of him?" he said.

"Weeeeell, he's difficult to ignore, isn't he? I mean, he's larger than life, and not just because of the money. I don't trust him. I haven't a clue why. I don't even know if I like him, but he's funny, and smart and interesting. I guess all that counts for something."

"He can't look at me," said Tony.

"I haven't noticed you look at him yet."

Pat laughed. It was true. Latham, the man who loved women, had reacted to the startling good looks and the youth of Tony Valentino with all the enthusiasm of a farmer for the presence of a fox in his hen coop. In return, the tortured, focused Tony, his faraway eyes set on his faraway dreams, had treated Latham like an elderly pedophile at a children's picnic. Latham, aggressively charming and dangerously urbane, had missed no opportunity to patronize his youthful rival. Valentino, his lip curled in a semipermanent snarl of superciliousness, had treated the billionaire like a joke in bad taste. Pat Parker had become their natural battlefield.

"You know, in some ways he's like me," said Tony.

"*What?*" Pat's mouth dropped open.

"Yes, he is. He's in pain all the time. He wants. He tries to disguise the fact that he does. He's addicted to proving something. All his bits and pieces, the trains, the boats, the planes, mean nothing to him. He's haunted. That's what he is."

Pat took a deep breath. He hadn't talked like this before. It sounded like a weakness he was discussing, but from his lips it was majestic too, like the suffering on the cross, pain for a higher purpose, a greater good.

He sat before her, and the water lapped around the faded blue cotton of his swimming trunks. His hands were splayed out Buddhist style across his legs, their palms imploring her to understand what he was saying. He was revealing himself to her. It was personal. She should realize that. His eyes cut into hers. He was talking about Latham, but he was also talking about himself.

"I hate him. He disgusts me. But it's me I see. He has to have the spotlight, but it's mine. I must have it, but he thinks it's his. He's pathetic. I'm pathetic. But the world thinks he's wonderful, and that's what it's going to think about me. Can you begin to understand that, Pat? Does it sound crazy?"

"Yes," said Pat suddenly. "It does. Crazy, but majestic. You're talking about the opposite of comfort. You're talking about antisecurity, and screw happiness, and the awesome power of the will. It's having your own way, isn't it, Tony? That's what you and Latham want. The stuff of your dreams are different, but it's the dreams that fuel you both. It's obsession that binds you together underneath."

He seemed calmed by her vehement profession of understanding, but he was still troubled by something. Pat knew instinctually what it was. He was troubled by her. He was troubled by them.

"And you, what do you want?" he said at last.

"Thanks for finding the time to care," she said gently.

She meant that. It wasn't a rebuke.

She looked up at the sky. What did she want? Him? Yes, but more than that.

She spoke haltingly as the thoughts came. "I guess I want in the abstract. I want like the little people want. I want to be happy. I want to be loved. I need to love. Working and making beautiful things seems to deliver the goods best. So that's what I do. But it's a means to an end, and the end is satisfaction, and security, and belonging and having someone belong to me . . ."

She peered up at him to see how her thoughts had landed.

"That's right," he said. "That's the right way to feel." He seemed unaware of his patronization, and the fact that he didn't recognize it made it go away. "It makes us opposites." He smiled to show that he'd hoped for that, because it meant they had a chance.

"The kind that attract?" said Pat, smiling back at him.

"The kind that attract," he said, and his voice was lower as he spoke, and his eyelids sank down over his suddenly smoldering eyes.

She couldn't resist it. It was crazy, but she just couldn't. He had to be teased, despite the dangers. Nobody should take himself that seriously.

"An opposite like Dick Latham," she said.

His voice stepped back from the edge of intimacy.

"Don't play games with me, Pat Parker," he said.

"Oh, but I *want* to play games with you, Tony Valentino. Sometimes I feel you've been seriously deprived of games." She laughed to taunt him, and she scooped up another handful of sand and she threw it onto his thighs to show that she wasn't afraid of him, but that she liked him more than was entirely safe.

For a second the war raged on his face, and then she saw herself win and the triumph surged within her. His smile was little-boy-sorry as he admitted to his crippled sense of humor. But it didn't linger long. Fun was to him an alien world. Lust wasn't. He leaned forward and he reached out to touch her.

She didn't move. She was frozen in boiling ice. Only his finger could release her from the numbness that gripped her. It was on her arm, and its touch was more real than mind and body, than the bright sun in the heavens, than the cold ocean that had turned them into a volcanic island of passion, waiting to explode in the bliss of union.

His eyes danced in her soul, and she made the music for him. It was slow dancing, clear and low, and the notes of the melody were sweet in her body. Lazy, loving, far now from the panic to come, the sounds of desire built within her. They cascaded out through her own eyes, and they swayed in tune to his. Her fingers tingled, the sweat rushed to bathe her upper lip, the salt air was deliciously nervous in her flared nostrils. His finger traced the contours of her arm. It wandered across the smooth muscle, lingered on the hot skin, reached up to her shoulder. There, the flat of his hand rested, feeling her gentle motion. She was breathing for his hand. It rose and fell, so near the loveliness of her neck, waiting there, with all the time in the world. She turned toward his hand, and she leaned her head to one side to capture it, her cheek crushing it softly like a flower in a book. He could feel her warm breath on his face. It was the beginning of the negotiation of bodies, the give and take, the threat and promise, the war and peace that would abolish all boundaries and obliterate all distinction, until there was only surrender and togetherness in the awesome harmony of eternal joy.

He inched across the sand toward her, until his face was close to hers. She was bathed in his breath, and she inclined toward him, eager for all that he would do for her, greedy for his love. He cupped her head in his hands, holding it reverently. The wonder shone from his eyes into the love light that blazed from hers.

"Tony," she whispered, her voice breaking. "Tony," she murmured again, loving the sound of his name, lusting for the intimacy he offered with his eyes.

His finger was on her chin, lifting it up to him. His thumb was at her lower lip, slippery on the sweat there, washed by the currents of her breath. She opened her lips to taste his salty skin, and she put out her tongue to touch the finger that hurried to be touched. Her mouth was parched as the summer canyon, but her tongue was wet still, and it licked him gently, painting his sensitive fingers with precious saliva in the tender prelude to the making of their love. His finger waited, passive, and she played with it, nuzzling it with her teeth. She eased it deeper into her mouth, pushed it back again, clasped it tight to tell him about the prison of her body, and how it longed to hold him in its velvet walls. She moved her head from side to side and her neck swayed to the secret rhythms of romance, craning nearer, stretching back. And all the time the messages from her body came winging in, the delicious fear in her stomach, the rushing blood in her taut nipples, the aching void at the core of her.

His hand moved behind her neck, and the finger she had tasted burrowed into her hair. He drew her toward him, and she pushed back against his hand, making him force her, forcing him to admit that he wanted her as much as she wanted him. She was still fighting him. She was his equal, courageous, determined, giving nothing away. Her resistance made him stronger. His hand was rough now as he drew her in, and his lips were tender no more. They closed over hers, crushing her mouth, and his tongue pushed into her, invading her rudely in the way that part of her longed to be invaded. She reached for him and drew him to her, bruising his lips with hers. He pressed against her, battling her tongue with his, using his wetness to slake the thirst of her longing. Their teeth clashed in the kiss. Their mouths became one. It was war. But it was a conflict that both would win, and they gave no quarter and demanded no mercy as they battled for the pleasure victory that each must have. His whole body was plastered against hers now, the power of his muscled chest heavy against her breasts. Slowly, inevitably, he forced her back until she was prostrate beneath him, her back buried against the hot sand, his body above her, framed by the beauty of the pale blue sky.

At last his mouth freed hers, and she lay still below him, captured, as she had been in her dreams, by the man she loved. She smiled in triumph, and the breath rasped between her throbbing lips, her chest rising and falling beneath his. She could smell him. She could taste him. Oh, dear God, she could feel him—rock hard against her hips, his legs heavy on hers, his dripping, sweat-soaked skin melting on her body. But there was a new expression on his face. No longer was he the cruel conqueror. The harshness had left his features. There was a softness in his eyes that she had not seen before, and she knew that now a more subtle, more delicate wind was blowing, one that would whip her to a frenzy of ecstasy more complete than she had ever known.

His hand was on her chest. He reached for her breast, tracing its lines to the nipple. Beneath the cotton of her swimsuit, her flesh quivered beneath his touch. She pushed out at his hand, and her eyes pleaded with him to be bold. He heard her. He hooked his finger beneath the material until she knew what he would do, and he paused to use up the moment. Memory must have this. It must never go away. Through all the years of familiar intimacy, this second would be remembered. Slowly, almost sad that there would never be another first time, he unveiled her. The shuddering sigh rushed from him. His eyes were filled up with the vision. She lay flat, but her breast did not. It rose up at him, a white triangle of perfection, pure and lovely as snow on a distant mountain. The paleness in contrast to the syrup brown of her skin, its firmness against gravity's invisible pull, the crowning glory of the shell-pink cone that capped it—all merged in the mist of passion, and Tony Valentino bent down in homage before its savage beauty.

With his tongue he touched the tip of her nipple, and it reared against him, impossible in its tightness. He waited there, vibrating with her, feeling her blood course against his, amazed by the rhythmic thrusts of her pulse. He could feel her heart beating through his own delicate skin, as her nipple expanded and contracted, pushing out, retreating, ebbing and flowing against his wetness. Gently, in wonder, he licked at her, moving his tongue across the slippery surface of her throbbing breast. He nuzzled against her, rubbing the silken softness with the roughness of his cheek. He took the petal pinkness between his teeth, threatening it, loving it, pressing down, marveling at how the tautness sprang back against him, at the power of her fragile skin to cage the blood that rushed so furiously beneath its surface. And all the time he listened to the low moans of satisfaction that sprang from her, as his body caught fire, and his roaring mind planned new acts for the drama of love.

She pulled herself up, supporting her body on her elbows in the wet, warm sand, and her breast thrust out at his mouth. She groaned her pleasure, but all the time she was wanting more. How could this go on forever? How could it be speeded, how slowed, how, dear Lord, could it be intensified? She reached behind to untie the top of her swimsuit, but already the focus of her mind was moving away from her pulsing breasts. She threw the strip of material onto the sand and, exhausted by the effort, she fell back, half-naked, totally open to the man who now owned her body.

He buried his head between the firm mounds of flesh, and his mouth roamed over them, feeding from their fullness, his tongue sliding deliciously over the creamy skin. They were wet with his wetness, gleaming and glistening with his moisture, and damp, too, with the sweat of her desire. He burrowed in, losing himself in the warmth of her, as if he wanted only to be buried inside her body, to merge with her, to become her so that his terrible need would be a need no more. But there was no turning back in the dance of commitment. There was no standing still. There was only the headlong advance toward the moment of glory.

His arms were pylons in the sand beside her. He pressed himself up above her, and then his head was moving down toward the place she longed for it to be. His tongue weaved a slippery track on her stomach, pausing at her navel, heading down again to the edge of her bikini bottom. She knew what would happen now, and her heart raced as the lust fountain exploded inside, making a river of the silvery stream that slid from her.

She arched her back, and she pulled her bottom upward. Her hands found the elastic of her bikini briefs. She thrust them down, without shame, without guilt. They straddled her thighs, a sensual bridge between her straining legs, and she thrust out at the material as she fought to open herself up to him. For long seconds he hovered above her, a hummingbird eager for the nectar of the dew-soaked flower. The wisps of her shining hair were watered with the scented juice of her. Her pouting pink love lips nestled in the liquid, downy sea. He breathed in the steam heat of her, as she sizzled on the burning plateau of desire. Then he lowered his face to taste her, to please her, to love her, and her moan of acquiescence was the music for their sweet communion.

His lips touched hers in the alien kiss. Shy, she pushed out at his mouth. He breathed gently against her. Her radiant heat beamed back at him, the musk of her passion floating into his mind.

"Yes, yes," she whispered, her voice husky, her eyes closed tight to seal in the excitement. She was melting for him. All the warm wetness of her body was drawn to his lips. Her essence lingered in love at the edge of his tongue.

She felt the still tip of it, soft against her softness, and then it began to move. She shuddered from the shock of his touch—the enormity of what he was doing, the wonder of what it meant. In the ultimate intimacy, his tongue was speaking to her in the language more honest than words.

There would be no retreat from this. It was the firm foundation on which everything would be built. It meant everything, yet its meaning was a slave to the feeling of it. Sensation and commitment had merged in the magic of the moment.

His tongue slid upward, swimming on the flood tide of her, and it came to rest at the throbbing center of her world. It stopped, aware of where it was, knowing so well what it could do now. She moaned to reassure him, but he needed no reassurance. His bones, his muscles, his mind were there for her alone. Over the nerve-racked minutes he must build the mighty castle of her ecstasy, and then he must demolish it in the explosion that would set the sky on fire.

His tongue moved against the millimeters of her sexual flesh. Gently at first, then harder, his tongue grew firm, more pointed, more insistent. He swept against the core of her, licking at her, milking her of joy, and his whole face bathed in the bath she had become, as it submerged itself in the sole purpose of her pleasure. Rhythmically, his tongue rubbed at her. It darted, random, in her depths. It slipped against the slick of her, and his hands snaked beneath her. He reached for the tight skin of her buttocks, and he drew her toward him, increasing the pressure of his head in the heart of her, and she shouted out sharply on the breeze as ecstasy blanketed her mind.

He picked her up and forced her to his mouth, like a chalice to the lips of a desert traveler.

His tongue was desperate now in its quest for her. It left the pleasure center and dived down into the molten sea, plunging into the dark recess of her, drinking, exploring, licking, as it loved her. His mouth closed over the opening of her, sucking the sweetness from her, and then every part of his face joined the battle for her joy. She arched her back and thrust her pelvis at his head, greedy for sensation, wanting only more. He thrust back at her wonderful, airless prison, and he listened to the music of their love, the wet sounds, splashing, dripping, foaming, as he swam on the river she had become.

"Oh! Ooooooh!" she moaned. It was running away from her. She was out of control. Her legs heaved against the bikini bottoms that straddled them, and she heard the material tear as she fought to open herself wider to his mouth. Her stomach was flat as iron, the muscles of her ass tight, as she battled for the strength to squeeze yet more pleasure from his tongue. Her mouth was dry, as all the liquid of her body turned into the love that was drowning him. Soon, so soon, it would all dissolve and the steel purpose would fall apart in the thrashing dissolution of her orgasm. And she would be empty. The void that ached in her depths would not be filled. Fanned to a furnace by his lips, the fires would grow cold all alone, isolated from *his* pleasure by the separateness of her body.

"Tony," she whispered. "Make love to me. Put yourself inside me."

She opened her eyes and stared into his. He must know how much she wanted this.

She wanted to see his face at the moment they were joined together forever.

In answer, he rose up above her, and she was aware of his hand at the waist of his swimsuit. She felt his body wriggle once, twice, sensed the wonderful touch of him against the slippery skin of her thigh. She reached down, unable to stop herself, and she stared into his soul as she held him for the very first time. With both hands she clasped it, and her heart seemed to stop as the wave of adrenaline broke within her. It was so big, vast and angry, its tautness pulsating against her fingers, threatening her, promising her fulfillment beyond the reach of wild dreams. For a second, in the conspiracy of lovers, they fought to hold the moment. But already the head of him was straining at the mouth of her, and she was opening, wide, wider than was possible. The muscles of her legs heaved against the bikini bottoms, and the ripping, tearing sound of the material was the signal for the union. Her legs snapped apart, and her bottom rocketed upward from the sand. With a cry of delight, he plunged forward. He rammed into her, filling her full, bursting her open with the hugeness of his lust. Her mouth opened, as the breath rushed from her lungs. Inside she was delirious, as the most intense pleasure flirted with the sharpness of pain. She opened wider, but there was nothing left, and still he reached in, deeper and deeper, farther and farther, more and more. He forced her apart, making the space for himself, and her sleek sheer walls stretched around him, her skin merging with his in a closeness made possible only by the abundance of her liquid love.

Now at last he was at the roof of her, and it seemed as if there was nothing else but him in her body. He had taken it over. The rest of her was isolated in some forgotton corner of the envelope that was flesh and bone. He was her child, growing in her womb. He was the unforgiving marauder, pillaging her bowels with the cruel delight of his alien invasion. He was her lover, stiff and wonderful in her belly, in his rightful home at last, safe in the land she prayed he would never leave.

Her eyes were wide as the part of her that held him. In wonder, she watched him. Pinned on the point of his purpose, she looked down from the brink of the abyss. He moved inside her, and, as she was acclimating to his presence, he began to withdraw. But before the panic of emptiness could replace the joy of fulfillment, he was back. Her whole body shook with the rhythm of his strokes. Out to the brink, back to the ceiling of her world, the piston action was terrible in its reassurance, conjuring up blissful visions of the release that was its goal. She clamped down on him as far as her body would allow and she moaned her pleasure as she welcomed the climax she feared. This first time was too intense. There was no controlling it. Later they could become clever lovers. Now they were hungry novices, enslaved by the experience that was stronger than either of them. Faster, harder, he tore into her. Softer, more welcoming, she relaxed for him and their stomachs slapped together, greased with sweat and love, in the musical rhythm of lust.

His eyes told her of his moment, as her body howled of hers. She was rigid at the second the music soared to its crescendo. Every part of her sang in harmony. She was whole. She was perfect in the time before the truth was told. She was dimly aware of his furious body, but her inner eyes were staring at the brilliant light that had illuminated her mind. At the peak the breath was full in her lungs, and the message from God was alive in her heart.

"I love you. I love you," she screamed at the heavens and at him, and then, happy now to die, she leaped from the cliffs into the boiling sea of her orgasm.

Dick Latham peered over the stern and his smile was as natural as the Joker's. Below, the crew were attaching the davits to the wave runner. Pat and Tony stood on the afterdeck, their fingers intertwined loosely, and they talked quietly to each other, oblivious to the orderly confusion around them. Latham's knowing, suspicious eyes roamed over them. He noticed Pat's ripped bikini bottoms, tied at her hip by what looked like the drawstring of a man's swimsuit. He took in Tony's trunks, held up by a rough knot formed from the loose material that had somehow lost its means of support. They had missed lunch. Hell, they had missed tea. And it didn't take a Sherlock Holmes to figure out why. Somewhere out there, on the sands of Catalina, Pat Parker and Tony Valentino had been doing it on the beach.

Through clenched teeth, Dick Latham called out to them. "Where were you? We missed you. We were beginning to get worried."

They looked up at him, but the breeze had taken his words.

"What?" said Pat. Tony Valentino said nothing, his sullen face turned up in disdain at his rival.

Latham wasn't the sort of man to repeat himself.

He beckoned them, his arm darting up and down in a gesture that gave away his irritation.

They took their time. The back of *The Hedonist* was layered like a cake. The lower deck was where the toys were loaded and unloaded, the Riva ski boat, the windsurfers, jet skis, the small sailboat, the wave runners. It was used for swimming, skiing, and scuba diving, and its transom doors opened to the ocean where a vast platform extended out into the swell. The deck above was indented back and comprised the outside dining area where lunch and dinner were eaten on the few days when the coastal Southern California weather rose above its normal Mediterranean climactic range. Latham stood on the deck above that, the sitting area where communal drinks were taken before meals, and where batteries of telephones kept him in touch with the outside world. Precisely sixty steps would deliver the lovers to his face. About a minute. He waited at least three.

Tony came first. He swaggered into Latham's view, holding his hips like a dangerous weapon, and the pseudosmile around the corners of his mouth spoke volumes. Pat followed, languid, lazy, her body relaxed, moving with the sleek, liquid motions of a well-fed cat. Latham had intended to be coolly supercilious, but the sight of them revised the emotional possibilities. He was deeply pissed off. The trick would be to hide it. At first he said nothing, hoping for the apology that wouldn't come.

"I wish you'd told us you were taking off on that thing. It would have been polite. There were four of them last time I counted. Some of us might have liked to come along," he tried.

"We wanted to do a bit more than just make circles around the boat," said Tony. The words plus the gestures could have run as a short play off-Broadway. He twirled his fingers in the air in a circular motion to signify the fatuous route that all the safe, silly fatuous people would have taken as they trolled around the safety of the floating gin palace with its wall-to-wall crew. People like you have no guts, he was saying. Your idea of adventure is boats in the bathtub. You're old, old man. You're old and safe and secure, and your money has drained you of excitement and interest as surely as the years have drained away your youth. The only thing that was missing was a middle finger raised in mockery . . . and Dick Latham spinning on it like a nursery top.

Latham watched him. It was personal now. It wasn't just Pat Parker. It was everything. It was the generation war. It was sexual combat. It was the vital necessity of winning, whatever and wherever the conflict. The excitement welled up inside him, replacing the anger. In the oceans in which Latham swam, *he* was the great white shark. There was no competition anymore, just smaller fish to eat. Now, here, swimming among the plankton and the groping grouper, he had found a killer whale. It was wonderful. He could flex his mental muscles, get back in shape, and experience the satisfaction of humiliating someone who was very nearly his own size. There was even a prize, as there was in all the best contests. It might have the Valentino fingerprints on it now, but they could be gotten rid of in the wash. Then, polished, retooled, and carefully engraved with the Latham initials, Pat Parker would take her rightful position on the Latham mantelpiece, with the other trophies. Who knew, she might do a couple of months there, before he hit her with the sledgehammer he used for breaking the hearts. Yes, she would be a glorious victory in the endless war he waged against the female race.

He laughed, and this time his face read "mirth."

"God, Tony, you make me feel like a geriatric. Any minute now you'll be calling me 'sir' and pulling out chairs for me. Let me just say right now that if it comes to the kiss of life, I'm allergic to men."

They all laughed at that, Pat in relief, Tony in victory, Latham inside. "Anyway, you two must be thirsty," he continued. " 'Boating' is thirsty work!" He smiled to show he knew. He pulled the cellular phone from his waistband and pushed a button for the steward. He flopped down in a chair, Fred Astaire casual, and made a motion for them to join him. Their "impoliteness" was apparently forgotten. Latham had slid on, creamy smooth, to a role other than that of offended host.

The lovers joined him. Tony sprawled confidently against the cushions, Pat by his side, her hand resting casually on his leg. She had to keep the contact. Inside she was still full of him, and her heart sang as she thought of it. She felt deliciously and uncharacteristically passive. Tony was in control. Of himself. Of the mighty Dick Latham. Of her. The gulls soared overhead. Strauss warbled from the sound system. The only problem in the world was what to order to drink.

"When I said we were worried, what I really meant was that Allison was worried." Latham smiled easily as he dropped the note of discord into the lovers' harmony.

Was that a flash of guilt in the surly eyes of the Adonis? Was there a tinge of green in those of the photographer?

The steward padded across the deck to take the orders.

"Oh, Johnson, have someone tell Ms. Vanderbilt that her friend is back. I think you'll find she's in her cabin," he said casually over his shoulder. The veiled insinuation was unmistakable. Vanderbilt and Valentino had been an item. Valentino and Pat had cheated on her. It was no big deal, but it *was* a little shabby. Not at all the sort of trick that the Lathams of this world descended from the moral high ground to play. He had effortlessly cast himself in the part of the responsible adult, patiently explaining about right and wrong after the kids had pulled the wings from the fly.

Tony shifted on the white terrycloth of the banquette. Pat's hand drifted from his suddenly restless leg.

"Allison's a big girl," he said, cutting through to Latham's meaning.

"But a little vulnerable, no?" Latham smiled. He looked at Tony. His laughing eyes found Pat's. Accusation lingered amid the humor.

"I have a feeling you'd know about the vulnerability of women," she laughed, in retaliation.

"What would you like to drink, miss?" asked the steward.

"I can recommend the peach juice. I had a Bellini before lunch. Of course they'd make it fresh," said Latham, ignoring her jibe as he swam easily in the undercurrents of the conversation. She was sticking up for her man like a lover should. He liked that. He liked her, liked the salt-matted hair, the jutting breasts, the hard boy's ass that platformed out at the top of her long, luscious legs.

"Yeah, okay," said Pat. "What are you having, Tony?" In answer, Tony waved the steward away, shaking his head from side to side. It wasn't the time to be accepting a glass of water from Latham. That his butt was on his boat was a compromising enough position.

"So, Tony, apart from riding the dangerous waves, what other activities can we find for your amusement?" asked Latham, baiting the trap. A wave runner was no problem for a biker with a sense of balance. There were toys down below that would be. How would the Big Apple Thespian play on a mono-ski with Dick Latham at the wheel of the boat? Would he score points at skeet shooting as the clay pigeons curved and curled in the wind off the stern, and the Latham Purdey's blazed inaccurately at his shoulder? How complete would be his downfall on the windsurfer, that graveyard of a novice's self-confidence? Dick Latham excelled at all of the above. He had endured long hours at the Holland and Holland shooting school near Heathrow, and wet, longer ones in Scotland Augusts as the cunning grouse flew in waves above his guns. He had windsurfed with Baron Arnaud de Rosnay before his death, and he had taken lessons with his beautiful widow, speed windsurfer champion Jenna, off her beach in Mustique. Ivana Trump had been his instructress on the mono. Oh, yes, years and billions were not the only things that Dick Latham had over the cocky Tony Valentino. The name of the game would be to demonstrate it.

"What I'd really like to try is scuba diving," said Tony easily, picking his way through the Latham minefield. Strong lungs and a stronger body were all it needed.

"Yeah, we can do that," said Latham, trying to hide his disappointment. "The best place is Santa Cruz, a few miles up the coast off Santa Barbara. They have some amazing caves. We can go up there this evening, while we have dinner. Go out first thing in the morning if that sounds like fun."

"Fun? Fun? I'm not against fun," said Melissa Wayne.

In all her short sharp life, Melissa Wayne had never said a truer word. Fun she knew about, and pleasure, and the inflicting of cunning, delicious pain. She stood there on the edge of the group, and as she spoke she became its center. It was as if some celestial spotlight had picked her out, and as it lit her, she began to shine with a brilliance of her own. She was small in stature, but in no other way, and her multifaceted beauty gleamed like a priceless cut diamond bathed in starlight. She wore Chanel crocodile sneakers, velvet soft jeans around her drum-tight butt, a silk Yves Saint

Laurent shirt falling away from pert, pushy tits. But clothes were not her point. Her personality was. It dwarfed her body, reaching out like a tentacled aura to touch her audience. The perfect face, the freckles around the turned-up nose, the heart-shaped mouth, the neat little ears were merely props for the main event called Melissa Wayne, and the three who watched her sniffed at her X factor with the fascination she had come to regard as her due.

"Ah, Melissa," murmured Latham, visibly affected by her presence. "I don't think you have met Tony Valentino and Pat Parker. Pat is a very famous photographer"—he paused—"who works for one of my magazines, and Tony is . . . Tony is an 'actor.' And Melissa is, well, Melissa is Melissa, isn't she?" He laughed easily.

"Hi, Tony," said Melissa Wayne. She didn't deal in women, period. If the entire female sex vanished in a flash, leaving her the sole survivor, to Melissa it would be a slow news day. She walked forward quickly as she put out her hand to him. When he reached up to take it, she didn't give it back. She kept it, as if it were a painting on loan. Her tongue snaked over lipstickless lips.

"I don't know your work," she said.

It was a masterpiece. She was deadly serious, matter-of-fact, her words as far from flirtation as her body was close to it. Her message was unmistakable. Tony was an actor. That meant he was a serious artist, as she was. The female "photographer" and the billionaire had ceased to exist. In the world there were only two people—she, and the boy who should be on the menu for dinner. The fact that Melissa Wayne was bought by the households of America as sexual breakfast cereal was overlooked. In this role, she was Streep and Fonda in Oscar combat. Somehow her presumption elevated Tony to Nicholson and Hoffman status. That was exactly what she had intended.

Tony smiled his pleasure, his hand happy in the Wayne one. He stood up.

"I've just finished at the Juilliard," he said. "Next stop is Steinbeck's *East of Eden* off-Broadway." He ran off the attenuated curriculum vitae as if it were Olivier's. He was completely unfazed by its shortness. Latham had to admire it. Belief in yourself was contagious. He'd always known that about himself. Now, with a modicum of surprise, he realized it could be true for others.

"The Juilliard's the best, and improving on James Dean should be a challenge," she said. "If I'm in town I'll come to the opening night."

"Hi, I'm Pat Parker," said Pat coldly. "I'll see you there . . . if you're in town."

"Hi," said Melissa Wayne with a half nod in the direction of Pat's hello. She didn't turn around.

"How was the trip? Did they look after you?" asked Dick Latham, enjoying himself thoroughly.

"Fine," said Melissa. She continued to stare at Tony. He continued to hold her gaze. She had tuned into his wavelength with the expertise of the woman who lived for men. That was flattering, and it was flattery with topspin, because the actress had long ago dropped the *-let* from her *star*.

With reluctance Melissa relinquished Tony's hand. She sat down on the edge of a director's chair, knees together, legs splayed out, her hands resting on the faded denim. She was silent, but her quietness did nothing to detract from her stunning appeal.

"Did you helicopter in?" asked Pat. The instant jealousy was receding. She liked women. They were at least innocent until proven guilty. The Wayne come-on had been a work of art, but then she was famous for that. It was why she was a box-office creamer. It was why she got two-point-five per pop. She was a pro playing a pro, and she had to practice. After all, Pat had to take photographs. Anyway, Pat was the one in possession. The body memories said so.

"I didn't swim," said Melissa. She turned to face Pat, and scorn for her small talk was all over her face. She smiled to take the sting out of her rudeness, effortlessly emphasizing her patronization.

"I thought maybe you'd been beamed in from fantasy-land," said Pat.

"You're not a paparazzi, are you?" said Melissa in retaliation. She wrinkled her nose.

"Pat's a very brilliant photographer," said Tony Valentino.

He was absolutely definite about it. There was no compromise. His tone was not angry, but his sentiment was clear. If Melissa Wayne didn't climb down, she would be pushed, her fame notwithstanding. He liked her. He respected her. But Pat Parker was off-limits.

Melissa looked at him, back at Pat. For a second or two she was undecided. Fantasy-land! Jeez! The dreamy boy won. God, he was sure of himself. That was good. It made it better during the sex games when they crawled across the room wearing the saddle she kept in her closet. This one might even take the bit. Whatever, sooner or later, she would make sure the photographer girl got to see the Polaroids if not the videotape. She wouldn't be best pleased by the insight into the Wayne fantasy-land they provided.

"That's a relief!" she said with a laugh. It wasn't totally clear what she meant. That Pat wasn't paparazzi? That the conversation was over? That she and Tony had avoided a falling-out?

"Well," said Dick Latham. "I'm going to get a bath, have a massage, and then we'll meet back here for drinks before dinner. Say about seven?"

He stood up.

"*What* fun!" he said, and with a chuckle he was gone.

"God, dinner is going to be rough," said Pat. She stared into the mirror to check her makeup, but she was watching Tony, as he lounged in an armchair catching Diane Sawyer fresh via satellite on the ABC news.

"Yeah, Melissa's a loose cannon. But I admire her. She's taken some shots to get where she is. I suppose she feels she has the right to hand out a few. You can't judge people like her by the same rules."

Pat turned around. She knew what he meant. Hard-chargers put up with a lot of bullshit on the journey to their place in the sun. Sweet dispositions got left behind. Humility, generosity, sense of humor got discarded with the other excess baggage. Right now, however, it suited her *not* to understand. Tony had stood up for her when Melissa had gone on to the offensive, but he had been flattered by the star's attention.

"You mean one law for the Melissa Waynes, another for the rest of us," she said, letting the sarcasm hang out.

Tony sighed. He closed his eyes. It was a part of life he didn't like. Pat was on the verge of picking a fight, because she had seen him shine out to the girl who shone at the world. Big deal. Why did she have to be so predictable? Neither her body nor her mind were.

"Okay, she liked me. I liked her. There's no need for a philosophical discussion about it."

He crossed a blue-jeaned leg over the other one. He raised his arms above his head. He didn't actually yawn but he went through the body motions. In a test of attentive powers half the audience would have described the sound he wasn't making.

Pat started to frown, but it turned into a laugh. She loved his refusal to be drawn into games. Around him, everything was simple and honest. All was on the surface—the good, the bad, and the ugly, although there was precious little of the latter. It was true she'd been jealous of his liking Melissa Wayne, but what sort of a guy wouldn't fancy her? The girl made Basinger look like a hot dog. Compared to her, Meg Ryan had all the vulnerable charm of a leper in a Jacuzzi. Side by side with Melissa Wayne, the Playmate of the Millennium would have possessed the subtle sensuality of a road drill.

"Okay, okay, I'm sorry," she said. "Actually she *is* a turn-on. And it would be great if she showed for your opening. It'd for sure help with the PR."

Pat regretted it immediately. They'd had this conversation before. But hell, he was so other-worldly, and she was so worldly-wise. To get by in this life you needed a little help from your acquaintances. You didn't get much from your friends, unless you were in a mess and short of an enthusiastic audience.

He looked like he'd respond—a staccato blurb about not needing a tart to help with his art—but he passed on it. "Why do you think she's here?" he said instead.

Pat cocked her head to one side. Tony so seldom asked a "why" question.

"I'd have thought she was just Latham's speed. I mean he bought Cosmos, even if he raped it for the real estate."

"You think he's a star-fucker doing coitus interruptus on Hollywood?" mused Tony. "I wonder. Somehow I don't think so."

"Well, he can't stick her in a movie. Now that he's dismantled Cosmos, he doesn't have a studio. And I don't think Latham's the sort of guy who'd stoop to finance indie production. Melissa's box-office performance means there's money for her films anywhere. Maybe he just likes her. Maybe she likes him. After all, you two did."

Tony smiled at her halfhearted attempt to resurrect the argument in embryo, as he continued to think out loud. "I mean, Latham's still got the Cosmos logo, the library, the goodwill. All he's missing is the buildings, the product, and the people. Plenty of those in L.A."

"Cecil B. de Latham? I don't think so somehow. He's too WASP . . . East Coast . . . too smooth. Most likely he'll sell the bits and pieces to the Japanese. They've already got the banks, and a rising sun over the Cosmos spinning globe would look real dandy. Jeez, wouldn't it have been wonderful to have lost the war?"

Tony wasn't persuaded. Latham was up to something.

"We'll see. But I can't help feeling that something's going down. That guy Havers helicoptered in with six or seven suits who had to be bankers or lawyers or both. They've been stuck below deck like they were cabin class since yesterday morning. I walked by the communications room this morning and there were fax machines going nuts."

"It's probably like that all the time. We one-fax families don't understand how the other half lives. I mean the relaunch of *New Celebrity* is probably worth a message or two."

Pat was proud of herself. That had segued in nicely. Sooner or later she had to bring up the question of the photographs. The deadline for the prestigious first issue was approaching. The lead time could not be chipped away indefinitely. If the photo spread was to have maximum impact, it should coincide with the barrage of publicity that would accompany the launch. Already the awesome Latham PR machine was grinding into gear. The gossip columns were full of it, each morsel placed lovingly by Marilyn Evans or Rogers and Cowan where it would show best. Billy Norwich, Liz Smith, Suzy carried it most weeks, and the seminal incorruptibles, the George Christys of this world, were passing the message in the rarefied grapevines that twined across the heavens joining star to star.

"Have you thought about what you're going to do for the magazine?" said Tony suddenly.

She took a deep breath. He'd brought it up. This was the moment. There were two ways to go. She could tell him the naked truth or she could dress it up. The second way would be easier. The trouble was that Tony would rip right through the packaging to the bare flesh, and she would be left looking devious.

"I thought maybe . . . . you," she blurted out.

He said nothing. He looked down at his hand. He looked back at her.

"And when did you have that idea?" he said.

Before or after the photographic session, he meant. Before or after this afternoon. "Are you using me, Pat Parker?" asked his eyes. "Are you for real? Or are you for yourself?"

She bypassed the question.

"They're just so *good*, Tony. You know that. Alabama said so. When something's that great, you have to use it. It's a responsibility."

"It's a *responsibility* to show America my dick?"

She shook her head from side to side. Oh boy! It was going to be worse than she'd thought. "Listen, Tony, I don't know how to explain this but—"

He held up his hand to cut her off. "Don't shoot me some crap about the photos making me a star, okay? I know you're hung up on that stuff. If they're as good as you think, they'll make *you* a star. That's the bottom line, isn't it? Maybe it always was."

Pat tried to stay calm. Part of what he said was true. The spread would be good for him. It would be better for her. But so what? They were technically lovers. If that meant anything, and she wanted desperately to believe it did, then he should be as eager for her success as she was for his. Art was beauty. It could do no wrong. It would be brilliant for everyone—for her, Tony, Latham, Emma, for *New Celebrity*. She was going to fight for it.

"Why do you object?" She launched into the attack.

"They were personal, Pat. They were mine. They were me. You took them for *me*, remember? Not for the world."

"Yes, I did, and they're still yours. I won't use them if you tell me not to. I just want to change your mind. I want to stop you from making a mistake, because I do care for you, not because I don't. They started out as pictures, but when they were printed—when I saw them—they were something else. It's like Ansel Adams's *Moonrise* photograph. The stupid moon's there over Hernandez every night. It never misses. But the photograph is more than its subject. The beauty is in the angle, the point of view, the emphasis on some indefinable part of the reality that only the artist sees. Artists make the others see. They open their eyes. It's like you, Tony, in that *Streetcar* you told me about at Juilliard. How many schoolkids have murdered those same lines you spoke? But you made the words live. When you said them the audience *understood*. You gave them your perspective, Tony. You made them art. I've done that to your face and your body. Those photographs have captured something that's bigger and more fundamental than you. It's the *idea* of you and what you represent. Anyone can look at them and they know you, they feel you, they have a relationship with you. Maybe they're sad and lonely and fed up with their lives, but when they see those photographs they'll feel better inside for just a moment or two. And they'll pick themselves up and hold their stomachs in, and maybe they'll remember what it was like to dream in the days before the music died. That's what I'm talking about, Tony. You've got to understand. You've got to believe me."

She sat forward, her whole body leaning into her words as she fought for what she must have. But at the back of her mind she had made an awful decision. She might not have persuaded him, but she had persuaded herself. If he said no, she was going to betray him. She was going to publish and be damned.

Tony's face was quizzical. He'd heard her pitch, and she was sure he was impressed by it. It had weakened his resolve, but it hadn't turned him around.

"I wonder if you're right," he said at last. "I don't know that the world's ready for mainline male pinups. I don't know that I'm ready for it, whether it's me or not, whether it's art or not. Look at the fuss about the Mapplethorpe photographs. People *can* disagree about art, you know."

Pat took a deep breath. The Mapplethorpe name could stop her heart.

"Listen, I knew Robert. He was my friend. I loved him. When he was alive he was just another photographer to the rest of the world. Now that he's dead, the art crowd wants to make him a hero. *He* used to make the distinction between his art and his pornography. *He* knew they were different. 'That's my pornography,' he'd say. I heard him say it a thousand times. But the portraits of you are beautiful because your body is beautiful and because you're pure and untouched by crassness and mediocrity. And that makes you difficult as *hell*, and impossible, and cruel sometimes . . . and it makes me love you."

There were tears in her eyes. For her dead friend. For her so-new lover. For the art that must see the light of day.

"You're more like me than I thought," said Tony, and he stood up, and he walked across the room to her.

Searchlights picked out the silvery wake, and the moon shone down on the ocean, bathing it in a phosphorescent glow. The hum of the engines made the deck vibrate gently, but otherwise there was little sensation of motion. That the 120-foot megayacht was powering through the swell at close to forty miles an hour was a well-kept secret. On the aft deck of *The Hedonist* the dinner table gleamed with Georgian silver, the starched linen was Four Seasons pristine, and the Waterford crystal appeared to have been cut yesterday rather than at the tail end of the eighteenth century. Scented gardenias flown in from Florida swam in individual bowls in front of each place setting, damask napkins sat sedately on Crown Derby side plates, and a low conversation-friendly orchid centerpiece crowned a table that would not have looked out of place at Buckingham Palace, but which here, on the Pacific Ocean off Catalina Island, looked like very hard work.

The group drinking Krug on the afterdeck had made a sartorial effort, with one notable exception. Tony had come as Stanley Kowalski. His one concession to the opulence of the setting was that he had washed. Nobody seemed to mind. After all, the nearest mainland was Malibu, where overdressing was a criminal activity.

"Ready for the caves of Santa Cruz?" said Dick Latham, the banter beneath his words. He was dressed in the Palm Beach uniform of navy double-breasted blazer, bright green pants, highly polished Cole-Haan loafers, no socks. He sipped pensively at the vintage champagne.

"Are you?"

"You bet. They're pretty deep, you know. We'll dive sixty feet, maybe more. We'll have to be careful. I've ordered a decompression chamber, but it won't be installed for a month or two."

"Tony, are you sure you should be doing that? You've never dived before." Pat knew Latham was using psychological warfare. It might not be working on Tony. It was beginning to faze her. She held on to his arm as tightly as the hour-glass Anne Klein jacket clung to her torso, above the full-length see-through Perry Ellis silk chiffon skirt.

"It's just swimming. I'll copy Dick. I'm sure he'll be doing all the safe things."

Latham laughed. The guy didn't stop. He was fearless. "That's right. Follow the old man and you can't go wrong. That's the ticket, isn't it, Havers? You're the expert."

Havers, white-tuxedoed, white-faced from the hours below deck making the empire work, laughed at his own expense. He was Gromyko to his boss's Khrushchev. The top Russian had once boasted that his henchman would drop his pants and sit on a block of ice if ordered to. But then Gromyko had been there to crack a rare smile at Khrushchev's funeral.

"It's always the clever thing to do," agreed Havers as he gulped at a neat Glenlivet.

"I'm always looking for clever things to do," said Melissa Wayne. It didn't look to be a lie. She had come as the Golden Girl. Her shoulders were bare, and her toffee-brown lickable skin slid into a matte gold sequined mini-sheath dress. The best legs in the business ended in Isaac Mizrahi gold rubber boots. Gold and rubber!

Peaches and cream as a harmony cliché was history. Her hair was piled up on top, waiting only for the word to come cascading down. Conversation faded away in her presence, as it was supposed to.

Dick Latham's eyes ate her as a first course, despite the iced silver bowls of packed beluga that waited on the table. A movement on the edge of the group broke the spell.

"Ah, Allison, there you are. We're complete. What have you got down there in your cabin? *War and Peace?* Ha! Ha! Now, I don't think you've met Melissa Wayne, a fellow Thespian. Allison was a student with Tony at the Juilliard, Melissa. She's a bona-fide member of the American aristocracy stooping to conquer, despite familial lack of enthusiasm. That's about it, isn't it, Allison?"

Allison Vanderbilt was pale as snow, but she made a beautiful ghost. If Pat was on-the-nail stylish, and Melissa Wayne at-the-edge trendy, then Allison Vanderbilt was cashless class. She wore a simple black cocktail dress that might have been Yves Saint Laurent or Givenchy, but was actually run together by a little woman in Seal Harbor, where her parents, who thought the Hamptons common, kept a summer vacation home. She was barefoot. She knew about teak decks. The Vanderbilt twelve-meter had been a contender for the Americas' Cup.

She looked hopelessly at Tony, helplessly at Pat. Her unseeing eyes played in panic over the golden condom that was Melissa's dress.

"Hi, Allison, you look just wonderful," said Pat.

"Doesn't she just?" said Latham.

"Terrific," agreed Havers, hoping he would draw her at dinner.

"Mm," said Melissa Wayne, a noise that might have meant very nearly anything.

The only person whose opinion Allison cared about said nothing at all. Part of her thanked God for that. One more "Are you all right, Allison?" and she'd have burst into tears.

"Some champagne for you, Allison?" asked Latham solicitously. The connoisseur in him loved her look, vulnerable, pure, transparently good. The snob in him liked it even more. He had come a long way since his father had stuck his first mall together. Yale had been okay, and now of course there was the Racquet, the Union, and the Knick. But he was short of a good prep school, and the cradle-to-grave buddies that the old money had. And the Brook had never let him in. That hurt. Lots of things did. The megabucks could make most things right, but they couldn't give you the belief in your own superiority that a Scottish nanny could. If you hadn't fought with the upper classes as kids on the dunes of New England, if you hadn't learned to dance with them, slept over, stood next to them as an angel in the nativity play, you would remain forever an outsider. You might be invited to their houses, befriended, permitted to marry their daughters even, but only your children would be considered their equal.

"What I'd really like is a glass of scotch," said Allison.

Latham heard the secret class language. It was the sort of thing he picked up from the British in the bar at White's. You didn't say "a scotch." You said "a *glass* of scotch." It was the aristocratic mistrust of conversational shorthand, the suspicion of champagne as a nouveau-riche drink, the total lack of concern about whether or not others might think whiskey an unladylike choice. If she'd felt like drinking piss, Allison Vanderbilt would have asked for a *glass* of it, and everyone in the room would have somehow felt themselves to be with the wrong drink. You had to admire it. The girl was in emotional pain. A peasant had let her down, but the safety net of her background had caught her. She might have fallen, but she still dangled in the air above the heads of the rest of them, superior, ultimately untouchable, and, at the end of the day, aware of it.

"A glass of Famous Grouse for Miss Vanderbilt," said Latham.

"What I want to know," said Melissa Wayne, irritated by Latham's solicitous attention to the powder-puff drama student from the East, "is why you are keeping a whole barrel load of men in the bowels of the ship. I saw a couple of them come up for air. Are they reserves or something? I think we should be told." She laughed flirtatiously, eying Tony, as she let him know what men were for.

"Ah, my guilty secret is out of the bag." Latham laughed mysteriously. "I was saving that for the dessert, or rather the pudding, as my English friends would say." His eyes flicked toward Allison in an attempt at forming class solidarity. She continued to stare forlornly at Tony.

"Well, I have to admit there *is* a deal cooking. Rather an exciting one as deals go. But let's wait. As this is still L.A. County and we're not allowed to eat anything fattening, it'll do as the bombe surprise."

He ushered them toward the table.

"Now, let's see, Melissa here, on my right. Pat, if you could bear to take my other side. Then, what about Tony next to Melissa, and then Allison, and last but not least Tommy, between Allison and Pat. Isn't this fun—the grownups get to eat with the children." He laughed as he spoke to show that he at least was a child. Somehow he allowed the impression to linger in the air that at least one of the children was as old and as serious as God.

Six stewards moved forward to draw back six chairs, and drop six napkins into six laps. The glistening caviar, served only with quarters of lemon, stared up at them. Crystal shot glasses were filled with freezing, viscous Absolut vodka. San Pellegrino burbled into the Waterford tumblers.

"I hope the caviar is all right," said Latham. "It came down with Tommy from Petrossian and then with Melissa in the helicopter. If it's not, we'll blame them." He chuckled as he small-talked his guests, scooping a spoonful of caviar onto a slice of butterless toast.

"I had a call the other day from someone named Emma Guinness," said Melissa Wayne. "She claimed to be the editor of one of your magazines, *New Celebrity*. I didn't know there was an *old Celebrity*."

"We're revamping it," said Dick Latham pleasantly. "Emma's from England. My new broom. I suggested she do a profile on you, Melissa. What did you tell her?"

He turned to the star. She smiled provocatively.

"Ah, a hands-on owner. I like that." Her expression insinuated that the Latham hands were already on her. "I said 'maybe.' I never trust Brit journalists. Anyone who's a success is an outcast in England. The papers make their lives hell. I have it in my contracts I won't tour there. Several of us do. I hope she's not going to turn *Celebrity* into a watered-down *Spy*."

"That's certainly not my plan," said Dick Latham, banging back the vodka in a single gulp. He didn't like anyone bad-mouthing *Celebrity*, especially a hot star like Melissa Wayne. These days when the name agencies—CAA, ICM, Morris—ran the town, gossip and hearsay could metamorphose instantly into the gospel truth. A magazine that depended for its lifeblood on star access could be blackballed out of existence in seconds, and then the only people who would appear between its covers would be desperate unisex bimbos from the daytime soaps. "But don't ask me about it, talk to Pat Parker. She's on the masthead. She's under exclusive contract. Hers and Emma's hearts beat as one."

He gestured extravagantly to Pat, as if introducing a prizefighter. He had set up round two.

Melissa turned slowly toward her former adversary. Pat stared back at her across the table, an anticipatory smile playing around her lips. She didn't intend to start anything, but if something was started, then she was going to finish it—with or without the help of Tony Valentino.

"So, Patricia," said Melissa. "*Tell* us about *New Celebrity.*"

She sat back in her chair like a studio boss waiting for a minion to pitch a script. The impression was left that whatever was now delivered would be found wanting. Her right hand twiddled a lock of hair, her left drummed impatiently on the immaculate tablecloth. Her sultry eyes fastened onto Tony Valentino across the table. "Watch me," they said. "Who do you want? The woman or the mouse?"

"Emma would be able to tell you better than I can—but I know what she's aiming for. It's going to be a fearless magazine—not bitchy, not gossipy, but artistically dangerous, cutting edge, something entirely new. It's going to be very visual, and the 'people' articles are going to dig deep into motivation, into weaknesses and strengths. You know, like, What made you want to be a movie star? What does it mean to you to be famous? How do you cope with it? What terrifies you? What turns you on? What turns you off?"

Melissa Wayne laughed. She threw her head back to do so.

"Well," she drawled, "I'd have no problem at all answering the last two questions." Her meaning was unmistakable. To emphasize it, her eyes flicked to Tony and her tongue slipped out to moisten her upper lip. Then they swiveled back to Pat, and the wet lip curled.

Pat took a deep breath. Okay, she'd tried. Now she slipped off the gloves.

Dick Latham stepped metaphorically between them. A catfight would be fun, but he didn't want Melissa Wayne painting herself into a corner in which she would be honor-bound to refuse to appear in the magazine. Social blood sports and business were better not mixed.

"On a more specific level, have you given any thought to your first photo spread, Pat? I'm just longing to see it," he said.

Pat's mind stopped in its tracks. The confrontation had been avoided. A far more significant one was brewing. This mattered. Was the dinner table the place for it? Who knew? When at last she spoke, she herself was quite surprised by what she said.

"I want to do a photo essay on Tony. The prints are brilliant, but I'm having problems persuading him to let me use them."

She couldn't look at him as she played her dirty trick. She was using the others against him. It was unfair, but it might just work. Her heart hammered in her chest. Their relationship was on the line.

Melissa Wayne came right in on cue.

"My God, how wonderful," she said. "I was beginning to wonder about *New Celebrity* from what you said. Now I'm converted." She patted the Latham arm as she stared at the furious face of Tony Valentino. "Write me down for a subscription. Does my piece get to rub shoulders with his?"

Latham smiled. "Sounds great. Tony as the spirit-of-a-generation. Focused, drug-free youth, and something the women can relate to. I like it. Yes, I like it very much."

Despite himself, he did. Tony was unique. The fact that Latham would have liked him atomized was beside the point. He was visual dynamite, and the chemistry that bubbled between him and Pat would have lit up the photo session. He looked at his rival, and there was curiosity on his face that mirrored the ambivalence in his heart. Tony would be good for *New Celebrity*, and therefore good for Dick Latham. It was a new angle on the young actor, and it jelled with the grudging respect Dick already felt for him. The guy was powered by ambition, but had never crawled. On the contrary, he had gloried in being confrontational. In the ordinary way Latham would have put that down to the unthinking bravado of youth. But with Tony, it seemed to spring not from a denial of insecurity, but from an extraordinary self-confidence. You didn't have to like it, but you had to admire it.

"Why the objections, Tony?" asked Havers.

Tony said nothing, and for a second it looked as if he would ignore the intense interest that now sparked around him.

"Maybe Tony felt that the photographs were personal," said Allison Vanderbilt suddenly.

Her face was white, her knuckles whiter. The mist in her eyes was tears. Her voice was heavy with accusation. She was accusing Pat of betrayal of trust, of disloyalty, the ultimate crime in the code of the upper classes. And as a subsidiary felony, a misdemeanor really, she was accusing Pat of stealing the man that Allison loved.

"They were," said Tony. His eyes were daggers in Pat's as she dared at last to look at him.

"Oh, nonsense, you mustn't be so bourgeois," laughed Melissa, flicking her head at Allison, but talking to Tony. "That kind of thinking is for the silver-spoon brigade with nothing to protect but their privacy. Those of us with talent have an obligation to display it, be it beauty, brains, or both." She pushed out her pointed breasts at the table and giggled to show that she came in the last category.

Pat fought back the temptation to come to the rescue of the distraught Allison. But Melissa, for all the worst reasons, had ended up on Pat's side. And she was bringing her powerful cannon to bear on Tony.

"Would you take your clothes off for *Playboy?*" asked Tony, zeroing in on Melissa. His question tried to be hostile, but ended semiserious. He admired Wayne, and he fancied her. She was what a woman should be—up-front, determined, and with something to aim at.

"I did," said Melissa simply. "It was how I got my first part." The humor had gone from her voice. She had moved on. "Did you take off your clothes for Pat's pictures?"

There was silence at the table. It was broken only by Allison Vanderbilt's sharp intake of breath. Pat looked up at the starry sky. Its peace was a dramatic contrast to the dinner for which it was the ceiling. Havers coughed. Dick Latham sat forward, alert, waiting for the reply. On Melissa's face was a half smile of anticipation. Tony Valentino had become a thundercloud full of hidden lightning.

"Yes, I did," he said at last.

"Good for you," whispered Melissa Wayne. Her breath was coming faster. "I can't wait to see them," she added.

"That was brave," muttered Havers, horrified by the male lapse of taste.

Latham digested it. Artistic danger. Cutting edge. Emma had gone on and on about that. Pat had just mentioned it. Well, apparently they all meant what they said. He thought fast, and as he did so the printouts cascaded from the computer of his brain. And they all ended up in the tray marked "brilliant."

"I think it sounds very, very interesting," he said. There was no trace of sarcasm in his voice.

"You do?" said Pat. If he felt like that *before* he saw the photographs, he would be over the moon afterward.

She had feared his ridicule, first because of the publishing risk involved, second because he so obviously disliked Tony. Clearly she had underestimated him. He wasn't an ordinary man with ordinary prejudices like Havers. He was an original. He thought for himself. He didn't let his feelings get in the way of his judgment. It was as if she were seeing him for the first time. Dick Latham had made his billions the newfangled way. He had earned them.

"I would consider it a very great privilege to be allowed to see them," said Latham. He looked straight at Tony. Man to man. Equal to equal. Professional to professional.

Tony looked back at him. It was a powerful pitch, especially as it came from a man who had no reason at all to like him, and every possible reason to rejoice in his humiliation. Latham had been handed the perfect ammunition, and he had refused to use it. Instead the billionaire was asking for a personal favor. Already he had paid Tony a difficult male compliment by predicting that the world would enjoy the sight of his body. It was an impressive and unexpected turnabout, and it had taken courage. Tony liked that. You had to dare to change. You had to seize the moment. You had to lose the past, and look only to the future. Inside, a weird feeling was on the verge of being born. Could he end up *liking* Dick Latham? Anything was possible. Because he was well on the way to hating Pat Parker for the unforgivable thing she had done.

"I think Pat's decided to publish them, anyway," he said at last, letting the bitterness hang out. He turned toward her, and his words were cold as ice when he spoke. "I didn't know who you were," he added.

Pat shook his eyes from hers. She had won. She had lost. She had sold him for her art. The photographs would be used now. Latham would ram them past Emma Guinness, if she objected, and it was far from certain that she would. The deed had been done, and she had lost her lover. She wished he would understand. She had been ruthless, as he was ruthless. There, across the table, weeping gently, was Allison Vanderbilt, whom he had used. But he wouldn't see that. He wouldn't take it into consideration. With blinkered vision, he would hold this against her, despite the fact that in the same situation he would have done precisely the same thing. The crazy part was he would benefit from this. Her pictures would launch his career as they sank the relationship they shared. It was so mad, so bad, yet so deeply necessary. Never before in her entire life had getting her own way felt so pointless.

She looked up at the sea of blurred faces. The caviar had gone, but the halibut bonne femme and the Puligny Montrachet had landed. Dinner still had to be endured. So did the rest of her life. She straightened herself up.

"Perhaps this is the time for my little announcement," said Dick Latham into the curious mood that had descended over the table.

They tried to look interested, but they didn't succeed. Allison was way past surprises. She looked like she was about to faint. Havers was clearly in on the secret, whatever it was. Tony was lost in the proud fastness of his private world. Pat suffered in hers. Only Melissa Wayne retained the energy to register excitement.

Latham wasn't fazed by the poor response. The expression on his face said he had the cards. When he played them everyone would sit up and take notice.

"You may remember that recently I bought Cosmos Pictures. When I took advantage of a real-estate play and closed down production, people concluded that my interest in the studio was over. That is not the case. Far from it." He paused to allow the message to sink in. Tony drifted up toward the surface from the depths in which he'd been swimming. Melissa cocked her head to one side. Pat slipped her mind into forward gear.

"In fact it is my plan to rebuild Cosmos—to create a brand-new studio from scratch in the style of the old Hollywood. I intend to turn it into the best and most influential studio in the world. I'm counting on you to star in some of my pictures, Melissa, and who knows . . . maybe Pat will one day direct, and perhaps Allison and Tony . . . will act in a Cosmos movie . . ."

He opened his arms to all of them, as he signaled the wide-open possibilities of the future and his eagle eyes inventoried the faces at his dinner table. He had them all now. They were hooked. He could reel them in. He could throw them back. He could fillet them and cook them and eat them up.

Melissa let out a whoop of excitement. More work. More glory. More cash and the cachet that could be turned into sex. All the studios courted her, but Cosmos was special. Despite its string of flops, it was old Hollywood aristocracy, and she had never worked for it before. Allison heard the siren movie call across the rocks and ruins of her life. The word *director* spun in Pat's mind, as moving images replaced the stills. But the most dramatic effect of the Latham words was on the face of Tony Valentino.

He seemed deeply shocked by the news, and yet it was impossible to tell whether he thought it good or bad. His expression defined ambivalence. In his eyes shone the light of excitement. At the same time his mouth curled down in an expression that could only be disgust. His other features alternated uncertainly between the two extremes of emotion. Fascinated, Pat watched him across the table, acutely aware of his dilemma. Latham, a man he despised, had offered obliquely to make Tony's dream come true. Would he accept? Would he put career before principle, as she had just done? Yes, he would. Pat knew that. And in his brilliant future there would be no place for her. The anger flooded through her. Damn! It was so unfair, so hypocritical. He was just like her. He would betray his own feelings to get what he wanted just as she had allowed her own ambition to turn her into a traitor. Didn't two wrongs cancel each other out, even if they didn't make a right?

Then, suddenly, another thought occurred to her, cutting into her mind like a thunderbolt from the blue. "Where are you going to build the new studio?" she said.

"Oh, somewhere in the desert," said Dick Latham with an airy wave of his hand.

"Isn't Pat coming?" said Dick Latham, pretending a surprise he didn't feel.

"No idea," muttered Tony, as if he hardly knew who Latham was talking about. He picked his way through the piles of diving apparatus that were laid out on the bottom deck of *The Hedonist*. "Do we really need wetsuits?" he asked.

Latham smiled. It was beginning. Tony was trying to score an early point. The Pacific water off Santa Cruz Island was around seventy. It was cold, but not *that* cold. If Tony could shame Latham into leaving the rubber suit behind, the older man would have an uncomfortable morning. Tony's younger and more efficient body-temperature-regulating system would give him an advantage.

The diving instructor, who was a full-time member of the yacht's crew, answered for his boss. "The surge tides can throw you against the walls of the caves. You can rip yourself to shreds in there if you're not careful. You need wetsuits, boots, heavy gloves, especially if you want to pick up a lobster."

"Oh," said Tony with a smile. "I see we'll have to be *very* careful."

Latham and the diver exchanged glances. "You *have* done this before, haven't you, sir?" asked the diver warily.

"In my sleep," said Tony, ambiguously.

The summer fog lay like a blanket across the sea, wrapping Santa Cruz in a cotton wool mist. It was warming already, though, and the blurred ball of the sun was fighting to peep through the haze. The water was calm, the swell rolling in gently, but the diver seemed nervous. His anxious eyes scanned the water.

"Going to be okay, Joe?" asked Latham.

"You know how it is, sir, it's unpredictable, and the tide's really too high. Are you sure you don't want to try this later?"

He was aware of Tony's eyes on him.

"Can't. We've got to get back to Santa Barbara this afternoon. I'm in New York first thing in the morning."

"Well, I'll be right behind you," said Joe.

"To hold your hand," laughed Tony.

The muscles rippled on the forearms of the diver. He turned toward Tony, his eyes flashing.

"No need for you to come, Joe," drawled Latham. "Our young friend likes to live dangerously. I think we should accommodate him." He laughed. The caves were not to be trifled with. It was crazy to explore them without an experienced diver and speleologist.

But that was what a part of life should be about, wasn't it? There should be a time for excitement, and pitting your wits against the elements, and for doing things that weren't strictly sensible. It was a lesson the old could learn from the young.

They climbed into their wetsuits as Joe checked the bottles and the regulators. The small diving boat, lowered already into the water, bobbed off the stern.

"I'll be anchored off the Lobster Caves, if you're doing them first, then I'll move across to the Bat Cave when I see you swim over. Look after yourself."

"If the asshole gets himself into trouble, leave him behind" was the unspoken message. Professionals loathed glory boys. They were always having to clean up their messes.

Dick Latham nodded. It was exactly what he intended. A half-drowned Tony Valentino being sucked from the water by the unforgiving Joe would make an excellent end to the morning.

"Okay, Tony, let's do it." They climbed into the boat and Joe manhandled the heavy bottles into the stern across the swimming platform of *The Hedonist*. He started the outboard, and soon the dive boat was cutting across the swell toward the Cavern Point shore of the island.

"Let's do the Bat Cave first," said Tony.

"Fine, in at the deep end," agreed Latham.

They hauled on the bottles as the boat anchored, adjusted their masks and mouthpieces, and took up their positions on the edge of the boat. Then, together, they toppled over backward into the water and the bubbles and the dark ocean swallowed them. The cold took away their breath as they cartwheeled in the water, but soon they were oriented and swimming strongly toward the jagged opening in the cliffs. Dick Latham felt for the underwater light at his belt, and he tensed his shoulders, adjusting the air bottle on his back. Bat Cave was the second largest on the island, and, he remembered, a safe one, but you could never tell. Here there would be no minions to smooth his way. His billions would be as relevant as bird droppings.

The entrance loomed up, black against the brown cliff, and his flippers caught briefly against sharp rocks that guarded the cave's entrance. His head broke the surface of the water, and he turned around to see Tony's beside him. He reached down for the light and shone it above his head into the cave. The interior seemed at first to consist of a single chamber, at the back of which was a dry platform of pebbles and piles of rotting wood. He half swam, half walked into the cave, ducking down low in the water to keep his air bottle beneath the surface so that the ocean's buoyancy would take its weight. He aimed his light at the ceiling, and there, hanging upside down in the darkness, were the reason for the cave's name. A bat, caught in the spotlight, uncurled its wings and in seconds the air of the cave was full of them, darting and jinking in the gloom above the heads of the explorers. Tony, too, reached for his flashlamp, and for a minute or two they tried to catch the furious bats in their beams like fighter planes in the fingers of wartime searchlights. Tony laughed and Latham joined in, two boys locked in an adventure, boys who had been rivals, even enemies, minutes before. Away to their right, a narrow passageway led off from the main atrium of the cave. The water lapped near its ceiling, leaving little headroom above its surface.

Dick Latham pulled out his mouthpiece.

"Let's try that." He pointed at the internal exit to the cave. "I'll go first." He ducked down below the surface, holding the light in front of him in the blackness, and began to swim toward the opening. As he did so, he felt an underwater current suck at him, pushing him off course. His shoulder touched the rocky wall of the cave. His head brushed against it. Damn! You couldn't predict the swell. They should have been wearing helmets with mounted lights. Thank God for the heavy gloves. He turned around. Tony, too, had been caught by the unexpected motion of the sea. His thumbs-up gesture said it was no big deal. For a second he paused in the opening, but he felt Tony's shoulders on his fins. It would have been wise to wait. Swells came in sets. The smart diver would hang around to see what would unfold before pushing on. But, caught up in the atmosphere of male competition, Latham didn't wait. He took a deep breath of air, and he pushed into the narrow passageway between the rocks, Tony following close behind. There was no space to turn around. The only way was forward.

The light pointed ahead, reflected from the sharp, ragged walls, disappeared into the darkness of the tunnel. Dick floated toward the surface, but now the roof of the channel merged with the surface of the water. There was nothing to breathe but the bottled air on their backs. For long minutes they swam on, and Latham tried to calculate in which direction they were heading. It was no good. The tunnel twisted and turned. It was impossible to know if they were running parallel to the sea, heading back toward it, or burrowing deeper into the ancient rock of the island. Dick Latham felt the first fingers of alarm, in the pit of his stomach, at the nape of his neck. He wasn't frightened yet. It was a pleasant feeling, with the advantage of strangeness. His body was tingling, on maximum alert, and his mind was cool, running faster than it did in a tough negotiation with a worthy opponent. To his right the light picked out another tunnel, heading off at right angles to the main channel. His gut told him it might cut through to the ocean. Or it could be a cul-de-sac. If they made the turn they would have to be careful. A few more and they could get lost. They had used maybe fifteen minutes of air. There were fifteen left. He angled himself into the opening of the tributary, which was when it happened.

The slapping water began to boil around him, and a powerful jet erupted from the tunnel. It picked him up like a leaf in a hurricane and hurled him bodily at the wall. It was as if he had taken a direct hit from a hidden fire hose in a riot at night. The pain exploded in his shoulder where he banged against the rock. His left flipper was torn from his foot. His mask was sucked from his face, the mouthpiece of his air line was dragged from between his teeth. He tried to right himself with his hands and to protect himself with his feet, but the rocks sandpapered against him. A glove disappeared into the boiling caldron of water, and his hand was crushed against the sharp surface of the wall, ripping the skin from his fingers and exposing the bone of his knuckles. A light exploded in the middle of his mind as the nightmare began, and around his brain a ghostly voice was repeating what he knew. "You're in trouble, Dick Latham. You're in deep trouble, and it's your own fault."

He righted himself in the lull as the current subsided, but he knew as he did so that it was the end of nothing but the beginning.

He reached over his shoulder to grab at his floating mouthpiece, and he jammed it back into his mouth. He steaded himself along the wall, noticing the cloud of blood that spiraled from his injured hand, and he tried to hang on for dear life against the countercurrent that he knew was coming. He moved his arm frantically to signal Tony to keep back from the entrance to the side channel, and then he tried to find a purchase point on the jagged rock face.

The water sucked at him. It plucked at his legs, drawing him away from the rock face. Stronger and stronger it pulled at him, peeling his bleeding fingers from the wall to which he clung. He looked over his shoulder into the black hole that wanted him, and suddenly he knew with the certainty of the damned that he would die. There would be no escape from the vacuum trap. Once inside the churning hellhole, he wouldn't have the strength to swim against the swirling currents. If he wasn't battered unconscious against the sharp rocks, he would be held captive beneath the water, watching in panic as the gauge of his breathing tank flicked toward empty. Out there on the deceptively smooth surface of the ocean, Joe would be waiting, oblivious to his danger. Even if Tony was able to turn around in the narrow passageway and get back to the dive boat, there would be no time for the rescue. Dick Latham held on, but as he did so he could already feel his fingers, and his life, slipping away.

His past didn't flash before him as it was supposed to. Instead, the black bile of anger surged up within him. Damn it to hell! He wasn't ready yet. There were too many people out there to be glad about this. There were enemies to be destroyed, women to be devoured, magic deals to be done. He would never get to see *New Celebrity*, never cut the ribbon on the Cosmos studio, never hear the noises that Pat Parker made in the final surrender. So he threshed with his feet, and he tore with his hands, and he filled his lungs with air for the superhuman effort to avoid his fate. Shit! Tony Valentino would watch him die. There was nothing else he could or would do, and Dick Latham didn't blame him. So much for the generation game. He hadn't expected it to end like this. Game, set, and match to love with no replays on the first encounter and in record time.

The surge tide scraped him off the wall. It bundled him into a ball of chaos and swallowed him up. He corkscrewed into the darkness, and his head crashed against a rock, sending bright stars fireworking into the blackness of his mind. There was a terrific blow behind his shoulder, and suddenly there was no air in his mouthpiece. In panic, he realized what had happened. The collision with the rock face had knocked the entire first stage from his air bottle. The only breath he had left was already in his lungs, and now his mouth was full of salt water. His heart drummed in his chest, as he fought to stay calm in the short seconds before death. He had one chance. If he could wait for the ebbing current to flow once again, it might catapult him through the narrow opening he had just entered. Once outside, he could share Tony's air. He peered through the gloom as he tried to get his bearings. He grabbed for the light, but it was no longer on his belt, swept away in the maelstrom that had engulfed him. In desperation he braced himself to plunge into the unknown, and he pushed down hard with his heels to gain forward momentum. The sharp pain shot up from his ankle, crowding into his breathless brain. He was stuck. His foot was caught in a crevice. His last chance was gone. Dick Latham gave up. It was supposed to be a pleasant way to go. You drifted away as if falling asleep. You took a deep breath and the water bubbled in. You floated above your body in the famous death experience, glad to be shot of it, free at last from the flesh-and-bone prison that foolish mortals were so attached to.

The hand gripped him. A face loomed up against his. A mouthpiece was thrust against his lips. Dick Latham bit at it, and life flowed into his lungs, as relief and oxygen coursed through his blood. It was Tony. He'd braved the whirlpool to join Latham in the watery grave. In an act of superhuman courage, generosity, and foolishness, he had sacrificed his own future so that a man he hated could have a few more minutes of his. The thoughts kaleidoscoped in Latham's mind as warmth and gratitude battled with fear and hopelessness. But Tony Valentino had other plans. His fingers were buried in the flesh of Latham's upper arm, and it wasn't the grip of panic or desperation. It was the grip of determination. His other hand hovered in front of Latham's face. His finger jutted out, pointing back over his shoulder in the direction of the bottleneck entrance. His finger jabbed emphatically. They were going to attempt the impossible. They were going to try to swim against the force of the current.

The urgency of Tony's fingers and the emphasis of his gesture stiffened Latham's backbone. The young man had always looked strong, but Latham had imagined his muscles to be designer ones, all pumped up for show in some narcissistic Manhattan gym. Now they would be put to the test. Tony jerked Latham's hand down toward his belt, and he crunched up his body, placing both feet on either side of Latham's midriff to get maximum thrust from the wall. Latham hooked his other hand into the belt and, steadied by the younger man, he maneuvered his trapped foot free of the crevice that held it. Tony reached for the mouthpiece, took a lungful of air, and passed it back to Latham. His hand jerked up. His hand jerked down. His legs pistoned straight. He shot like a bullet into the foaming water, and Latham was dragged in his wake, kicking furiously to provide additional forward momentum. They arrowed toward the exit, into the teeth of the countercurrent. Every millimeter they achieved, their speed slowed. Then, three feet from their target, they stopped. Tony's arms churned the water. Latham's legs threshed up and down. It was no good. They weren't moving. Once again the wave of fatalism passed through Latham. So near. So far. Thirty-six inches in some godforsaken cave was the difference between a glorious future and oblivion.

Latham realized that Tony had a decision to make. Without Latham in tow, Valentino would have a chance. Carrying the excess baggage, he was doomed. Latham should let go of the belt. It was the right thing to do. Already Tony had done too much for him. Whatever. He didn't let go. In fact his knuckles tightened on the belt that was his lifeline, and in extremis Dick Latham smiled grimly as he realized what a very unpleasant man he was.

Tony turned to look at him. He could see the Valentino eyes through the foaming gloom. They bored into him with all the scorn of the winner for the loser. I've won, they said. I was right. You were weak, and I am strong. If we die now it will change nothing. You didn't even have the decency to let go. It was the most effective message. Somewhere in the depths of Dick Latham's soul the fountain of adrenaline began to play. Damn it! Damn him! The power coursed into his legs. Suddenly they were light as feathers, and they thrashed the water with renewed vigor. Together they inched forward and Tony, encouraged, redoubled his efforts. His arms hammered at the sea. His legs crashed up and down beneath Latham's body. Then, quite suddenly, like Jonah from the whale's mouth, they were vomited through the opening. They tumbled forward, cascading over each other, and crashed into the wall outside.

Their velocity, and the shock of the impact, threw them sideways out of the suction of the deadily side cave. In the calm, they sank to the sandy bottom, and the joy rushed through them. They hugged each other, holding on tight in mutual congratulation, and the tears of gratitude sprang from Latham's eyes. They shared the mouthpiece, and it was the pipe of peace between them. They were friends now. Whatever happened, they were joined together by a bond more powerful than any other. Latham owed Tony his life. Tony had risked his for the billionaire in his arms. Their closeness was more than physical. Later there would be words, but now they were not necessary. Through the mist on the inside of their masks, their eyes were talking.

EIGHT

Emma Guinness sat behind the desk in the thronelike chair and peered around the meeting she was taking.

"I'm into class," she said. "It's going to be the new American thing. I want writers from Harvard and Yale, but they've got to look good enough for a Calvin Klein ad. Brains without beauty isn't going to hack it in the 1990s."

She leered pugnaciously around the room. Was there any dissent? Who dared raise the flag of rebellion at her court? Who wanted the order of her boot? Not anyone. Their silence was golden.

"And I want lots of subtle sex. The fact that you and I don't like it means nothing. Everybody's terrified to screw, and yet the urge hasn't gone yet. One day it will, and we can ride a nice Puritan wave, but the early nineties will be glossies with naughty bits. So I want art dirt, okay? You know, whoever's the new Newton. *Playboy* with sex. Look, don't touch."

She tapped on the table as an accompaniment to her stream of consciousness, and all the time she wondered how best to wound, to sow the seeds of misery among the best and brightest she had hired.

"Now I don't want anything too camp, Howard," she said sharply to the art director she had stolen from *Vogues Hommes*. "Camp's okay for the odd article as long as it's haute camp, but not for the visuals. Eyes-wise, *New Celebrity*'s strictly straight. Fashion?" She paused. As always, the curtain was descending.

"Well, fashion's Michael, isn't it? Just keep it young and energetic and not too *dull* . . . but not too daring either . . . I mean, like, use . . . Oh, God, use whomever you like, just don't screw up, okay? . . ."

Michael smirked. It was the Guinness blind spot. In the whole magazine he would be the only person with carte blanche. He tried not to look at her clothes, but his eyes kept scurrying back to the red-button booties that kept peeping from beneath her desk. What was so fascinating about the disgusting? It took real originality to be a genuine fashion victim.

"Now, novelizations. We need a few of those upper-class privileged kids wittering on about how dreadful it is to have cash, nice parents, and a rich education that allows them to get paid for tapping out drivel on typewriters. You know, lots of drugs, sordid bits about bodily functions, and the hopelessness of life when you've got it all. That's *definitely* nineties stuff. 'Downhill All the Way' type rubbish, 'Straight Run to the Grave,' 'Dead in the Night'—if you can't find an author, hire an Ivy League Social Register model and I'll rattle off his autobiographical first novel during my lunch break."

"What about Maria Gonzales?" tried Jacosta, the sharp features guy.

"Okay. I don't mind her. At least she's young, and young's coming back. She doesn't even seem to share the journalistic horror of adjectives. She doesn't copy that lush Hemingway, even if the rest of America is hanging on to him as if he invented writing. I can't quite work out whether the fear of descriptive passages is to do with a short attention span or dislike of reading period. I know readers are supposed to use their imagination to fill in the blank spaces themselves, but I've always considered books to be a spectator sport. Anyway, give Gonzales a go. Is she still screwing that girl at Ford's?"

Jacosta thought she was. Howard from Paris hadn't been in the Big Apple long enough to know. Michael was able to provide a definite yes.

"Good for her. Go up to five for a first serialization. She's a 'serious' writer, so she shouldn't cost more than that. If she's greedy, come back to me and I'll call her agent. It's Mort, isn't it? He loves me. Don't you all?" She laughed to show that she knew they loathed her, and that she didn't mind. It was the friction she needed. It brought out the best in her, and her best was brilliant.

The telephone rang. She frowned. "I said no calls," she muttered, sweeping it up and scowling out over Central Park.

"Oh, Dick, well . . . *hello!* I thought you were in Malibu. How nice . . ."

She beamed around the room. They all knew who Dick was. Now they'd get to see how close she was to the boss.

"Why that's *wonderful!* So *soon*. I never thought Pat would come across this early. Great! Yes, the first edition. Absolutely. What's the subject? I didn't know there was one in Malibu." She laughed, and her whole face shone with an other-worldly vivacity. A Pat Parker spread for the relaunch. Dick Latham sweet-talking her on the telephone in front of a room full of minions. It was turning into a delicious day.

"Oh . . . oh . . . a boy, you mean they're all of a boy . . . the same one . . . I see." The bounce had gone from her voice. A boy, a *Malibu* boy, didn't sound too kosher. But then, Pat Parker had shot the pix, and photos didn't translate well into words. "Anyway, *you* like them, that's the important thing. No, you've got an incredible eye. I mean it. I'm not bullshitting you . . . okay . . . in five minutes, terrific. I'll get right back to you."

She eased the receiver back onto the phone as if she were tickling Latham's back with it. She peered around the room. It was time for an update, an interruption to normal programming. A big story had broken.

"We have a Pat Parker photo spread for the first edition. Dick's got the prints upstairs. He's sending them down. He's wild about them."

"Of a boy from Malibu?" said Michael, whose fashion portfolio came with built-in bravery. He let the sarcasm out.

"Yeah," said Emma defensively. "I don't think Mr. Latham is likely to be wrong," she added icily. The "Dick" had become "Mr." for the hired help.

"Now, where were we? Oh yes, trendy writers. Well, the trouble is the lead time. They'll be out before we get them in, but one has to try. Just remember nasty is nice, okay? Babies are history, families are dull, singles are back. The world hasn't caught on yet, but *we* know, don't we, campers? Booze is dying, health is hot, and we don't take orders from Euro-trash anymore . . . except . . ." and she laughed a brittle, threatening laugh, "from me."

"I don't know that you're totally right about families," tried Jacosta. "I mean *parenting* is a pretty seminal issue, especially fatherhood." He shifted in his chair, waiting for the lash of the

Guinness tongue. Sometimes he experienced a modicum of pleasure from pain. He must talk to his shrink about it. Trying to keep the old buzzard interested was a problem these days.

"Seminal? *Sem*inal? Balls! Semen is more seminal than 'parenting.' Forget all that Spock schlock. Now semen skin rejuvenators, *that's* an issue. Didn't Jackie Bisset have one in that Beverly Hills class-struggle flick? Whatever. Somebody write me a memo on semen, okay? Well done, Kit. There you are, all those long words paid off at last."

The knock on the door interrupted her. The secretary who entered the room was beautiful and haughty as befitted God's handmaiden. She didn't wait to be invited in. She held a manila envelope.

"Mr. Latham asked me to deliver this," she said. She walked across the room like a model on a catwalk and laid the envelope in front of Emma Guinness.

"Thank you," said Emma with the coldness she reserved for good-looking women of a lower status than herself.

She reached for the envelope and eased open the pins that held the flap.

She pulled out the handful of prints and leaned forward eagerly to look at them. The face stared back at her. The face, the body, and Jesus Christ, the dick. It was one of the most beautiful photographs she had ever seen. The dangerous eyes held her. The shades of black and white sang in the sweetest harmony. It was magic. It was brilliance. It was hotter than the burning fires of Hades. She swallowed hard, because it was other things, too. It was searing memories. It was chaotic discord. It was the plucking fingers of dread trampling up and down her suddenly sweating spine. The print swam before her eyes. A red mist had descended. Her heart was hammering beneath her heaving breasts. Never, ever again had she expected to confront this face, this body. She had wiped it from the forefront of her mind, and it lingered only in the dark place where all the humiliations lived—in the basement of the id, from where the occasional muted scream taunted her. Tony Valentino! The name exploded in her brain as the sweat leaped to her upper lip. The lowlife who had crossed her was to be the photo spread in the very first issue of her magazine.

"Are they a disaster?" asked Michael hopefully. He couldn't hold back his enthusiasm for the promising situation. Emma Guinness was white as the ghost she had clearly seen. The print trembled in her hands. Her unseeing eyes wandered over it in panic.

Emma didn't answer. The points that pricked at the skin of her butt were the horns of a dilemma. As she handed the photos across to the fashion editor, she was already confronting it. On the one hand, the photos were wonderful. They were pure art—heart art, not dirt art, and they would be an asset to the magazine. Alone, they would guarantee the success of the relaunch. *New Celebrity* and Emma Guinness's career would be off and running. But at the same time Emma was determined not to use them. This boy had humiliated her. He had spurned her advances. He had insulted her in public. No way did she intend to help him. The photo spread would appear over her dead body, despite the fact that Latham, whose word was law, loved them, and that Pat Parker had the contractual right to demand that they be used. And there was another angle. It was crystal clear from the photographs that Tony and Pat were lovers. Their chemistry sizzled from the surface of the prints. They were a celebration of sensuality, the ultimate gift to the voyeur who would not stoop publicly to snoop. So jealousy was added to revenge, and both battled self-interest, as Emma wondered just what the hell she would do.

"Wow," said Michael. "These are hot." They all crowded around him, looking over his shoulder as he flicked through the prints. The chorus of acclaim was as predictable as wasps at a picnic. The people assembled in that room had only two things in common. They had all been picked by Emma Guinness, and they all knew how to pick winners. It was back to square one. The hirelings she had personally assembled were against her, and so was the ultimate arbiter upstairs.

"Too strong . . . male nudity . . . too sophisticated," she tried.

"Nooooooh," they all chorused.

"Not the first issue . . . sets an unfortunate precedent . . . upset the straight men . . ." Her wild eyes scanned the room for support.

Those who normally would not have dared to disagree with her, did now. United they stood. Divided on these photographs they had no desire to be. Their voices rose in a Tower of Babel refutation.

Emma Guiness shuddered. She breathed in deeply. There was no time like the present. She picked up the phone and punched three numbers.

"Emma Guinness for Mr. Latham," she said.

*   *   *

She went in at a trot, as if physical momentum alone would give her the psychological edge. He sat back at his desk and smiled his welcome. He looked as if he had been born again. The life positively vibrated from him, despite the bandaged hand, and a colorful bruise high up on his brow.

"Emma, sit down," he said, standing up and waving her into a chair. "Aren't they great? That was what we needed, wasn't it? It's a wrap now. I couldn't be more pleased."

"That's what I wanted to talk to you about, Dick. I know they're good photographs, very good actually, but I don't think this is the right image. I mean the boy looks a bit Latin, I mean a bit cheap, I mean he looks a bit too . . . oh, Malibu. You know, sort of obvious, don't you think? I'm sure Pat can do better. It is the *first* issue, and he's not exactly a celebrity, is he, whoever he is."

She realized that her syntax had fallen apart. She realized that he realized it. Words were her transport through life. Usually she kept them in tiptop working order. Now, at the moment she needed highly greased grammar, her motor mouth had seized.

"What on earth are you talking about?" Dick Latham laughed, eying her tits. "You sound as if you're on Dexedrine."

"The pictures," blurted Emma. "I don't think they're right for the magazine."

"He's called Tony Valentino," said Dick Latham, cutting through to the bottom line. He was still smiling, but he was watching her like a cat—her face now, not her chest.

Emma paused. He couldn't know, could he? But why the fuck were these pictures coming through Latham? Why hadn't Pat Parker submitted them to her? That would have been the right way to do things.

"Well, whatever he's called, I don't think he's *New Celebrity* material, and I don't think his bits and pieces are either." Her eyes slipped away from his as she spoke.

"There's a theory that you met him once," said Latham. His voice was amused.

"Tony Valentino? I don't think so. He looks sort of male bimboesque. I guess I could have seen his head shot if he was a model. Was he ever in England?"

Emma shifted in the chair. She knew her face was giving her away. Her cheeks were on fire. She had to brazen it out, but he knew. He knew. Would he let her off the hook?

No, he wouldn't.

"He was an actor, at the Juilliard. Word is you visited his end-of-term play, *A Streetcar Named Desire*. He played Stanley. Odd that you don't remember his face. It's rather a memorable one, don't you think?"

"I vaguely remember," muttered Emma, gazing out of the window in desperation. "I hadn't put the two together."

"The only reason I mention it is that Pat was worried because apparently there was a falling-out between you and Tony over something or other. She thought you might hold it against him vis-à-vis these pictures. Of course, I told her that you were far too professional for that. Business is business in this company, I said, and nobody believes that more than Emma Guinness. She'd shoot her grandmother for circulation, sell her son for the right advertising, said I." He paused, and he leaned forward across the desk. The smile had gone. His expression was cruel. "I wasn't wrong, was I?" he added.

Emma Guiness swallowed. There was only one possible answer to his question. She laughed a gallows laugh.

"Of course not," she managed through strangled lips. "How did you get to meet Valentino? Through Pat?" She struggled to change the subject.

He ignored her question.

"So now what were you saying about these photographs?"

"Yes, I see, well on second thought they're very dramatic, and, of course, they *are* beautiful. I wasn't questioning that. I think maybe my initial impression was a little hasty. They're so strong, maybe they just took some digesting. Thank you, Dick. You've opened my eyes on this one. Pat, too. Isn't she clever? Yes, the more I think about it . . ."

She was dying inside. Tony Valentino had wounded her soul. She was going to make him a star. His career would be launched in her magazine. What she had promised to trade for his flesh, she was about to give him as a reward for his insults. And no longer would it be a piddling quarter page in the all-but-invisible "Stars of Tomorrow" section. Now it would be page after steamy page of celluloid charisma burning into the eyes of every agent and casting person coast to coast.

But Dick Latham's mind had wandered on. He had bludgeoned his employee into submission. His objective was achieved. Now, in his own time, he was prepared to answer her question.

"You asked about myself and Tony Valentino," he said. "I'll tell you. Do you know what he did?"

Emma didn't know.

"He saved my life," said Dick Latham.

"You're not happy, are you?" Alabama gazed out over the mountains, their lower slopes wrapped in coastal mist. He didn't turn around as he spoke.

Pat Parker kicked out her legs and lay back on the outsize sofa as she planned her answer. No, she wasn't happy. She was miserable. She felt like an orange from which someone had sucked the juice, leaving her dry, empty, all used up. The last few days she had gone through the motions of living, but it had passed like a bad dream, full of cul-de-sacs, traps, and things happening to her that she couldn't help. Unrequited love might not be the most original feeling in the world. Knowing that didn't help.

"No, it's not a good time," she said at last, smiling bitterly at her understatement.

"You did right," said Alabama. "When fame hits the fan Tony will be grateful."

"He thinks I betrayed him."

"You did, but it was an end-justifies-the-means thing, you know, like Arnold Newman's portrait of Krupp. The kraut thought he looked just fine, and Newman had turned him into the pictorial symbol of evil. The moment you stop shooting trees and get into people you catch all the ego rubbish. Blast through it. Keep your eyes on the art, and everything ends okay."

"Happy endings?" Pat laughed doubtfully.

"I've seen less promising situations turn into happy families," said Alabama.

"For*get* it. Mrs. Tony Valentino would have to have the moral purity of Joan of Arc, *and* the strength."

"The girl was a schizophrenic," said Alabama dismissively. "Listen, are we shooting today? You wanna go down to the Rock House and do some bikers?"

"You mean do some beer."

"Whatever." Alabama smiled, turning around to face her.

"Nah," said Pat. "I just feel like hanging around and having you tell me photography stories—like about Kertész, tell me about Kertész." She curled up her legs like a child waiting for a favorite story at bedtime. Alabama, tough and terrible to the outside world, was so soothing to her. He was chamomile tea, warm muffins, and woolly bunnies at dusk. Was everyone like that—showing different faces to different people, not really a single person at all?

"One day everyone will say Kertész was better than Steichen, Stieglitz, and Weston. He could find beauty where no one else could see it. *That* is the ultimate genius. I cheated. I took obvious beauty, and I made it more beautiful. André saw a leaf in the wind, snow on the ground of an ugly square, and his lens made it something else. Cartier-Bresson and Brassaï both acknowledged their debt to Kertész. The world didn't know him till Szarkowski's MOMA exhibition in the sixties, and poor old André never forgave the world for its oversight. He was one of the most bitter men I have ever met, and with the least reason. Imagine, inventing the photoreportage style, and then worrying about whether or not people give you credit for it."

"I can sympathize with that. It must be so *frustrating* to know that you possess something that nobody else can see. Tony feels like that. It eats away at him. He hasn't mentioned it, but I can see it in his eyes." Pat couldn't stay away from Tony for long.

"Like everything else in life, the emotion can be used or abused. You can make it work for you, and use its energy to help you get what you want. Or you can point it inward rather than outward, and let the acid drip away at you until there's nothing left. Toward the end André could talk about nothing else but how the Americans had failed to appreciate him. He was the unhappiest artist, but the greatest. I find that the most unbelievable paradox." Alabama shook his head.

"Except that dissatisfaction is the sharpener of your art. You judge it yourself, and the more harsh your judgment the harder you try. I suppose that in the end only by thinking your work is rubbish do you get to perfection. The trick is to be able to live through the discouragement, and not pack it in."

Immediately, Pat wished she could take back her words. Alabama turned back toward the mountain. He said nothing. She hadn't meant to, but she had struck a chord within him. Had he really stopped taking photographs because there were more of them in the world than bricks?

"Yeah," he said at last. "It was the other way around for me. Everybody loved my stuff. I just wasn't so sure about it myself. The fact they all went belly up for it, made me doubt it. They trash the mountains, pollute the rivers, and screw the trees and then they shell out hundreds of thousands for my pictures of the things they're ruining. It seemed a good joke to plow their money back into the environment, and con them at the same time."

"Take my portrait, Alabama."

"What?"

"Take my portrait." She jumped up, excited. "I want you to. I want you to work again. Please. Do it for me. Just one portrait. That's all I'm asking for. Will you? Please, Alabama. Please."

She ran across to him, as he turned toward her framed by the picture window against the mountains.

"It's not a small thing," he said, avoiding her eyes.

"I know that. I know it. You're frightened. You're nervous. You think it might turn out like *shit.*"

She dared to goad him. It was dangerous, but he responded to that.

"What the *hell* do you mean? Nervous? Of a photograph? Me? Jesus, girl, have you forgotten who I *am?*"

"Have *you?*"

"Listen, I never wanted to be a Picasso—a 'paint-till-you-faint' artist. I gave up because I was fed up. If I wanted to, I could take a better portrait than you've seen in ten years with the frigging lens cap on."

"Do it. Prove it!"

"I don't have to prove anything to you."

"I wasn't talking about me. I was talking about proving it to yourself."

He was pacing up and down now, irritated, hesitant, and yes, fearful.

"And what the *hell* would you do with this portrait? Peddle it for a stinking Porsche?"

"No," said Pat simply. "I'd send it to Tony."

NINE

Tony Valentino stared into the mirror and scowled. It wasn't the reflection that made him do that. It was the stuff inside his head. To do this part he had to hate, and to hurt. He had to feel the raw emotions that gave Cal his exposed-nerve personality. Then he had to project them outward so that all the world could feel how it felt to be rejected. Everyone must know for themselves the dread reality of a world without love. He had read Steinbeck's book half a dozen times. He had walked the fields and the hills of Salinas, smelled the scent of the hot grass, lain down gratefully on the rich earth as he would sink into the lap of his beloved mother. "Mother"—the word lasered into his mind as he meant it to, and it set light to the feelings that were Cal's feelings. This dressing room was no longer on Broadway. No more was he an actor waiting for a curtain call and a hushed, expectant audience. He had ceased to be Tony Valentino. He was Cal Trask. He was Steinbeck's Cain on whom the Lord had set his mark. He was Adam's son, Eve's offspring, and he dwelled in the land of Nod, to the East of Eden.

The tap on the door was insistent.

"Two, Mr. Valentino," said the disembodied voice.

In the cunning artificial dream Tony Valentino stood up. He sleepwalked to the door and opened it. He ambled into the corridor and loped along the passageway toward the stage. His shoulders were hunched to protect himself from the slings and arrows that humanity liked to throw at him. He flicked his fingers as he lied that he didn't care, and a smile of scorn played around the edges of his mouth. He caught sight of himself in a mirror, and he hated his beauty, so he crunched up his face into a crushed cardboard expression that was supposed to mock his good looks but only succeeded in emphasizing them. The women would love him out there, damn them. They always loved Cal. They were frightened of him. They were in awe of his unpredictable moods, yet fascinated by the way he recoiled from them until the very moment of their knee-trembling surrender. He despised them for loving him. He was so unlovable. That great truth he had gleaned from the stony ground of his childhood. He kicked out at a rubbish bin that was a metaphor for the world, and he heard the muted hum of the audience behind the heavy curtains. The men out there would loathe him. They knew his secret. They recognized that he was deep-down bad, and, although they would always be his enemies, he respected them for being right. They were the half of humanity who had his number. They were the gender of his father, and his ambivalent love for them lay curled up tight in the womb of his hatred.

In the front seat on the darkened auditorium, Pat Parker's gut was tangled as Medusa's hair. James Dean had played this role in the famous Elia Kazan movie, and Pat could understand why girls committed suicide when he'd died. Tony's Cal was deeper than Dean's, and it wasn't just that she was involved with him still, and therefore the very opposite of a disinterested spectator. There was all the vulnerability of Dean's character, the shy, wounded charm; the touching eagerness to be accepted, standing beside the brittle defensiveness of the boy-man who had learned in the hard school of childhood that grownups could not be counted on for love. But there was more than that. Tony's Cal was strong in the midst of his weakness. His scars were deep inside and the battles he fought were not with the world, but with himself. He was walled away from people. They could whip his flesh, but they couldn't touch his soul. His essence was unavailable to them, and it was his essence that she wanted. Pat breathed in deeply, astounded at the depth of the emotions that sloshed around within her. She was part critic, part psychiatrist, and all the time she was the one-time lover who recoiled from the possibility that the boy she still worshiped would never love her again.

"What do you think?" Dick Latham leaned in toward her like a priest in confessional.

"I can't describe it," said Pat.

She cocked her head to one side, rolled her eyes to the ceiling, and splayed out her hands in her lap to emphasize the inadequacy of mere words.

Dick Latham chuckled. Tony Valentino's virtuoso performance was hardly a peak moment for the male sex. All around the auditorium husbands had lost their wives, boys their girlfriends, women their hearts. But for Latham it was different. He wasn't wearing the hat of Romeo competitor. He was wearing the halo of successful angel. On his return from Catalina, reborn as a result of Tony's unexpected and selfless bravery, he had attended the rehearsals of the off-off-Broadway stage adaptation of *East of Eden* in which Tony was appearing, and had been electrified by what he'd seen. Hours later, he had bought the whole production, closed down a struggling mainline musical by making its grateful backers an offer they couldn't refuse, and moved Tony's play lock, stock, and barrel to Broadway proper. His personal PR, Jay Rubenstein, had overseen the play's prelaunch publicity, and the vast advertising budget had done the rest. The first night was a major social and literary event. Every critic in New York was there, and the literary lions had prowled the aisles before the curtain had risen. Mailer, Vidal, Wolfe had shaded into Plimpton, Didion, and Dominick Dunne. Society had run the gamut from nouvelle Gutfreund greenbacks to the A and B class of Astor and Buckley. And everyone knew that they were present at a triumph.

"He's playing himself, isn't he?" said Latham.

Pat shook her head, half in denial, half in wonderment. It wasn't as simple as that. Tony was *using* bits of himself, but Cal wasn't him. Cal's prostitute mother had deserted him. Tony's beloved mother had defined decency and faithfulness. Cal struggled to win the approval of his distant father. Tony had been a fatherless child. Yet, despite the differences, Latham was right. It was the similarities that had her nerves on edge. It seemed that Tony had somehow been bathed in lovelessness, and that his aloofness, his untouchability was the result. There was something almost psychopathic about him—a cruelty, a single-minded sense of purpose that excluded others, even lovers, perhaps especially them. He pushed people away, and the closer they came, the harder he pushed. Pat knew. She had experienced it. Okay, maybe she had behaved badly. She had done the "wrong thing," but did she deserve to be excluded from the life of the man she loved? Wasn't that overreaction by a person who took himself and his ideals far too seriously? Then doubt bubbled up inside her. Could it be that Tony had used his uncompromising moral code as an excuse to ditch her? Men did that. No! She recoiled from the possibility. Tony didn't need excuses. Only the weak needed those. Tony, above all else, was strong. It was what she loved most about him. There was even a part of her that admired the way he had reacted to her betrayal of him. He hadn't stood for it. She hadn't measured up to his high standards and he had rejected her because of it. She respected him for that, but it didn't make life any easier. It wouldn't be long before she was face-to-face with him at the Canal Bar party. What should she say? How should she behave? What the *hell* should she feel?

"What do you think, Emma?" Pat turned to her right. Somehow the more people who got into this conversation the better. It would dilute its strength.

"Not a lot, quite frankly," lied Emma. "It reminds me of those plays we had in England in the fifties. It was part of a trend called 'kitchen sink' drama. This is the same sort of thing, only with fields instead of sidewalks. You know, nasty people doing nasty things to each other in nasty surroundings. You get art points for the degree of nastiness achieved on the principle that only degradation is real and anything fine is false."

"Emma doesn't like the play, Dick," said Pat immediately, dropping Emma deep into it. It was a reflex action. Emma was her friend, but nobody was going to get away with criticizing Tony or the play that was his vehicle.

"What?" barked Latham.

Emma's cheeks reddened. "What I meant," she spluttered across Pat at her boss, "was that personally, for me, the subject matter is a little depressing, but the play itself is *very* powerful. Very. I think it's going to be a huge success. I *know* it is. And of course, synergizing with Pat's pix in *New Celebrity*, it's going to make Tony the toast of the town. No question." She bit on her lip as she uttered the unwelcome words. The worst thing of all was that they were true. The evening was turning into a disaster of cosmic proportions, and it promised to plumb deeper depths. Latham had coincided the play's opening night with the *New Celebrity* launch party at the Canal Bar. The moment Tony had taken the bows at this triumph, they would all be traipsing downtown to watch him taking them at a second. At the instant of her magazine glory, Emma Guinness would be upstaged by the nobody she had turned into the biggest somebody in New York. Even the Almighty wouldn't have had the nerve to dream up a script like that. The man who had humiliated her had saved Latham's life, and become a star overnight. To add insult to injury, he actually had talent. The only good news was that his relationship with Pat was on the rocks. Maybe that would provide some consolation bad tastes amid the sugary menu of wall-to-wall congratulations that looked destined to be the diet of the evening. She took a deep breath. Soon she would have to confront him for the first time since her humiliation in the Juilliard. Their respective situations could hardly be more different. What on earth would happen?

"I hope you're going to be able to learn to think American, Emma," said Dick Latham coldly. "England has produced some great writers certainly, but precious few of them *this* century. I don't know how anyone can fail to appreciate Steinbeck."

He knew he was misinterpreting what Emma had said, but he did so on purpose. No hireling could get away with trashing his play.

"No, I agree," babbled Emma. "Hemingway, O'Neill, Fitzgerald, Faulkner, Tennessee Williams, Steinbeck—I mean, they're tremendously impressive. Shaw, Maugham, goodness, Wilde, are minnows by comparison, drawing-room stuff against the power of the American greats. The English admire your writers *enormously*." She leaned across Pat, her expression absolutely slavish in its subservience.

"The *middle*-class English, maybe. The upper classes have never heard of them," said Latham curtly.

Emma Guinness recoiled from the tongue lash of the Latham whip. He was one of the few Americans who could make an English class crack like that. Obviously he had learned a trick or two in the Whites bar, because his comment was right on the money. The British aristocracy were enormously proud of their intellectual poverty. They left the business of writing to the dreaded middle classes. When the king had been introduced to Gibbon, author of the monumental *Decline and Fall of the Roman Empire*, his only comment had been: "What is it, scribble, scribble, scribble, eh, Mr. Gibbon?" At a stroke, Emma, by her erudition, had revealed herself as a card-carrying member of the bourgeoisie rather than of the upper classes to which she had always aspired. Americans weren't supposed to know the difference. This one did. Latham, her boss, the most powerful man in her world and the one she dreamed of marrying, knew her social secret. Salt burned in the old wounds.

"Thanks a *lot*, Pat," she hissed sotto voce.

But Pat wasn't listening. Quiet descended on the audience. The curtain was going up.

Tony Valentino stared across the room toward the desk where the woman sat. She was bathed in shadow. Brittle blond hair wreathed her small, sharp features and the black lace dress, so prim and prudish, lied about the lewd woman she was. He peered through the gloom, and his heart stopped as he saw her for the first time. A lifetime of longing hadn't prepared him for this. On the one hand was fantasy, the world of his desperate childlike dreams, as he had constructed the perfect woman from the void of fact. But here was reality. Here, in the "proper" Victorian study, among the ferns and the spotless antimacassars, was the whore who was his mother.

"What do you want from me?" she said, her voice harsh.

"I don't want anything." It was the biggest and most grotesque lie of all time. What did you want from the woman who had borne you? It wasn't as simple as "love." In the love desert he had learned to do without. There were ways to survive its absence. You pickled yourself in the vinegar of hatred and you learned not to trust. You schemed and you planned and you skulked in the dark places among the dark people who were your kith and kin, and laughter was a sneer, and happiness was just an illusion. The dearth of love was the death of hope, but you could live with hopelessness and it gave you a wild courage because you had nothing left to lose and nowhere to fall.

"Why come then? Why follow me? How long have you known?"

Her voice was petulant. She wasn't pleased to see the son she had hardly seen. She wanted information that she could use. Even now her wants had precedence over his, as they always had.

"Why did you leave us?" he blurted out, but it wasn't the right question. "Why did you leave me?" he added. It was right now.

He waited for the answer as if for the kiss of the ax's blade, and he knew it wouldn't satisfy. It was the abandonment. That was the source of the pain. He had been so small, so defenseless, so innocent and yet, even in the first hours and days, so deeply unlovable that the woman who had borne him would all but kill to escape from him. She had shot his father because he tried to stop her from leaving. She had risked murder to get away from him. What mark was upon him? What dread aura signaled his worthlessness? For God's sake, why was he so impossible to love? Tony felt the tear swell in his eye, felt his heart heave in his chest because he knew this agony. It was his. It always had been. His father had left him all those years ago. Even now, he could scarcely believe that it was not his own fault. There must have been some deficiency in him that had pushed his father away and condemned his beloved mother to a lifetime of poverty and loneliness as she struggled against all odds to bring him up on the open road.

The tear squeezed out and ran down his cheek as he drew the emotion from the reservoir of pain. But at the same time his white-knuckled fists clenched by his side because there was room for another feeling now. There was space for anger. Whatever the cause of their leaving, deserters were traitors. As such, they were enemies to be hated and punished. Cal and Tony had learned how to survive in the cruel world, but their crippled hearts cried out for revenge as others lusted for happiness and security and the love of families. Cal needed the idea of his mother, but already he was beginning to loathe the fact of her. Tony wanted his father, but there was a part of him that dreamed of patricide.

"I left you because you were in the way of what I wanted."

She lifted up her chin, and she smiled as she said that, showing the sharp incisor teeth of the wolverine, her eyes flashing in the dull light.

"I was a baby, Mother. I was just a baby."

The reproach was solid in his words, and his heart was breaking for the helpless thing he had been, and for the helplessness that lived on, buried deep beneath the veneer of his toughness. But, as he spoke, he knew that he was not reaching her. There was space where her heart should be. She was psychologically deformed, as stunted and as warped as if her limbs had been twisted and misshapen in some terrible disease or by some accident of birth. There were words for it. Evil. Wickedness. The devil. But they had no meaning, because she was still his mother.

She didn't answer. Instead she looked down and studied the back of arthritic hands, their skin dotted with brown spots, hands aged before their time, hands that his father said had once been beautiful.

"Did you leave us for this? Are you glad?"

He signaled with his hands to summon up the bogus gentility of the brothel, the disgusting tawdriness of the shame house that his mother had preferred to him. He was giving her a chance to apologize. Long after love had gone, and after all the years on the emotional rack, he wanted her formal admission that a great wrong had been done. But she didn't know how to say sorry, because the sorrow she knew did not involve the insubstantial shadows who were other people. It only involved her, and the decay that was the legacy of her rotten life.

She leaned forward and both her hands were on the green leather of her businesswoman's desk. Her face poked out from the shadows into the mind of her son.

"Yes, I'm glad. I'm rich and I'm free and I do what I want. I'm free of snot-nosed kids who only want things, and I'm free of your saintly father and his selfish goodness, and I'm free of all the cant and the hypocrisy of the slime that run this world. I see them in here, you know. I've got photographs of the rubbish who rule us, writhing under the whips, lusting for pain and humiliation at the hands of big, dull women who only want to eat chocolate and rest their feet. They ask for our votes, but they want the heel marks of my girls on their crotches. Do you realize that? Have you any *idea* about the world out there? Yes, I left you for this, because this is *mine* and in the hell of families, women are *owned*. They're slaves to the babies they produce and the men who father them. Drudges. Victims. Servants. Do you hear? Do you hear?"

She was screaming now. Cal recoiled from her as he was directed to do, but then Tony felt the feeling deep within. Her words touched him. He had read them a hundred times in the script, but he had not been emotionally prepared for them as he was now. His intellect saw a poor, psychologically damaged woman. But his heart saw the mother whose blood was his blood. And there was a message in her words that he understood. She was talking about freedom. She didn't mean freedom to vote, freedom under the law, freedom to speak freely. She meant *real* freedom. His mother was talking about freedom from conscience, from responsibility, from guilt. She had wanted to be free of babies and poverty, from worrying about what other people thought, free to create her own personal, idiosyncratic world in the land of the supposed free where in fact conformity was the universal goal. At a stroke, she was no longer evil. There was an odd logic in her behavior, that only an anarchist like Tony could understand, that only an outsider like Cal would appreciate. A hundred years separated the two men, and it was the difference between walking toward the woman who had just spoken and walking away from her. The stage directions called for the latter. But Tony Valentino wanted with overwhelming strength to take her in his arms.

He walked across the stage, and the surprise was there in the eyes of the actress who had become the father he had never had.

Pat Parker was dimly aware that her feelings were the feelings of the entire audience. It was as if in the silence, emotion had become universal. She knew what she wanted. With all her heart she wanted the mother-and-child reunion. But at the same time, the stage was electric with a sense of terrible uncertainty. The immediacy was total. There was no predicting what would happen, because the characters were as alive as life itself, and because there were no scripts in the real world. This was the ultimate in the art of acting. Tony had lifted them up in the palm of his hand, and they had journeyed through the vale of his emotional sorrow. Most of the crowd had forgotten they were in the theater.

Pat was excited. Now that she had seen Tony act, so many things made sense. She could see where the charisma came from. It flowed from an other-worldly ability to communicate dramatic art. Deep in the theatrical experience, she was hardly able to see Tony as the boy who had once been "hers." He had become public property like the ocean and the beach, and the wide-open sky. Later, as the thrill subsided, there would be time for memory of ownership, and for regrets at the loss of it. Right now, she could only admire him.

Emma Guinness was beside herself with rage. She shifted about on her seat and cursed the thing that was happening all around her. He had been good at the Juilliard. Here he was brilliant. Then, she had thrilled to his performance as she had dreamed of his body. Now, he was an untouchable. He was in the process of being anointed with the success that would take him beyond her reach forever, and the revenge she wanted so badly was receding into the dim distance. Next to her was Pat Parker, the girl who had loved him. The relationship might be over now, but Pat had experienced the flesh that Emma wanted. Somehow that made her a rival—a *successful* rival. And it wasn't just Tony. Latham had chosen Pat to sit next to. Latham's eyes never left the beautiful photographer, as he laughed at her jokes and hung on her words. Yet Latham was Emma's target, and Pat knew that. Maybe she wasn't encouraging the billionaire, but she wasn't discouraging him either. The mean little business of repeating Emma's criticism of his play was an example of the undercurrent flowing beneath the surface. Pat Parker had better watch out. She was creeping toward the Guinness enemy list. Those who reached that, lived to regret it.

Five seats farther along the front row, Melissa Wayne was ecstatic. She hadn't forgotten the moody nobody on the boat off Catalina who had had the luck and the good judgment to save Dick Latham's life. There had been chemistry between them, despite the fact that he had belonged to the photographer who was too good-looking by half. When the invitation to *East of Eden* had arrived in tandem with the one to the Canal Bar launch party for *New Celebrity*, she had immediately accepted. Somewhere down the line she was due to give Emma Guinness an in-depth interview for the already successful revamped magazine. That, and the fact that Dick Latham was apparently planning a new schedule of movies at Cosmos, made the evening interesting from a career point of view. Seeing Tony Valentino again was to have been just icing on the cake. Not anymore. He had become the main event. She couldn't take her eyes off him. Anybody could recognize the power of his performance, but as a professional she knew exactly how difficult it was. Not for one minute did he seem to be acting. He had become Cal to such an extent that one could be forgiven for thinking the whole thing wasn't very clever at all and that he had simply had the good fortune to find a part that was the mirror image of his own personality. Melissa, however, was sophisticated enough to know that was not true. His brilliance was to make it *seem* so. It was a whole new dimension to the boy whose chief attributes until now had seemed to be his flesh and blood and his touchingly insolent self-confidence. So Melissa Wayne licked her lips in the darkness and squeezed her legs together, as she waited for all the good things that would surely happen to her on what promised to be a memorable evening.

Directly behind Dick Latham, Allison Vanderbilt's eyes sparkled through the mist of her tears. She was glad that her date, Jamie Leavenworth, hadn't made it back from the bar. That was good because it meant that she was alone with the man she loved. All around her the audience thought they had a lease on Tony Valentino as he seemed to show the public his most private feelings, but Allison Vanderbilt knew it was a sham, perhaps the most beautiful, brilliant confidence trick that had ever been played. Alone in the crowd she knew him. She had crawled inside his wounded soul and wandered in wonder in its secret places. Oh yes, Pat Parker had been with him, but she had only wanted to use him for her own career purposes. Allison's love was pure. She needed nothing from Tony. His dreams were her dreams. She would die for him, do anything for him, and the magnificence of her selfless obsession filled her up. He didn't love her, but that didn't matter. The only thing that mattered was Tony and the things he wanted. Two days ago they had walked in Central Park and he had held her hand in a gesture that said she was his dearest friend, as he had told her of Pat Parker's mean betrayal and of how upset he had been by her disloyalty. It had hurt to hear him talk of the woman he had loved, but it had been wonderful once again to be so close to him. Later on, they would sit at the same table at dinner and she prayed to the Lord that she wouldn't cry, like now, damn it, because it was so hard when you loved so much . . .

Dick Latham wondered if he had ever had such a good time in all his life. In his heart there was an odd affection for the massed humanity that surrounded him. He loved them because they were reacting in the right way. He loved them because they so obviously agreed with him. They were wise and wonderful because they loved the play that he had backed and because they loved the boy who had saved his life. *East of Eden* would be sold out for months. On his first foray into Broadway investing, he had struck gold. Once again the Latham touch had been the Midas one. Later, they would celebrate the first sell-out issue of *New Celebrity*. Already there was an advertiser's feeding frenzy as the upmarket products queued to get into future editions of the magazine. Subscriptions were going through the roof. God was in his heaven and his hated father was spinning like a top in his grave. He felt invincible. He was the man who could do no wrong. There wasn't even a problem about finding something for an encore. He had backed a hit play and launched a wildly successful magazine. Making a blockbuster movie would be a cinch. Tony Valentino would star in it. He was made for a celluloid crossover, and it would be no problem to pull him from the play that Latham owned. It didn't matter that he was unknown. His talent transcended such petty considerations. Melissa Wayne could carry that part of the deal. All that was needed was for the man of the moment to dream up the package, and the lights sparkling in the Hollywood firmament would all be green.

He turned toward Pat. She was on the edge of her seat, leaning in toward the stage. He had been going to say something, but he didn't want to interrupt her intense concentration. So he watched her, in the stage glow, as she stared at the boy she loved, and an even better feeling wafted over Dick Latham. The worst thing about happiness was wondering how it could be improved upon. Now, suddenly, he knew.

Tony Valentino had reached his mother. He knelt down. Tears poured down his cheeks. She didn't pull back from him when he took her in his arms. Instead, she rocked from side to side in the alien embrace of tenderness. All her life she had never known she had needed comfort. All his days, he had yearned for it. He looked up at her, his face dissolving in hope and longing for a better future.

"I forgive you, Mother," he whispered. "I understand. I understand."

TEN

Tony Valentino sat back in the limo and poured himself a large drink. He knew intellectually that he had produced the performance of a lifetime. He had seen it in the eyes of the audience. They had clapped till their hands were numb and the curtain calls had gone on and on. In the dressing room afterward, the congratulations had been transparently truthful, and yet, the bizarre feeling that made no sense gripped him. Tony Valentino couldn't escape the weird sensation that he had bombed. It had happened a couple of times before, and he had discussed it with his teachers at the Juilliard. They hadn't been much help, because they hadn't been used to dealing with talent like his. Tony had tried to analyze it, and unhampered by false pride, had concluded that perhaps it had to do with genius. For most people, doing things really well was a reward in itself. To the tortured genius, everything was an uninteresting stepping-stone toward the perfection that could never be achieved. Horowitz had endured nervous breakdowns and addiction to tranquilizers in an attempt to escape the pain of creation. Goya and van Gogh had lapsed into madness. The majority of America's literary Nobel laureates were alcoholics. The fact that he had done well was pushed to the back of his mind by the agonizing thought that he could have done better, and the places he had failed filled his brain at the expense of the moments in which he had triumphed. The applause of the crowd and the hyperbole of the critics meant nothing to him. His jury sat in silence inside.

It handed down its verdict, and the verdict was guilty. He could think only of the rare times when his words and gestures hadn't matched, and of the tiny instances when there had been a time lag between body and tongue, and more important, between heart and mind. By his own stratospheric standards, his performance had been a failure, while by any rational ones it had been a stupendous success. The trouble was that only his opinion mattered. His art had never been the trick of instilling confidence in others. So he drank deep on the neat Glenfiddich, allowing the alcohol to burn against the lining of his empty stomach. He caught his breath and stared moodily from the car window at the steamy streets of the darkened city. The gloom filled him. It was going to be a bad evening. He felt evil. The trendies at the Canal Bar had better watch out. So had Melissa Wayne, who sat beside him, thin and lovely on the fat cushions, and tricky Dicky on his other side, and busty Emma Guinness with her sandpaper tongue, and Pat Parker, too, Pat who had made love to him on the sand and traded his trust for a slick career move. He had thought she was special, but she had shown herself to be like all the other rats in the stinking city, buying and selling each other, foraging for advantage in the sewers and gutters as they turned their faces away from the stars. In their fashion they had all made their moves on Tony Valentino. Well, tonight the devil was in him. Future moves had better not be false ones.

Melissa Wayne sat quietly, surrounded by the aura of her spectacular beauty. She wore a richly embroidered black velvet jacket over a torso bare except for a purple moiré bra top, from which African coins dangled on beaded chains. A faux emerald necklace separated her exposed upper body from the pallor of her exquisite face. Her blond hair was piled up high in a young Barbara Hutton cut, and her eyes were hidden by diamanté-rimmed sunglasses above pert scarlet lips. A pencil-thin black crepe skirt hid the rest of her above Manolo Blahnik gold lattice grosgrain shoes. She reached out and hooked her hand inside Tony's thigh in a gesture that was both a threat and a promise. "This belongs to me" she was saying.

Tony ignored the Wayne hand. Not many people could do that. Melissa's fingers resting on an inside leg were not usually a take-it-or-leave-it phenomenon. They set wheels in motion, hormones bubbling, the blood rushing headlong to places from which it couldn't escape. But he genuinely didn't mind. Okay, so the bitch wanted him. Way down on the list of priorities, maybe he wanted her. If it happened, it would be cool. If it didn't, the world would keep on turning. He was aware that his indifference was turning her on, but that wasn't the reason for it. His mood was. Black as the night outside, it sat on his shoulder, full of thunder, tight with lightning, thick with the storm of pent-up irritation that must erupt before the evening's end.

"Can I get you a drink, Melissa?" said Dick Latham, his eyes fastening onto the errant hand. The diversion was a reflex action. The man who loved to defeat women couldn't bear to watch another playing his own game. He had other plans for tonight, and Melissa was not part of them, but still it rankled that her hand was stalking somebody else.

"Is there any champagne?"

"There usually is. Let's see." Dick Latham didn't move a muscle. In the rare air of his plutocracy he had only to speak. Actions were for others. In New York State the limos were no longer allowed to serve alcohol, but that law applied only to the *hired* limos that the mere millionaires used. This stretched Mercedes was a Latham possession. So was the blessed Dom in the icebox. So was the bodyguard, huge on the tiny bucket seat, who now reached for it. The *pop* of the cork unglued Melissa's hand from Tony's leg, as if the mini-explosion had occurred beneath her fingers. She accepted the wine and put it to her lips provocatively, leaving a scarlet half-moon of lipstick on the Baccarat flute.

"Have we taken over the whole restaurant?" she breathed.

"Yes and no," said Latham, precise in his assault on the law of excluded middle. "I told Brian to let in a few of the better-looking regulars. I find that adds *tension* to a party. The best ones need loads of that."

"Somehow," said Melissa Wayne, "I don't think lack of tension is going to be the problem tonight." With the skill of the really good actress, she insinuated both that she knew Tony Valentino was a ticking bomb, and that she didn't mind a bit.

"Our little table should be fun," said Latham. "You remember Pat, don't you, Melissa? The photographer who took the wonderful photos of Tony."

"Is she a lesbian?" said Melissa suddenly. Her ambush had the virtue of total surprise, as it was supposed to.

Dick Latham choked theatrically on his glass of chardonnay. Tony Valentino sat up an inch or two from his slouched position. Even the bodyguard, giving his "hear-no-evil" impression, seemed to perk up.

"No!" Latham laughed. "What on *earth* gave you that impression?"

"Oh, I don't know. Just her vibes. She seemed sort of sexually indeterminate, and on the boat she was hostile in that way that people in gender turmoil often are."

"Pat wasn't hostile. You were," said Tony Valentino.

Melissa smiled. It was *exactly* what she'd wanted—a reaction from the target. He flashed his accusing eyes at her. She smiled radiantly back.

"Oh, I'm so sorry, sir. I was *hostile?* That's very unlike me. How gall*ant* of you to stand up for the wronged lady. Quite the knight in shining armor."

She laughed as she mocked him, far from fearful of his dangerous mood.

She implied effortlessly that his championing of Pat Parker had nothing to do with setting the record straight, but everything to do with the way he felt about her.

Tony shifted in his seat. God, she was hot. It was like sitting next to a radiator. He could smell her sex beneath her Paloma Picasso. The Rifat bra was losing the battle to hold back her breasts. They were weapons in offensive mode. He could just about see her nipples. Despite himself and the memory of Pat Parker, the feeling began to build within him.

"Actually," said Latham, "Tony and Pat don't get along."

He sounded far from worried about the falling-out.

"She went back on her word." Tony was irritated. He didn't appreciate comments on his private life.

"That's something I can't *bear*," said Melissa enthusiastically. Her hand sneaked back. She licked wet lips. In the real world, word-breaking was her second favorite exercise.

"Here we are," said Dick Latham.

There they were. The street outside the Canal Bar looked like the dangerous part of Gotham City—tack on seed on sleaze—the perfect camouflage for New York's hottest restaurant. The sidewalk was littered with paper, old pizza, and paparazzi. The latter swarmed around the limo, sensing the serious money from the cut of the carriagework.

Melissa sighed, adjusted her underwear through the crepe skirt, and waited for somebody to open the door. She pretended to hate what she loved. Being an actress made her good at that.

On the pavement she stood her ground, making no effort to push through the milling crowd. The flashbulbs lit the night. A cocklike mike sidled up to her lips. " 'Entertainment Tonight,' " said Leeza Gibbons unnecessarily. Melissa turned quickly to Dick Latham, smiling on her arm. Her expression flashed a "well done." The prime-time nationwide show didn't do a lot of hanging around outside restaurants. It was a neat PR move. Now she looked around for Tony. She wanted him in frame. He would be grateful for the coast-to-coast exposure. He wasn't there. She looked back. He wasn't in the limo either. He'd slunk around the crowd, in the classic Penn pincer move. She shrugged. It was a way to go. She slipped into gear for the sound bite, mentioning her current movie in every sentence so that it couldn't be edited out. Then, micro-seconds before they cut her off, she smiled a full frontal good-bye, and sliced through the blazing cameras toward the Canal Bar.

Inside, Dante and the gang were already on fire. The room was packed, the decibels were on positive feedback, and the Run-D.M.C. rap music sprayed over the black-uniformed crowd like machine-gun fire.

A Greek god loitered at the maître d's lectern. At the sight of Dick Latham and Melissa Wayne, he metamorphosed into a body servant.

"Sir, Ms. Wayne, welcome to the Canal Bar. I'll show you your table."

As it was supposed to, the sound faded as they made their entrance. But New York wasn't as impressed as L.A. The vast, dirty city was a great leveler. Star status hardly protected you from the accusing eyes of the beggars and homeless, the static and the neurosis, the beady eye of a Saturday night special. In Beverly Hills by now, the boys and girls would be polishing their pitches. In the Big Apple they were too busy getting high.

There were three empty places at the table.

"Hi," crowed Emma Guinness from the depths of a nerve-racking Isaac Mizrahi silver sweatshirt.

"There you are." Tommy Havers smiled from a too-well-cut Cerruti suit.

"Hello." Allison Vanderbilt waved, stylish in a no-name navy-blue sheath dress. "May I introduce Lord Leavenworth."

Jamie Leavenworth tried to stand up, but with difficulty. He was drunk. He burped once, laughed, burped again, and sat down. He looked like a chinless cherub, shining bright, lost in terminal self-admiration as he reached for his gin and tonic. Melissa Wayne ignored him. Dick Latham nodded. His father, the earl of Swinley, was a fellow member of White's.

"Hi, Dick," said Pat Parker.

His eyes zeroed in on her. The rest of the table receded. Dick Latham took a deep breath. She looked like she had invented animal magnetism. Her hair was lion wild, back-combed into a tawny mass of jungle excitement. She wore a Katharine Hamnett shaded leather jacket bearing the ecological legend CLEAN UP OR DIE above a black velour body suit, and the material gripped her skin like it wanted to *be* it. She stood up, like a skyscraper growing in time-lapse photography, and her unusual height was emphasized by the Cuban heels of her black patent leather ankle boots. Dick Latham reached up to kiss her with the reverence of a communicant.

"Where's Tony?" hissed Melissa Wayne.

"Is he sitting with us?" whined Emma Guinness.

Pat Parker's leonine eyes scanned the room over the Latham shoulder, wary, like those of the animal she resembled.

"I think I see him over there," said Havers.

"Tony who?" slurred the incapacitated aristocrat.

"Ah, Tony, there you are. You gave the photographers the slip, and after my publicity people had sold grandmothers to get the right ones to turn up. What shall we do with him?" He aimed an affectionate punch at the shoulder that had appeared next to his.

"Hi, Tony," said Pat.

"Hi." His voice was flat, dull, devoid of emotion. It was a duet. The room was no longer the set. It had become the distant backdrop.

"You were great in the play," said Pat simply. She smiled, giving him an opening, opening the rest of her life to him. Boom, boom went her heart—ram, bam against her ribs.

He waved away the compliment. His eyes shut her out. "Hi" was all she was going to get. In her memory his stomach was against hers. She could smell his sweat. She could hear him moan while he came.

"Hello, Allison," he said. He walked over to kiss her.

"Careful," growled Leavenworth, putting his hand over his drink as if Tony had endangered his most valuable possession.

Tony's eyes flashed fire at him. "How have you been?" he said to Allison.

"Oh, okay," she laughed bravely to show she had handled it.

"Loved the play. You were really cooking, especially in the second act. It was a difficult part. You were great."

"I wasn't happy with it," he said. There was a bond between them stronger than the "love" they'd made. She would get his true feelings, because she deserved it and because she would listen.

"I thought it was even better than your Stanley Kowalski," said Emma Guinness. Tony looked at her for the second time in his life, and she stared back at him, her face expressing an extraordinary mixture of emotions. She was defiant, determined to put a brave front on the unpromising meeting. She was trying to be cute —"We-can-rise-above-this" style. There was a carrot—"Like-me-and-I'll-forgive-you." There was a stick—"Keep the feud going and I'll bury you under my words in front of all the people who invented you."

"I like the silver tent better than the ballet-dancer rig," said Tony, his voice thick with sarcasm.

"I think we should get hold of some wine," said Dick Latham cheerfully.

"Fab," gurgled Lord Leavenworth.

"Don't you think you've had enough, Jamie?" whispered Allison quietly to her date.

"What?" said Leavenworth loudly. He spun around on her. "Don't dare . . . ever . . . tell me what to drink. Do you hear? Mind your own fucking business."

"What did you say?" said Tony into the shocked silence.

"It doesn't matter. Please, Tony," said Allison to avert disaster.

"Tony," said Pat.

"People, people," admonished Dick Latham, far from disturbed by developments.

"He told her to mind her own fucking business," said Emma Guinness, oiling oily waters.

"Yes, I did," agreed Leavenworth, a fatuous smile on his face. He leaned back in his chair belligerently.

Tony hovered above him. He lowered his head until it was inches from the Englishman's.

"Apologize," he barked.

"Tony, he's zoned," said Pat.

"So what?" said Melissa Wayne.

"Piss off, you fucking wop," said the fifteenth Viscount Leavenworth.

Tony hit him. It was a vicious blow. Starting from the shoulder his arm pistoned out, downward, at an oblique angle, and his fist collided with the cheekbone of the lush. It didn't stop there. It traveled on. The nose was a definite obstacle, but not an insuperable one. It disappeared. The lower lip didn't fare much better. It was a ripe mango falling from the tree, and the seeds that spilled from it were a couple of teeth from the already depleted lower jaw of the chinless wonder. A fine spray of blood wafted across the immaculate table, and a particularly large globule attached itself to one of the understated white daisies that formed its centerpiece.

"Oh, dear," said Dick Latham. Thank God the English upper classes disliked their children. Otherwise Swinley could have caused all sorts of difficulties for him in the bar at White's.

"Direct hit," crowed Melissa Wayne, enormously impressed. The last decent fight in Morton's, Richard Zanuck's, had been an age ago. L.A. didn't approve of them.

"Fisticuffs? Before the soup?" said the cheerful voice of Brian McNally, who had materialized at the table with the sixth sense of the superb restaurateur.

Lord Leavenworth hadn't finished bleeding. He slid gently off the chair and continued to do it on the floor.

"I wonder, Brian," said Dick Latham, holding the arm of the restaurant's owner, "if we could find someone to scoop him up and chaperone him to Lenox Hill."

"I'll go," said Allison. "He's my second cousin," she added by way of excess explanation as she dabbed with a napkin at the place where her relative's nose had been.

"I'm sorry, Allison," said Tony, rubbing his skinned knuckles.

"It's okay," she said, as two large men arrived from nowhere to pick up the comatose peer. Her tone of voice implied that it would have been just fine if he'd confessed to being the Night Stalker.

"He ought to use Hoefflin," said Melissa Wayne enigmatically.

Even her impenetrable remarks carried weight. Everyone looked at her.

"For the plastic surgery," she amplified. "He's the only man. Even better than Michael Hogan."

"Will he sue? Assault charges, maybe?" asked Emma hopefully. A viscount bleeding on the floor was bliss to her. The possibility of bad things happening to Tony Valentino was even better.

"The English don't go in for that kind of thing," said Latham. "But it may well be that Tony is asked to resign from some of his clubs." He laughed at the ridiculous thought, as the divine waitress from an Ethiopia-equivalent country removed the bloodstained flowers. He beamed around the depleted table. The surreal feel was tangible. The earl's heir was disappearing through the disinterested ranks of Manhattan haute café society, leaving a trail of blue blood on the linoleum floor. The trademark McNally decorative minimalism had paid off once again. Tommy Havers escorted Allison and the unconscious body.

The eaterie entrepreneur still hovered at the table, thoroughly at home in the atmosphere of transcendent sangfroid. That his countryman had taken a pratfall didn't faze him. Male East-Enders liked nothing better than to knock the noses off earls' sons, not least because female East-Enders liked to go to bed with them. In Bethnal Green there was permanent open season on hooray Henries. Anyway, to give good restaurant you had to deliver drama, and so far this evening it was lights, camera, action all the way.

Tony sat down at last. Dinner had officially begun.

"You didn't have to do that, Tony," said Pat. She dared to accuse him across the table.

"No money in it, you mean?" He smiled insolently back at her.

Her cheeks reddened as they signaled the hit.

"He was drunk. He didn't know what he was saying. He couldn't defend himself." She tried to stay calm, but the anger was rising inside. The money crack was *so* unfair. But *was* it? What he was really saying was that he was spontaneous, direct, honest, while she was devious, calculating, cunning.

"Who cares that he was drunk? Who cares that he couldn't defend himself? He was insulting. I like men who don't put up with that." Melissa Wayne's tongue sneaked out to emphasize the last bit. Her eyes daggered into Pat's.

"We all know you like men, period," Pat shot back at her.

"And you don't. There. I was right all the time." Melissa smiled triumphantly around the table.

"*I'll* handle this," snarled Tony. He didn't need a champion.

Pat felt the bile explode at the back of her throat. She didn't know what the hell the hooker meant about her not liking men, but the remark insinuated that she had been discussed behind her back, and in a not-very-flattering way.

"The trouble is," said Pat slowly, "that you're not very civilized, are you, Tony?"

"That from the wild animal look-alike."

"At least I don't *behave* like a wild animal."

"No, you behave like a roach. Creepy, crawly, and always getting into places it's not wanted."

"Like your pants?" said Pat.

"Goodness," said Emma, "this is the first X-rated dinner party I've ever been to."

"Shut the fuck up," said Tony.

"See!" said Emma, mock demurely.

"Like my *life*," he added, turning back toward Pat and spitting the words at her across the table.

"Now. Now. Tony. Pat. Let's all calm down. We're all excited. I know I am. And let's remember we're here to celebrate *New Celebrity*, and Tony's success, and Pat's pictures. Let's have some food and learn to love each other again. Okay. *Okay?*"

There was steel in the last okay. Latham liked to walk on the wild side, but there was a limit. Now he was letting everyone know it had been reached. The fight had had one welcome dividend. It had scared off the massed table hoppers who had been gathering on all sides.

Havers walked back to the table.

"It's all under control," he said. "I sent Allison, the Englishman, and one of the bodyguards in the limo to the hospital and I alerted the company medical people to smooth things along. Also, the lawyers. Another limo's on the way in case there's a mess in the Mercedes. I'll have someone talk to the limey in the morning when he's sober so there are no complications." He sat down, fixed a smile to his face, and prepared to act as if nothing had happened.

"I don't want anybody covering up for me. . ."

"Relax, Tony." Latham's arm was firm and definite on the arm of the man who had saved his life. "It's detail stuff. It's no big deal. Forget it. These things happen."

He waved away the Leavenworth nose as if it didn't exist, which of course it no longer did.

"Now," he continued, "let's get these chairs cleared away. Pat, you move in closer to me. Tony, you shift around a bit so that Melissa isn't so isolated. There, that's better. And Tommy, you let Emma in on all the company secrets, okay? All the ones that you keep from me. She's such a gossip, I'll pick them up from her later on."

He chuckled to camouflage what he'd done, but everyone at the table knew. The couplings he'd suggested slipped on the mantle of inevitability, as beneath the surface the subplots raged.

Emma Guinness drank deep on the bitter cup. She'd drawn Havers, who was as interesting and as appetizing as old broccoli. The guy wasn't a man, he was a thing. He was the engine that made the Latham companies go, and as such was well oiled, powerful, and in perfect working order, but compared to the captain on the bridge, he was nothing. Across the table sat the man she wanted. Sure, it was aiming high, but she had always done that. And she had the brains for the job, the nerves of steel, the rubber-ball ability to bounce back. Not many who aspired to Latham had her attributes. They might be better looking, more charming, sexier, but they couldn't run his magazines. At the end of the day when Latham crawled between his sheets, it was his business, not romance, that he thought about. Anybody who made it successful would be his close friend.

The trick would be to turn the dreaded *F* word into something else. There had been no action replay of the mile-high coupling, but she was counting on the advertising figures and the *New Celebrity* subscriptions to rekindle his interest in her. Then, once the sexual bridge had been well and truly crossed, she had plans for the rest of it—the relationship; the live-in-lover stage; heck, wedding bells and the leverage of bloodline kids before the supersettlement. Yes, that was it. Marriage was not her end game plan for Dick Latham. Divorce was. She would cut him in half and walk away the richest woman in the world, pushing the queen of England into second place. Then, dear God, the streets of Belgravia and the hills of the Cotswolds would be red with the blood of those who had humiliated her. And most of all, a terrible fate would be found for the jumped-up actor on the other side of the table.

But as the wonderful daydream peaked within her, it began the slow fade. Across the table was the reason. Dick Latham's head was inclined toward Pat's. He was talking intensely into her face. She was nodding back at him, engrossed by his pitch. His hands waved before her eyes in a myriad of clever gestures. He smiled. He frowned. He ran through his entire repertoire of expressions. It was clear what he was doing. He was trying to pull her. Emma Guinness, wife to be, mother of his children, future recipient of fifty percent of his fortune, simply did not exist in his world. She swallowed hard and the malice flowed out of her toward Pat Parker. The girl was making a move on her guy. Already the photographer had captured the actor Emma had wanted, and then proceeded to turn him into a star and a Latham protégé, safe from the Guinness revenge. Pat was playing a dangerous game. Emma had wiped people out for less.

"What do you think of the plans for Cosmos?" said Havers, cutting into her thoughts.

It was just about the only remark in the world that could have gotten her attention. She turned toward him and her face lit up.

"I'd like to know more about them."

"Specifically?"

"Specifically, personnel, as in Who's going to run it?"

"No decision yet. Any ideas?"

Emma pretended to be thinking. It wasn't difficult. She was going to run it. She hadn't been in the States long, but she had America's drift. America was about movies. It always had been. It always would be. Movies were what the country cared about, movies, and their watered-down surrogate, television. America was bound together by celluloid muscles. Its skeleton was made in Hollywood. It was fueled on dream power. The movies made Montana like Manhattan, and allowed Americans to know and understand each other in a country too big for intimacy. Stars were what Americans had in common. They loved them. They revered them. They were fascinated by them. In Hollywood two hundred players controlled the movie game, and there was a sense in which they were the most powerful people in the land. They manufactured the country's self-image. They ran the propaganda machine. In the free world they, more than anyone else, controlled the minds. To run Cosmos would be to be an integral part of that elite. In comparison, the editorship of *New Celebrity* was nothing.

"What about me?" she said.

"You?" He laughed. "You're not serious."

"Maybe I'm not." Emma laughed too. She wanted to sow a seed, nothing more. "But I could do it better than the usual team of suspects—the agents, the lawyers, and the movie politicians they always end up with."

"Aren't you a little short of experience?"

" 'The name men give to their mistakes,' as Oscar Wilde used to say. Yes, thank God, I am. That would be my saving grace. Listen, the only thing that's important in running a studio is picking movies that the public likes. Nobody knows how to do that for certain, okay? But who are the experts on trends? Who makes their living from anticipating what the public wants and giving it to them, all glossily packaged, dripping with style, and with no rough edges?"

"The editors of successful magazines?"

She patted his hand. "How did you ever guess?" she said. "Actually, it's not even a new idea. Disney has been sniffing around *Esquire*, *Premiere*, and *New York* magazine for lower-level executives."

"Don't call us, we'll call you—when *New Celebrity's* winning awards." Havers laughed dismissively.

"That won't be a very long wait," said Emma Guinness, staring moodily across the table at the man who could make all her dreams come true.

Dick Latham was letting himself go. He could smell Pat's breath, strawberry sweet in his nostrils. He could see in her eyes the ambivalence, the tough vulnerability, the defensive sense of humor that she used to deflect the pain. He was under no illusions. She didn't like him, but at least she wasn't indifferent to him. There had been less promising beginnings. Occasionally her eyes would flick away from his, and although he didn't turn to follow their direction, he could sense where they were aiming. She was watching Tony, Tony and Melissa, Tony with whom she could only fight, Tony whom she wanted only to love. Dick Latham was a veteran of all the lust wars. He knew what was going down. Tony and Pat, their hate and their love merged in the most explosive mixture of all, were trying to make each other jealous. Latham and Melissa were the tools of the time-honored game. It was an invidious position, but it could be used. The rules said that Pat must appear fascinated by Latham. For greater credibility, it would help if her feelings could go halfway toward matching her actions. So she was allowing herself to like him more than she did, and Dick Latham was taking advantage of the situation for all he was worth.

"Any thoughts about your next spread for us? I can hardly wait." He stared deep into her eyes, a dreamy expression on his face. He meant it. In the chase, everything must be meant.

"Not really. It just happens. Keep the mind prepared and the eyes open. Give luck a chance to kick in." The half smile around her lips said she knew his game, and that she didn't mind. He could keep going. He'd have to do very well, better than he'd ever done before, but she wasn't shutting him out. She could surprise herself, if he could surprise her.

She was hot in the catsuit. Her body itched. The whole of her was sensitized to everything. She was still cross, still indignant, hell and damn it, still in love.

Across the table the impossible Tony was allowing Melissa to vamp him. She was draped over him like a cloak, and Pat knew without hearing it the sort of shit Melissa was ladling out. It would be movie-time stuff—the big names littering the floor around her neat little ankes as she tried to impress Tony with the bits of her that he couldn't see. Which didn't leave much. She was Parental

Guidance at the least, and that was just her clothes. The body language was hard core. Her fingers fiddled with the nape of his neck. Under the table her foot would be footling with his. Already she had spooned some of her avocado mousse into his ridiculous open mouth. Had he *any* idea what a fool he was making of himself?

Pat forced her eyes away from him. What was slick Dick going on about? Lord, he was as smooth as an actor playing a middle-aged God—authoritarian, all-knowing, deeply caring, supremely self-confident. He kept running his fingers through his graying hair, as if proud of the fact that he wasn't vain enough to dye it, and every time he smiled he seemed to think he was dishing out a present. But he *was* good-looking. And powerful. And he was enormously easy. She never felt he was going to run dry, say something that jarred, or do something uncool. In a situation like this it added up to quite a lot.

"You know I've never met anyone like you before."

Pat smiled as she watched him notch up the rheostat of his come-on.

"Me neither." The way she said it wasn't necessarily a compliment.

He sensed it.

"What do you want, Pat Parker?"

"Can you give it to me, if I tell you?" she said at last.

"Try me!"

Her eyes flicked across at Tony. For a second they faced each other, their expressions saying they wanted only to hurt and harm. Neither gave an inch. There was no mercy, just the cold steel of revenge. He turned toward Melissa, and she leaned into him, red lips parted, her hands playing with his thigh. It was certain what would happen. In hours they would lovers. Pat's stomach turned on the wave of nausea.

She decided fast. This dreadful game was for two players. Tit for tat. The sacrifice of the nose to spite the face. But first there were concessions to be won and conditions to be agreed.

"Do you remember, a few weeks ago, in Malibu . . . ?" she began tentatively.

He finished her sentence for her. "I told you about my plans for movies at Cosmos . . ."

He smiled in triumph, as her eyebrows arched up in amused surprise. He was on to her. He knew before she knew.

"Okay, yes, Cosmos, and the movies and me getting a chance to direct . . ."

"You want that?"

She took a deep breath.

"Yes, I do."

"Do you think you could do it?

"I know I could."

"Yes, I think so too."

For long seconds he said nothing, as he savored his victory. The deed was as good as done. Pat Parker was on the verge of surrender.

"Do you mind my asking why you want it?"

Pat took a deep breath.

"Because it's there. The challenge. It's a way to move on, to get bigger, to have more effect. Every still photographer dreams of it. They seldom get the chance, and most of them would be terrified if they did. But they all want it, in their beds at night."

"Is that what *you* think of in your bed at night?" Dick Latham allowed himself the gentle sarcasm, and he glanced quickly across the table at his one-time rival.

Pat didn't answer. She was about to make love for revenge, and in addition she would get something she wanted. It didn't have to be spelled out. A strange detachment wafted over her. Mentally she inventoried her body. Was it ready for this? Could it be done convincingly? What was this business called? Prostitution? Could it be *enjoyed?*

He smiled a cruel smile as he read her thoughts.

"Do you keep my Alabama portrait beside your bed?" he asked suddenly.

"Yes, I do. It was a promise, wasn't it? You gave the money to the Sierra Club?"

He nodded slowly. They were both people who kept their word. Perhaps that was all they had in common, yet they were about to be lovers.

"The directing thing is no problem," he said. "You can have that." He waved a dismissive hand. He stared hard at her. His voice was harder.

"I have an overwhelming desire to see my portrait again," he said. "Tonight."

E L E V E N

He picked up the portrait and peered at the person he had been. Twenty-five years melted away. Dick Latham was back in Paris.

"Why didn't you like it?" asked Pat. She stood in the doorway of her bedroom, and the feeling of unreality deepened.

"I didn't like many things in those days." He was quiet as he remembered. God, he'd been good-looking, and cruel, like some Nordic prince. It was all in the eyes. Alabama had trapped the truth in the molecules of the film. He could feel the feelings he was feeling then—contempt for the crusty, low-born photographer; disdain for the fellow American in Paris who hadn't been to the right schools, hadn't a "family," wasn't rigid as cardboard with cash; disinterest in the artist who wasn't dead—that potent contradiction in terms that labeled the poseur photographer as nothing but a jumped-up pavement performer, unknown to museums, collectors, and ancient money. It was all there on the face that Pat Parker woke to in the morning and went to bed with at night.

She walked to his side and watched him with him.

"You look kinda cocky," she said, laughing a little.

"I was," said Latham. He didn't laugh. He was still back in the distant days. Already his mind was reaching out from the photo session to the other memories.

"What happened to the girl Alabama told me about?" said Pat. It would help if she could get to know him. This would be the shortcut.

He looked up at her, then back at the photograph.

"She walked out on me. Wouldn't you have walked out on this son of a bitch?"

"Oh, I don't know. You looked like fun."

"If you were into sick jokes." She had never seen him like this. The confidence had gone. He was humble. It was as if he loathed himself, the veneer of his self-confidence covering nothing but a gaping vacuum. He hated the part of him that the picture revealed, because the careless boy of the portrait had blown *his* future happiness. All these years later, Dick Latham still loved the girl who had left him.

"She was that special?"

There were tears in his eyes, no question.

"Yes," he said simply. "She was that special. And I took her heart in my hand, and I . . ." His voice petered out, but his hand clamped down tight, and his knuckles whitened as he made the fist. Then his arm shot out, and his fingers opened and his crushed love flew away across the room, as the bird had flown so many years ago.

"Nobody since then?"

"Nobody since then . . ."

They both wondered whether he would add "till now."

It would have been so easy and so cheap to tell the lie. Say it and I'll despise you forever, thought Pat.

He stopped. He sat down on the bed, the portrait across his knee. He looked up at the girl he wanted, and the guilt pricked at him. He was amazed by the alien emotion. Others had such feelings, not he. So many people led lives thinly buttered with fear. Terrified of the world they lived in, they were slaves to fortune and hostage to the whims and caprices of others. They were shackled by the chains of their own conscience, too. When they couldn't find others to make rules for them, they made petty rules for themselves. Life to them was pain. The stick of the world's disapproval was laid semipermanently across their shoulders, and when nobody had the energy to punish them anymore, they scourged themselves with the whip of guilt. Mea culpa had never been a Dick Latham problem. His rule was to take what he wanted without thought, hesitation, or the expectation of remorse. He had bought the beauty who stood before him. The price was around fifteen million, the cost of a risky, bomb-able movie at his brand-new studio. The tag was the highest yet, and he had promised to pay it. Not to collect would be unthinkable. But now, on the edge of yet another meaningless conquest, he held back. Why the *hell* was he waiting?

Standing in front of him, Pat sensed his dilemma. Her head was on one side, her expression quizzical, as she watched his conflict.

He looked up at her, and suddenly, there was desperation on his face. "Listen," he said. "We don't have to do this. . . . I mean . . . the movie's fine anyway. You've got that. You'd be brilliant . . . ."

But Pat Parker had already made her decision. She was in the driver's seat. Perhaps she always had been. Dick Latham would never know how well he'd done. Vulnerability, sensitivity, decency had never been part of his arsenal. His best performance had been an accident.

Pat reached beneath her arm, and her fingers closed on the zipper of her catsuit.

Melissa Wayne picked up the photograph and stared at it suspiciously.

"Who's this?" she asked, her remote-control jealousy sensing a rival.

Tony took it out of her hand.

"It's my mother. She's dead."

His tone was matter-of-fact, but Melissa could tell it was a big deal.

"I'm sorry. She was very beautiful." As a rule she never spoke well of her own sex. For dead mothers she could make an exception.

Tony looked at the photograph as if seeing it for the first time. There was a longing in his eyes.

"Yes, she was beautiful, but she never used it. She didn't even know it."

Melissa sensed the accusation in his words. It wasn't a remark that applied to her. She wished she hadn't brought up the subject. It was extraordinarily unpromising. Sympathetic small talk was a million miles from her forte. Now she had to dredge up more.

"How long ago . . . was it?" she tried, without much enthusiasm. She couldn't get the *D* word out. She peered in desperation around the dingy apartment, searching for a diversion. Most things looked like roach haunts. It was best not to pick anything else up.

Tony didn't answer. He realized she couldn't care less about his mother. He didn't mind. The sorrow was his, not hers.

They sized each other up like two pieces of steak on a butcher's slab. Then, quite suddenly, the spark was back. Electricity fizzled in the fetid air of the room. There was danger, excitement, and there was the unknown.

"Come here," he growled.

He had stolen her line. This was supposed to be a Melissa Wayne production. As the star she had precedence. He was the bit player, not the director. Part of her wanted to get that straight. Another deliciously unfamiliar part wanted only to obey. She sashayed toward him, a smile of patronization on her face. "I'm indulging you," said her expression. "We'll start your way. We'll end up mine." Inches from him, she stopped. The points of her breasts nudged at the cotton of his shirt. Her breath fanned his face as she mocked him with her closeness. Her threat was everywhere, in her jutting hips, in the firm aggressive stance of her legs, in the tongue that slicked over heart-shaped lips. Any second he would reach for her, and from the touch of his fingers she would know at once whether he was man enough to control her. One hesitant move, one lapse from surefootedness, and he would be on the knees that God had given him, the better to worship her.

Tony wasn't thinking about any of that. Her feelings didn't matter. The minds of others scarcely existed for him. They were unknowable, and uninteresting. They were academic distractions. To spend time investigating them was to waste energy, and dilute the force of his will. In front of him was the movie star, ripe as a wet peach. She was cocksure and sassy. She was uncomplicated and ruthless, and as pretty as anyone had a right to be. Most of all, she was *there*, on his tacky carpet, next to his unmade bed with its grubby sheets, ready, willing, and fantastically able to make him feel good, to make him forget the pain—the death pain, the art pain, the Pat Parker pain.

He put out his hand and grabbed a handful of her hair. His touch was not rough, but it was absolutely masterful. He drew her head toward him, until the skin of their lips were millimeters apart. Her eyes drowned in his, and he could see the lust in them, and the wonder, and yes, the fear that would be a newcomer to the Melissa Wayne sexual repertoire.

He lowered his savage lips to hers. It was the kiss of an enemy, terrible in its intensity and ruthless in its aggression. He invaded her mouth. His tongue ransacked her. His teeth ground remorselessly against hers, as he fed from her. It was close to pain, far from gentleness, and, ravaged by him, her head a prisoner in his powerful hands, she stood stock-still in awe of his lust. His body was crushed against hers. His male smell was thick in her flared nostrils. The throbbing heat of him thrust rudely against her stomach. She couldn't breathe, but breathing was not important anymore.

One hand twisted in her hair, the other reached behind her back for the strap of her bra. He unhooked it, and it fell away from her pulsing breasts. He drew her into him, plastering her chest against his.

"Tony!" she tried to say as his mouth freed hers. *Slow down. Be careful. Don't hurt me.* But she didn't want any of the things for which her eyes asked. Her body was calling the shots. Her mind was a mere servant. She needed more cruelty, more passion, more of his gloriously selfish lust.

He knew that. She was a mustang to be tamed, and first there must be the hell and the heaven of ecstasy before she trotted meekly into the corral, happy to be led, delirious beneath the saddle of her rider. So he put both hands on her shoulders, and stared deep into her eyes as, firmly, he pushed her down. She sank to her knees, full of wonderful despair, and reveled in the alien humility. Nobody had done this to her. Not like this. There had been no one to dare. Her face was tight against the burning heat of his blue-jeaned crotch. She could see the shape of him, enormous in its threat, rock hard with its promise. She rested her cheek against it, and her fluttering hands reached for the snare-drum tightness of her nipples. She pinched them until she could recognize pain in the sea of pleasure that engulfed her. She was full of dread, stuffed tight with longing, proud to be made to do the deed she would do. She reached for the straining muscles of his thighs. She ran her hands against the soft cotton. Her fingers found the buttons. She moved reverently, bravely taking this small initiative, fearful that he would forbid it. His strength hovered over her, threatening, formidable. Slowly she undid him. It sprang from the tightness of his jeans, leaping and rearing from the shorts that draped it. Like a dagger it glistened against her cheek, radiating heat, big, vast, pulsating with purpose in her face. She held the base of him in her hands, and she took a deep breath, filling her lungs with the precious air she would need. Around her fingers, his hair was wet with sweat, the shaft of him slippery in her grasp. She moved her hands upward, her skin burning with his heat. She could feel the blood pounding through the arteries that stood out on the shining surface. Up toward the tip she traveled, close to the angry point of him, and she bent in close and breathed in his musk as her lips moved toward their destination. At the back of her head she felt his hands take up their position. They rested there gently, but their presence had purpose. There would be no turning back from this. No second thoughts. There would be no avoiding the sweet conclusion. She shuddered at the thought of the delicious coercion.

There was the slightest pressure behind her head, propelling it forward. It was a command. She moved to obey. Her tongue snaked out and rested against the point of him, bathing the heat, but fanning the lust. She moved it against him, savoring the taste, sliding it gently over his tense flesh. Round and up and down, her tongue traveled, darting into the opening, lapping lovingly at the still miraculously expanding shaft. His low moan encouraged her, and the jerky movements at the back of her head and neck ordered her to the next stage in the slow dance of desire. She opened her mouth wide, so wide, and he slid gratefully into her. At first just the tip entered her, but already she knew his plan. Behind her the hands were tightening. Before her, the hips were thrusting. In panic she tried to look up at him, to tell him no, but the eyes that reached his screamed only yes, and the cruel eyes that stared back agreed. He slid deeper into her, and she opened wider to take him, until there was no mouth left for his hugeness . . . only throat. But still he didn't stop. Remorselessly, he advanced until he owned her space, and there, locked between his hands and his hips, she was nothing but the soft wetness that wrapped him.

For long seconds he stayed there as the air in her lungs vanished, and she fought to breathe through nostrils drowning in the sweat of his stomach. Then, at last, he was retreating and the oxygen howled into her lungs. She reached out to push him away, the flat of her hands thrusting against his pubic bones, but her mind and body wanted different things. The desire to breathe and be free of him was replaced by the far more powerful need for his return. So her hands snaked around to the firmness of his buttocks, and she drew him in toward her once again, throwing back her head to receive him. She heard him laugh as he speared her, pushing to the farthest recesses of her throat, pulling back, pounding once again into the velvet softness. Now they were in rhythm and her panic receded as her passion grew. There was a time and a tide, an ebb and flow, a time for breathing and emptiness, a time for stillness and fulfillment. He was making love to her mouth with the same intensity that others had made love to her body. The only difference was the part of her he had chosen for his entrance. Already she was thinking of one thing. How would she deal with the bittersweet ending? As if sensing her concern, he showed her. There was little warning. He didn't speed. He didn't slow. Quite suddenly, he withdrew to the opening of her, and there he waited.

Behind her head his hands were rigid. She was trapped in the vice of him, helpless as she secretly longed to be. All her ecstasy would be his ecstasy, every shuddering spasm of his delight would be her surrogate joy. She stiffened for the moment and her mouth was dry around him as fear and wonder merged before the pent-up torrent that would be released. Everything had stopped in the lull before the storm, all was calm in the hurricane's eye. She didn't dare to move. He didn't deign to. Her eyes, wide with fright and excitement, twisted up toward his face. His, hooded with cruel lust, peered down at her.

And then he nodded. His head jerked up, jerked down, and she knew what it said. He was giving himself permission. This was the advance warning of the honor he would bestow.

Her mouth was a surge tide at sea. It was an undammed mountain river. The waterfall was inside her, and she was drowning in the flood of his liquid desire. There was no time to taste him. It was hardly possible to feel him. There was only the battle for survival in the storm, and the mad, clashing emotions as he pumped her full of the passion that would never be love. She tried to swallow but she couldn't, and he flowed out of her as he poured into her, soaking her, anointing her with his blissful essence. He soared against the walls of her throat, thrusting, pushing, spending himself in her, washing her with the sweet feed of his soul. And all the time his fingers twined in her hair as he rode her mouth, twisting the reins in time to the rough rhythms of his climax.

It was over. Like a rag doll she sagged on the stick of him. Her head lolled sideways, and breath sucked into the vacuum of her lungs. The present was past, but it would never cease to exist, and Melissa Wayne shuddered with the sublime feeling that was as near as she had ever been to commitment.

He slipped from her mouth, and she smiled up at him, awash with his intimacy. Now he would subside, and there should be some small pretense of tenderness, a touch, a caress, in the gentleness charade that manners required. She started to get up, and she reached behind her neck to hold his hands. They had been introduced to each other at last in the most fundamental way possible, in the clash of bodies. Now it was time to build some kind of a relationship on that firmest of foundations.

She opened her mouth to say something. But he held up his hand, demanding silence.

He placed both hands on her shoulders and he turned her around, until she faced away from him toward the edge of the bed. Once more, her heart hammered against her ribs, forcing the blood through her reawakening body. Before, there had been time only to monitor the feelings from the top of her. Now, the messages screamed in from below. She was still half-clothed, but she was damp with desire, hot as the fires of hell in her panties beneath the skirt. Had he the strength to do this now? She dared to hope for it, and the butterflies flew in her stomach as she prepared to obey his most outlandish request. He pushed her forward, firmly but gently, and she lost her balance as she was supposed to, falling toward the edge of the bed. She steadied herself against it, and she waited, bobbing on the adrenaline sea of superreality that surged within her.

He lifted her skirt, unveiling her legs, pushing it up roughly over the back of her thighs, where her stockings merged with the black garter belt. She tried to visualize herself in his eyes as he unwrapped her. Apart from her face, her bottom was her best feature. Pert, rounded, firm yet resilient, and basted honey brown by the sun. The snow-white silk panties, cut like a Brazilian thong, ran in the thinnest pencil line across the divide of her buttocks. He paused to savor the sight of her and she was pleased. And then, quite suddenly, she was frightened as the thought occurred to her. Surely not. Surely he wouldn't . . .

She twisted around to forbid what he had made no move to try, but his hand was on the back of her head, pointing it forward, disallowing her attempt to assert control. Whatever he wanted, he would have. The choice was his alone. She swallowed, and the taste of him lingered, giving her strength at the moment of her passivity. Strung out on the edge of the ultimate abandon, she tried to let go of herself, to give herself to him totally, to do with as he willed. She would ask nothing so that she could receive everything. She must trust that there was mercy in the man that ruled her, and she thrilled with delicious horror at the thought that there might be none.

His hands were on her buttocks. They traced wet patterns on her skin, making circles on the soft surface. They wandered freely into the divide, hooking beneath the silk of the thong, dipping boldly down to feel the shy entrance. Down, down between her trembling legs went the fingers that ruled her, skin diving into the treasure pool, shameless as they investigated her, rude with their boldness. At the lips of her they paused, separated, and then his finger dipped inside, and his thumb reached back to hover at the brink of her most alien place, pushing down gently into the furrowed, yielding skin. He held the core of her, and she couldn't see his face. She was trapped as she had never been trapped before, defenseless, wide open, utterly and completely unable to influence what would happen now.

"Tony, please," she murmured. She didn't know what she meant. She just wanted to say his name. It wasn't a plea for cruelty or kindness. It was a hopeless request for both. Until this terrible, marvelous moment, Melissa Wayne had never known the true meaning of ambivalence. She could actually feel herself pulse beneath his fingers. They would be burning in the caldron of her, melting in the bubbling Jacuzzi fountain of her lust. She pushed back at them, and in response they thrust at her, luxuriating in the welcome of her passive passion. Then, suddenly, they were gone. She was untouched by him, and she pushed out her bottom, searching for some part of his body, arching her back as she thrust her butt into empty air. She ground her pelvis in the void, pleading with him not to leave her alone on the brink of union. She was without pride now, the movie star no longer, just a victim of a need more awful than she had ever known.

"Please, Tony, please," she pleaded, groaning as she ground herself toward him, pushing back with both hands on the edge of the bed to find some part of him to touch her. She looked down, through silver-slicked thighs, and she could see his blue-jeaned legs, the scuffed suede of his ankle boots. He was still there. He hadn't left her. There was still hope. Surely he wouldn't be that cruel. He wouldn't walk away now, would he, leaving her to conjure up her own understudy orgasm? In answer to her unspoken question, Tony Valentino lowered himself into the divide of her buttocks. He didn't slip off her panties. He left them where they were. Throbbing with heat, rock hard once more, she felt him push into the cleavage, down into the wetland, and she moaned her encouragement as she swayed her pelvis from side to side, the better to grip him. The length of him lay against her, bathing in her steam, sizzling on the platter of her bottom. Then, it slid lower until the tip of him threatened her illicit place, hovering above the pulsing ring. The dread filled her. She shook her head in hopeless defiance and in alien longing. There was nothing she could do. It was his decision. Already she was relaxing against his touch. Her muscles were his friends, not his enemies, and slippery with her longing, they were barriers no more. For long seconds he paused at the forbidden entrance, flirting with the pain, playing with the possibility, sampling the pleasure of the humiliation. He leaned against it, felt it give, heard her juddering moan of aquiescence and terror. She felt his stomach muscles tighten across her butt. She sensed his body draw tight like the string of a bow. All his energy and power seemed to surge into the part of him that threatened her, and she readied herself as best she could for the assault to come. He lifted away from her, the hammer drawing back for the mighty blow, and her whole body was the nail . . . and the nether place where the tip of him rested was its quivering, defenseless head.

When he came at her, it was as if he had been shot from the barrel of a gun. The breath was crushed from her lungs as his chest crashed down on her back. Her bottom shook with the force of his momentum, and she fell forward pinioned to the edge of the bed by the power of his velocity. But at the very last millisecond he changed his direction. He swooped down, and up, and the weapon of his passion rampaged in glory into her dripping core. She was spared. But at the same time she was executed. His sword had speared her to its hilt. She was split apart. She was full, wrapped tight around the invader like the second skin she wanted to be. No longer did she have a body of her own. She was the clothing of another's body. She was his home and his shelter. She was the flesh-and-blood prison for the part of him that must never leave.

The orgasm was the sky through which she flew. There was no waiting, no savoring, no building toward a conclusion. There was only the truth of the climax. It was instant. It merged with the moment of his entrance, and by the time he collided with the roof of her world, the celestial choirs were lost in descants of swooping, soaring ecstasy. She was on her knees as she should be at this moment of supreme beauty, and she screamed into the wild music, burying her head in her hands, as the tears poured down her cheeks.

Then, in the jingle-jangle aftermath, there was a new feeling to be felt. Slowly but surely the sobs of joy turned into something else. Her head was buried deep in the far-from-clean Valentino sheets, but Melissa Wayne had something to say.

"Tony . . . you bastard," she growled.

TWELVE

Melissa Wayne lay back on the sun bed on the pool terrace of her home and looked out over Beverly Hills. It was hot at the top of Benedict Canyon, but the air was fresh and clear and she could see a patch of silver ocean across the rolling hills. She adjusted the volume of the Walkman until the Stones were rolling into her mind on muffled steel wheels, and she tried to make sense of the chaos that had turned her world upside down. There was only one word for it. Actually two. Tony Valentino. She had never thought it would happen. She was too selfish. She was too ambitious. Her career came before sex, before everything, or at least it had until the extraordinary *East of Eden* evening when she had finally met her match. She ran her hand across her flat stomach, her fingers trailing among the downy hairs over the brown skin and the firm muscles, and she remembered the touch of him. It was so cruel. It was careless. It was rough and unloving, devoid of respect. It was hungry, greedy, completely lacking in tenderness. When he touched her his hands roamed free like marauding conquerors, interested only in gratification, and she felt helpless and unloved. It was dreadful. It was humiliating. But it was also the most exciting and erotic sexual experience that she had ever had. She knew what was happening. She was experiencing what her former lovers had known. In her increasingly exotic S&M world, the boys had always been the toys. She, the superstar, had always been the *S*. They, the miserable males, had inevitably been *M*. A touch of the whip, the key turning in the lock of a handcuff, lovers chained to the foot of her bed while she slept with a rival, had been the stuff of her games. There had been tongue baths, and cunning torture, tattoos saying embarrassing things in embarrassing places, and always the beautiful boys of beautysville had queued up to be used by the star for the status it bestowed and for the wild, alien delights of submission.

Tony had forced her to make the switch. She had fought against it, but desire had been too strong and the power of his persona had thrust her into a sexual role she had never imagined she would play. She was obsessed by him. He was there all the time, in her dreams at night, in the more fevered dreams that came by day. Latham had pulled Tony out of the Broadway play, and his part had been taken by an understudy to the fury of the ticket holders. He had moved to Malibu to help with the preproduction of Latham's first Cosmos movie, and so now he could and would swoop down on Melissa's house, stride into her bedroom, and drag her from bed to make "love" anywhere, anyway, anytime he chose. Then he would leave. He would simply disappear, and she wouldn't be able to find him to scream at him and tell him what a pig he was. The hours would pass, and then the days, until she could only pray that the noise in the driveway was the crunching of his bike's wheels, that his was the hand on her door, that the rough voice in the dark night belonged to him, ordering her to please him as if she existed to do nothing else. Sometimes he would have her standing up by the side of the bed, not bothering to undress, merely undoing his fly and using her like a cheap envelope to receive his lust. At others he would take her on the floor of her clothes closet and then leave her, locked in for the rest of the night, awash with his sex, until her embarrassed maid freed her the next morning. He made love to her in the pool; leaning over the leather seat of his bike; in the kitchen, standing against the cold door of the kitchen fridge. He wouldn't wait for her orgasm. He would leave after his, and the delicious humiliation tied her up in the silken chains of human bondage as it was destined to do, until her very mind was a prisoner and her will enslaved. For two terrible, wonderful weeks the sensual torture had continued, and Melissa Wayne was unhinged by it.

She took a deep breath as the sun beat down on her gorgeous body. Every sound made her start. Every noise made her salivate. Every cracking twig, each creak of furniture, every footstep turned on the capricious fountain inside her. She was a Pavlovian dog, and her bell was no longer Tony Valentino. It was the thought of him. But at the same time, Melissa Wayne had reservoirs of strength. She was flirting with the boundaries of love addiction, but she had not yet reached them. She was that toughest of all creatures, a successful actress in Hollywood. And there was a part of her that could still say no. Right now, the game of obsession suited her. She was between parts, and she liked to use her brief vacations for mind and body expansion of one kind or another. It was all part of the vital life experiences that no actress could afford to miss out on. You needed range in your repertoire. So, although Tony Valentino loomed over her mind like the Phantom of the Opera, there was an extent to which she was playing the role of love slave rather than actually living it. And that had one curious, but absolutely compelling, result. There was a part of Melissa Wayne that would never forgive Tony Valentino for the way he was treating her. Her body might lust for his passion. Her mind vowed vengeance for it. Somewhere down the line, when the time was right, the star would punish the zero for his lèse-majesté. It might be achieved in a groveling role reversal, in which Tony himself was forced into the part he had cast for her. More likely, it would take another form. She would simply destroy him. It wasn't personal. It was a power trip. It would be fun to blot him out and watch him hurting. It would be nice to see him cry, as his world fell apart and bad things happened to those he loved. It would be delicious to watch his dreams die and his soul burn, to see his essence wither and perish like a leaf in an oven. Yes, he should realize that the stakes were high in any game he played with Melissa Wayne. And her heart beat faster as she contemplated the trouble she could cause for the boy who had dared to be her sadistic lover. The intercom by the sun bed buzzed once. She picked up the receiver.

"Damn! I forgot. Okay, send her out to the pool. Oh, better bring some coffee, and some champagne about an hour later."

She banged the receiver down and reached for the terry bathrobe. Jeez! What a time for an interview. But was any time good? She sat up and pulled on the robe as a small, determined figure erupted from the dark of the house.

Emma Guinness marched across the grass toward the star. She wore a floral dress whose vast rhododendrons dwarfed anything that could be found in nature. An outsize flower tried unsuccessfully to cover each enormous breast, and the unfortunate pattern was continued on hideous shoes. She tripped over a sprinkler head but didn't take her eyes off her target as she narrowly failed to fall.

"Hi," she said cheerfully.

"Hi," agreed Melissa, with less enthusiasm.

"I'm sorry I'm early," said Emma, hovering over the star like a human bouquet.

"Actually, I'd completely forgotten you were coming," said Melissa, who liked to get the upper hand early in an interview. Later you could always stoop graciously to the level of the interviewee. At the start, it was best to establish superiority.

"Is it a bad time?"

"It's always a bad time for an interview, but no, it's fine." Melissa laughed to take the sting out of her words.

She motioned to the chair beside her, and Emma sank into it, notepad across ample lap, the Beverly Hills sun threatening to wilt her flowers.

"How's Tony Valentino?" said Emma Guinness.

"What!" said Melissa.

"I heard you were seeing him." Emma Guinness never accepted the role of second string for long. She had known her question would put Melissa on the defensive.

"I hope this interview hasn't started yet," said Melissa coldly.

"No, of course not. We're off the record. I only asked out of personal interest. It fascinates me how a little guy like that can travel so far so fast."

Melissa's face relaxed into a smile. The Guinness girl was refreshing. It was very un-Hollywood to give so much away. Being rude about a Melissa Wayne boyfriend was a dangerous game. Guinness couldn't have known that Melissa would share the sentiments she had just expressed.

"You think Valentino is a little guy?" said Melissa. "After selling all those magazines, the rave reviews on Broadway, and saving the billionaire's life?"

"Listen, he's got a pretty body, loot fixed the reviews, and saving Latham was luck. He can act a bit, I admit that. But you know the media. He's this month's flavor. Not next month's."

Emma's face twisted as she spoke. She couldn't keep the bitterness out of the words.

Melissa laughed. "I'm not so sure you're right about that. It looks like he's going to star in a Melissa Wayne movie."

Suddenly, all Emma Guinness's color was in her dress. Her face was white.

"What?"

Melissa smiled to see the effect of her words. Emma Guinness might run the most successful Latham magazine. Information-wise, however, she was clearly out of the company loop. And what the hell had Tony done to upset the flower bed? Something pretty unspeakable, that was for sure. Melissa was beginning to enjoy herself. Who was interviewing whom?

"Yeah, it's sort of secret, but you work for Latham, so I guess you can know. He's scheduling a new slate of movies at Cosmos, and the first one is a Melissa Wayne vehicle, with Tony Valentino supporting. He has some crazy idea about getting that dyke bitch Pat Parker to direct, but I'll undo that part of the deal."

"You can't allow that," spluttered Emma Guinness.

The Wayne eyebrows arched up. People didn't tell her what she could and couldn't do.

"What I mean is, surely it isn't a very good idea to risk your career appearing in a movie with an unknown like Tony, and especially with Pat. They were together, you know . . ."

The horror was behind Emma's eyes. Tony as a rave centerfold was one thing. Tony as a hot Broadway actor was another. But Tony as a movie star was something else altogether. It couldn't be permitted. It mustn't be.

"I think," said Melissa grandly, "that it would take more than one poor movie to 'risk' my career. Anyway, I think Tony would be very good in the part. It's made for him. The chemistry between us is . . . well, interesting. It's about a young would-be actor who gets obsessed with a successful actress he meets in Malibu. Hardly a reach for Tony, I would imagine, and the younger-man/slightly-older-woman thing is hot right now. I think it'll play. My box office'll make sure it opens. It'll be the first production of the revamped studio. That means there'll be no skimping on the advertising budget and no problem with distribution. Billy Diller's done a steamy script. Could have been hotter, I guess, but one can always get those things right on the night . . ."

As if to emphasize that aspect of the deal, Melissa threw back the bathrobe and allowed the sun at her body. Emma's eyes crawled jealously over it. It was another flesh field that Valentino had harvested. Those hands had felt this body. These hips had ground against his. Was his seed in there now, the legacy of last night's passion? She shifted in her seat at the unsettling thought, and the Wagnerian music began to play inside her head. God, not *The Ring*. It was bad news when she heard that. It was so real. It wasn't like a song in her head, a tune on her brain. It was like a whole sodding orchestra in there, tuning up. The shrink in London had been quite interested in her orchestra, especially the fact that she heard it loudest when things upset her badly. He had wondered if it was an auditory hallucination, and had put her on a quietener pill called Fluanxol. She'd only gone to see the silly old fart because she'd had trouble sleeping and the stupid G.P. had suggested it. But the tablets had helped. It was a pity she hadn't brought some with her to America.

"It might make him a star," said Emma Guinness, her voice wrapped in horror.

"Why would that matter? What have you got against him? He's not very nice to women, is he?" Melissa sounded amused, but her tones were soft and inviting. With the skill of a superb actress, she intimated that any confessing that Emma might do would be to a sympathetic and far from powerless ear.

Emma cocked her head to one side as she picked up the message. *The Ring* had become *Tannhäuser*, loud and insistent, the horns blaring dangerously in her head.

"He behaved very badly to me once," she said at last.

"Sometimes he tries to do that to me," said Melissa in the understatement of her week. She actually had his finger marks in bruises on her butt. Her tongue licked nervous lips at the thought of it.

"He does?" said Emma carefully, trying to hide the hope in her voice. Two important women had been treated badly by a man. It was the stuff of which evil alliances were made. One thing was certain. Emma and Melissa working in tandem could bring tears to the Valentino eyes. *Tannhäuser* was louder now, its strains soaring grandly through her mind. She almost wanted to conduct the music.

"Sometimes," said Emma softly through the Wagner, "I dream of paying him back."

"Do you ever think of how you might do it?" said Melissa with anaconda innocence.

"Just dreams," laughed Emma mirthlessly. "Unlike you, I'm not in a position of power over him."

"Power?" said Melissa.

"Yes, the ultimate power. You're the star. The only thing he wants is to be one. You can stop that. You could ruin his movie career before it ever takes off . . . if you wanted to."

"You mean in the movie we're making together."

"Yes." Emma laughed.

"Ha. Ha," laughed Melissa, "that would be funny."

What a good joke, they agreed. Nothing had been said. Nothing had been promised. No commitment had been made. It was just two girls laughing about a tricky boy who was a bit too big for his boots. No more. No less. Like *hell!*

"What would be *really* funny," giggled Emma, "would be if Pat Parker had to direct you and Tony doing steamy love scenes. She's potty about him, and deep down I think he's still gone on her. Can you just imagine that?"

Melissa's smile had gone cold. Yes, Valentino probably would still love the serious-minded photographer with her artistic airs and graces. His treatment of Melissa certainly had nothing to do with love, and much more to do with disgust. It was as if he were punishing her for her role as a female sex symbol. By humiliating her, Valentino was avenging himself on all the women, perhaps especially on Pat Parker, with whom he was still deeply involved despite some silly lovers' tiff. Pat Parker. What was it the cow had said to her on the Latham boat? "I thought maybe you'd been beamed in from Fantasy-land." She'd topped that by screwing Valentino on the beach. Mmmmm . . . Pat Parker was not a favorite person. There was poetry in the suggestion of the limey who looked like a wreath.

The coffee arrived, but already Melissa Wayne felt like champagne. She said so, and she wasn't at all surprised to find that Emma Guinness felt like it too. The interview remained, but the interview was no longer important. The secret alliance was.

"Okay, Melissa, what do you want me to say about you in my magazine?" said Emma.

"Whatever your magazine wants to say about me," said Melissa.

And they both laughed in the bright Beverly Hills sunshine, because both had received good news from each other, the good news that would be bad news for Tony Valentino and Pat Parker.

"You deliver on promises, don't you?" shouted Pat above the noise of the helicopter's engine.

"Only when they make sense." Dick Latham mouthed the words, refusing to compete with the roar of the chopper. He slipped his hand into Pat's and they watched as the jet-copter came to rest on the graded pad, the wind of its blades ruffling their hair and fanning their faces. The pilot cut the motor. Silence descended on the canyon. Doors opened, and in seconds the passengers were walking down steps to the bright red dirt of the newly bulldozed landing strip. They peered around in the blazing sunlight as they accustomed themselves to the alien environment of the deserted mountains. They carried briefcases, cameras, notepads, and, with the brittle bonhomie of their species, they tried to pretend that they were at home when they weren't. Jesus! What a place for a press conference—stuffed up in the heavens, so near to civilization and yet so far. Latham had better deliver on his promise of hard news. If there was any letdown they would rain on his parade for a year and a day—despite the freebies and the handouts, the bribes and the bountiful bimbos and all the other arm-twisting, mouth-watering delights that the Lathams of this world showered on the fourth estate.

Dick Latham walked toward them. Behind him Tommy Havers consulted his clipboard. The mountaintop press conference was coming together like clockwork. This was the fifth incoming flight of the morning, and there were two more on the way. Half a mile up the hill fifty journalists were already getting plastered on the Krug and bourbon in the sort of high-end tent a genuine Bedouin would never want to leave. It looked like a hundred percent turnout and this wasn't just a California thing. The nationals were there in force and it hadn't been easy to get them there. Havers had walked the tightrope between whetting jaded press appetites and giving the game away. Luckily, over the years he'd never squandered the capital of believability, and the media had learned to trust him. Even NBC had sent a crew. Soon, with luck, Brokaw's locked jaw would be struggling to tell the world what Latham wanted it to hear.

"Hi, Lawrence. Comfortable trip?" Latham called out to a *Wall Street Journal* scribbler he recognized. The journalist screwed up his eyes in the glare and peered suspiciously back. He wasn't particularly impressed at being singled out for recognition by the billionaire. A few years back he'd scored a Pulitzer, and in the American pecking order writers who'd won those deferred to nobody. Anyway, one thing was clear. In laying on a bonanza like this, Latham was admitting that he needed something. The *Journal* scribe was about to be a brown-nosee, not a brown-noser.

"I hope this isn't some environmentalist shit," he said, threateningly.

Latham laughed. If they only knew. "No, Lawrence, I can safely say that this hasn't to do with the environment, and that's the way I'd like it to remain."

Havers shepherded the press toward a trio of jeeps that would carry them on the bumpy half-mile ride to the mountain-peak marquee.

Pat kicked at the red soil. "Is this where you're going to build your house?" she said. "It's one helluva pad."

Latham avoided her eyes when he answered. "Yes, it is big," he said evasively. Before the day was over she'd know the truth. How would she deal with it? She thought the purpose of the press conference was to announce publicly the reincarnation of Cosmos, and to reveal the details of its first daring movie schedule, including the film that she would direct. She didn't know that the dynamite had been saved for the punch line. The real news would be the studio's location. They would all be standing on it—back lots, front lots, wardrobe, props, production offices—all nestling happily in the middle of the once beautiful Malibu hills that Alabama had spent his life trying to protect. It wouldn't have to be spelled out. These ink merchants might look like a load of street people, but they had the noses of claret connoisseurs when it came to sniffing out the information that would sell the papers for which they worked. The moment they hit Pacific Coast Highway, they would telephone their offices and the story would break. The next person they would all call would be Alabama, Pat Parker's friend and mentor. It would be make-your-mind-up time for the girl whose body he could still feel against his. On the one hand would be the friend she admired, the moral high ground, the nature she now loved to photograph. On the other would be the billionaire she had bedded, and the brilliant career in movies he could open and close like the covers of a book. He smiled grimly as he mapped out her dilemma in his mind. Which way would she go? With a frisson of surprise he realized that he really cared.

"What style are you going to build in?" asked Pat.

Damn! The house again, the house that would be a sound stage.

"Come on," said Latham, hurrying toward one of the jeeps. "We ought to get back to the others. Melissa can't be left alone for a moment without making a scene, and God knows what Tony'll be saying to the news hounds—something uncomfortable, uncompromising, and uncalled for, I expect."

He watched her wince as he played the Tony card. When that hit the table, all desire for architectural discussion should disappear. It did.

"You made Tony's dream come true. Was it because he saved your life?"

"Does there always have to be a reason? Don't you think he's right for the part? I do. I thought you did."

He spoke sharply to emphasize that he was looking at things objectively, that he was a businessman, the kind of guy who wouldn't let personal factors influence an important decision. Pat laughed to show she saw through the bullshit.

"Listen, Dick. He's incredibly talented. But there are lots of actors out there who are that. Ditto directors. You're way out on a limb, and everyone knows it. I happen to think you're right, and the trust you've put in us won't be misplaced, but you're winging it. You must have reasons for doing that. Personal ones."

She squeezed his arm like a lover could. Not that she did love him. She still wasn't sure whether she even liked him. But she *was* close to him. The body memories said so.

Dick laughed ruefully. It was a new feeling to have someone around who could see inside him. Normally that might be irritating . . . and dangerous. With Pat Parker it was fun . . . and dangerous.

"Listen, motivation is pretty much of a mystery, despite what the psychobabblers say. But yes, I suppose there are noncommercial reasons for using both you and Tony. I guess I want to show everyone, and myself, that I can do this thing. Making movies is supposed to be rocket science, but it's really smoke and mirrors. I reckon my gut is as good at predicting how something will play as anyone else's. Okay, I could guarantee an opening by using Cruise, Hanks, or Murphy, but that hardly makes me a hero, just a megabuck banker. And ultimately an opening doesn't guarantee a flick will have legs. If my show runs, *our* show, I'll be the only one on the planet who predicted it. Sure I'm taking a hell of a gamble, but there's a window of opportunity here, and I'll only get this one chance. It's the first movie of the revamped Cosmos slate. The distributors, the reviewers, even the public will have to suspend common sense and give believing a try, just this one time. The curiosity quotient will be phenomenal. At least it'll get sampled. That's in the cake. If it's brilliant, I'm a star. If it's not, I'm a rich hick who went Hollywood, to give his glands and his ego an outing. That's the way I like to live. On the edge, but with insurance. Your skill, Tony's skill, are my secret weapons. And it ain't insider trading to profit from the information."

"It should be. I'm going to reinvent the movie genre. I'm going to teach the world how to watch. They'll see things they've never seen," said Pat excitedly.

She climbed into the back of the jeep, swinging her long legs up, the blue denim of her shirt sweeping open to show most of her braless breasts. Dick Latham swallowed. Her peep show was totally innocent, but it added emphasis to her words. Teaching the world the art of voyeurism seemed suddenly well within the Pat Parker reach.

They set off, bumping, grinding, winding toward the sky. Pat was quiet. Saying it was one thing. Delivering the goods was another. You had to believe in yourself, but at the same time the memories of past artistic struggles lingered to highlight the difficulties. She would have to learn a new medium on the job. She would have to handle Melissa Wayne, whose reputation as a troublemaker was as legendary as her mistrust and hatred of women. And she would have to deal with Tony Valentino—deal with his prickly pride, with his hatred of her, deal with the pain of the past, and the certain pain of the future as she directed his on-screen passion with the woman who was already his off-screen lover. Then there was Allison, psychologically wounded by Tony, as she, Pat, had been wounded. Why the hell had someone stuck her in the movie, and why did the script call for her suicide? Jeez! Life had better not imitate art on this one. And moviemaking was a deadline business. There could be no luxuriating in the angst of "block," no hanging around while inspiration slept late. She would have to crack her whip, and the wild celluloid animals would have to jump on cue if the whole shebang wasn't to end in blood, tears, and a horrible destruction. So she took a deep breath and hung on to the side of the jeep as it threatened to wobble off the corkscrew road, and the delicious dread and the terrified excitement filled up her mind.

"*New Celebrity* went off with a big bang," said a journalist, turning around from the front seat of the Wrangler.

"Yeah," smiled Dick Latham, as if it was no big deal. "We're way ahead of the old one on subscriptions and advertising already. It's a hit, and you ain't seen nothing yet."

"What's Emma Guinness going to do for an encore after male nudes?"

"You'll have to ask her. She'll be at lunch."

Pat swung around. "What's Emma doing here?"

The spear of guilt lanced into her. She hadn't forgotten the time on Broad Beach when the feisty Englishwoman had admitted her plans for surfers and Dick Latham—not necessarily in that order. Emma had been her friend, and she had hired Pat for more money than she had ever imagined she was worth. In return, in the Canal Bar, Pat had allowed the man that Emma daydreamed of marrying to make his moves on her. It hadn't needed a Columbo to get the picture. While Emma had been bored to death by Tommy Havers, Dick Latham had poured his charm all over her. The Guinness eyes had narrowed as they registered the slight, and without being able to do anything about it, Pat Parker had watched an enemy in embryo grow in front of her. It made her uneasy. Emma Guinness was a dangerous woman to cross. Beneath the joky malice of her exterior lurked the iceberg capacity for genuine hatred. When talking about her English class enemies, Pat had seen its tip. Now Pat herself was a Guinness target, no question. It was only a matter of time before the arrows came winging in.

"Emma likes to be where the action is," said Dick.

"Likes to be where you are," corrected Pat. If Emma was to be an adversary, Pat had better start her own undermining operation.

"Same thing," said Latham easily, no stranger to the sin of pride.

"We'd better keep her away from Tony," said Pat.

"And you," added Latham with a laugh. His response was purposefully ambiguous. Emma away from Pat? Pat away from Tony?

"Here we are," said Pat, ignoring the double entendre.

The jeep crunched to a halt at the very top of the world. The marquee had been set up on a graded platform at the tip of the mountain ridge. The vista that unfolded around them was spectacular. You could see to Santa Barbara, west to the coast of Catalina Island, east across the Valley to the Santa Susana and San Gabriel mountains, south to the sparkling Santa Monica Bay. It was a forever view, breathtaking in its bright loveliness, and the hills shimmered in a heatscape cooled at the edges by the blue of the ocean. Down below, in the canyon, another helicopter was winging in, and hawks rode the thermal currents in competition, swooping and soaring above the chaparral in lofty disdain for the outsiders who had disturbed their tranquillity.

The hum of animated conversation erupted from the tent, as the tongues of the word merchants loosened with the booze. Nobody was much concerned with the breathtaking view, despite the rolled-up sides of the marquee. Latham and Pat plunged into the melee, the jeeploads of semifresh journalists led by Havers in their wake.

A large conversational knot separated to reveal Melissa Wayne at its core, incredibly edible in a Gaultier pin-striped miniskirt and soft leather jacket.

"Hi, Dick," gushed Melissa. "Hello, Pat," she managed in an entirely different tone of voice. She hadn't forgotten the confrontations on the yacht trip and at the Canal Bar, but all sorts of things had happened since then. She had signed for the Cosmos movie that Pat would direct. She had been used and abused by Tony, who'd had some sort of relationship with the photographer. And Pat, and presumably Tony, clearly had unspecified secret deals with the billionaire, which explained his dangerous decision to stick them in his movie. It was enough of a psycho minefield to make walking carefully a necessity. Later, when she was carrying the flick on the broad back of her name, there would be time for starry fireworks. In the meantime, she would keep her usually stratospheric profile at sea level.

"Hi, Melissa. I'm really pleased we're going to be working together," lied Pat. She looked around. Where was Tony? The bitch had screwed him. He'd screwed the bitch. Which one did she hate the most?

"Tony's over there," said Melissa with psychic accuracy.

Pat's eyes followed the Wayne finger as if they were attached to it by string. Immediately her head snapped back as she realized too late that she had been wearing her feelings on her sleeve.

Melissa's smile of triumph said most of it. Tony Valentino's screw-you expression of disgust as he caught her eye had said the rest.

In retaliation, she slipped her hand into Dick Latham's. The moneybags are mine, said her gesture.

Inside, she was worried. How the hell would this get done? She had to make peace with Wayne for the sake of the movie. She had to mend bridges with Tony for the sake of . . . Well, never mind.

"What did you think of the script?" Pat turned to Melissa. "Please, let's be professional," said her eyes. "Let's bury the crap. Let's make a movie they'll all remember."

"I signed, didn't I? It's okay. It's not great, but it's fine. We can redo a lot of my stuff."

Pat shuddered. The script of *Malibu* wasn't set in cement—no script was—but Melissa Wayne wielding a pen was a nerve-racking thought. Melissa Wayne rewriting her own part was far worse. Still, this wasn't the time to say so. Press receptions were about harmony. If it couldn't be faked at this early stage, then a disaster of cosmic proportions was definite.

"There you are," said Emma Guinness. She smiled the smile of the Damien child. "Pat and Dick. Dick and Pat. All my favorite people. Hello, Melissa. Where's the brilliant James Dean remount? Pouting in a corner somewhere, I expect, besieged by kamikaze women who saw his willie in *New Celebrity*. *What* a success they were, those pictures, weren't they, Pat? Didn't you just love them, Melissa? Almost as good as the real thing, I imagine, but I'm no expert. Dear me, no! Ha ha! I have to defer to others on that one. Goodness, what fun this is. Movie time. The big league. The genuine nitty-gritty. And us poor journalists allowed to hover around the edges of the action. *What* excitement! I feel quite *faint*."

"Can you get me a drink, Emma," ordered Dick Latham abruptly, ignoring the waiter who hovered at his shoulder. "Oh, and get a glass of champagne for Pat, will you?"

The dismissal was absolute. Nobody made fun of Dick Latham and his friends, however well the abuse was camouflaged in the clothes of humor. Emma's face fell like an elevator, as she realized her miscalculation. But inside she was strangely elated. She felt weird, detached, other-worldly. It was as if, at some fundamental level, nothing mattered anymore. All the scheming, all the cunning plans had added up to zero. She had arrived but she still wasn't *there*. She had made a brilliant success of the magazine. She was the toast of New York. Yet she was the gofer who got the drinks for the billionaire and his screw. She had money, acclamation, minions to serve her, but her true objective had eluded her. She was no closer than she had ever been to the global revenge she wanted so desperately. Her enemies survived and flourished—all those hated English girls who had humiliated her, Tony Valentino for whom she dreamed of a special hell, and now Pat Parker, who had hijacked the money mountain that Emma had intended to marry. It wasn't enough to be brilliant. Mere brutality didn't deliver the goods. While she played the game by the rules, however well, she could never win. The realization broke over Emma Guinness like the surf on a lonely beach. To get her own way she would have to up the ante. There was room for moderation no longer. Drastic situations demanded drastic solutions. From this moment on, she wouldn't shrink from them. She would sign her personal pact with the devil, and whatever the price she would pay it. So she smiled to cover the evil that bubbled so suddenly from her soul, and she walked away through the crowd to collect the poison chalices for the enemies she would destroy.

"Dick!" Pat's tone of voice said he had gone too far. The smile on her lips said he had hardly gone far enough.

He smiled back at her, proud of his cruelty, secure in his strength. East Coast people weren't supposed to be like this. Up-front ruthlessness was an L.A. thing. Way out West, brutality was the instrument that measured the diameter of your balls. But Dick Latham had already adjusted to life on the rim. He was in Rome and he was out-Romaning the Romans.

"So, Melissa, I'm thrilled that we managed to talk your agent into letting you do our movie," said Latham. He smiled at his conceit. When the old owl had seen the size of the check, he'd had to pop a popper for his angina.

"It'll be *fun*," gushed Melissa. She smiled seductively at Latham, wickedly at Pat. Her "fun" sounded like the kind cats had with mice. "Where will we be shooting? Right here in Malibu, I guess."

"For the location scenes, yes. Until we can build a new studio, the inside stuff'll happen at Universal. I've done a deal with MCA."

"Where exactly in the desert are you building the new Cosmos?" said Pat suddenly.

"Yes, yes," said Latham, rubbing his hands together to conceal the inappropriateness of his response.

"Where?" said Pat sharply. The premonition was pricking at her.

"That was a topic I wanted to save for the press conference," said Dick Latham after a pregnant pause.

Pat frowned. His eyes had flicked away from her. He was hiding something.

"I think we ought to mingle a bit," he said. "Spread the good word about how brilliant we all are. Remember, this is L.A. County. Understatement is a sign of mental instability. When you're talking telephone-number money, don't forget the area codes. The locals always divide by six anyway. Tell the truth and they'll think you're a minus quantity."

He laughed brightly and disappeared into the crowd.

"Isn't he great?" Pat laughed.

"Isn't he *rich!*" countered Melissa.

"Look, Melissa. We've got to work together," said Pat, taking the bull by the horns. "Can we try to be friends, for the time it takes to make the movie at least?"

"Friends! Friends?" Melissa Wayne curled her tongue around the word as if it were a dirty one. "There are only two sorts of people in my life." She sneered. "The ones I don't like, and the ones I go to bed with. Sometimes they overlap."

Pat shook her head as if the cause were lost. She stuck out her chin. If Wayne wanted hardball she could have it. Bullies often reacted better to the stick than the carrot.

"Is Tony Valentino an overlap?"

Melissa Wayne's head shot back. Her cheeks reddened. Damn! She'd been trying to keep that part of her life under wraps.

"Mind your own business," she replied. She turned and walked away, but as she did so, she was running over the plans she had made for the beautiful boy who had dared to abuse her.

"Your drink, madam." Emma Guinness's voice was thick with sarcasm. She held out the glass of champagne to Pat.

Pat debated whether to apologize to Emma for Latham's rudeness, but the glint in the Guinness eyes told her not to bother. A sign of weakness might make things worse. "Thanks, Emma," she said, reaching for the glass. The champagne never got to her outstretched fingers. Emma pitched forward, pretending a passing waiter had caught her from behind. The Krug splashed from the glass as it was meant to, soaking Pat's hand, her wrist, and the John Richmond tattoo on the long sleeve of her shirt.

"I'm *so* sorry. I'm afraid I'll never make a waitress," intoned Emma Guinness theatrically, the smile twisting her features. "Where's Dick? Has the lord and master deserted his mistress?"

Fire blazed in Pat Parker's belly.

"Listen, Emma, don't give me that bullshit. You and Dick had nothing going. You work for him, that's all. Anything that existed was all in your mind. It's the best place for it."

She waved her hand up and down to shake off the champagne. God, the girl was a chameleon. She was fun, and bright and amusing . . . and then she was this.

"You work for him too, Pat. I just hadn't realized you did it on the horizontal. There's a name for that kind of job, isn't there? For sure it isn't photographer—but it does begin with a *p*."

"Careful, Emma. Your ugliness is beginning to show. I mean the inside stuff." Pat's eyes dusted the horrendous purple silk bugle-beaded coat-and-shirt disaster that was Emma's sartorial statement of the day. Thank the Lord, Guinness had nothing to do with her movie. No way could Pat have been diplomatic after a remark like that. She'd been called a few things in her time. A hooker had never been one of them.

Emma Guinness started to contract. She made tight fists. The color drained from her champagne-reddened face. Her lips were tight and mean around her mouth. She'd gotten the message. It was a taste dig. Through the years she had acquired a hypersensitive allergy to those. She searched the word processor that was her brain for the appropriate insult, but already she was moving past mere language. The bitch was daring to defy her, after throwing a wrench into the delicate machinery of the Guinness future. All the ancient hated ones were suddenly lumped together in the parcel of flesh and bone that stood before her. Pat had become Victoria Brougham and the *Class* enemies of England. She was Tony Valentino and the Nantucket/Vassar girls of old *Celebrity*. She was the entire world that existed only to thwart Emma Guinness and to deny her her rightful place in the sun. The conversation roared and receded in Emma's mind. The Wagner thundered in her head. Nothing seemed real anymore. There were only blood-red colors, and bright sharp smells, and at the tips of her fingers the space-program lacquered nails tingled like the talons of a tiger at bay. She could rip this girl apart. Before they hauled her from the twitching body, she could rake those cheeks past plastic surgery. It would feel so good to plow the bleeding furrows, to gouge the eyes Shakespeare-style, to hear the screams of the stricken enemy. That was where she was going. She didn't care any more about cheap, clever remarks. They were for silly, civilized people who played the game by the rules. Now, she was black as the night, and in league with the devil and his secret ways. She was going mad, of course. But she was embracing her madness. That was the point. To be superhuman you had to soar above convention. You had to dream crazy dreams, and you had to dare to do dreadful things. You didn't fear retribution, because society's miserable revenge was painless compared to the agony of not having everything that you wanted. She was free at last, swimming unencumbered in the icy lake of pure hatred, and, at the moment of her weird epiphany, Emma Guinness cooled down.

"I'm sorry," she said. "I didn't mean all that. I think I must have had too much to drink."

Pat, astonished, tried to catch up with the mood change.

"That's okay. I understand. Forget it." She managed a lukewarm smile.

"I'm sorry Dick wasn't here. He'd have loved that little conversation." Emma Guinness laughed. The charm was back. The poison gas that had bubbled from the swamp of her id was blowing away in the wind.

Pat could hardly believe the character change. Mentally, she filed it away. One thing was clear. Emma Guinness was near to some sort of breakdown. Underneath the brilliance, her psyche was in ruins. She was terribly unstable, and yet nobody who hadn't witnessed the outburst could be made to believe how dangerous she had become. Should she try to warn Latham? Hell, no! He'd be suspicious of her motives. Anyway, Latham needed about as much protection as a black widow spider needed from its unfortunate mate.

For now, however, she would hold out the olive branch.

"Listen, Emma. You know Dick and I aren't really . . . an item. I mean . . ."

"Well, you did a little better than a john in a cloud over Wisconsin." Emma laughed, dreaming of deathrays, smelling the blood.

"Less novel. More mundane." Pat laughed, conjuring up visions of straitjackets, men in white coats, Thorazine syringes.

"Hi, Pat. Hi, Emma. Remember me? Allison Vanderbilt." Allison Vanderbilt did not look like someone who would be easily forgotten, nor did her tone assume she had been. She was coolly beautiful in a cream Alaïa pantsuit, and her ostensibly humble demeanor was a class weapon she carried like a club.

"Hello, Allison. How wonderful to see you," said Pat, grateful for the interruption. "Isn't it terrific you're working on the show? I love your part. You're going to be perfect. Is your family pleased?"

Somehow the Vanderbilt family was a topic that hovered like an aura around Allison.

"Oh, they think it's a tremendous joke. Deep down, I think Mommy's quite impressed. She has this crush on Sylvester Stallone, and now she imagines I'll be inviting him to stay. Daddy keeps boasting about some starlet he used to take to El Morocco way back in the Stone Age, and he's threatening to turn the orchid house into a screening room. He actually warned me about casting couches, you know . . ."

"It's great to see you so happy," said Pat.

"Have you seen Tony?" said Emma Guinness, congenitally opposed to happiness wherever she found it.

The fleeting expression of pain across the Vanderbilt features was her reward.

"Yes, he's over there. I'm so pleased we're going to be working together," said Allison with unnecessary sincerity. Pat was much easier to like now that she and Tony were no longer lovers.

"You and Melissa should be great chemistry," said Emma, "especially with Pat stirring the mix." Nobody felt the urge to agree with that.

Pat had had enough. "I haven't said hello to Tony yet," she said quickly. "I mustn't ignore my leading man."

Her heart bumping around in her boots, she cut loose from Emma and Allison and aimed herself through the crowd at Tony.

Tony Valentino was equal parts agony and ecstasy. The press reception was a hell constructed with him in mind. The reason for it was sweet dreams. He shifted from one foot to another and tried to say things that were both true and inoffensive, while around him the hardboiled press veterans lobbed their bombs. What did it feel like to be a male pinup? What would his dead mother have thought? Were male sex symbols airheads, like female ones? Why did the possession of a passable body suggest that the boy bimbo should be able to *act?* He sipped on the tomato juice, breathed deeply, and tried to keep the Latham faith. His instructions had been straightforward. Don't blow it. Don't bust nose. Play Saint Sebastian until there were no arrows left. Dick Latham's advice had been polite, but there had been a threat in his words. Tony didn't mind. He was where he dreamed of being. He was in his rightful place at last. Here, on the brink of fame, he could take anything that they threw at him.

"What's *Malibu* about, Tony?" sneered a columnist. He wanted to find out if the idiot could *speak*.

"Obsession. It's a film about wanting—about the pointlessness of ambition, and yet its absolute inescapability. It's an essay on success, fame, making it, and their relationship to happiness and contentedness. It contrasts quiet lives with noisy lives, peace with war, the struggle to reach goals that never stay still with the passive acceptance of fate. It asks the question, 'Which is the better way?' "

"And which is the better way?"

"There are no answers in films or in life. There are just worthwhile, carefully drawn questions."

"Like, 'Why the hell are we all stuck up this mountain listening to psychodrivel from rent-a-dick?' " said someone in a slurred voice from the edge of the crowd.

Valentino's fists whitened. He swirled around to locate the endangered lush.

"Because of the emotion that killed the cat—curiosity," said Pat Parker. "And what Tony just said is very far from drivel. It's the most intelligent statement of the film's highest concept I've heard. You should write it down, if you're still capable of writing."

She stood beside him, and when their eyes met the old solidarity was back. Whatever they had been to each other, whatever they would become, they were the same people on the same side. They were out there, on the limb, living dangerously. They were taking the shots and hunting for the rewards, daring, dreaming, gambling with life. Unlike Cohen's bird on the wire, his drunken midnight chorister, Tony Valentino and Pat Parker were free. It wasn't pleasant. It wasn't comfortable. Perhaps it wasn't even wise. But it was inevitable. Around them clustered the fact men—the experts on the status quo, on what could be done, on what was impossible. Short on will and long on education, they dealt in the currency of safety. They constructed their lives on apparently firm foundations from the bricks and mortar of security and they paid for predictability with the hard cash of boredom. Here was the dilemma at the heart of *Malibu*, the movie. Should you embrace an obsession, or recoil from it?

Imperceptibly, Pat and Tony moved closer to each other. Their shoulders touched, swayed away from each other, touched again. It wasn't the tightness of the crowd. It was the passion they still shared. Surrounded by the sea of mediocrity, they clung together, and both realized at the same time that the second stage of their lives was beginning.

"You haven't directed before. The only brand-name star in the movie is Melissa Wayne. What makes you think this isn't going to be a disaster?"

"What's Dick Latham up to?"

"How long have you known him?"

"Is this going to be a trend at the new Cosmos—using unknowns?"

The questions came in fast and furious, and Pat held up her hand to fend them off.

"Please, gentlemen, be patient. There are press people who haven't arrived yet. There's going to be a formal question-and-answer session later on. All your questions will be answered then. Let's do this thing right."

She slipped her hand into Tony's, pleased that he didn't resist, and she led him away from the gadflies who had been tormenting him.

"Let's go outside for a while. I need to talk," she whispered.

He went with her. Outside the tent, the heat and the quiet closed in on them. Pat walked to the edge of the hillside, and the vista stretched away from them like a magic carpet. They could see to the Sierra Madres and beyond, the majestic mountains shimmering in the heat haze.

"God, it's beautiful here," said Pat. "It's moments like this that I feel I really know Alabama."

"How is he?" said Tony. Alabama was neutral ground, safe, unthreatening. Tony liked him. Pat loved him.

"The same. He never changes. He's furious I've agreed to do this movie, but he's not really mad, he just pretends to be."

"He doesn't believe movies are art? Maybe he's right," said Tony.

"Some are, some aren't. Ours will be." She turned toward him and smiled. Our movie. Yours and mine. A joint project for two people who had been joined together before fate had separated them. Her eyes hinted she was thinking that. His recognized her thought.

"It's going to be tough as hell," said Tony suddenly. The pain of future torment flashed across his face.

"Me and you . . . and Allison . . . and Melissa?" she both said and asked.

He nodded, staring out into the brightness of the heatscape.

"We need to be friends," said Pat. "You need to forgive me. You need to trust me."

Again he nodded, avoiding her gaze. Pat took a deep breath. Would words make it better or worse?

"Should trusting be so easy?" he said at last. There was reproach in his voice, but not terminal reproach.

She reached out and took his hand once more, and she stared deep into his eyes. She would only have this chance to state her case. Her heart was on trial.

"Tony, listen to me. I'm not proud of what I did, but I *had* to do it. You of all people must understand that. When I took those beautiful photographs, I had no idea of what would happen to them. Please believe me. It wasn't a calculated thing. It just happened in the most natural way in the world. It was the sort of thing that could never have been forced. You must have felt that. I never asked you to do what you did. You did it yourself, because it felt so right. That's how great art happens. And when it does, you can't ignore it. I couldn't, anyway. It's too rare. It's too important. It's bigger than people and their feelings, because without it people can't grow. Am I making sense? Okay, maybe I was wrong, but look what's happened because of what I did. I knew it would. *New Celebrity* is a sensation because of us. This movie's happened because of it. Everything you ever wanted to happen has happened. I may not have done the right thing, but can't I take some credit for all the good things that are showering down on us?" She squeezed his hands. "Tony, look at me. Tell me it's okay. Tell me *we're* okay. If not the same, at least friends, close friends."

His face was a mask. She searched it for clues. Nothing stared back at her. Deep down she knew he was playing with her. She was being forced to predict the expression that would come next. The embryonic director in her had to admire it, as the woman and the lover screamed their dissent.

She couldn't leave it to chance. She had to influence him. So she stepped close, into his space, until her body was close against his. She was risking rejection. She knew that. He could humiliate her for this, and he was good at that. Far too good. Still, he remained an enigma. His emotions were locked away. But they were there. Millimeters beneath his skin, she could sense their presence. He had not moved back. He had stood his ground. In the absence of straws to clutch at, she squeezed the hand he was allowing her to hold.

"I thought the leading man was the star's perk," said Melissa Wayne.

The cold water of her sneering words poured over Tony and Pat. They snapped apart as if separated by a steel spring.

"I'm sorry to interrupt such a . . . private moment," snarled the star, "but as at least three photographers have captured it for posterity through their telephotos, and as you are standing in full view of most of California's paid gossips, I thought I should swing by and say hello. I know you're new to the movie game, but on a set we have no secrets. We'll be one big happy family of professionals, doing our job, oblivious of personal feelings, having no favorites." Her lips positively curled with malice as she cast her sarcasm at what she firmly believed were the born-again lovers. Her threat was everywhere. She wouldn't forgive this. Her face had been publicly slapped. The gauntlet had been thrown down. She was picking it up for a duel to the death.

Pat cursed inside. Melissa Wayne had only one attribute. Her sex appeal. She hated only one class of thing. Women. She had jumped to the premature conclusion that Pat had stolen back "her" lover. It was a capital offense. As the result of this misunderstanding, the director and her star were set on a collision course, and principal photography was weeks away. There were no words to explain what had happened. The body language had done the talking. Pat couldn't apologize. So she just stared at Melissa in helpless defiance.

Melissa glared back. Then suddenly she laughed, throwing back her head and tossing her hair in the sunlight, pushing out her pert breasts.

"I'm going back to the party. Dick is limbering up for some kind of an announcement." She turned as if to walk away from them. Over her shoulder she let rip with the Parthian shot. "See you in the love scenes, Tony," she said, but she was looking at Pat Parker as she spoke.

"Don't worry about her," said Tony. "I can handle Melissa Wayne."

"You've had practice?" Pat bit her lip, but she could not resist the jealous dig.

"That won't help." There was anger in his voice. Melissa might have forced them into some kind of alliance, but he hadn't forgiven Pat. His tone said she shouldn't assume too much.

"I know. I'm sorry," she said. "Maybe you can handle her, but I wonder if I can."

"Melissa's a bully. You just have to stand up to her. She's ambitious. At the end of the day she won't wreck the movie. She can't afford to be in a stinker. Nobody can."

"I hope you're right." Pat's mind was whirling. "See you in the love scenes," she'd said. It was a loaded remark, because everyone had heard the rumors about Melissa Wayne, about how she was a reality freak, believed in the whole Method bit, couldn't stand faked sex. Directing steam and sizzle was difficult enough without having the guy you loved on the wrong end of the lens . . . with a souped-up nympho who didn't believe in briefs and G-strings beneath the sheets, whose box-office clout could deliver the things she wanted.

"We can control her," repeated Tony, his voice hard and forceful, as if saying it would make it true.

"Yeah, I guess so, and Dick'll be a help. We can always lean on him."

"Yeah, we can always depend on Dick," he sneered.

She felt the coldness. Nothing had been forgotten. Up ahead, there would be only stormy waters. Dick Latham and Melissa Wayne were hot topics that could not be avoided.

Pat reached out to hold the arm that had just left her.

"Come on, Tony, let's go and hear what the old boy's going on about." The "old" was a concession. She'd wanted to come up with more of a putdown to show that Latham wasn't important to her, but at the last minute she hadn't been able to find one. Why? But this was no time for self-analysis. Life was off and running. She and Tony weren't back together again, despite what Melissa thought, but they had achieved some sort of armed truce. For the sake of the movie? As a prelude to something more? It was difficult to know.

They walked toward the tent.

Dick Latham was on the rostrum, talking into a microphone.

"I expect some of you are wondering where I am going to build the new Cosmos studio," he said. "Well, I'm proud to be able to say that the answer is . . . here. We are standing on it now. Cosmos Pictures will be built in the Malibu hills."

The roar of interest exploded around the room as the meaning of his words sank in. A studio in Malibu, in the mountains where war raged between the developers and the environmentalists. Dick Latham was about to carve up the canyons. He was going to try to build the new Cosmos slap bang in the middle of Alabamaland. Armageddon was about to be unleashed.

The words rushed into Pat Parker's mind. Her mouth opened and her hand flew to it.

"What!" said Tony Valentino by her side.

"Cosmos! In Alabama's hills?" she whispered, half to herself, half to him. Already she was beginning to understand the implications. She was working for Cosmos, for Latham. She was on their side. Her whole brilliant future, Tony's future, their future together was bound up in the success of the movie that would be the keynote for the revived studio. If it failed, everything would fail. But Cosmos in Malibu meant that Alabama, her friend and mentor, would become her bitter enemy. He would fight with all the fearful force at his disposal to derail Latham's plans. She would be forced to choose between the hare and the hounds. No way could she run with both. In desperation she looked at Tony. In shock he stared back at her, as gradually he, too, became aware of her dilemma.

She looked back at Latham. Surely it was a joke. He'd told her Cosmos was destined for the desert. He'd gone on and on about his concern for the environment. There had been the model of the house he was intending to build in the canyon. But even as she tried to hope that it wasn't true, Pat knew it was. Deep in her heart she had sensed that something like this was afoot. She had never trusted the billionaire she had allowed to love her. His eyes had avoided hers earlier when he had ignored her questions about the home he never planned to build. He had conned them all. The bastard had bought, used, tempted, and manipulated her, and now he was laughing as he dared her to fight back. The anger flared up inside her.

She pushed forward through the excited crowd. As she did so, Dick Latham's eyes caught hers. He had been looking for her, and now across forty feet their faces locked together. It was clear from his expression that he wasn't proud of the trick he'd played. He wasn't crowing, mocking the dilemma he had forced upon her, as he rejoiced in yet another hollow victory over a woman. Instead, he looked frightened, and the sight of Dick Latham's fear stopped Pat in her tracks. She had never seen it before. Probably no one had. She understood immediately. Latham still wanted her. He wanted her more than he had wanted anyone since Paris all those years ago. He had been unable to resist the Cosmos-in-Malibu deal, because it had made brilliant business sense, but now he was terrified that it would cost him the woman he loved. Across the heads of the boozed-up journalists, he was pleading with her. His face was talking with an eloquence that even Tony would envy. Pat took a deep breath. Anger had been so simple. On its wave she could have ridden toward the decent thing—the mountains, Alabama, and the good-bye to Hollywood dreams. But now, melted by the humanity of Dick Latham's bizarre love, anger was going, going, gone.

For the first time in her life Pat Parker was a spectator. She hadn't a clue what she would do next. She turned to Tony, who had caught up with her. Tony looked at Latham. Tony looked at Pat. He saw the communication that Pat and Latham shared.

When he spoke, there was sadness in his tone—sadness and resignation.

"The bastard's got you," he said.

THIRTEEN

Alabama twisted the top off the Corona with his teeth and spat it into the fireplace.

"The dentist told you to stop that," said King absentmindedly.

"The *dentist*," growled Alabama, "is praying that I fall off the Harley and catch a mouthful of road. That way he can spec the house on Winding Way *and* stick some concrete caissons under that broken-down piece of shit he's bought under the landslide at Big Rock. Bottlecap damage is merely a new Porsche."

He burped to accentuate dentist scorn, and stared out over the panoramic view.

"So what do we do today?" said King.

"Same as always. You print some more money, man, and I dream up ways to spend it."

King laughed. His eyes flicked back to the paper on his knee. "Some chick named Finke's written an article on Malibu in the *Times.* Says it's in danger of turning into Miami Beach." He sat back to enjoy the fireworks he had lit, flexing his pecs and stretching his quads. Alabama loathed Malibu exposés written by glib outsiders who thought of themselves as seers.

Alabama puffed himself up. "I've read more of that bullshit than you've done chest repetitions, man. A little history, lists of celebrity homeowners, interviews with a gossip of verbally incontinent rent-a-mouths, a couple of eyecatching headlines, and it's another deadline met in mediocrity land. All you need for that crap is press clippings, a jaundiced eye, and a paper with a name that gets you the entrée to people who otherwise wouldn't piss on you if you were on fire. What I can't understand is how some reporter—"

The telephone cut into his diatribe. He ambled across to it and scooped it up. "Hello," he barked.

"This is Richard Brillstein of the *L.A. Times.* Is this Ben Alabama?"

"The *Times?* Jesus, I was just talking about the *Times.* Yes, this is Alabama. What do you want?"

"Well, uh . . . Mr. Alabama . . . I've just attended a press conference given by Richard Latham, the new owner of Cosmos Studios . . . you know who I mean?"

"I know Latham." Alabama was suddenly wary.

"And he's just announced . . . I mean, literally an hour ago . . . that he's intending to build an entire studio right here, next to your ranch, in the Malibu hills."

"WHAT!" Alabama shouted the word down the line. King sat up.

"That's what I imagined your reaction would be. It was mine, too. There would have to be considerable environmental impact. He's talking about hundreds of acres of sound stages, back lots, front lots, you name it. Then there'd have to be access roads, whole mountaintops graded, and central sewers, of course, which would put him on collision course with the cityhood people. I wanted your reaction, Mr. Alabama. I'm glad I'm the first to give you this information, although I realize it must be bad news for you . . ."

But Brillstein didn't get the scoop of the Alabama response. In the middle of his sentence, Alabama put down the phone. He stood still. Movement was impossible as the fury built. Anger for him was a way of life, an affectation, even. It was seldom personal, nothing more than a useful character ploy that paid dividends in terms of people intimidated and his own way achieved. This was different. This was rage. It was hot and cold at the same time. It was the freezing ice block that plucked the skin from bleeding hands on some snowy steppe. It was the branding iron hissing and sizzling on bare flesh in macabre ritual torture. The fury tore at his ancient gizzards. He clamped his fists tight. He screwed up his eyes, and great gusts of air billowed in and out of his bellows lungs. The blood was everywhere. He could see it as a mist before his screwed-up eyes. He could hear it rushing in his ears. He could feel it pumping like a fire hose in the cavern of his chest.

"What's the matter?" said King. Alabama's face was red. Now, before King's eyes, it was whitening. "What's Latham done?"

"He's a dead man," breathed Alabama. "He's committed suicide," he whispered. "He's gone, history, he's an ex-person," he wheezed.

He faced King, as if seeing him for the first time. His voice was incredulous, as he amplified his answer.

"He's dared . . . he's *dared* . . . to try and build his godforsaken studio in the middle of my mountains."

He stared in defiance at his assistant. There! He'd gotten it out. He'd actually said it in words. It was a considerable achievement. There ought to be applause. Inside, the idea was scurrying around his brain like a rat in the night. A studio, a *movie* studio, sitting like some hideous neoplastic growth in the heart of the beautiful hills. Never in his entire life had he contemplated such a perversion. All the horror in the universe was encapsulated in it. Cosmos was the epitome of the tawdry tinsel of cheap illusion. Latham was the disgusting devil of capitalism rampant, the crass cash mountain, the symbol of the mammon and materialism that Alabama had spent his years decrying. Now they had come together to threaten the love of his life. It was mind-bending. It was the firm foundation on which a crusade could be built. The billionaire must be stopped. It didn't matter how. The cost was immaterial. If it took murder, then so be it. The gas chamber was an incidental detail. Alabama's own life was an inconsequential irrelevance, in contrast to the monumental abortion that threatened to color the world blood red. His eyes darted around the room, mirroring the ideas that darted across the computer screen of his mind. What should he do? What must be done? Resolve wasn't enough. Superhuman cunning would be needed to defeat the billionaire's evil. He must calm down. He must think.

"He can't do that," said King, appalled.

"No, he can't. He won't. I won't let him," muttered Alabama.

He walked across the room and threw himself down on the outsize sofa. Good. His thoughts were sorting themselves out in some form of sequence, as his brain recovered from the chaos of shock. Latham had made a public announcement at a press conference. That meant his ground would have been carefully prepared. Billionaires didn't stay billionaires by failing to deliver on their promises. Staying megarich was a confidence trick. Billions were a banking pyramid. For as long as they remained believers, the moneylenders would hold it up. When doubt crept in, Kashoggi-style, they pulled the rug. That meant Latham had gotten permission to build Cosmos in the mountains. He wouldn't actually have the zoning, but he would have the secret promise of it. Clearly he had worked miracles at the normally environmentally conscious California Coastal Commission. Was it already too late to intervene? That was the first question. How could the die be uncast? That was the second.

"Do you think Pat knows about this?" asked King.

Alabama sat up. He hadn't thought of that. The Cosmos thing had wiped everything from his mind. Pat had agreed to direct a Cosmos movie. She was thick with Latham and the dreadful English girl who ran the stupid magazine. It seemed impossible that she wouldn't know about Latham's plans for the studio. That made her the very worst sort of person, a traitor. No! Alabama recoiled from the idea. She couldn't have known. She was an artist. She'd learned to love the mountains. Heck, she'd photographed them. She wouldn't be a party to their brutal rape. After all, he, Alabama, who usually knew everything, had heard nothing about the diabolical plan. Lathan knew how to keep a secret. He must have kept it from her. There was a way to find out. He would call her. She would tell him how horrified she was. She would back out of the movie, tear up her *New Celebrity* contract, and she would never speak to Richard Latham again. She would volunteer her support, and she would work with Alabama to undo what must be undone. But as he laid out the scenario in his mind, Alabama already knew it wasn't as simple as that. Pat Parker was a go-getter. As far as it was possible, she was on the side of the virtuous, but when good clashed with the ambition that fueled her, which would win? Then there was the joker in the pack, the one called Tony Valentino. More than grace, Pat wanted him. Would she give up her own and her lover's fame and fortune for the flora and fauna of some parched hillside? Like *hell* she would. Valentino and Latham would work together as the magnet sucking Pat Parker toward her dreams. What could Alabama offer as a counterattraction to a lover's gratitude and artistic acclamation in the minds of the masses? Snakes and doe-eyed deer, hawks and canyon mice, stark rocks, barren land, and the still heat of the high chaparral. To side with him, Pat Parker would have to be more than a saint. She would have to be the angel she so closely resembled.

"I don't think she knew," said Alabama. "But I think she knows now."

King was silent as he thought about it. He idolized Pat. Somehow he sensed she was on the verge of exclusion from his world, that the decision would be hers, that it would not be an easy one.

"How can you stop Latham? Call the president?"

King could never get over the fact that Alabama and the president were friends. Alabama was *his* friend. He was real. He could be touched. He smelled. He got drunk. The president, however, was, well, the president, like God was God, the pope was the pope, and Orel Hershiser was Orel Hershiser. The concept of Alabama and the president was for King the place where reality met illusion. Okay, so the president had run on an environmentalist ticket, and had once owned an Indian motorcycle, and loved to take bad photographs, but that still didn't make his friendship with his boss any more believable.

"Yeah, I can call the president, and my friends in the Congress. I can spend days on the telephone calling in the IOUs. I can do the media, and put a bomb under the PR people, but all that takes time. It's my guess that time is something I don't have too much of. Latham knows that a lot of powerful people won't want this. If he's ready to go public with it, it's because it's on the verge of happening."

"So what can you do?"

"I could kill him."

King laughed. Then he laughed nervously.

"Seriously, Alabama."

"No, I'm serious. I could blow the bastard away. I could waste him."

King said nothing. He had never seen Alabama in such a dangerous mood.

"Or I could do something that would mobilize public opinion in a way that it had never been moved before. Something that nobody could ignore. Something that would get through to people, make them visualize the potential tragedy, make them feel it in their hearts and minds, make them see it . . . see it . . . make them *see* it . . ."

There was a Damascus light burning in Alabama's face. It was illuminating him. In its clarity, he saw. At once he knew what he must do. In the purity of his personal epiphany, he was filled with an awesome resolve. He stood up.

"Where's the Linhof?" he said.

"It's in the camera room. In the safe. Why?"

"Is it in shape?"

"Yeah, sure it is. All the cameras are, Alabama. They always have been. You told me to look after them."

Alabama felt the shudder run down his spine. He had never

imagined he would reach this moment. He had longed for it, dreaded it, recoiled from it, and now he was on the brink of embracing it. For so many years he had made his excuses. Bricks, he'd said. Nature, he'd lied. Too many photographs, too many photographers, he'd bleated. He'd dreamed up all sorts of reasons why he'd given up photography, and they had all had one purpose —to hide the real one. Fear. Now, he faced the truth. He had put away his cameras because he was terrified that he had lost his artistic skill. Ten years ago there had been a bad patch, a period when nothing had seemed to work visually. For most artists that was a daily demon to be wrestled with. For Alabama, however, it had been a first, and it had scared the living daylights out of him. He had gone dry, and he had reacted to the cessation of the fountain by refusing to try to turn it on. Days without working had dragged into weeks, months, years, and, as each second passed, his artistic courage had drained away. The excuses and rationalizations had gained in strength. He had learned to live with the lies and the cheating, and in King, the brilliant printer, he had found the willing codependent. Together they had constructed the façade that hid the truth so well. And what was the truth? That the mighty Alabama, the art hero of three generations, was a fake, a cheat, and a coward. Beer helped disguise that. So did the bikes and the brawls. So did the protection of the mountains that he had made into his own personal cause. Well, now it was over. The time had come to confront the demons.

"Do you know what I'm going to do, King?" said Alabama.

King knew the answer was coming.

"I'm going to make photographs. I'm going to make pictures of that canyon that Latham's trying to wreck, and the world will weep when they see their beauty. I'm going to make photographs that I've never made before. I'm going to take all the photographs that for years I was too terrified to take. I can do it. I must do it. I will do it."

He stood there, shaking with the power of the moment, wanting to shout out in joy and pain at this, the instant of his rebirth. As King watched, in awe of his friend's transformation, tears of determination and relief poured down Alabama's cheeks.

The sun came up over Saddle Peak, sending sleepy fingers of light poking into the canyon. It hung there, underlined by the mountain, as if pausing for breath after the long night journey to the top of the world. The ground stirred at daybreak. The blackness softened, the shapes formed, and the valley, cool and moist from the dew of the sea, gathered its strength for the heat to come.

Alabama was ready for the magic of the new beginning. For two hours he had clung to the mountainside, his feet wedged in a rock ledge, his shoulder numb against a bleak boulder. In front of him the mahogany view camera had all the space. It gleamed in the glow of the earliest light. King had not forsaken it during the barren years. It was polished, oiled, and loved. Now, the 10/8 plate nestling in its bowels, it was ready to be used. Alabama took a deep breath. This was a million miles from Nikon land, leagues from Hasselblad territory, where motor-drive was a dirty word and where there were no second chances. He had the picture in his head, where it needed to be. Nine-tenths of the work was done. But still there was the mechanical part. It mustn't be allowed to destroy the consummate beauty that was alive in the eye of his mind.

He processed the information, using Ansel's zone system. He didn't have to think. Experience thought for him. Luminance value of the weak sun, say Zone VII. So, if 250 candelas per square foot was on VII, 60 candelas per square foot would fall on Zone V. He was using Isopan film which indicated a basic exposure of 1/60 of a second at f/8. The 3X yellow filter, which he now added, would reduce that to 1/20 of a second. He let the pent-up breath whistle through his nostrils, disturbing the silence. He could almost see the sun grow. The moment would be gone almost before it arrived. It had to be anticipated. The second it was experienced it would already be too late. Alabama reached forward. He stopped down to f/32. His finger hovered on the release. Then, quite suddenly, he seized. A wave of panic broke over him. He was numb, paralyzed, bathed instantly in clammy chaos, and the cool professionalism that ruled his mind degenerated into discord. A voice boomed in his brain. "You can't do this," it said. "You've forgotten how." It laughed—a horrible, mocking laugh. "You remember all those bad photographs you despised, Alabama? Well, join the club, you old phony. There's another one coming up. Moon in June. Red sails in the sunset. Say cheese and watch the birdie. Into the drawer with it, Ben, baby. Stick it in the family album. Bore the relatives with it on a wet Sunday afternoon." The voice was cackling with helpless mirth in his mind. "You got up in the middle of the night to shoot this shit? You climbed the mountain to blaze away at the mediocre? Oh, Alabama! Stick to the beer and the memories and the might-have-been. Leave the photography to those with balls that still work."

"No," he said out loud, wiping the sweat from his brow with the back of his hand. He fought to concentrate. The pastel shades were painted onto the hills now. The light was growing in the womb of darkness. His gut said, "so soon"—but his gut didn't know anymore. How could he break the block? How could he make the confidence grow like the beauty that was erupting all over the canyon? He searched for allies in his loneliness. But in the art void, there were no friends, only doubts and fears and the ghostly intangibility of the feckless muse.

Then it came to him. Through the mystery of the magic moment, he saw the vision across the canyon. It was white stucco. It was squat. It was ugly. Smoke billowed from its chimneys. A vivid red neon sign uttered the obscenity. COSMOS STUDIOS it read, and it seemed to Alabama that the sun itself recoiled from the ugliness of the mirage. His mind cleared. The voice in his head receded. Here was something worse than failure and the scorn of the world. Here was the prospect that the mountains he loved would be destroyed. Once again he could "see." Once more he could "feel." It wasn't too late. The time was now. He squeezed the shutter release and gave the picture a "long" one-second exposure. Even as he captured it, he knew what he had. This would be better than *Moonrise Over Hernandez*, more dramatic than Ansel's glorious *Black Sun*. Already he knew that it would need water-bath development to preserve maximum density in the foreground. Even now he could see the cut of the print, calculate to the last millimeter the photograph's depth of field. God, he had done it! He could *do* it! The goblin of doubt was no longer perched on his shoulder. And in the bag on his back were twelve virgin plates.

Ben Alabama let himself go. He entered the nature he loved, and at the same time he opened up to allow it to enter him. The sun was rising over the mountain, but the sun was also rising in his heart.

Splosh! The pelican dropped from the sky like a thunderbolt and disappeared beneath the surface of the sea. He reemerged instantly, and the flash of silver at his beak said he'd scored. Beneath the balcony, a forty-five-year-old beachboy adjusted the fishing rod that stuck up from the sand. Apart from these competitors, Carbon Beach, the one they called "Deal Beach," was deserted.

"What am I going to do, Allison?" said Pat. She turned back from the balcony. Allison Vanderbilt was stretched out in a chair, her long legs hitched up on each other. She wore dark glasses as a concession to California. Otherwise, she was pure New England from the cut of her classic hair to the tips of her perfect toes.

"God, Pat, I don't know. Isn't it what people call a moral dilemma?"

She laughed helplessly. Manners replaced morals in the upper-class high ground from which she operated. Appropriate and inappropriate courses of action were laid down in the unwritten constitution of the aristocracy. Murder, rape, arson, torture were all covered by the shadowy rules you learned from Scots nannies in the nursery. Things were done. Things were not done. In every conceivable situation you knew how to behave because the regulations had dripped into you by osmosis during a thousand tailgate picnics, a hundred horse shows, at scores of balls as you danced with class fellow travelers in shoes that were always too tight. If Pat herself didn't know what to do, Allison wouldn't be able to tell her.

Pat screwed up her eyes against the brightness of the early morning sun, and she sighed. She had gotten to know Allison, and she really liked her, but the beautiful rich girl's relationship to the real world was as close as that of a dyslexic to a dictionary. On her Alice in Wonderland planet a career was what you had to irritate your family, money grew in trust funds, and friends were nearly always cousins.

"The way I see it," said Allison, trying hard to be helpful, "is that Mr. Latham is rather ruthless. I mean, he's the sort of man who would . . . who would . . ." She cast around in her mind for a definition of ruthless behavior. "Who would . . . haggle in a store," she managed at last. She wrinkled her nose in disgust at the thought. Arabs did that. And nouveau riche people like Latham. *So* demeaning. After all, it was only *money*.

Pat laughed at the touching naïveté. Allison made her laugh, and at this particular point in her life, there were few enough people who could do that. It was amazing that the friendship had developed at all. Allison must have despised the way she had treated Tony, and, as a would-be rival, she had reason to be jealous. But it hadn't turned out like that. Instead, Allison had been drawn to her precisely *because* she had loved Tony, and because Allison sensed that she still did. In the Vanderbilt book, loving the same people as they did meant you had good taste. And people with taste could be forgiven anything.

"Okay, so he's an iron man, a hard charger. How does that affect what I do?"

"Well, perhaps you should be tough with him yourself. You could tell him you think that his plan to build Cosmos in the mountains is a *really* bad idea. You could tell Alabama you've told Mr. Latham that. Then Alabama would know that you'd done your best, and he couldn't be cross. If Mr. Latham doesn't listen, at least you've tried and it's not your fault."

Again Pat laughed. The thought of Latham giving up his deal because Pat thought it was a *really* bad idea was about as funny as the bad-tempered Alabama being satisfied by her weak-kneed intervention.

"And do you think I should go on working for Latham? Should I go on directing the movie as if nothing has happened, while they pour concrete all over the hills and Alabama has apoplexy?"

"But the hills are Alabama's charity, aren't they? Not yours. I mean, if he wants to blow a fuse it doesn't mean you have to hold his hand while he goes up in smoke." Allison knew what she meant. Charities weren't interchangeable. If Aunt Miffy was spina bifida, then you bought a table at her party. You didn't bother with the retinitis pigmentosa Eye Ball, because that was run by the awful pushy woman who kept pretending she was a Whitney when she wasn't.

"Alabama would think I was disloyal," said Pat, wondering why she had to explain the obvious.

"Oh," said Allison, puzzled. She cocked her head to one side as she tried to understand it. *Loyalty* was a class buzzword. It was the most important attribute of all. Dreadful deeds were done in its name. The most extraordinary things were left undone because of it. But somehow it was out of context in this conversation. Why?

"Surely they don't really *have* loyalty in California," she said at last.

She knew it sounded a bit odd, but it was sort of true. Out here, people prided themselves on their lack of sensitivity and their toughness. Nothing was allowed to get in the way of their bottom lines, whatever those were. Conscience and codes had been what they'd come to California to escape. There were no school friends here, no family, and the only thing familiarity bred in the Southland was contempt. Alabama was one of "nature's gentlemen," that potent English euphemism for someone who was likable, but of inferior social status. He had the insubstantiality of servants, inhabiting that strange buffer zone between reality and illusion that existed beyond the green baize door. Of course, he was feisty and wonderful, and admirable because he loved okay things like art and conservation, but at the end of the day he was a shadowy figure who was in no position to ask for loyalty, let alone demand it. It was funny that Pat Parker felt otherwise, but then she *had* been born in New York, which was careless of her.

Pat peered out at the pounding surf. Allison had rung a bell. Maybe she did understand things after all. Sometimes ostriches had a better view from the sand than the shrewdinis from the treetops. She was right. This was California, Los *Angeles*, damn it, not Lynchburg, Virginia. And it was the movie business, where people gambled, where they won and lost. She looked down the beach. There weren't very many losers on Carbon, where Latham had rented her a house for the duration of the shoot. Bruce Willis. McEnroe. Disney honcho Jeff Katzenberg. All-purpose mover and shaker Freddie Fields. Hard Rock Café owner Peter Morton. Over the years, they'd probably stepped on the odd toe. Hypersensitivity was the mortal enemy of high-end property on Deal Beach.

It was time to get "real." If she wanted to commit hara-kiri and give up her dreams for somebody else's, nobody would care. Tinsel didn't know how to cry off camera. If she walked out on the Latham flick, she'd never work again in Hollywood. And for what? Mickey Mouse points from a rag bag of environmentalists, who'd never pay her bills or remember her name? The gratitude of an old man who didn't have the balls to take photographs anymore? The moral glory of doing the right thing? Whatever she did wouldn't make any difference. The mountains would be raped with or without her. She wouldn't even be an accomplice. Like Pilate, she could wash her hands of the whole sorry business. She took a deep breath and tried to ignore the guilt that pricked at her.

"Yeah, you're right, Allison. The hills are Alabama's fight, or 'charity,' as you put it. Not mine. Why should I throw over the movie just to show solidarity with him? It's too much of a sacrifice. And, hell, how do I know that if I quit I won't be dropping everyone else in it? Latham might just hire another director, but he might shelve the entire project. Then you wouldn't get your chance, and Tony wouldn't get his . . ."

Pat recoiled at the thought of Tony's terrible disappointment, but not so far and so fast as Allison Vanderbilt.

"God, I hadn't thought of that. Tony might not get the movie." Quite suddenly, Allison had been touched by the conversation. No longer was it mere social metaphysics and ethical philosophy, it was flesh and blood. The color drained from her face. Her expression was haunted.

"Perhaps you should say nothing to Latham," she added in a strangled voice. Deviousness was as foreign to her as soul food, but this was life and death.

"No, I'll call him. Why not? He's conned me. I'll tell him he's got no taste and less manners and that he's a jumped-up bastard who wouldn't know a fine feeling if it sat on his face. I'll get it off my chest, and then in the morning I'll punch in as if nothing has happened. He won't mind. He likes people who stand up to him, especially if they intend to back down when it's time to count the cash."

Allison wasn't sure. These people were aliens, Pat Parker included. How could anybody predict their behavior?

"Whatever you do, you wouldn't put Tony's career at risk, would you?" she pleaded.

"You love him very much, don't you?" said Pat.

Allison nodded. She didn't trust her voice to say those words.

"So do I," said Pat simply. "He thinks I don't, and that I just used him for my career. You probably think that, too. But it's not true. I love him as much as I ever did. Perhaps more."

"I know," said Allison. "At least I think I know. You're like him in many ways. You want. You need things. I respect that, but I don't really understand it. I just want whatever he wants."

"What if he wanted me?" Pat's question popped out.

Allison paused. It was a test. Whose love was the greater? It was like the story of Solomon and the baby and the rival mothers.

"I'd want him to have you. I'd help him to get you. If that was what he really wanted . . ."

It was true. Tony was her obsession. Possession wasn't a part of the deal. Her feelings were too strong for that. They soared in the high sky far above such petty considerations as jealousy and greed, beyond ownership, togetherness, and reciprocity.

Pat walked toward Allison and knelt down by the side of her chair. She took the patrician hand in hers as she would the wing of a wounded bird.

"I think he does love me, Allison. Deep down I think he still does," she whispered.

Allison stared straight ahead. She knew what she was being asked for. She was being asked for help.

"I'll be seeing him tonight, at the Getty," she said.

Pat's breath flowed out of her. Nothing had been said, but she knew Allison had granted her silent request. The relief filled her up, but at the same time there were other things to worry about. She, too, was going to the mysterious party at the Getty Museum. So was everyone else. Especially Alabama. He was giving a surprise showing of his "latest" work, presumably King's rehashes of his vintage sixties stuff, passed off as new. There would be no avoiding him. He would force her to take sides, and by the end of the evening he would be her enemy. Latham, too, was a guest, and the president of the United States, Alabama's old friend, was coming down from the vacation ranch he owned in the Sierra Madre mountains. His presence guaranteed a Malibu media beanfeast of epic proportions. Every star in the heavens would be turning out for the party at which Alabama and Latham would meet for the first time since the announcement of the billionaire's plans for the studio in the mountains. For sure, fireworks would be on the menu. But most important of all, she would be seeing Tony again. Could Allison make things right between them? Would they once again be lovers?

Dick Latham pushed back against the jets of the Jacuzzi and watched the gulls wheeling over a sea in which a school of dolphins played. His East Coast friends would laugh at this kind of decadence—a hot tub on his bedroom terrace with a view down Broad Beach all the way across Zuma to Point Dume—but secretly they would envy it. It had to do with the finely tuned survival instincts of the old money. Those who had made their loot the original way, by inheriting it, had never forgotten the lessons of the French Revolution. Conspicuous consumption made the peasantry restless. These days they didn't need to chop off your head. Their weapon was the ballot box, and with it they could cut off your assets when the party got too boisterous. The new-money arbitrageurs of Wall Street had discovered the truth of that when they had shown the unacceptable face of capitalism. It was something Mellons, Vanderbilts, and Rockefellers bent over backward to avoid.

The intercom buzzed.

Latham flicked open the channel. It was amusing to do business in the Jacuzzi while watching babes on the beach. A tub with a view was *so* California.

"Yeah," he drawled.

"It's Tommy. Can you spare a minute?"

"Come right on up."

"Great! I'll be up there in two."

Latham reached for the Lalique decanter of Joy de Bains. Why should bath essence be a female thing? It was too good for them. He upended a generous quantity into the foaming water and twiddled the knobs to increase the power of the jets. What brilliant news would Havers bring? More millions made? More rivals cast down? More personal triumphs for the man with the platinum-plated everything?

Havers advanced across the acreage of the Latham bedroom. He winced at the prospect of a tubside interview. A cerebral child, he had always felt out of place in the jocker-room. There, male nakedness, and the way you dealt with it, was some kind of a subterranean test of character.

As if reading the Havers mind, Dick Latham readjusted himself ostentatiously below the bubbles. It was his mission in life to amplify male discomfort wherever he found it.

"What have you got, Tommy?"

"I just wanted to bring you up-to-date on the fight about the Cosmos zoning. I thought you should have the latest before the Getty party."

"Yeah, how's it playing? Seems the opposition are a load of pussycats. They haven't got their act together. Instead of mobilizing the opposition, Alabama's kissing up to the president and throwing some boring retrospective at the Getty. The old goat must be all shot to pieces by the booze. Full of sound and fury signifying nothing. All mouth and trousers, as my British friends would say."

"That's the message I'm getting. I've just talked to Fingleton at Coastal. They had their heads down, expecting all kinds of heavy artillery, but there's next to nothing—two or three liberal congressmen sounding off, a few extra letters in the politicos' mail bags, a couple of scathing articles in the left-wing press. Nothing heavy duty. It just isn't orchestrated. What I can't understand is Alabama. He issued one over-the-top statement and then disappeared from the face of the earth. Unless he pulls a hat rabbit, we're home free on this one. We'll have the go-ahead in a week or two, and the bulldozers up there in three."

Dick Latham stared out to the sand. A girl was pushing a windsurfer into the waves—G-string bikini, a taut body, snow-white hair. God! Why did anyone live anywhere else? At eighty thousand for an undeveloped oceanfront foot, the land was a steal. Hell, you only needed 125 feet of frontage to build something respectable. Then there was nothing to do but sit back, watch the women, and count the capital gains until the tidal wave took you away—easy come, easy go in the Southland where "security" was an expletive you deleted, and where the game's name was "reach-for-the-sky." Then, in the midst of his reverie, he frowned. A cloud had appeared on his spotless horizon. Formed from instinct, it was growing fast, darkening, moving toward the center of his mind. It was wishful thinking to categorize Alabama as a lush and a loser. Underestimating enemies had never been a Latham failure. Somewhere, out there, Alabama was up to something. Sooner rather than later, he would find out what it was. His gut told him it would not be pleasant.

"What's the schedule for the weekend?" asked Latham, forcing the anxiety from his mind.

"Well, Emma Guinness and the *New Celebrity* people are coming down tomorrow. I guess they all want to be patted on the head, given raises, etcetera. I must say they've done a fantastic job. The magazine's doing gangbuster business."

"That's Emma's work. It's all due to her. And she's all due to me."

Dick Latham spoke sharply. At the end of the day you followed the flow of money to find out where the credit belonged. It wasn't an infallible pointer, but usually it was accurate. Credit was something he could never get enough of. It was his father's legacy.

"Yes, that was a brilliant hiring, Dick. Absolutely brilliant."

"Listen, I'll have all the hired help over for lunch tommorrow, but keep dinner free, okay? I'll take Emma to La Scala. The sea bass is great there, and it'll be fun to hear her being beastly about the Saturday night celebrities. How are things at Cosmos?"

"We desperately need to find a CEO. Did you see the short list I sent you?"

"It's shorter now. I crossed everyone off. They're all losers,

Tommy. They're the sort of guys who only know two words. Yes, for anyone above them. No, for the guys below. I need someone who isn't afraid to take a measured risk. Lawyers and agents don't like doing that, and the so-called creative people are happy with risks but aren't too kosher at calculating them. What about hiring a celebrity shrink? At least they'd know where the bodies are buried, and they might have a line on what'll play in Pomona."

"Maybe you'll find one at the Getty this evening. All the usual suspects'll turn out for the president," said Havers.

"I wonder why the president's turning out," said Latham.

"Isn't he some sort of photography buff?"

Latham didn't answer. The world and his wife knew that. The old boy had actually had an exhibition of his rubbish at the Corcoran Gallery in Washington when he'd been a senator. Latham had been to the opening night and had tittered behind his hand with the rest of the glitterati at the brazen presumption of the politician's ego. Okay, so the posturing old fake fancied himself a celluloid aesthete, and had been a friend and admirer of Alabama's from way back. It still didn't explain the presence of the most important man in the Western world at an elitist museum in Malibu.

"Anyway," said Latham, "if I get a chance to talk to him, is there anything I need to bring up? What about those TV license applications in Chicago? Aren't they up before the FCC?"

"Yup, it wouldn't hurt to mention those. The chairman of the FCC was at Yale with him, and he's a new appointee. You never know what a word in an ear can do."

Dick Latham frowned. A very unpleasant thought was forming. Into whose ear was Alabama whispering?

FOURTEEN

For an ordinary mortal the gates of the Getty were more difficult to enter than the eye of a needle, but Alabama was not ordinary. He had been waved through them as befitted the God he was. Now, he stood like Colossus on the brick-paved entrance to the peristyle garden of the museum, and he peered grandly down the pool toward the main building of the reproduction Roman villa. He hadn't bothered to dress for the party. He had come as himself.

All around him the heavy hitters whispered like the scheming courtiers of ancient Rome. In traditional Malibu style, they had arrived on time, so that they could leave early. What was not traditional was the nervous tension that crackled in the crystal air. You could feel the angst. The president was coming. And there was Alabama in the clothes that Oxfam would have turned down, with his muscle-bound sidekick and his art armor all around him like a halo. Any minute now, the billionaire would show up to join Streisand, Cher, Spielberg, and Johnny Carson, and everyone would watch as the cold war that had been raging in Malibu for as long as anyone could remember burst into flame. There, before their eyes, in the museum that tried to be tranquil, Latham and Alabama would square off for the fight of the millennium, with the president of the United States of America as referee. A studio in Alabama's mountains! It was as inflammatory as the famous brushfires that raged at the end of the Malibu summer.

"King, my man, this is going to be just like the old days," said

Alabama. His heart swelled in his barrel chest. On the edge of war, he had never felt so at peace. The reason was upstairs, on the walls of the photography room. After so many years of art infertility, he was potent once more. In the early morning, as the sun had come up over the hills, he had fought his demons and won. A part of him was actually grateful to the philistine money man. Latham had provided the tough going that had enabled the tough to get rough. When the devil had driven, all Alabama's psychological creative blocks had melted away and the work that had sprung from his soul was the best he had ever done. Right now, the doors to the exhibit were locked. Presidents liked to have something to open, and the impact would be greater that way. The photographs would have a dramatic effect as the opinion makers feasted on the visual banquet he had prepared for them. He had distilled and concentrated the beauty of the mountains. It shone from the surface of his prints more brilliantly than it did in the nature that had been his inspiration. There, in black and white, was the wonder that the wrecker was planning to destroy. No seal beneath the hunter's club, no child staring at the barrel of a murderer's gun could have spoken more eloquently for the cause that was his, and would become the world's. He knew he would win. The pictures were too powerful for the billionaire's billions. The environmentally conscious stars would rise up on the tidal wave of their fame and sink Dick Latham like a toy boat at sea. He never should have messed with Alabama. Not in Paris all those years ago. Not now. Not ever.

The Secret Service men were scattered among the crowd like raisins in a fruitcake. Transmitters pressed to their ears, sunglasses glinting in the late afternoon light, their eyes darted that way and this as they waited for the arrival of the president. A helicopter clattered overhead, drowning out the party small talk as its pilot monitored the progress of the presidential motorcade down Pacific Coast Highway. Some bothered to look up. Most didn't. Malibu cool demanded low-key response to everything except major disasters like dented cars, invasions of personal privacy, and weaknesses in the property market.

"Good luck, Alabama," said Cher.

Alabama smiled and held out a gnarled hand. She was renting in Malibu right now, but she would buy soon, and she was persuasive, and environmentally sound.

"I can count on your support?" he asked with a smile.

"Anytime. Anyplace. I'll sing. I'll act. Have you seen me tap? Who does the loonie think he's messing with? Mere money doesn't cut it around here. He should wise up and go home."

"Maybe we can arrange that. The president's in our corner. When he leans, you feel the weight."

"You're not exactly light, Alabama."

"We'll see. We'll see." Alabama chuckled. He felt so good. It was like a biker rumble in the old days, a poker game when you had the cards. Any minute now, Dick Latham would cream through the doors on his charm cloud, and Alabama would let him have it right between the laser beams of bogus sincerity that would be shining from his eyes. He hadn't rehearsed his speech. Righteous indignation would do the talking. When the dust settled, Latham would know both that it was personal and that he had lost. Paris would be avenged. The mountains would be safe.

"Would you like a glass for your beer, sir?" said the waiter hovering beside him. Clearly, he was new to Malibu.

"Naw," said Alabama, placing the bottle to his lips and drinking deep. His eyes scanned the crowd. They had all showed up as he had expected them to. Norman and Lyn Lear's Environmental Media Association were well represented. Its thirty-five high rollers paid around twenty-five thousand a year each for ecological causes such as Alabama's. Redford was there, over by the Flemish marble figure of Bathsheba, talking to Disney boss Michael Eisner and his wife Jane. All were EMA members. The rival Earth Communications Office was represented by Tom Cruise, John Ritter, and its evangelical founder, the charismatic Bonnie Reiss. And the hard-core environmental agitants-litigants had showed. Alabama noted members of both the Natural Resources Defense Council and the Environmental Defense Fund deep in conversation with Bob Hattoy, L.A. regional director of the Sierra Club, as they rubbed shoulders with a nude Greek youth from around 530 B.C.

But Alabama was looking for someone else in the crowd, and he couldn't see her. Pat Parker had been invited. Would she come? What would she say? What would she do? The doubt welled up inside him, as his exhilaration faded. He could deal with the president. He could handle Latham. But how would he fare with Pat Parker, the only person on earth he considered an equal? She had stood up to him before, a hundred times, and mostly she had won. But in those days she had always had right on her side. Would she now? She had much to lose by doing the moral thing, and a lot to gain by avoiding it. If she stood by him, he would admire and respect her more than ever. If she didn't . . . well. Alabama tried not to think about the awful thing that would have to happen. Then, on the edge of the crowd, he caught sight of two people who might not be far from Pat Parker. Tony Valentino and Allison Vanderbilt were deep in conversation.

"She still loves you, Tony," said Allison. "Really. I believe her."

"Did she ask you to tell me that?"

Allison Vanderbilt wasn't good at lies. There were so few people, apart from her parents, that she could be bothered to make them up for.

"Not exactly. But she probably knew I'd tell you." She stared straight at him, unafraid of his sarcasm, because she wanted him to be happy and because she believed that Pat could make him happy.

"She just wants the movie to go smoothly. She's only interested in her career, and what I can do for it. She's proved that already. Now she's trying to use you. That's probably why she made friends with you in the first place."

"Is it so terrible to want things, Tony? Is it so awful to use people to get them? Haven't you ever done that?"

She didn't spell out her accusation, but it was there between the lines. Allison didn't mind his using her. Allison prayed that he would. But it didn't alter the fact that he had.

Allison saw the mini guilt cloud scud across his features. She pressed home her advantage.

"Sometimes, if you love very much, it's an honor to be used. And ambitious people can genuinely love people who are good for them. Perhaps it's the only way they can love. I know love is supposed to be pure and without ulterior motive and all that stuff, but that only happens in romance novels. In the real world, people love the people who help make their dreams come true."

"So says the great expert on the 'real' world."

Allison had set herself up for the rebuke, but she didn't mind, because she knew she had gotten through to him. Tony and Pat were soul brother and sister. For them, career and love would never be separated like church and state. If such a love was their goal, then each was destined for a loveless life.

"Maybe I understand the world a bit better than you, Tony," said Allison. "At least I think about it from time to time."

"Meaning I don't?" He smiled to show he wasn't picking a fight. Allison was no fun to fight with. Winning made him feel like a jerk.

"I mean you don't really care what other people think, so you're not the world expert on human motivation. It's fine not to be. It's not a criticism."

She smiled at the ridiculous concept of her criticizing Tony.

"You're right," he said ruefully. "People are Martians. They're a total mystery to me."

Allison laughed. "And to other people, too. It's just that most people have all sorts of clever theories about what makes other people tick, and they pass them off as fact. Nobody knows the truth, so nobody can prove them wrong. How else do you think shrinks make their money?"

"I guess Pat's less of a mystery than anyone else," he said, almost to himself. What the hell did he feel about Pat Parker? He found it so hard to analyze things like that. A part of him still loved her. Another part believed she had betrayed him. The trouble was, he didn't have much of an angle on love. Sympathy, empathy, and understanding didn't loom large in his emotional life. When he thought about her, he wanted her. Her body had set him on fire. He had always felt good when she was near to him, less good when she was far. She made him feel strong. He loved to fight with her because she stood up to him, and she wouldn't put up with his bullshit. He admired her spunky determination, her quick temper, her artistic talent, and he really liked the greedy way she ate, the clothes she wore, and the jokes she told. She never irritated him, and nearly everyone else did. He actually *liked* her. That was the most remarkable thing of all. She had been the friend who could become the flick-of-a-switch lover, and he had never known when some ghostly finger was going to turn on the current. Was that love? Or did the Greeks have a more subtle word for it. Whatever! For good or ill, those seemed to be the feelings inside him.

"Forgive her, Tony. She didn't mean to do a bad thing, and only good things have come out of it. For her, yes, but for you, too. And for me."

Tony said nothing. He trusted Allison. She was so pure and she loved him purely. Nothing she said was ever intended to mislead. Anything she wanted for him would only be wonderful. Why the hell couldn't he love *her?* She was beautiful, incredibly beautiful, and she made love with an intensity he had never experienced in any woman. To love her should be so easy, and yet something made it impossible.

"Is Pat coming this evening?" he said at last.

"Yes, she is."

"What's she going to say to Alabama?"

"God, I don't know. I think she's going to tell him she can't help him."

"She shouldn't do that."

"Why? What do you mean?" There was alarm in Allison's voice.

"It would be the wrong thing to do. A studio doesn't belong in those mountains. Alabama's her friend. She shouldn't let him down. Hell, she's supposed to be an artist. She should care about those kinds of things."

"But if she doesn't side with Latham, she'll be off the movie, and then the movie might not get made. You'd lose your big chance. She can't risk that."

Alarm was becoming panic. Allison only cared about Tony's dreams. Nothing must wreck them.

"Screw the movie. At the end of the day, it's just entertainment. And screw Latham. He's a bastard. He always was. He always will be. All he cares about is his stinking cash. Somebody ought to tell him that."

Allison looked at him in horror. Maybe she didn't understand him after all. She had always thought he cared only about becoming a star. Now, he seemed to care more that Pat Parker shouldn't betray her ideals. Heavens! Had her pep talk been *that* successful? Perhaps the man she loved knew how to love after all. He had actually expressed a selfless emotion, or so it seemed. Well, if he wanted Pat Parker more than his name in lights, that was fine by her. It would just take some getting used to.

But their conversation was over.

"Look, it's the president," said new hot realtor Lori McGovern.

And it was.

President Fulton was pulling off a "low-key" entrance that was effortlessly high profile. He swept through the doors of the Getty on a wave of Secret Service men and he pumped hands and exchanged greetings with half a dozen potential campaign contributors en route to Alabama.

Alabama walked forward to greet him. Anyone else of his appearance would have been gunned down before he had taken another step. He looked far more sinister than an assassin, but he was the president's oldest friend.

"Alabama, my old buddy," said the president, arms open wide for the bear hug. Really powerful men knew the value of public admissions of friendship.

"Fred, Fred, it's good of you to come." Alabama didn't stand on formality. A Fred was a Fred, not a "Mr. President." He'd actually gone biking with Fred Fulton in the days when he'd owned an Indian, before he'd ever thought of politics as a career. They'd drunk beer together, and shared dreams of earning a living from photography. Even in those ancient days, they'd worried about the environment, way before it was cool to do so, and before there was much to worry about. Now old friends had come together in the face of a threat, in the greatest tradition of friendship. On the telephone, Alabama had laid it on the line. He had asked for help in the expectation of getting it, and he hadn't been disappointed. In the ordinary way, a billionaire like Latham would not be a man that even a president would want to cross. But this wasn't the ordinary way. The life or death of Alabama's mountains was at stake.

"Where are the photographs, Alabama? That's what I want to know. And what are we going to do about this guy who's trying to steal away our birthright?" Fulton liked to dramatize. His trumpet always sounded certain. That was why his followers won so many battles for him. He looked around the crowd, clustered about the Roman garden, and his words floated over them so that they would be in no doubt where he stood on this matter—shoulder to shoulder with Alabama. Fulton's finely tuned political antennae picked up the message that the crowd consisted mainly of Democrats. They were his people. Many of the stars had turned out for his campaign rallies. They would do the right thing. Or would they? After all, it wasn't a theme park that Latham was planning to build in the hills. It was a movie studio. It would be a potential source of work to people who could never get enough of that. To side against it would be to put ideals before career. It was a choice that film people found difficult to get right.

"Come on, I'll show you," said Alabama. He led the way through the parting crowd, the president in tow, and the Malibu celebrities trotting along behind. Excitement was mounting. Exhibitions usually contained few surprises. They were advertised, reviewed, and expounded upon until everyone knew exactly what to expect. This one, however, was surrounded by secrecy. The doors to the photography room had been locked for two days, and no one had the faintest idea of what was inside. Soon they would know.

The crowd surged through the Roman columns of the re-created Neapolitan villa into the marble-floored entrance vestibule. Following their leader, they filed up the stairs. The oak doors of the photography room were locked. A large key materialized in Alabama's hand. Now he opened them. He stood back, gesturing to the president to pass him. It was not a large room, and there were not many prints on its plain white walls. There didn't have to be. They were original Alabamas. The president looked around at his friend and smiled.

"Where should I start?" he said.

Alabama gestured to a nearby wall. The president walked up to the print. He stood back. He stood up close. He leaned in to savor the detail. He stood back once more. Alabama was at his shoulder. The president repeated the performance for five more prints in total silence. Then, at last, he turned toward Alabama. His eyes were alight with excitement. He opened his mouth to speak, but for once words failed the old campaigner. His hands were dragged in to the rescue. They splayed open. They fluttered, they hovered, they dropped back to his side in the gesture that said what was coming would be woefully inadequate.

"Never . . . never . . ." he mumbled, "have I seen such beautiful pictures. Is this . . . is this . . . the canyon that Latham is trying to destroy?"

Alabama nodded. Malibu leaned in to hear the great man's sentiments. They were not long in coming.

"Well," said the president of the United States, "he won't be allowed to, will he?"

Dick Latham was late. He jumped from his car and he hurried across the gravel toward the doors of the Getty. Havers and a couple of lawyers scurried at his side. He was immaculate in a pinstriped white and dark gray worsted suit, and only the worried expression on his face hinted that all was not well with his world. It was instinct. Things had been too quiet out there, beyond the perimeter of the Latham Enterprises wagon train. Had the Indians been gathering in the silent darkness? Was this Getty Museum cocktail party/exhibition in the presence of the president the perfect place for an ambush? If so, he was prepared. He had brought his own law, not in the shape of six-guns, but in the form of their latter-day equivalent, a brace of shiny attorneys with the notches of rich court settlements on their butts. Whatever harsh words were said, they had better not be slanderous. There should be no hint of impropriety, and no veiled insinuations that anyone would attempt unduly to influence the zoning decisions of properly authorized agencies. Simple abuse he could deal with. It was water off a duck's back. All he cared about was winning. And the way things looked at the Coastal Commission, who had the power to give the final yes or no, he had as good as won. And yet, and yet . . .

The garden of the Getty opened up before him. He stopped. Apart from a few wandering waiters, it was deserted.

He grabbed the nearest one by the sleeve.

"Where is everyone?"

The waiter pointed. "Up there in the photography room, looking at the photographs," he said.

Dick Latham set off again at a furious pace. Damn! Why the hell hadn't he allowed for the PCH traffic and the added disruption of the President's motorcade? Everyone else had. It was a beginner's mistake in Malibu. Presumably the president was up there already. The shiny-suited hit men hanging about had "Secret Service" in neon on their chests. They watched him suspiciously but didn't approach. He'd passed the door check, and he looked vaguely familiar.

He clattered up the stairs. The line to the photography gallery snaked along the passageway.

"Hi, Dick," said the appalling Broad Beach agent who had once told Latham his party was a nonevent because Alabama hadn't showed. "Alabama's inside with the president." The bearded freak name-dropped loud and clear, and Malibuite Rich Little, standing a few feet behind, couldn't help mimicking him.

Latham fired himself toward the head of the line. He wasn't waiting for anyone. If things were being said behind his back, he wanted to hear what they were. He barged into the packed room, pushing ahead of Olivia Newton-John, who was far too polite and charming to object. There, he all but collided with Alabama.

He bounced back. Their eyes locked like the antlers of rutting stags.

"Tricky Dicky!" barked Alabama.

"Ben Alabama," countered Latham. He was off balance. He'd rehearsed this in his mind, but here was reality. Alabama looked as mean as ever. The difference was that this time he had good reason to be.

"You lied to me," said Alabama fiercely, between clenched teeth. It was the deep end. Before everybody who was anybody in Malibu, i.e., the entire movie industry, Latham was being publicly branded as a liar.

"I have attorneys here," said Latham coolly. "That's a slanderous defamation."

"That's the gospel truth," growled Alabama. "You told me you wanted that land to build a house on it, not a stinking studio."

"I changed my mind," said Latham.

"You're gonna have to change it back," said Alabama, leaning forward menacingly, his eyes small with his vast hatred.

"That's for the California Coastal Commission to decide," said Latham. He wasn't going to be bullied. If Alabama lost his temper, Latham would win. He looked to be on the verge of doing just that. He was acutely aware of the silence in the room. Everyone was catching every word of this. Hundreds of versions of the conversation would be circulating the Southland within the hour.

"That studio will go up over my dead body." Alabama's voice was quivering with scarcely suppressed anger.

"I hope not, but if that's what it takes . . . ."

Latham smiled a tight smile. It was shifting his way. He could feel it.

"You always were a bastard, Latham. You haven't changed. You're still the same snot-nosed little rich kid you were in Paris. You think the world is one of your nursery toys that you can break if you wish, don't you? Well, it's our world too, and we're not going to let you touch it."

"Hello, Latham," said the president. He had materialized at the billionaire's elbow.

"Hello, Mr. President," said Dick Latham, wilting slightly at the production of the biggest gun of all.

The president smiled a threatening smile. His pseudofriendly manner was the most dangerous thing Latham had ever seen. He had met the guy three or four times before, and he'd never thought much of his leftist politics and folksy style, but he had never underestimated the toughness of the man. Fulton had a reputation for furthering his friends and burying his enemies. Latham's policy had been to steer clear of him and work for the future election of a Republican. But there was no avoiding him now.

Quickly he introduced Havers and his two legal eagles, managing to mention that they were attorneys. He saw the old boy's eyes narrow as they sensed the point he was making. Anything said now would be on public record. Words would have to be chosen carefully.

"Have you any idea what I've just seen?" said the president. He leaned forward, clearly expecting an answer to his impossible question. It was one of those maddening "Guess-what-I'm-thinking" interrogations to which pompous superiors subjected their inferiors. Latham hadn't a clue. A partridge in a pear tree? The beauty of holiness? The CIA file on Gorbachev's mistress?

"I don't know," he blurted into the silence. A mist of unreality was descending.

"I'll tell you," said the president as if to some small and willfully stupid child. "No, better than that, I'll show you." He reached out for Latham's arm and he gripped it firmly. Then he dragged him through the rapidly parting crowd to the wall of the room. "On these walls," boomed the president, "are some of the finest, most beautiful, most moving photographs I have ever seen in a life at least partially devoted to the study and practice of photography. These are not snaps. These are art. Fine art. The finest art I have ever seen. Look at them, Latham. You look at them."

Latham knew what was coming. He looked at the photographs with the enthusiasm he reserved for messes on roads. The beauty stared back at him. In the normal way it would have touched him, as it was supposed to. He had never seen the mountains look like that before. They were revealed. Before, he had seen them through the biblical glass darkly. Now, it was face-to-face. He recognized the canyon, of course. It was the Cosmos back-lot-to-be. The strong, silent photographs had accomplished an extraordinary feat. They had painted a gory red sign above his head . . . and it read ATTILA THE HUN.

"Well?" boomed the president.

Latham swallowed. The old fool might be a left-wing hooligan and a class enemy, but he was still America's leader. The power of his office was draped around him like an aura. There was an extent to which he *was* America, the country that Latham loved. He had to be answered. But how? He was aware of the Malibu crowd pressing around. Necks were craning, ears were flapping, tongues were preparing to wag.

"They're very good," he managed at last. His body had stopped. His lungs were still. His heart, if it was still pumping, was keeping a desperately low profile.

" 'Very good'? 'Very good'?" said the president in incredulous tones. "Damn it, man, you're planning to stick your movie studio slap bang in the middle of this beautiful canyon. These pictures actually *show* the damage you're going to do. And all you can say is 'They're very good.' What sort of a guy are you, Latham? Have you got a heart? Have you got a soul?"

The president was puffed up like a balloon. His eyes were staring. Latham could have sworn he was beginning to shake. It was an awesome sight. Fulton had wound himself up into one of his famous and much-feared furies. All that was needed now for stratospheric lift-off was a word—any word—from Dick Latham.

The Latham mind was starting up again. He had been lured into a trap. He had underestimated Alabama, and now the devious old buzzard had turned the tables on him. The photographs were a wonderful idea, but they were brilliant chiefly because they were so beautiful. They spoke directly to the gut. Intellectually, one might be for or against development in the hills. After seeing these prints, there was only one possible emotional verdict. Hell, Latham felt it himself. Still, he mustn't be beaten. He must never be defeated. This was business, and he had to win. Right now, what was needed was damage control. He fought to find the words that wouldn't blow the presidential fuse.

"The last word is with the California Coastal Commission . . ." he tried.

It was as far as he got.

"The *Coastal* Commission . . ." sneered the president, his voice thick with amazement. "The Coastal Commission," he repeated, as if it were a hilarious joke. "Listen, Latham," he barked, "I carried California, and I didn't carry it small. California's my state. The people that make California work are my friends. Now, *you get this.* I can't influence a zoning decision. That would be improper. But no two-bit local bureaucrat who votes for your stinking studio in Alabama's mountains is ever going to end up a friend of mine. You hear what I'm saying? And another thing. I've got a state-of-the-union coming up and a press conference, and the environment's a hot issue, and you know how the media loves examples. Well, there wouldn't be a better one than Alabama's prints on blackboards around the room. And a mug shot of yours for good measure. How's that going to play at the newsstands where they sell your ink, Latham, and with the FCC, where they license your TV stations? You tell me that, Latham. You just tell me that."

But Dick Latham didn't want to tell the president how it would play. Dick Latham knew exactly how it would play. It would not play well. He was cool now. He was back on target in his mind. Cosmos was only a small part of his empire. Latham Enterprises itself could not be jeopardized. There was no telling where a thing like this could end. The president had done his homework, and he had slipped in a spine-chilling threat. He knew about the Chicago TV licenses. Latham, imagining a harmonious meeting, had actually been going to bring them up himself. Now it was crystal clear just what message would be whispered into the ear of Fulton's old chum who ran the FCC. It wouldn't have to be spelled out. Nothing incriminating would be said, but the net effect would be the murder of the Windy City cash cow that figured so prominently in the profit projections of Latham Enterprises. And the threatened presidential press conference would not be the happiest of moments. The editorials of his rival newspapers would tear him apart. So would the liberals who peopled the publishing industry. In the Park Avenue drawing rooms, the shoulders would be as cold as the buffets.

One thing was certain. To press ahead with his plans for Cosmos in the mountains would be criminally stupid. But even as he admitted that to himself, Latham knew that he couldn't give up. It was personal. It was him against Alabama. It was Latham locked in the infinite war with his father in the grave. Hell, he could fight the president. The old fart was hardly God. And he could survive the media and the loss of the Chicago deal. What was the point in having money if you couldn't afford to lose it to get your own way? His last words had been correct. It was down to the Coastal Commission. If they said yes, as still looked more than likely, he would get what he wanted after all.

He drew himself up. It was High Noon. He was facing the commander-in-chief, the most powerful man in the world, but he didn't flinch.

"I have listened to what you have said, Mr. President, and you must do what you must do. But it doesn't change my plans. History is full of those who have fought change and resisted progress. I don't intend to be one of them."

The president's eyes narrowed as he listened to the totally unexpected Latham response. The robber baron had taken his best shot, and he hadn't surrendered. That it was crazy didn't detract from the billionaire's courage. Fulton was the supreme political animal. He had used his temper. He had bullied and blustered to get his way. It hadn't worked. That meant losses must be cut. Presidential power and prestige must not be squandered in a squalid public slanging match. He turned on his heel without saying another word, and, surrounded by his entourage, he stalked from the room.

Alabama hadn't caught the last bit. He had left when the president was ahead and Latham on the ropes, because he had seen the face in the back of the crowd that he had wanted to see. He pushed through the people toward her, coming at her obliquely so that she would have no warning of his approach. As he did so, he palmed the Leica that swung from his belt. He wasn't worried. He knew it would be all right, but he had to hear it from her. He had to know that Pat Parker was on the side of the angels, was on *his* side. Three feet away from her, and behind her, he paused. He bent down and caught her in the viewfinder, angling for the best position as the computer in his mind calculated the light. Then he waited. She would have the portrait she had asked for, the one he had suggested she would flog for a Ferrari or was it peddle for a Porsche, the one she said she wanted for Tony Valentino. She was more beautiful than ever in the lens of the Leica, her proud head held high, the animated sparkle shining in her eyes. Something was making her smile. It reminded Alabama of the sun coming up over the mountain, and, as it broke around the edges of her mouth, he called out softly to her, "Pat!" She turned toward him as he had intended, and her smile deepened as she saw him and what he was doing. *Click!* There it was. A perfect portrait by the man who had rediscovered his art.

"Alabama, you've taken a photograph!" she said.

He laughed as he stood up, letting the Leica fall to his side.

"I've taken several," he said, throwing out his arm to the prints on the wall.

"I know," she said simply.

"You could tell they were new?" he said.

"I could tell. They're magnificent. They're totally different. They make me want to cry."

He laughed. She was the only person in the world apart from King who knew his secret, and the only one whose magic eye would have known for certain that these photographs were new, not old.

"You like them?"

"It's beyond 'like,' beyond love, Alabama." She reached out and touched him. "How did you do it? How did you break the block?"

"You helped. You softened me up. You told me the truth I hadn't dared to tell myself—that I was scared—that I was a coward. But Latham pushed the button. He had to be stopped. He still does."

He watched her closely. Decision time was near. They were pleased to see each other. For how long would pleasure last? Which way would it go?

Pat swallowed. She still hadn't decided. She was on the edge of the razor. There was Tony. There was Alabama. There was Latham and the movie she would direct, and there were the photographs of the mountains, haunting in their precarious loveliness, on the walls of the John Paul Getty Museum.

His eyes glinted. She didn't have long. It shouldn't be that difficult. The jury in her heart should need no extra time. Then, over her shoulder, Alabama saw him. Tony Valentino stood close, watching them, and Pat Parker had no idea that he was there.

"Where do you stand, Pat?" he said.

Pat took a deep breath. Even now she didn't know what she would say. She was about to find out.

"With you, Alabama," she said.

The relief flooded into his heart. He wanted to take her in his arms and bear-hug her until she cried for mercy. But before that, he wanted more. He wanted chapter and verse. He wanted it spelled out so that there could be no room for doubt, and no going back.

"You won't work for him? You'll give up the movie, and the *New Celebrity* thing?"

"Unless I can persuade him to drop his plans for Cosmos in Malibu."

"Latham might scrap the movie. Tony might not get his chance. You'd risk that?"

As he spoke, Alabama stared into Tony Valentino's eyes over Pat's shoulder. Tony's lasered back fiercely, giving no inkling of the feelings inside.

"Tony's talent will get him where he wants to go. He doesn't need my help," said Pat. Nor my hindrance, she thought. Had she betrayed him a second time? Could you betray people by doing the right thing? She tried to work out what she felt, but she couldn't. There was relief that the decision had been made, but it was balanced by anxiety about her suddenly so uncertain future. Her old job was gone. So, most probably, was her new one. And she had lost Tony forever. It was a stiff price to pay for virtue.

Alabama moved toward her, and she leaned into his embrace.

That, at least, felt safe and good. It was wonderful to be back, in the base camp of his arms, after the no-man's-land of moral uncertainty.

"Let's go and tell Latham now," he said. "He can't stand up to all of us. We'll make him give in."

Over her shoulder, Tony's eyes still held his. Alabama smiled gently. Was his premonition correct? Time would tell.

He steered Pat through the stars to the place he had left Latham, impaled on the subtle spear of the president's threat. Now, he stood alone with his henchmen, shell-shocked and forlorn amid the fascinated crowd. The president was nowhere to be seen.

"Hello, Dick," said Pat.

He smiled wanly. "You, too?" he asked. He seemed to know.

"Give it up," she said. "It's bad. It's the wrong thing to do. Everyone can see that now. Alabama's shown them."

"I can't," he said. His eyes dropped from hers. He didn't seem angry, or even stubborn. It was as if his hands were tied by his past, by his personality, by all the forces that had shaped his extraordinary life.

"I can't work for you, Dick, if you do this. I can't work for *New Celebrity*. I can't even be your friend."

Did he shudder at the very last bit? Had that at least touched him?

"Whatever," he said.

The anger welled up in Pat. "Whatever"? Hell! "Why do you always have to play God, Dick Latham?" she exploded. "You'd be better off playing the little boy that deep down you are. You tear the wings off flies. You lie and you cheat and you steal to make miserable money when you've got an obscene amount of it already, and you make me *sick* with your pride and your power and your terrible emotional poverty. You ought to learn how to *care*, Dick Latham, because otherwise, nobody, but *nobody*, is ever going to love you."

"Hear, hear," said somebody in the crowd. It was Robert Redford. Dick Latham looked up and saw him. Redford had played the mountain man, Jeremiah Johnson, in a movie once, a character who looked a lot like Alabama. He had fallen in love with Utah and, through his Sundance Foundation, he worked harder to preserve the beauty of nature than he did at his career. Now, publicly, he had sided against Latham.

"Don't be a hick, Dick," said someone else. It was Martin Sheen, unofficial mayor of Malibu, and once the recipient of Latham's gentle scorn at his Broad Beach party light-years ago. He was the soul of the beachland, or at least its conscience. *He* knew how to care. He had given the world lessons in it.

The stars crowded in on him, pushing closer.

"If you do it, I'd never work for Cosmos," said Mel Gibson.

"None of us would," agreed Barbra Streisand. The chorus was taken up. "We won't work for you." "We won't work for you." It was becoming a chant. At the back of the crowd, arms began to sway in unison.

Dick Latham swallowed. There was a time and a tide in the affairs of man that, if taken at the ebb, led straight down the john. Such a time was now. Such a tide was surging all around him. Before him, plastered tight against him by the mass of stellar humanity, was the girl that he had come nearest to loving after the only true love of his life. The words of the president still reverberated in the air. The threat to his media empire still rang in his ears. Now, he had started a celebrity strike. The stars of Malibu were about to picket his studio. If he continued on his disastrous course, he would be risking everything he had ever created, and then Pat would be right. Nobody, not *anybody*, would ever love him.

He held up a hand, and the voice that sounded hardly seemed like his.

"It seems I have miscalculated," he said. "I have decided to withdraw all plans to build a studio in Malibu."

The howl of approval rent the air, as, slowly but surely, the anger started to form in Dick Latham. It burned softly at first, but then it burned brighter, and soon brightest, banishing his disappointment like the sun the marine mist from the midmorning Malibu shore. Alabama had won. He had lost. But he didn't have to like it. And the word that kept going round and round in his brain was *revenge*.

He pushed toward the exit, thrusting roughly at the crowd. He brushed past Alabama, whose face was alight with the smile of triumph, and Latham's voice was tight as a noose around the neck of a dangling man as he spoke. "I wonder if you'll ever take another photograph," he snarled.

Pat Parker watched him go, and the relief at his surrender was at war with the fear of what would happen now. She had blown her top, in public. Latham would never forgive her. From this moment on he would be her enemy. That frightened her, but it also saddened her. There was a part of Dick Latham she liked very much, perhaps too much. It was the part that reminded her of herself.

Suddenly, she wanted to get away from all the people. She didn't even want Alabama's congratulations. She didn't want to hear him crowing in triumph, because his victory was also her defeat. She wanted to be alone. She wanted to think, and to get things into perspective. She had to make plans. She had to adjust to the fact that her world had been turned upside down and that she had nobody to blame but herself. So she allowed herself to be sucked through the exit on the river of fame, and, in the corridor outside the photography room, she turned right when everyone else turned left toward the stairs. The sign on the door ahead said simply—PAINTINGS AND SCULPTURE—but the most important thing was that the gallery into which she walked was empty.

Or rather, it had been, because now it was full of her, and of the man who had followed her into it. She realized she was not alone when she heard four footsteps on the marble floor instead of two. She spun around. He stopped.

"Tony!"

He said nothing.

She stared helplessly at him. Would the recriminations and the accusations start now? Should she try some kind of explanation, some sort of apology? It was all too much, too soon. She felt drained, but she still cared—God, how she cared! She tried to read his expression. What was there on the face of the boy she loved? Would she ever know? Would it help to know? But his face was blank. Long and hard, he looked at her, the perfect mask of his expression hiding the mystery of his persona.

And then, quite suddenly, he began to smile.

The smile started like a spark of fire in the high chaparral. It caught from the corners of his mouth, and it spread inward and upward to engulf his lips, his eyes and his suddenly wrinkling forehead. Fanned by wind, it burned across his face, until the smile was a furnace, brighter than sunlight, warming Pat's heart with its radiant heat.

"Oh, Tony," she murmured, and she fell forward into his arms. He was ready for her. He caught her, and held her with a strength that said he would never let go. He hugged her to him, squeezing out the doubt and the pain, and she buried her head in his power, smelling the warmth of him, nestling down deep in the body she loved.

"It's over," he whispered. He meant the anger, the frustration, the bitterness.

"Is it starting? Is it beginning again?" she said softly, meaning their future, the union that would be their marriage, the eternity they would share. His eyes said yes.

For long seconds they were happy merely to be close after the long parting, but then their bodies began to stir. The greed was growing. Touching had made them hungry. She pulled her face from his chest, and she looked up at him through the tear mist that filled her eyes.

"Tony!"

His fingers ran through her hair, feverish in their hurry to experience her once more. His eyes roamed over her beauty, desperate to capture it forever. Then he drew her to him, and he bent toward her, and his lips rushed to her lips. In the cool gloom of the art temple, the kiss was their wedding ring, as their soundless mouths screamed the vows of faith. Their moisture merged. Their hard bodies clamped close. Their tongues lapped together. She clasped her hands around his waist and, in reply, he thrust his hips against hers, grinding into her. She felt him grow. She felt herself open. Bigger, wider, harder, softer, taller, wetter, oh dear, so very wet. Beneath her skirt, she was burning. Beneath his jeans, he was on fire. His leg forced itself between hers, and she bent down, half sitting on his thigh, rocking on it, hungry for friction. Her heart was hammering, her mind was roaring. She pushed against him, caressing his throbbing heat with her crotch, teasing it, urging him on, thrilled by the pounding blood that rushed next to the core of her. Her hands squeezed him in toward her. Her thigh jammed itself between his legs, and she swayed from side to side, rubbing him as her tongue searched the back of his throat, and her breasts flattened against his chest. Through the denim of his jeans she could feel the tip of him. Through the folds of her skirt, through the silk of her panties, he could feel the slicked velvet of her heartland. Molecules of material separated them. It was not enough. They had dared to reach a rhythm now. They danced in time to the music of lust, and they knew what they wanted. They wanted orgasm. Somehow that mattered more than anything else. In the crash of souls the past would be forgotten. Forgiveness, explanation, the hollow excuses—all the shallow, sullen tricks of words—would be rendered unnecessary by the shower of liquid flesh. Their new day would dawn in the glorious explosion of bodies. It was so very near. She held her breath as she tiptoed close to her conclusion. He was rigid on the edge of his. They clung together at the brink, determined to drown in each other. Closer, harder, they forced themselves together. They must be each other, become each other's skin and bone and blood. Later, their child would formalize their union. Now, there was only the promise of all the happiness to come.

FIFTEEN

They wandered back from the sea, savoring the fading heat of the late afternoon sun. The beach was quiet on the Malibu, a lazy, laid-back place of strollers, old friends and young lovers, and the surf washed the sand clean as the mountains watched and the birds wheeled in the powder blue of the sky.

She took his hand, and he squeezed hers, as they reached the steps. He stood back to let her past, and she walked up to the faded wooden terrace of the beach house, her long legs pointing to the hard perfection of her butt, and the strong slope of her back. He noticed her beauty, and he swallowed as he followed her.

She turned and smiled to show that she knew his thoughts, and she loved them, and then she walked across the balcony that separated the house from the beach, and she leaned over it, certain that he would join her there. For long seconds they said nothing.

"I couldn't forgive you, and I couldn't forget you," he said at last. They hadn't discussed this.

"And now?"

"It's moved on."

"What do you mean, 'moved on'?"

She smiled calmly. The language they both wanted was the language of bodies, not these words and sentences.

He laughed to show that he hardly knew what he meant, and that it didn't matter now.

"You were incredibly brave . . . with Latham. I've never seen a woman do that."

Again she smiled, in gratitude, in relief. She had done the hardest thing. So often, it was the right one.

"I thought he'd fire me, fire you, fire everyone. And then he calls me and says 'Nothing's changed.' I still can't believe it. What is he, a masochist or something?"

"Nobody ever told the bastard how to behave. No one ever cared about him enough to bother. He respected you for what you did. *I* respect you for it."

"You do?"

"I said I did." Tony smiled lazily. Compliments didn't come easily to him. Repeating them was harder. He tried, as he had tried a hundred times, to work out why he had forgiven her, why her betrayal no longer mattered to him. Was it her incredible courage with Latham? Her decision to put Alabama's mountains before her career? Was it Allison, who had made him see that Pat really loved him?

"Did Allison speak to you about us?" said Pat, reading his thoughts.

"You mean, did she tell me what you told her to tell me? Yes, she did. She was word perfect. She believed you."

"Do *you* believe me?"

"Believe what?"

"Who's fishing now?" She reached over and poked him lightly on the brown skin of his forearm. "Believe that I love you," she added, her voice lower, husky.

"*Do* you love me?"

"Yes. Very much. Very, very much. I never stopped." She looked into his eyes.

"In your fashion." He was beginning to understand that Pat and he loved in a different way from everyone else.

"In our fashion." She realized that, too.

Her eyes probed hungrily into his.

It was almost time, but there was something she wanted to do first.

"Hey, I've got a present for you," she said as if she had just remembered it.

She walked to the edge of the terrace and picked up the photograph from beneath the shirt that had covered it. She handed it to him.

"Alabama took it yesterday at the Getty," she said. "He sent it over this morning. I want you to have it."

He looked down at the photograph, then back at her, then once more at the image of her.

"It's beautiful," he said. "There's only one thing in the world I want more than this." He laid down the photograph.

"What?" she whispered.

"You."

He smiled a slow, easy smile. The current was running. He played with her fingers as they reached for his. He ran his hand gently across them, as if he had never felt them before. Her shoulder was heavy on him, and she leaned over and lay her head against the side of his neck, nestling there, warm and wanting. He breathed her in, the sweet aroma of her merging with the salt breeze, with the subtle scent of sun oil from bathers on the beach. Then he bent down until his head was against hers, and for long seconds they were content to be close as the surf crashed on the sand beneath them and the gulls wheeled in the sky above. Waves of alien tenderness coursed through him. The pulse of total love beat within her. They were more together than ever.

"Tony," she whispered. "Tony . . ." But he put his finger to her lips, telling her that this was no time for words. Her uneven sigh hurried past his fingers. He could feel her breath, heavy with its message of desire. Inside, he knew her heart would be in time with his, rapping out the dangerous drum riff of body purpose and flesh longing. Her eyes were languid—wide and willful as they laid bare her dreams. She longed for him. She would have what she wanted.

They drifted into the kiss. Mouths open, tongues so ready, they fell toward it. Nuzzling at dry lips, they were content to wait for wetness in the luxury of so-slow love. They bit at each other with all the world's tenderness, their teeth roaming over the vulnerable skin. Then their hands were allies, reaching for each other's heads to fine-tune the passion. Their fingers entwined in each other's hair, rubbing, pushing, pulling to make the magic grow. Malibu went away, the beach beauty receding into a backdrop of beige and blue. Now it existed only to frame them, and, in the forefront of the photograph, they breathed their love into each other's mouths.

They clung together. Their hands had become arms, and already their soft bodies were tensing as they feared to lose the moment they had. Rougher now, they tied each other tight in ropes of limbs, and the delicate kiss was already hungry, greedy for more, determined to have it. They dived into the sea of lust, refreshed by the abundant wetness, as the liquid intimacy swallowed them. Tongue on tongue, they swayed together. Hip to hip, they shared the hardness. Souls on fire, they trembled at the gates of ecstasy.

He pushed her away, and she allowed the parting because she knew what it promised. He led her back from the sun's glare into the darkness of the house, and she went like the willing victim of a pagan sacrifice. In the gloom at the back of the room, he stopped, turning once more to face her. He reached out and unbuttoned her shirt. He watched her closely, savoring every nuance of expression as she stood so still, so passive, at the mercy of his unhurried fingers. He peeled back the cotton shirt, and her breasts stood there, humble in their defenseless beauty. He touched them, to show he owned them, and his hands were the masterful hands of the general inspecting the spoils of victory. He cupped her breasts. He held her nipples between his forefinger and thumb. He ran an insolent finger up the gentle slope of their curvature, down the underside, where they sprang vertically from the hot skin of her torso. These are mine, said his gestures. These are a piece of the property that you have sold to me. You have no rights anymore, apart from the right to give pleasure, and the right to receive it. She shuddered with delicious acquiescence. Her breasts trembled beneath his touch. Her chest heaved with the effort of breathing, as her blood surged in the adrenaline high.

His hands dropped lower, to the belt of her blue jeans. He undid it. Gently but firmly, he lowered her pants. She didn't help him. He didn't want her to. She moaned as the material slipped below her butt, and she looked down past her bare stomach to the silk panties. She was ashamed that they were already wet in front, and yet she was pleased too, because he'd done that. It was his fault. The spring of lust and love that spilled from her was his creation as much as hers. So was the heady scent of her musk that wrapped them both in the cocoon of intimacy. Her upper body was still tented by the shirt. Her lower legs were still clothed by her jeans, but the heart of her was now nearly revealed. Its damp warmth was on the silken surface of the bikini briefs, exposing the guilty secret of the throbbing core it covered.

He reached into the elastic of her panties. He pulled them down, until they were buried in the rumpled denim that veiled her upper thighs. His hand hovered near to her, basking in her radiant heat, tantalizing the glistening down beneath it. Her love lips shone in the triangle, coral pink, gleaming in the slippery ocean of lust. They were so shy, so beautiful, so desperately in need of his touch. Again she moaned on the edge of abandonment, and she pushed out, her hips moving millimeters toward him in the gesture of surrender. Her body was pleading for his, yet still he held back, knowing that every millisecond of joy postponed would multiply a hundredfold in the bliss to come. His hand crept closer. It touched the soft, soaked hair, withdrew, touched it once more. He stared into her eyes, and she nodded the permission he didn't need. Again she moved out at him, more insistent now, as shame faded into the urgency of desire.

He lay the flat of his palm against her. She groaned her pleasure at him, throwing back her head and showing him her long, white neck. He massaged the abundant wetness, and she rubbed herself against his hand, loving it, demanding more. Gently, he explored the brink of her, hooking his finger into the edge of the silken opening, laying it back, pushing in deeper. She bent down at the knee, following his finger, as if trying to capture it inside her, encouraging it to explore further the secret parts of her that belonged to him and always would. In answer, he moved higher, until his fingers rested on the place that had become the center of her body. Reverently, he moved against it, exploding the stars in her mind.

"Oooooooh," she moaned as he milked the ecstasy from her. Her legs were weak. Her knees buckled. Her whole body pivoted around the pleasure source. The sweat sprang from her upper lip, trickled in drops around her breasts, stood out in a sheen of passion around her tense nipples. Still he moved against her mystery. He seemed to know the privacy of her. He was roaming across her body, unlocking its forbidden places. He had keys to all the doors. Already, he had stolen her heart. Now he was taking the rest of her.

Her hands reached for him. She must have more than this. She must have all of him now. She reached for his jeans, but he stopped her. There would be only one leader, only one led. His hands were on her shoulders. He guided her backward toward the sofa, and she sat down, half losing her balance, falling back across the cushions. Her legs splayed open. She was pleading with him to take her, fast, hard, as cruelly as he wanted, as cruelly as *she* wanted in the desperate limbo in which he had left her. He stood over her, staring in awe at her conquered body. The smile of longing played across her lips, and danced in her wondering eyes. Her hand reached for her nipple. The other moved between her legs. In the full frontal power of his gaze, her finger slipped inside. She was daring him. She was showing him what she wanted. He must do this, or she would. It had to be done. There could be only one escape from the steam pressure that filled her body. Release must come. He had to understand that.

For long seconds Tony Valentino left her alone on the plane of her longing. Joined only by eyes, their need grew. She could see the might of him expand. She could see his passion pounding and throbbing. Please, her eyes asked. Do it now. However you want to. I exist for you. I have no other purpose.

He reached for his belt. He undid it. He flicked open the buttons of his 501's. He was free. He slipped out of his jeans and shorts and walked toward her. He knelt beneath her open legs and rested his hands on her thighs. She eased herself down toward him, tears of love misting up her eyes. He rose up to meet her, and they slid into each other, each in their natural home at last, joined together, as they were meant to be.

"I love you, Pat," he murmured.

"Always love me," she whispered back.

Emma Guinness dropped the microphone between her breasts. It disappeared, and for a second she wondered if she would ever find it again. Thank God for the wire it was attached to. She peered into the mirror. Nothing showed—neither the hidden microphone already warming up in her cleavage, nor the angst in her mind. In half an hour she would be having dinner with Dick Latham, the target in which she'd once dreamed of being embedded. Days ago, marriage had existed as a distant possibility in her imagination. It existed there no longer. Latham had humiliated her in public, before a rival, before Pat Parker, her employee, and the Guinness world had turned nasty. From that moment on, she had changed. She had surrendered to her darkest dreams. Now, the world that specialized in plaguing her was about to find out that when the going got tough, the clever got evil.

She picked up a bottle of Paloma Picasso and splashed it over her shoulders. Damn! She was already beginning to sweat through the Dior underarm deodorant. It took super glue to block her armpit pores when the Wagner was tuning up. She picked up the belt with its Velcro attachment and its little pouch. The Pearlcorder nestled inside. She attached the jack plug to the microphone socket and bundled up the spare wire, tucking it into the belt. The high-tech industrial counterespionage shop off Grosvenor Square had been quite specific. The recording device was voice activated. Running time on the super-long-play tape was three hours. If a mouse farted during dinner, it would be captured for posterity in quadraphonic sound. She smiled a vicious smile. She had played this game before in the old *Class* days and Victoria Brougham had bitten the dust as a result. Even now she could see the hatchet-faced bitch doing her takeoff on the owner's North Country accent. She'd sat in the chair, legs apart, knickers showing, in the English upper-class way, and she'd looked like a milk-laden Guernsey in a wet field, as she'd bad-mouthed her employer and social inferior with the earth-shattering arrogance of her species. Emma's hidden Phillips recorder had caught it for posterity. Things were better now. These days, she could afford a state-of-the-art Olympus for her electronic eavesdropping.

Her smile broadened. It was quite possible that nothing would come from the dinner-table conversation. But the harder she worked, the luckier she got. The prepared mind was chance's friend. One fine day, if she was ready for it, the words would be dropped that would change her future. She pressed RECORD. "One. Two. Three. Testing. I hate you all." She said it softly. "I hate you all." She repeated it loudly. "I HATE YOU ALL." She pushed the rewind button, and then the replay, and her smile was Cheshire cat wide as the recorder repeated her truth. She looked at her watch. Dinner was at eight. Drinks on the sand first. She must hurry. What the hell should she wear?

She waddled to the closet, blissfully unaware of the mirror's view of her copious rear, her dumpy legs, her bull neck. She sighed. There wasn't a cheap dress in there. The labels were cutting-edge trend. Nearly all of them had appeared on slinky models in the better glossies. But as she looked them over, she knew that on her they would fail. Over the years she had tried to analyze it. She'd never succeeded. Was it her shape, her deportment, the awkward way she moved? Perhaps it was her skin, her personality, the pheromones she gave off. Maybe it was simply that her aura clashed with clothes, although to be frank she didn't look right when she was naked either. Again she sighed, as she reached at random into the dress rack. The Bruce Oldfield number she pulled out looked a dream on Princess Di. The flowers that bloom in the spring, tra! la!—light, summery, frothy as a well-timed soufflé.

Pah! On her, it would look like an over-the-top floral tribute at a nouveau riche crematorium.

She climbed into it, as she would a turnip field in winter. She ripped up the zipper, breathing out as she did so, and she smoothed down the protesting silk, before resuming normal lung activity. Good! Nothing had actually torn, although it was far too tight. She'd been eating for comfort and putting on weight. It wasn't hard to do in America, where the major addiction was sugar, and where sweet things tasted best. The tape recorder bulged noticeably. She rooted around for some kind of a shawl. The sun had gone down. The Malibu evening would be cool. She might look a trifle dowdy, but that wasn't the point. Dick Latham had already had his last shot at her.

She was ready. In her mind she ran through a list of possible subjects for blackmail. Anything to do with tax would be promising. Rich people couldn't bear paying those. "Only the little people pay taxes," Leona Helmsley had said. If she could trick Latham into revealing a Swiss bank account, a Liechtensteinian company, or something shady in a sunny place like the Caymans, she would be on a winner to nothing. Then there were all the run-of-the-mill billionaire crimes—like parking, stock manipulation, insider trading, breach of fiduciary trust, and more exotic peccadilloes like antitrust shenanigans, illegal campaign contributions, bribes to foreign governments. It wouldn't be easy. Latham was an American, not a loose-lipped European, who would trade any secret for an easy laugh. It would help if she could get him pissed. Again that would be no problem back in the old country, where nondrinkers were regarded with the suspicion reserved for acquaintances who called you by your first name.

Once more, she checked the inventory in the mirror. Did she look like a spy? No. She looked like a sack of potatoes that some lazy sod of a gardener had left in the flower bed. The hell with it! She was ready for dinner. Dick Latham, Pat Parker, and Tony Valentino had better watch out. Their guts would be her garters as she danced on their graves.

"I'm not taking any more calls. I don't care who the hell it is. Do you understand? The Speaker, the governor, especially not the president, okay? I'm out. I'm taking a meeting. I'm dead. Tell 'em whatever you like, but don't bother me with it."

Dick Latham slammed the telephone down, and thrust out his glass toward Havers. "Fix me another scotch," he barked.

Havers hurried to obey. He had never seen Latham like this. The guy was on fire with rage. He could all but see the smoke pouring out of his ears. And he was drinking. This was his third in the half hour that Havers had been in his office. He had good reason. The moment he had gotten home from the Getty the evening before, the storm had broken. The telephone was ringing off the hook. The courier vans were lined up on Broad Beach Road. The press were beginning to gather like vultures on the sand. Already there were a couple of live TV vans parked outside, and one of them was CNN. Alabama's photographs had exploded into the consciousness of the country's opinion makers with the force of a nuclear blast. All three network breakfast shows were clamoring for an interview with the would-be environmental rapist, and recently the calls had become more sinister. The bankers had started appearing on the line. Their tones carefully couched in lawyerly financial-speak, they had said one thing and meant another. They were worried, not by anything specific, but just worried in the way that perennially anxious people were when anything abnormal occurred. The Latham PR machine had moved smoothly into damage-control mode. Already some underling had been accused of masterminding the "Cosmos in Malibu" idea and had dutifully fallen on his sword.

Latham himself had televised a two-minute segment that was being made available nationally in which he had reassured everyone that the hills would not be touched. In a gesture of good faith, he had decided to give his entire mountain land holding to the Santa Monica Mountain Preservation Trust. They would be park lands forever—nature and horse trails for the people to enjoy. He personally apologized to everyone he had upset, and particularly to Alabama, the grand old man of the mountains, whose vigilance and artistic genius had narrowly averted environmental tragedy. Latham admitted with all the considerable charm at his disposal that the buck stopped with him. He took personal responsibility for the near disaster. Yet, at the same time, he managed to insinuate that this had been a lower-echelon decision made by lesser mortals who had been prevented in the most final way possible from making the same mistake again.

He grabbed the glass from Havers and gulped at it.

"Jesus, Tommy. All these years of image building. All the work and the contacts. All the crap from the politicos, the payola, and the pretense, and now, at a stroke, I'm public enemy number one. This is going to cost us, believe me. Licenses, circulation, subscriptions, God knows how much influence. That broken-down old idiot up in the mountains has bent my business."

"It'll blow over," said Havers. "It's bad now, but people forget. A week, a month, and it's history. We've contained it. We were fast with the response. We've given something away, admitted we were wrong, had the balls to do that. It could even turn into a plus. You know . . . we're open, we're responsible, we don't cover things up like the oil boys and the chemical companies. We make our mistakes and we pay for them . . ." He petered out. From the fire in the Latham eyes he could see he was not making his point.

"Don't *give* me that bullshit," exploded Latham, sucking greedily on his Glenfiddich. "He's cost me. A hundred million. Maybe two. He's turned me into Slippery Sam. I'm in there with the toxic wasters, the polluters, all the cheap hustlers and scammers who'd sell their mothers to turn a buck they don't need. Me! Dick Latham! Shit, Havers, yesterday morning I was a *gentleman*. What do you think I am now? An untouchable. A zombie, creeping around under stones with the rest of the social undead. My father will be laughing in his grave . . ."

Dick Latham had gone pale. The thought of his father had done it. He white-knuckled his fist around the cut glass of the tumbler. His hand began to shake. He stared, his eyes unseeing, through Tommy Havers. Somewhere down deep in the fires of hell, his father would be chuckling at his misfortune. All the billions, all the success, all the power, and still he could be thwarted by a mere mortal while his father gloated, the father who had made him what he was . . .

"I want Alabama wiped out," said Dick Latham, his voice shaking with hatred. "Whatever it takes. I want him ruined."

Havers looked doubtful. "I'm not sure it would be wise to move against him now. Perhaps later. Right now, he could finger you. It could upset a delicate situation. The spotlight's on us. Anything we do will be noticed."

Dick Latham nodded. In the midst of his fury, in the woozy booze mist that was beginning to fog his mind, he could see that Havers was making sense. There was a time and a tide for revenge as well as fortune. It wasn't now. It would be later.

"Do you want me to stay here for a day or two?"

"No," said Latham. "Get back to New York. Life's got to go on." Through the red haze of anger, the thought occurred to him.

Did Alabama's life really have to go on? Would the crusty old scarecrow live forever to enjoy the memory of the time he'd bested the billionaire? Was it possible for Malibu to contain the two of them?

"Okay," said a relieved Havers, nervously looking at Latham's scotch. He hadn't seen his boss drink like this before. His words weren't slurred yet, and for sure he wasn't stumbling about, but there was a wild look in his usually calm eyes. There was electricity in the evening air, a contained desperation, that Havers, who didn't usually vibe in on such things, found deeply disturbing.

"You're sure you don't need me to take some of the heat?" he added.

"Meaning I can't?" snarled Latham.

He turned on Havers like a wolf at bay. The steam that had been building inside was coming out.

"No, Dick, of course I didn't mean that. I just meant—"

"I don't care what the hell you mean, Havers. Just go, okay? Earn the money I pay you."

Doormats didn't like to be walked on. Luckily they didn't possess voices that could frame complaints.

Havers hurried from the room. For the first time in his life he actually felt sorry for Emma Guinness. She was going to have the nastiest evening of her life so far.

Dick Latham exploded onto the terrace. Emma Guinness was there already. She turned to greet him.

"Oh, do look, Dick, there's a seal out there in the shallows. I haven't seen one before . . ." Across her face was a girlish smile as she posed awkwardly in the unaccustomed role of nature lover.

"Fuck seals," said Dick Latham. His momentum carried him toward the drink tray that the butler had laid out. He grabbed the Glenfiddich by the neck as if about to strangle it, and "freshened up" a drink that was way too fresh already.

Emma Guinness watched him. She could see he was drunk.

"Bad day?" she attempted.

Dick Latham let out a kind of growl as he pressed the cut-glass tumbler to his lips. He swallowed a mouthful of malt whiskey.

"Have you any *idea* what has happened today?" The words held together, but their emphasis was unusual, and their unnatural definition told the truth about the Latham mental state. He was zoned. He was also furious.

Emma took a deep breath and the hidden microphone rubbed against the clammy flesh of her cleavage. She aimed herself at him like a reporter on "Eyewitness News." Her tape recorder wanted to know *exactly* what had happened to the billionaire's day.

"I gather there's a certain amount of fallout from Alabama's counterattack on the Cosmos thing," said Emma.

"Do you limeys still think understatement is cute?" rasped Latham. "The bastard has screwed me." He spat out the words as if they would exorcise ghosts. They were thick with disbelief. He'd been screwed at last. Through all the deals, the wheels, and the haute finance, it had finally happened. The shafter had been shafted by a broken-down old man of the woods, who wouldn't know a leveraged buyout from a discounted Third World loan. Jesus! Was this the turning point? Was this the moment when the sweet turned sour, when the harmony became discord, when the long march up the mountain turned into the head-over-heels descent down the other side?

"You mean you're going to have to build Cosmos somewhere else? Is that the end of the world?"

Emma was living dangerously. Her gut told her to.

"It's not the point. It's not the point," shouted Latham, his voice pitched curiously high. "I was made to look like a fool. The president of the United States actually threatened me. Can you believe it? . . . The *president* talked to me like I was a child of ten. Just about every movie star in America lined up to dump on me . . . and all I'd done was gone to the Getty to look at some dreary photographs because I thought it was a Malibu thing to do." An intense feeling of unreality was gripping Dick Latham. It was like an appalling dream.

"What did the president say?"

The tape was listening.

"Who *cares* what he said? It's what he made me do. It's what that scumbag Alabama's made me do. He's wrecked my plans. *My* plans. My *plans.*" The outrage was everywhere. It hung in the cool night breeze. It scurried around on the dunes of the beach. Out there in the shallows, the seal would be sharing it. Nobody crossed Dick Latham. It was what the billions were for. It was the sole and simple reason for their presence in the world. But how could he revenge himself on Alabama? He couldn't sell the old biker's stock short. He couldn't bamboozle his bankers and pull the rug from the bottom of his debt pyramid. Alabama was outside and above Latham's financial world, and he was beyond the reach of his media one. He had never envied the Mafia before. They might never be able to spend the riches they possessed; might never do more than eat their wife's spaghetti in some tract home in Miami; might never graduate past platinum-plated playmates and heartless, low-end tarts; but by God, they could enjoy their revenge. They had people who would kill for them. They had minions who enjoyed it. They had people who specialized in providing genuine unpleasantness for their victims before the merciful release of death. All it took was an oblique word, a packet of petty cash, a cryptic call to some psychopathic hit man in the dark, and the deed was done. And what could Latham drum up in the revenge department? A gaggle of lily-livered lawyers who actually believed the brazen lie that the pen was mightier than the sword; a shrill of silver-tongued leader writers whose words would end up lining drawers if they were lucky; a drink-soddened circus of talk-show rent-a-mouths bleating on to an anesthetized TV audience with a nanosecond attention span and a couch-potato world view. It wasn't good enough. It was a disaster. The man who had everything couldn't afford to buy his enemies a really bad time.

"It's amazing that some broken-down old fart like that can have such an impact," said Emma, showing solidarity as she tried to loosen up his tongue.

He slumped down on the beach chair, and some of the scotch slurped out of the glass onto the white linen of his pants. "I'd like to kill him," he said suddenly. "Maybe I will."

The drink was talking, but the recorder didn't know that. It didn't have eyes. It only had ears.

Emma laughed softly. Inside, her heart was singing. She'd never expected this. Latham, Mr. Tight Lips himself, was running off at the mouth, and the magnetic tape between her tits was eating his words.

"I think I'll have a gin and tonic," said Emma cunningly, walking to the drinks tray. Drinking encouraged drinking. With her back toward Latham, she poured a tiny measure of Tanqueray into the bottom of a glass and filled it up with Schweppes. She turned around, sipping at it, and screwed up her face in an expression that said "strong." She smiled ruefully to show that she could never get measures right. Then she slid across the terrace and sat down next to him. The Pearlcorder could have nailed him at fifty feet. Half a dozen were safer.

"Where are you taking me to dinner?" she asked in what she hoped was a disarming, little girl voice.

"Dinner?" said Latham. "Oh, La Scala," he mumbled.

His glass was empty. He was feeling a bit better. Evil, but better. Grandiloquence was expanding inside him. The Mafia did it, and who the hell were they compared to Dick Latham? They were two-bit hustlers with funny names and ugly faces who would never smell the Rose Garden, or get to be threatened in front of superstars by the president in the John Paul Getty Museum. They were outsiders compared to him, small-change artists who wouldn't rate a halfway decent table at Mortons, Le Cirque, or San Lorenzo in London. They slipped and slid around the bottomland amid the ooze and the slime, and nickels and dimes could buy and sell them. Okay, so he'd never before attempted serious revenge, but it wasn't too late to learn. Nothing was. Leveraged buyouts had been Swahili to him a year or two back, yet he'd financed a couple of the bigger ones through the boys at Kohlberg, Kravis. If he could handle a heavy-duty LBO, he could pass some pain Alabama's way. He merely had to turn the might of his mind to it, and the job was done.

"Can I get you another drink?" asked Emma.

He stuck out his glass to her, saying nothing. She was an employee. As such, she was roach slime. From now on, the people who worked for him were going to have to learn a few serious things about loyalty. If they wanted to bask in the stellar rays that shone from him, they would have to start striking Faustian devil deals. When he said "Jump!" the traditional "How high?" response would no longer be enough. In the future he would be looking for an "Off which cliff?" type reply. He wanted Henry II's knights drawing his paychecks, the kind of people who weren't averse to a little murder in the cathedral if that was the whim of his day. Yeah, Alabama was a sort of souped-up California-style Thomas à Becket—a tough cookie on a morality jag and a collision course with a king. The more he thought about it, the more he liked it. He was feeling much better. He was feeling pretty good. Hell, he was feeling fantastic. What he needed was another Glenfiddich, and forget the rocks.

Emma upended the scotch. She'd already established her reputation for pouring outsize drinks. She didn't blow it now. The caramel-colored booze was way past finger measurement. It looked like a long drink. She spirited it toward the wobbling Latham hand. He embraced it as if it were an antidote for poison. Perhaps it was.

"Will we be taking a driver?" she asked. "If you didn't want to bother with one, I could drive you."

Latham didn't answer at first. He was drinking and thinking. Would Havers kill for him? Could he ask him? He laughed bitterly. Havers would happily falsify a tax return, handle an inside trade; he'd even live dangerously and bribe the odd official, but that was all. No, if the walk was to be on the wild side, he'd have to discover some cats that were at home in the dark. But he had no idea where to look. His money had insulated him from foul people and kept his hands squeaky clean. Now, when he wanted to dirty them, the billions were an obstacle. Once again, the gloom cloud began to descend. He drank deep to keep it at bay.

"We'll take a driver. Always take a driver," he mumbled. "Let's go. I'm fed up with sitting here on this goddamn beach."

He stood up too suddenly. He staggered. He righted himself. A fatuous smile played around his lips. He picked up a telephone.

"Is the car waiting?" He slammed it down. "Okay, we're outta here," he said. He was conscious as he spoke that he was trying to sound like a gangster.

He stalked through the house, ignoring the butler, the maids, and the chauffeur who loitered in the courtyard inside the front door.

"La Scala," he barked rudely as he passed the gray-uniformed driver.

Outside, he climbed into the navy-blue Rolls-Royce with the discreet R.L. painted in dark red on the front door. He pushed into the back. There was no nonsense about ladies first. Emma piled in next to him. The door clunked shut. In seconds they were nosing out onto Pacific Coast Highway by the Trancas Restaurant.

"What's that place like?" said Emma in bright conversational tones. She could relax. The Pearlcorder was going to get an earful tonight. There was no hurry.

"Cowboys and rock 'n' rollers. It's about as rough and tough as Malibu gets." Rough and tough. It was how he felt. It was how he wanted to be. It reminded him of Paris. He'd felt like this then, when women had taken the brunt of his aggression. Alabama floated back into the gunsight of his mind. Right now he would be up there in the hills, gloating and guzzling beer. He'd be reading the articles, catching the afterburn of his victory via his satellite dish, taking the calls from all the weak-kneed, bleeding-heart lefties who cared so desperately about nature from their high-rise condos in Metropolis. He pressed the button that wound the window down. Lights blazed from the Malibu Cove Colony beach houses, the surf crashed against the sand of Escondido Creek, the lazy breeze melded with the smell of tiptop leather. It was a perfect evening in Malibu. The Santa Anas were blowing, and the night was sultry, here by the ocean, the freshness of the salt air merging seductively with the hot, dry wind from the Mojave Desert. At moments like these, Malibu was heaven. But the drumbeats of Hades, deep and insistent, were already throbbing in Dick Latham's drink-sodden mind.

The Rolls purred sedately on, oblivious to the hatred it harbored in its bowels. The moonbeams were bright on the water by the side of the highway, and the lights of fishing boats shone on the horizon. They passed Pepperdine, snug and smug against the dark outlines of the hills. They made the left at Cross Creek, and the sleek car eased itself toward the restaurant lot, through the knots of late pizza-filled surfers, the wandering lovers, and all the other clever people who knew that late-summer Malibu was where God would choose to spend his vacation.

At La Scala they were ready for them. Jean, the son of the owner and the maître d', was hovering at the lectern as Dick Latham stumbled through the door. Emma followed in his wake.

"A very great pleasure to see you again, sir."

At La Scala, there was nothing they didn't know about status. Latham was up there in the rarefied air where Marvin Davis lived. So what if he'd just been forced to climb down on his studio location? He was still a social ten in Malibu, and anywhere else, for that matter. The best table was in the window overlooking the Serra Retreat. They headed there now. On every side, conversations quieted.

As they crossed the restaurant, a table to their right looked as if it was occupied by several different species of rat. There was a large albino, a very common brown, and a couple of mongrels. The whitest one of all said, quite clearly, "Alabama."

Latham stopped in his tracks. He twirled around, losing the maître d', who sailed on oblivious to the fact that he had lost his valuable convoy. He stalked over to the table, and its occupants looked up expectantly. Surely not. This was too good to be true. They were about to receive a megabuck table hop. If so, stock would rise; points would be scored. They exchanged glances. Which one of their number had been secretly harboring a billionaire acquaintance?

Latham hovered over the table like an avenging angel. Emma stood behind him. "Who mentioned Alabama?" he growled.

The rats exchanged furtive glances. This was not to be a friendly meeting. This was a visit from the exterminator. They said nothing. The brown rat managed a nervous laugh. If an effusive greeting from Latham was money in the bank, to be publicly insulted by him was negative cash flow. The snow-white rat who'd condensed the Alabama/Latham/Cosmos story for the table went a whiter shade of pale.

Latham's furious eyes twirled like tank turrets. He was way past sense. It never occurred to him that these guys might be developers who wanted the Alabamas of this world buried as badly as he did. That wasn't what his gut said. Paranoia was striking deep. The universe that had existed as his personal plunder ground now seemed peopled exclusively by enemies. This was the new Dick Latham. This was Danger Man and Captain Power, the guy the wise didn't mess with if they wanted to stay healthy. It was a brave new cosmos of blood and twisted bodies, of concrete overcoats and offers that couldn't be refused. That it existed only in his drunken fantasy was unimportant. The unreal could be made real. In Southern California it happened all the time.

"You can tell your friend Alabama," he hissed, bending over the table like a tree on a blasted heath, "that he hasn't got long to enjoy his minimouse victory. Tell him that Dick Latham personally guarantees it. You got that? Personally. I guarantee it." The delusions of omnipotence swirled in the Latham psyche, swimming free in the malt whiskey sea. He felt like a god. He could cast thunderbolts down from the sky. He could wipe out lesser mortals with a flick of his fingers. It was no longer a question of how. It had become a question of when.

The maître d', reaching the empty Latham table, turned to discover the disaster that was unfolding at his rear. The tourists from Vegas and his star customer were on collision course. He darted back to avert tragedy. He grabbed the Latham arm and tugged deferentially at it. He hadn't realized that Latham was wasted. He hadn't ever been before. On previous visits to the restaurant, his cool had dropped the room temperature a couple of notches.

Dick Latham shook off the man's hand. He had said his piece. The law had been laid down. Everyone knew where he stood. What he needed now was a drink. He allowed himself to be steered to the table.

"Bring me a bottle of single-malt scotch," he said as he sat down in the window to the hum of reanimated conversation.

Emma eased herself onto the banquette opposite. Food should be kept to a minimum if the Latham stream of consciousness was to be kept flowing. She made a mental note of what she had gotten so far. Threats. Violent, public threats against Alabama. It was titillating, but words were cheap. In bars from the redwood forest to the Gulf Stream waters, macho Marlboro men were mouthing similar promises they wouldn't have the nuts to keep.

The pretty waitress came back to wonder if Famous Grouse, a blended rather than a single malt, would do. Latham was past the connoisseur stage. He nodded curtly, and in a minute or two he was back in whiskeyland.

"I think we'll need a little time for the menu," said Emma to the waitress. She gave a conspiratorial smile that said she knew her date was zoned, but that she could handle it.

She looked around. The faces were out in force. Neil Diamond was dining with his realtor Carol Rapf, spirit of the Malibu, doubtless celebrating the sale of his Colony home for $5.6 million cash to buyers who'd closed escrow in an unheard-of twenty-four hours. Rob Lowe, Mr. Midnight Blue, was eating with another realtor, the spectacular-looking Betty Graham. Was Mr. Clean turned Mr. Dirty thinking of trading places? Up or down would be the question. Farther along the prime-table line, Batman Jon Peters, former hairdresser, Streisand friend, and now Hollywood's most powerful producer, held hands with a beautiful actress.

Dick Latham slumped like an oily rag against the banquette, nursing the glass in his lap. His unseeing eyes stared out across the creek and up toward the Serra houses, their lights twinkling in the darkness. He knew he was drunk, but he didn't know the significance of it. Drink melted insight, and he didn't realize that the strange thoughts that ebbed and flowed within him were an ethanol production. All he knew was that he felt alternately powerful and impotent. The scotch seemed to keep him positive. Abstinence had him veering toward the negative. There was a simple enough solution. He took another gulp.

"Why is it," he said, in the whiny voice of the spoiled child he had once been, "that I give everything, and I get nothing in return?" He leered at Emma, his face lopsided. He wanted an answer to his fatuous question.

Emma held back the smile. Dick Latham getting nothing in return for his bountiful generosity was a hilarious idea.

"Maybe you don't ask for enough," said Emma. Her words sort of slipped out, but as she uttered them, the idea came to her. It cut through her mind like a knife through butter . . . and it took her breath away.

"Ask for enough . . . I don't ask for enough?" slurred Latham, as if trying to translate a dimly remembered foreign language. "Must one spell everything out . . . chapter and verse . . . to everyone? Don't the people who live off me have enough initiative to anticipate my needs and get the job done that needs to be done. I pay enough fiddlers. Why the fuck should I fiddle myself?"

"What job needs to be done, Dick? I don't understand."

Dick Latham sat to attention. Quite suddenly, he banged the glass of scotch on the table. The whiskey leaped from it, soaking the white cloth. The sharp sound of tumbler on table hushed the deal talk all around.

"Alabama needs to be blown away, wasted, put to sleep. I want him dead, super dead, so dead they have to invent a new word to describe it. Is *that* clear? Can there be any room for doubt about that?" His eyes were narrow. Spit darted from tight lips. His knuckles were white. He had shouted the first bit. He whispered the second. "And because nobody I employ has the *guts* to do the job for me, I'm going to waste the bastard myself."

The microphone between Emma Guinness's breasts was in no doubt at all as to the message it had received.

Emma Guinness winced as she remembered Dick Latham's Technicolor yawn at La Scala. It had been a problem getting him out. Thank God, they'd taken the chauffeur. His semicomatose body had been dragged through the thrilled diners. It had reminded the old-timers of the golden days when Flynn and Co. had dared to raise hell before Hollywood had been sold lock, stock, cock, and its barrel to the gray corporations. He had parked another cookie of humungous proportions in the back of the Rolls, and now he summoned up a third as the butler and footman carried him up the marble stairs to his bed. Emma stood at the foot of the staircase, fingering the pouch at her waist, and chuckled to herself as the retching, puking billionaire disappeared from view.

"When you've put him to bed, you can leave everything," she called up to the retreating trio. "I'll look after Mr. Latham."

"Very good, miss," said the puffing butler over his shoulder, relieved to be shedding responsibility for what looked like an extraordinarily unpromising situation.

Emma looked at her watch. It was early, not yet nine o'clock. She walked through the house toward the beach, and out onto the sand. The wind was picking up. It plucked at her hair, hot and caressing, blanketing her face with its valley heat. Today Malibu had changed. It was Santa Ana season. The freshness of the air was still there, but now there was the promise of something else—of sauna sunshine, desert dryness, of the crisp unrelenting warmth that would make you sweat and toss beneath your Porthault sheets.

The plan was coming together in her mind like a child's jigsaw. It was incredibly simple. All she needed was steel nerves, and the world would be handed to her on a silver salver. As she walked out onto the deserted dunes, she hitched up her skirt and fumbled for the pouch at her belt. The sleek brushed-chrome recorder that she reached for was the ticket to an earthly Paradise. She pressed REWIND, and almost immediately she pressed STOP, and then PLAY. Dick Latham's dire death threat against Alabama was crystal clear. He didn't sound drunk. The adrenaline of his fury had overridden the tranquillizing effect of the booze as he had made his vicious promise. The motive for murder was already established beyond reasonable doubt. So, now, was a murderous state of mind. Probable cause remained. And the crime. That needed to be committed. No question. Murders always needed a victim. It was a sine qua non. Ha! Ha! Oh yes, it was. A corpse was required. A corpse like Alabama. Now, Emma Guinness laughed. She rocked and roared with laughter out there on the lonely sand in front of Dustin's place and Bernie Brillstein's and Spielberg's rental that had burned to the ground so soon after he traded in Amy for groovy Kate Capshaw. She held her sides to keep them from splitting. She held the Pearlcorder tight in her hand like the lottery winner it was.

Slowly her laughter subsided. She felt so good—so crazy, but so wonderful. She had slipped her moorings forever now, and cut the rope that tied her to mundanity. She was adrift on the mad, wild seas, where anything could happen and the danger and possible disasters paled beside the infinite possibilities that were opening for her. By morning, she would be in a position to make all her hateful dreams come true.

She stood still in the wind. She was thinking, remembering. Like everyone else in the world, she had planned the perfect crime. Unlike the world's wankers, she would carry hers out. It all hinged on one memory. A couple of days ago, when she had been driving with Latham in the Testarossa, it had run out of gas. Luckily, they had been only minutes from the Cross Creek Texaco. Latham, laughing and enjoying the pretense that he was a mere mortal, had paid his deposit like a regular guy and walked out of the gas station with a gallon can of gas. He'd stuck it in the tank, thrown the empty can in the trunk, and headed straight home to Broad Beach to give the chauffeur a hard time. The can would be there now, where he'd left it—a can of gas carrying the fingerprints of a man with murder in his heart.

She hurried back into the house, and headed through it toward the five-car garage. She stopped and listened, but all was quiet. Dick would be unconscious upstairs. The servants would be tucked away doing whatever servants did when they could not be seen. She had all the time in the world. The keys to the Ferrari were on the board by the garage door. She took them, walked over to the gleaming red car, and opened the trunk. The empty can stared back at her. It was where Latham had thrown it. She picked up a clean rag from the bench, and lifted it gingerly from the bottom, being careful not to touch the chrome handle where the billionaire's fingerprints would be. She placed it next to the car's gas tank. She looked around. Shelves lined one wall of the carpeted garage. They were bursting with automobile goodies. A parts store would have given anything for the inventory. She selected a piece of hose, stuffed one end in the tank of the Ferrari and the other end in her mouth. She sucked until she tasted gas and then she transferred that end to the empty can. The high-octane fuel bubbled into its new home.

She picked up the can and carried it over to the white Targa Porsche, placing it carefully on the leather of the backseat, next to the red leather gloves that Latham wore when driving his toys. Again, she looked at her watch. Nine fifteen. She had several hours to lose. She didn't want the butler and the chauffeur testifying that Latham had been too drunk to stand. He would need a few hours to recover before a jury would deem him capable of doing the deed that she was about to do. Anyway, the middle of the night would be the best time. People slept then. People who were about to be framed slept; witnesses slept; victims slept . . . the sleep of the dead, the sleep of the damned.

She tiptoed out of the garage and made her way through the deserted, dimly lit house to her bedroom. She changed quickly into jeans and a black polo-neck sweater, and then she climbed into bed. She would not sleep, but she closed her eyes to cover her racing mind. Step by step she went through the plan, the left on Malibu Canyon, the right on Piuma Drive up to the Saddle Peak. She knew exactly where Alabama lived. She knew exactly where he would die. And in the morning, when the world woke to the smell of flames, she would claim all the prizes that were rightfully hers.

And then the world would darken for the people who had crossed her—for Dick Latham who had spurned her, for Pat Parker who had dared to be her rival, and, most of all, for Tony Valentino, who had humiliated her and left the terrible scars on her soul.

Alabama knew that it was the middle of the night but hadn't a clue what time it was. It was like this when he was working. The world went away. Nothing existed then, but the images, the magic, and the wonderful surprises in the darkness as he astonished himself with the astounding talent that seemed to belong to someone else. The image was coming through now, a ghostly shape forming itself on the paper, and Alabama filled in the gaps from memory—a tree here, a shaft of light there, the brushed texture of the bushes on the mountainside. The photographs of the canyon had done their job, but the memory of their beauty had lingered on, lighting up Alabama's art-starved mind. That afternoon he had returned to the place that would now be safe forever, and he had taken more photographs in celebration of his victory. It had been more complete than he had imagined. Overnight, Latham had become a pariah. His social life was dead. His businesses were badly wounded. Oh, he would survive. But never again would he shine like a newly minted penny. He was used up, tarnished, yesterday's man, and Alabama had organized it all . . . with a little help from his friends.

He walked across the darkroom and looked at the clock: 3:00 A.M. That was good. Another hour or two and he'd turn in. Maybe he'd sleep late tomorrow. The GMA satellite interview he'd done that morning had worn him out. He rubbed his eyes and returned to the bench. He had forgotten the joy of printing. Even in the early days when he had been taking photographs, King had done most of that. It wasn't that Alabama was bad at it, merely that subcontracting it left more time for shooting. He thought of King, fast asleep in his room upstairs. The excitement of the last few days, and Alabama's return to photography, had proved too much for his muscle-bound assistant. Drained by the nervous tension, he had crashed out early, popping a couple of rare sleepers to guarantee him the unconsciousness he needed. Alabama smiled. How like life that was. In the days when he had lain artistically fallow, King had never faltered. He had been a tireless source of strength and encouragement over the years as the doubt and the guilt had swirled around in the beer mist, and Alabama had wrestled unsuccessfully with his demons. Now, as Alabama had burst into the sunshine of his brand-new day, King had allowed himself to fall apart. Well, that was okay. Alabama felt strong enough to rise to any challenge. It would do him good to look after others for a change. He had been too selfish for way too long.

The sharp crack brought him back from his thoughts. It had sounded like a whip, and it had come from beyond the closed door of the darkroom. Something had fallen over. A brush? Whatever. The possibility of burglars didn't enter his mind. It was too remote out here for the lazy robbers from the urban ghettos, and the local variety would have sooner raided the devil in hell than Alabama. Could King be cruising around looking for something? No way. He was deep in his chemical land of Nod, and he'd deserved his escape.

The second noise was louder. It sounded like a gunshot. Damn! Alabama looked at the print. It was at a critical stage. It couldn't be risked, and bumps in the night were always a disappointment. He'd kick himself if he ruined a masterpiece for the pleasure of scaring off some inquisitive coyote. He bent over the image, screwing up his eyes in the dim infrared glow, and then he smelled fire.

That was different. It was what hill dwellers dreaded. At this time of the year the canyons were powder dry. The daily prayer was for the rains to begin. Alabama hurried to the door. He paused. He listened. He breathed in deeply. Should he open the thick, light-tight door? The thoughts were coming fast. If the house was burning, he might be opening the door on an inferno. The alternative wasn't attractive either. He could leave the door closed and bake in the oven of his darkroom. He tried to stay calm. It was probably nothing. Most things were. And he'd survived fires in the mountains before. Hell, in retrospect, they'd been fun, and the chaparral recovered eventually. It was nature's way of fertilizing the soil and clearing out the rubbish.

He put his hand on the inside of the door. It wasn't hot. That was a good sign. He filled his lungs with air. He crouched down. He opened the door. The flames licked at him. Long and thin, like the heads of snakes, they shimmied toward him and the wall of heat crashed into his face and filled up his mind with its danger. The room was burning. The house above it would be burning. All around the canyon would be burning in the fire of hell. The noise of the fire roared in his ears, crackling, hissing, sizzling across the neuron pathway to understanding. He slammed the door shut, buying himself only precious seconds, as he tried to think what to do. He stared around him in the bogus safety of the gloomy womb. There was an apron hanging on a hook. The water bath was full of ice-cold water. He grabbed at the apron, plunged it into the water above the glorious print the world would never see, and wrapped it around his head and shoulders. Crouching once again, he headed back to the door. Smoke was more of a danger than the flames, and hot air rose. He would stay near the floor where the oxygen still was, and he would try to make the stairs. He mapped out an escape route in his mind. Halfway up the stairs was a glass window. If he could break through that, he might be able to get out of the house. But the mountain would be burning. There would be no place to hide. Except the pool. Yes, that was it! Some of the old-timers who lived in the hills waited out brushfires in swimming pools. It was considered a macho thing to do. You put on tanks if you were a sissy, and you sat out the blaze in the deep end. If you were a real man, not the imitation variety, you saved on the cost of the bottled air. A foot of hose would hack it if you didn't mind your air smoky —one end in the mouth, the other an inch above the surface of the water. An hour or two of that, and you had a story that guaranteed attention for a year and a day. The pool was about a hundred feet from the house, and Alabama used it as a reservoir. He remembered it was at least half full.

He tensed himself at the door. He reached for the knob with one hand, and he clasped the wet material around his head with the other.

He opened the door and sprang forward into the fire. He didn't have to see. This was his home. The heat seared at him, plucking at his clothes, but he ran on, praying the stairs would not have been destroyed by fire. The bottom step gave way as he put his weight on it, but it held him—just—disintegrating with a sharp crack as his foot left it for the one above. He climbed the burning ladder, one step ahead of disaster, until he reached the turn in the stairwell. The window would be to his right. He didn't feel for it. His hands would melt in the heat out there. He kept them wrapped in the damp cotton. Like a linebacker shoulder-charging an opponent, Alabama threw his whole weight sideways. The window exploded against his arm, and amid a shower of glass and fiery frame, he shot through it. It was a six-foot drop, and he knew he wasn't positioned for a safe landing. There would be damage on contact. There was. He crashed down to earth on the shoulder that had atomized the window. There was a sickening wrench as he felt it dislocate, but the pain was bearable, because pain was a luxury this close to death. He peered out into the firestorm. Up ahead, the orchard that led to the possible safety of the pool was a furnace, but the scrub had been cut back to bare earth as a fire break. Unless he was unlucky, he would make it. He set off, loping through the sparks and the flying cinders like the wounded bear he was. He had traveled a distance of about thirty feet when he remembered King.

He stopped as the dreadful thought hit him. He turned back toward the house. It was burning from top to bottom. It was blanketed in flames, swathed in a marmalade bandage by the all-consuming fire. And King was inside, in a drugged sleep. Alabama's mighty heart heaved in his chest. He calculated the odds. Most probably, King was dead already. Nobody could have survived the inferno. To enter it and to try to save his friend would have only one result. He should hurry on to the pool while he still had time. It was the only sensible thing to do.

Like *hell* it was! Alabama didn't think anymore. Thinking had always been a bad business. It confused you. The gut was a far more dependable organ than the brain. He turned around, and he charged toward the house.

The back door had conveniently disappeared, and Alabama aimed himself through the halo of flames into the bowels of his burning home. The stairway to the upstairs bedrooms was a more serious affair than the basement steps he had just climbed. The sturdier oak could resist the flames longer. He took them two at a time as he plunged into the flaming hell, and he knew that his clothes were burning because he could feel the darts of pain against his skin, feel the skin peel away, feel the flesh bubble as it melted on the inside that had become the outside. He struggled on, aware that he was slowing as the wall of fire in front of him thickened. But there was no going back. There was only onward, and upward in a journey toward the eternity that he knew was his destination. King would already be walking there—King, who had given his life to Alabama, as Alabama was dedicating his to King in this gesture of ultimate solidarity. The pain had stopped, and the wall of fire was beckoning. His feet were lighter as he reached the landing, and there was a new spring in his step, because now he was at one with the fire. He was in tune with it, floating on it, a blissful, wondrous part of it. Here, at the end of life and the beginning of death, Alabama had *become* the flames. He staggered, but still he sailed on and his mind was full of love for the world that had given him such a wonderful existence. There would be others after him to march the arduous marches to beauty. Others, like Pat Parker, would travel his path through the long nights of sorrow to the light that he was on the verge of knowing. They would fight, and strive and suffer and enjoy as he had endured those things, and then they would merge as he was merging with the nature source in the endless sleep of ultimate peace.

Brighter than the brightest part of the fire burned Ben Alabama. He sparkled in the heart of the hills that were his home, and the light that shone from him would never die. It would live on forever in the beauty he had created, and in the beauty he had saved.

SIXTEEN

The water hammers crashed in Dick Latham's brain. He'd forgotten what a hangover was like. In the old days there had been lots, but he'd been young then. This was a vicious killer. The room swam when he stood. His stomach churned when he lay down. He wanted water, but he couldn't face the trip to the bathroom. He needed aspirin, but he wouldn't be able to keep it down. He longed for death, but he hadn't the energy for anything so exhausting. The metaphysical element was a minor problem. Through the banging in his head, there were fragments of memories. In La Scala, embarrassing things had been said, inappropriate deeds done. The hell with it, even in extremis Dick Latham didn't worry about the idiots. What they thought of him was their problem, not his. Nobody ever said unpleasant things to his face, and he couldn't care less what was said behind his back. He held on to his forehead to prevent it from releasing his brains all over the bed to go with the other nasties that had accumulated through the night. He turned his head to left and right, wondering if movement would help. The wave of nausea rushed through him. The sun was peeping through the blinds. From the degree of brightness it was early, maybe seven o'clock. He groaned, but that, too, was a mistake. The ticking of his beside clock was deafening. He was reminded of Bob Newhart's plaintive cry. "*Please* don't fizz, Alka-Seltzer."

Then he remembered. Oh no! Any minute now the television was going to turn itself on. It was the way he woke up, to Bryant and Co., and dishy Deborah Norville, who always made for a sexy start to the day. God, that would be the last straw. Willard's heartiness, and all those geriatric birthdays would be a cruel and unusual punishment. Where the hell was the remote control? The preprogrammed TV turn-on could be aborted . . . if you had a master's degree in computer engineering from MIT, and a head that didn't hurt when you thought.

He tried to sit up. As usual, the remote control had vanished. He flopped down again. Resignation crashed over him. He had as much control over events as the man at the stake before the firing squad. At least that lucky guy would have a pain-free future.

Click! It had happened. The room was full of Toyotas and why you should hurry to buy them, of toothpaste that made you taste good, of a breakfast cereal that saved your life. Then there was Deborah Norville, queasily self-confident as she wrapped her luscious lips around the news.

"A brush fire in the Malibu hills claimed the life last night of famous photographer and environmentalist, Ben Alabama. Mr. Alabama, known to everyone simply as Alabama, died when fire destroyed his ranch house in the Santa Monica Mountains. Recently Alabama won a notable victory when he prevented the siting of the Cosmos movie studios on undeveloped land next to the Saddle Peak ranch where he lived. Police suspect arson. The president, a long-time friend of Alabama's, said that America and the world had lost a great artist and a great man. He will be attending the funeral later this week in California.

"In Lebanon . . ."

Again Latham sat up. This time he stayed up. His hangover had disappeared. Alabama had been burned. God had granted his wish. He'd never believed in prayer. He did now. He reached for the telephone. He should be thrilled. He *was* thrilled. No, he wasn't. Hell, he wasn't thrilled at all. Last night he'd wanted Alabama dead. Now that he was, Latham missed him. Somehow Alabama had been a part of his life. He had been a comfortable enemy to hate, and he went back a long way, back to Paris when life had meant something. There was nobody else in the whole world who had known Dick Latham in the good old days. It counted for something. Damn it, he was sorry the old buzzard was dead. Wasn't life extraordinary? Wilde had been right. The only thing worse than not getting what you wanted was getting it.

The telephone beneath his hand was ringing. He picked it up.

"Dick? Tommy. Have you heard about Alabama?"

"I just caught it on NBC. I can't believe it."

"I never believed in coincidence before," said Havers. His tone said that he was not totally prepared to believe in it now.

"Yeah, amazing." Dick Latham's mind stopped in its tracks. What the hell had he said to all those guys in La Scala last night? He'd threatened Alabama. And now Alabama was burned to death in a fire the police believed was started by an arsonist. The two and two made four. He might be a suspect. Thank God, he had an alibi. His skin was suddenly clammy. Sweat sprang from beneath his arms. What alibi? Someone had poured him into bed around nine. He had slept alone. And Alabama's ranch was only a twenty-five-minute drive away.

"Listen, Tommy, can you slip down here to California? I'd like you to be around. Drop everything, okay? Just get here, and bring that slick lawyer from Kruger, French. You know, the young guy with the sharp suits, Felderman or Federman . . ."

"Feldman? The one we used when the accountant at KBAC had his hand in the till? He's criminal law."

"Bring him anyway, okay?" said Latham. The premonition was building inside him. He tried to put the bits of the evening back together. He'd played most of it as Al Capone, the Mr. Big who could not be crossed without exacting a terrible retribution. His timing had been way off. Thank God there was no hard evidence of the things he'd said. The table of tourists in La Scala had seen him being carried out. Nobody would have taken him seriously. Everyone would have reckoned the drink was talking. Anyway, one thing was for sure. *He* wasn't the firebug. If the cops had evidence of arson, it wouldn't point the finger at him. No way, could it. No way.

"Are you all right, Dick? You sound like you've got the flu."

"Yeah, no, I'm fine, maybe some virus or something. Anyway, hurry on down and we'll see if we can salvage any of this Cosmos thing. Maybe now that the old boy's history, everyone'll relax on it. I wouldn't count on it, but we ought to explore it."

"I'll be there in nine," said Tommy Havers. He hung up. So did Latham. For a second or two he was thoughtful. He should get more information, perhaps call Arnold York, the publisher of the *Malibu Times*. He was a helpful guy and he'd have the police version by now.

The door of his bedroom opened. Nobody had knocked. Emma Guinness stood in the doorway. She was in blue jeans and a black polo-neck sweater. She looked like a dumpy cat burglar. There was something in her hand.

"What the hell are you doing in here? Didn't anyone teach you how to knock?"

The expression in her eyes stopped him. It was triumphant. The smile devoured her face. In all his life Latham had never seen anyone so transcendentally happy.

"Well, Dick Latham, aren't *you* the man who keeps his promises," she said.

Latham opened his mouth to pick up where he left off, but as he did so, his premonition began to focus itself. The blurry feeling was clarifying, taking shape, and the vision that it formed uncaged the flying insects in the pit of his long-suffering stomach.

"Exactly what do you mean?" said Dick Latham. But in his guts he knew. Emma Guinness was insinuating that he had killed Alabama, or at least had him killed, but it was more than that. Her whole manner suggested that she had something that could tie him to the crime he had never committed. He tried to get his mind working as he covered the possible angles. It had to be more than his drunken threats, but what? He had done nothing. He was innocent. The only crime he was guilty of was wanting Alabama dead. But the look on her face was curdling further his already curdled stomach. It was a spine-chilling look of the purest evil. Her face was twisted in an expression of total wickedness, and the blood ran cold in Dick Latham's veins as he realized that he had made a fundamental mistake that he might pay for with everything. He had always known that Emma Guinness was cruel and vindictive. Those attributes had counted for nothing, because of her incredible talent. He had failed, however, to understand the most important truth of all. He hadn't realized that Emma Guinness was mad.

"What I mean is that you burned Alabama last night," said Emma. She took a step into the room. She closed the bedroom door behind her.

"You know I didn't do that," said Latham, his voice shaking.

"Does it matter what I know? It's what the police know that counts, isn't it?"

"There's not a shred of . . ."

"Evidence to suggest that you did it?" Emma finished his sentence. She was standing at the end of his bed now. He could see her glow. She was radiant. She was totally in command. She held up her hand so that he could see the tape recorder.

"This heard you," she said simply. "It was listening when you told it what you were going to do to Alabama."

Not for one single second did he think she was lying. And he knew this was only the beginning. There was more. There was worse to come. He felt the blood drain from his face. His stomach turned. Over her shoulder Willard Scott was wearing something camp and cuddling an embarrassed Okie at a senior citizens' picnic.

"The cops will have found a can of gasoline up there on Saddle Peak," said Emma. "The one you picked up the other day when the Ferrari died on us. Remember?"

Latham swallowed hard. He remembered. He'd carried it a hundred yards. His prints would be all over it. The tape plus the can equaled a case, if not a conviction, and an arrest would be more than enough to destroy him. The psychopath at the foot of his bed held his future in the palm of her hand. He could take the recorder from her by force, but the tape would be long gone and well hidden. The can would be with Homicide. It would take nothing more than one call to link the prints to him. Dick Latham could feel the handcuffs on his wrists.

But even as he dared to contemplate the bleakness of his future, he recoiled from the horror of what had happened.

"You did it," he said, his voice quiet but shaking. "You started the fire that killed Alabama."

She laughed then, a hideous, vicious laugh, and it was more than enough as an answer. She had flipped. She'd gone crazy. God, he should have seen the signs. People were always talking about her paranoia. Several people, including Tommy Havers, had warned him that she was teetering on the brink of insanity. He simply hadn't listened. It wasn't a side of her that he saw, and there were always a ton of men to bad-mouth a bright, brilliant woman, especially when she was a success and had power over them. But that was then. This was now. He was in mortal danger. A murderess was standing in his bedroom, and she was threatening to frame him for the crime she'd committed. Facts winged into his mind. He had the motive. He'd declared his intent, both publicly and privately. His threats were on tape. If Emma had driven up to the mountains to start the fire, she'd have taken one of his cars. The tire prints would be up there somewhere. He had no alibi. He'd slept alone. His fingerprints were on the can. If she had the will, she could do it . . . and the will was painted in blood all over her face.

"What do you want from me?" he said at last. There was always a deal—always was, always would be.

Emma paused to savor the moment. Her request would be granted, and it would be the first of many. She had the stuff of which blackmailers dreamed. She puffed herself up. She was going to enjoy these words, because of all the things they meant and they would mean.

"I want Cosmos Studios," she said. "I want total power to run it as I wish."

"Emma Guinness? Running Cosmos? You're joking, Dick."

"I'm not joking," said Dick Latham. He wasn't. He had never been more serious. He looked out of the window to avoid Havers's eye. At this moment he would have gladly traded places with any one of the improverished surfers on the beach.

"But she wouldn't have a clue how to run a major studio. I wouldn't. You probably wouldn't. I mean, she'd be a disaster. We'd be the laughingstock of Hollywood, and everywhere else, for that matter."

"I've made up my mind," said Latham. "This isn't a discussion, it's a statement of fact."

Havers looked desperate. He wasn't about to give up, whatever the risk to his career of disagreeing with the boss.

"What about *New Celebrity?* It's running great, and it's Emma's baby. You've admitted that she turned it around single-handed. If she leaves to screw up Cosmos, what the hell will happen to the magazine? Don't do this, Dick. At least explain the logic of it. It just doesn't make sense."

Dick Latham kept his eyes on the sea. "She's a trendsetter. She knows what the public wants. If she can pick fashions, she can choose movies. There's nothing else to the job. Some lawyer can second-guess her on all the business stuff. It'll work. Trust me. My instinct says it's right."

Havers had never heard Latham sound so unconvincing and so unconvinced. He remembered the conversation he'd had with Emma in the Canal Bar when she'd pitched him the idea of her running Cosmos. He hadn't bought it. Apparently Latham had. Why? What the hell was going down? Maybe there was a grain of truth in what Latham was saying, but overall it was naïve. There was marketing and distribution, the vital business of setting up a film, costing it, anticipating the problems up front. And you had to have believability in the industry, a network of relationships with the people that counted, with the stars, the packagers, and the vitally important banks. It helped to have shake-hands integrity, or rather the ability to fake it, and it was a plus if you could develop an on-the-lot esprit that would get people working for less money and keep the unions sweet. Emma Guinness excelled in none of the above. She was ignorant of moviemaking, and she was psychotoxic on top. Dick Latham would regret his decision from day one. The interesting question was why he was making it.

"Well, Dick, you know best," said Havers. "It's your show, but I've always considered Emma Guinness to be dangerously unstable." It was his way of washing his hands of the whole business. "When does she take over?"

"She's taken over," said Latham. His voice seemed far away. He was strangely detached. "She's hard at work right now."

Havers couldn't resist it.

"Doing exactly what?" he asked.

Dick Latham turned to face him.

"Rewriting the script of *Malibu*," he replied.

There was a long silence.

"I didn't know that project was still on the go list," said Havers carefully. He had heard the Pat Parker diatribe against Latham at the Getty. It had been the catalyst to the explosive reaction of the Malibu movie stars. There was a sense in which it had been Pat Parker, not Alabama, who had finally derailed Latham's plan. At the very least, Havers imagined that she'd have been off the payroll together with Tony and Allison and anyone else who might have been guilty through their association with her. Apparently not. Why?

"There comes a point beyond which personal feelings shouldn't enter into these things," lied Latham. "If *Malibu* and Pat Parker were a good idea before our little setback, then they're still a good idea after it. I called her and told her so." He turned away to the relative safety of the sea. Pat Parker and personal feelings were *not* separate. She might have crossed him, but God, she'd looked magnificent doing it. It had taken his breath away. Not much did. At the moment of his groveling defeat it was the one bright spot. She'd called him a child. She had his number. That made her unique. She was the club to which he wanted to belong, the one with the guts and good taste to pitch him out. It was almost as simple as that.

"And what does the new studio boss think of *Malibu?* Wasn't there bad blood between Guinness and Valentino? What the hell's she doing fiddling around with the script? That's hardly what studio heads do. It all sounds pretty weird to me . . ."

Dick Latham took a deep breath. He hoped Havers would never know how weird it really was, that Emma Guinness was the only thing separating him from a murder-one conviction. Compared to the importance of that, who the hell cared what she was doing at Cosmos?

Havers, however, in the unaccustomed role of dog with a bone, couldn't let go. "I mean, what's she *doing* with the script?"

"She's beefing up the sex scenes," said Dick Latham, with a nervous laugh.

The helicopter swooped low over Saddle Peak. The charred remains of the Alabama ranch, still smoking in the early light, lay like a black carpet below. Pat Parker leaned out of the window, and the tears rolled down her cheeks in the gusting wind. She could see the remains of the house now, a gutted shell against the rocks of the canyon wall. Nothing could have survived the terrible blaze. She tried to picture his last minutes, tried to imagine his thoughts as the hellfire devoured him and the home he'd loved. Already she missed him. There was a void in her life where he had been, and she knew it would never be filled.

Pat leaned over to the pilot and signaled with her hand for him to go lower. All morning they had been scouting locations for the movie, but this pilgrimage had always been at the back of her mind.

"Can you land?" she shouted above the roar of the rotor.

He nodded and swooped in, the *wop-wop-wop* of the engine rebounding from the dense walls of the canyon.

As soon as the helicopter was still, Pat jumped onto the scorched earth. The path of the fire was clearly visible. It had started from the road, high above, and rushed down, cutting a swath of destruction across the valley as it headed for Alabama's house. It had probably been started by a cigarette thrown by some careless driver as he headed home, oblivious to the havoc he had left behind. Certainly nobody could have done such a wicked thing on purpose, despite fire department and police theories of arson.

She walked toward the deserted house, so well remembered, and once again the grief gripped her. The funeral was tomorrow, and it would be a media event of vast proportions. The presence of the president alone would ensure that, but so would Alabama's personal reputation. Today, she would say her private farewell, in the place where his ghost would linger, here in the hills whose beauty would last forever in his photographs. At least the prints were safe. Nobody who lived in the Santa Monica Mountains could ignore the possibility of brushfires, and Alabama's precious negatives were locked in a fireproof vault at the Bank of America in Century City. What would become of them? Alabama had no family. Presumably they would be left in trust to some museum, although he had hated those and the besuited art-business men who ran them.

She walked toward the gap where the big oak doors had been, and looked in. She could see right through the house, past the frames of the melted plate-glass windows to the vista that Alabama had loved. It was a forever view, big and grand like the old man who had watched it, and more than anything it reminded Pat of the friend she would never see again. The staircase had vanished, and there was no way to get upstairs to the place he had died. But she could sense him. She could feel the spirit of him in the place his soul would never leave. It was a comforting feeling. She was close to him, and there was warmth in her heart beside the sorrow for the surrogate father she had lost.

King had died too, near as always to the master he loved. Once again tears sprang to Pat's eyes as she thought of the gentleness of his strength. His muscles had not saved him from the flames. Nothing could have done that. It must have descended like a thunderbolt, total in its surprise. But there would have been time for panic in the frantic seconds before the end, and Pat tried to close off her mind to the horror of those moments.

On an impulse, she knelt down on the singed tiles of the floor, and she closed her eyes and clasped her hands before her in prayer.

"Dear God, protect them," she whispered. "Wherever they are, love them as they loved me."

Emma Guinness looked out to sea. The Santa Ana wind had picked up the San Fernando Valley smog, pushed it through the Malibu canyons, and deposited it—a thin layer of yellow fuzz—over the surface of the ocean. But Emma couldn't have cared less. What was a little pollution when all her blackest wishes had been granted? She leaned over the edge of the bluff and looked down to the jagged rocks ninety feet below. Surfers were riding the waves. A girl sunbathed topless on the private beach. The crash of the ceaseless surf caressed her ears. She breathed in deeply and turned around toward the state-of-the-art Point Dume contemporary home that Cosmos had leased for her. Here on Cliffside Drive the real estate was real. Down on the sand a tidal wave would one day drag the stilt homes out to sea. Most of the landside houses would be consumed by fire. But the bluffs would survive for a thousand years, until the rock-eating sea eventually triumphed over them.

The platform on which she stood was built on a promontory that jutted out from the cliffs. It had been organized as a sitting area with a Santa Barbara umbrella and some high-tech Tropitone sun beds. Compact-disc music warbled gently on the outside loudspeaker system. The portable laptop word processor sat expectantly on the table. Emma sighed. She'd taken a few minutes off from writing to savor her wonderful world, but she couldn't stay away for long. There was too much to do; too much misery to sow; too many enemies to be cast down.

She walked back to the Balans chair that spared your back and knelt down at it, flexing her fingers in the speckled sunlight of Malibu's Indian summer. She adjusted the page and ran off a riff of sentences to start the flow. It was the third day of her tenure at Cosmos, yet she had hardly been near the place. She had her priorities, and the birth pain of the new studio was low on the list of them. At the very top was revenge. She had spent the time here on the bluff, writing, while the trucks unloaded her meager possessions onto the marble and granite floors of her spectacular rented home. Somewhere inside, a brace of secretaries fielded the calls. Here on the cliff face, the temperature was a few degrees hotter than anywhere else in Malibu, and the steam heat was coming from the green screen of the Smith-Corona. She had never written sex before, but, boy, had she got the hang of it. The visions flowed freely across a mind alive with make-believe sensations as the smells and the sounds, the tastes and the touches, tumbled over each other in her fevered brain. She held back on the euphemisms —the proud urgency of his desire, the shy ventricles, the illicit amulets of love. Instead, she named names, crude, rude, and deadly shrewd, as she spelled it out so that nobody would need to use any imagination. This, after all, was a script. It was her direction to the director. When she called a spade a spade, she wanted there to be no mistake about recognition of the implement.

She chuckled to herself as her fingers flew across the keyboard. Sometimes writing was like this. At times like these she seemed to be tuned to some inner steam of consciousness, and her fingers could hardly work fast enough to keep pace with the manic dictation that spilled up from her creative well. It was rare, but wonderful when it happened, a total contrast to the gray, sad days when every word had to be chiseled from stone. But she wasn't surprised. Everything was working for her. It was coming together. The moment she had surrendered to her darkest dreams, she had triumphed. A little murder had been the smallest price to pay.

The ugliest secretary in Hollywood, chosen by Emma for her spectacular homeliness, called out across the lawn. "Mr. Richard Latham on the telephone, Ms. Guinness."

"Take a message," Emma shouted back. Tony was beneath, Melissa was on top in the cowgirl position. Camera pans across the lovers, then zooms in for close-up. She could see Pat Parker's face, see her tense body hunched in the director's chair, as her lover made love to the legend before her eyes. Melissa had to thrust up, had to push with her finger into Tony's half-open mouth, had to moan and groan with crazed passion as she readied herself for her celluloid orgasm. Close-up on Melissa's face. Soundtrack. Wind up the music. Close-up of Tony's face as he lost it in the sea of sticky ecstasy. Would Pat be watching through the hand lens to frame the shot? Would Melissa be coming for real as she performed the on-set party trick she was famous for? And what would Tony Valentino be thinking as the sexpert balled him, as his girlfriend watched, wondering how soon she dared yell "Cut"? Emma could actually feel the angst. It jelled with the groovy sweat beneath her arms. It hovered in the bright air. It fingered her spine with its delicious anxiety.

She whacked out the words with renewed intensity, and as she did so the switch flicked inside her. She was turned on. She was warming up. The juices were on the move, like the ones she was writing about. She had become Melissa Wayne, throbbing and pulsating beneath Tony Valentino's piston power. She had him at last, nailing her to the floor. She was wrapped around his hard body, sucking him dry as he surged into her. Ooooooh! She shifted her shins on the chair and waved her rump in the air, wiggling it from side to side as the screen rocked to her autoerotica. Jesus! She was melting as she wrote about them melting. She was all revved up, gunning in neutral, and the typewriter keys beneath her fingers were the substitute for the bits of bodies she so suddenly needed to touch.

Merely reading this would make Pat Parker cry. Directing it would drive her mad. And Tony, proud, arrogant Tony, wouldn't he just love playing a piece of meat? The scene was X-rated. The "serious" actor would be a Harry Reems dead ringer. The guy who'd already bared it all for Emma's *New Celebrity* would be doing it in the movies and the talkies. He'd be typecast for a hundred years. As a geriatric they'd be offering him senior citizens' sex-instruction videos. The laugh burbled up from her stomach, as she savored the magic moment and all the ones to come, and she tapped away like a woman possessed as she dreamed up the scenario of her fiendish retribution.

They had to get from the floor to the bed, from wide-open spaces to the secrecy of sheets. It was beneath the Pratesis that Melissa Wayne, queen of closed sets, could wreak the havoc she was so very famous for wreaking. She didn't like jock straps and bikini bottoms and all the bits and pieces the professionals used. She liked to do away with them for the greater glory of the "art" she performed. When Melissa Wayne did her orgasm in close-up, there was only ever one take.

Emma's fingers shifted the lovers.

> He picks her up, roughly, as if she is weightless. He walks to the bed. He throws her down. He tears back the covers and the sheets. She rolls gratefully between them. She turns to watch the lover she longs for. Her lips are parted, moist with lust.

There. They were there, where the damage could and would be done. Next, she would draw the sheets over them. She would melt into his arms. Her hips would thrust eagerly toward his. Emma stopped typing. It was almost too good to be true. Pat Parker and Tony Valentino's relationship would not survive the *Malibu* she was creating. The sizzling script would see to that, and so would the sexual athleticism and Method acting of Melissa Wayne. Then, when the relationship was in ruins, she would make her move, and Tony Valentino, who had turned her down once and humiliated her, would not do so again. He would crawl on his hands and knees across the floor to satisfy her. He would plead to please the studio boss, because, if he didn't, she would take away the future that was his obsession. She would have him where she wanted him at last, humble at her feet, and in his gritty, groveling surrender she would transform the hero into the body slave she had always dreamed of owning.

Emma's fingers snaked back to the keyboard, and once again the letters began to dance across the screen. They formed the language of erotica, but they spelled the death warrant for Pat and Tony's happiness.

Only one thing was needed for the great and glorious conclusion she planned, and the strains of Wagner surged suddenly in her head as she thought of it.

Melissa Wayne was already her ally. Tonight, when they met, they would sign their pact in Tony Valentino's blood.

Emma sat behind her desk in the power position. Covered in rhinestones from head to toe, she looked like the Lone Ranger in drag, but the invisible sign above her head read STUDIO BOSS, and it was Melissa Wayne who had made the journey to Malibu. She sat across from Emma in a blue-jeaned tangle of limbs, and she licked luscious lips as she spoke.

"Well, Emma, I won't say I wasn't surprised, but I *do* say I'm pleased. It's wonderful for you, for me, for women in general."

Melissa Wayne purred like the cat she was. She had never liked a woman, dead or alive, and she didn't intend to start now. But she had been around Hollywood long enough to appreciate the value of the right noises. The bitch across the desk had come a long way from magazine land. Clearly she had balls. She had to be humored, at least while she sat in the CEO's musical chair. Anyway, they had already established a common interest—the punishment and humiliation of the impossible Tony Valentino. If that item was still on the agenda, Melissa was Emma's enthusiastic ally.

"It's fun, isn't it?" warbled Emma Guinness, shifting around to avoid a rhinestone that had impacted her butt. "I mean, everybody's all caught up with the science of moviemaking, yet everyone admits they don't know how to do it. I plan to enjoy myself. That way the public will, too."

Melissa laughed. "That's always been my motto. I get on pretty well with my leading men."

Emma joined in the laughter, glad that Melissa had brought up the subject. She was aware that it hadn't been accidental. The interview she had shared with the star at her Benedict Canyon home had been "no holds barred." It had stretched over a couple of bottles of Krug and mostly it had been about Tony Valentino. They knew each other pretty well for two people who didn't believe in friendship.

"Are you still seeing Tony?" said Emma.

"No," said Melissa. She bit her lip at the thought of him, and the way he had behaved toward her. Their bizarre relationship had hardly defined tenderness and commitment, but there had been the closeness of bodies. At least he had bothered to be beastly to her. That took effort and energy. It had been an involvement of sorts. Then, out of the blue, it had stopped. There had been no explanations, no apologies, and no good-byes. One minute he had been her pirate lover, cruel, crude, and unpredictable, but at least *there*. The next moment he had gone. She hadn't been able to reach him on the phone. Her letters, faxes, and Fed-Exes had gone unanswered. His agent had given her the Hollywood runaround. For a time she had wallowed in hysteria. She had dreamed of sending him dead chickens and skewered dolls, and she had left terrible messages on his answering machine promising retribution, and then begging him to return. Finally, the heat of her feelings had cooled and, in the unforgiving light of her new dawn, she knew exactly what she wanted for her sadistic lover. Even in the days when she had lain used and abused on the floor, hosed down by his lust, she had wanted to hurt him. Now, deserted and discounted, she planned far worse things for the boy who had dared to humiliate Melissa Wayne, the star the sane world yearned for.

"He went back with Pat, I heard," said Emma.

"I heard that too," said Melissa through tight teeth.

Their glinting eyes locked together.

"But he's still the supporting actor in our movie, isn't he, Melissa? It's his one shot at fame, isn't it? Wild horses won't make him give that up."

Melissa smiled. She liked the "our movie" bit, and it was true. Melissa was the box-office legend. Emma was the studio boss. Between them they owned the film. If they stuck together, they couldn't be defeated.

"Meaning?" drawled Melissa, her smile deepening.

"I'm just stating facts," said Emma. "Tony's going to have to realize that we're the boss. If he wants the movie, he pleases us."

Melissa Wayne squirmed in her chair, pushing her pelvis down on the heel on which she sat. The *boss!* She was going to be Tony's *boss!* She was going to get control of him at last. Her bit would cut into *his* mouth; her whip would crack against *his* flank. She leaned forward into the conspiracy.

"That will be very nice," she said quietly, with an intensity that Emma could almost touch.

"I should say that I've made a few changes in the script," said Emma, a half smile playing around her lips.

Melissa was vibrating on her wavelength. The changes that Emma had made would be good changes. There was no question about it.

"What I've done basically," continued Emma, "is to beef up the love scenes between you and Tony. And I've strengthened the obsession element. Before, there was a certain equality in the relationship. Now, we have a struggling young actor, infatuated with a cruel and capricious megastar. Does that sound like you and Tony, Melissa?"

The expression on Melissa Wayne's face said that it sounded like sweet music. Her mind was racing deliciously, but there was a question she needed to have answered.

"What does Pat Parker think of that?" she said.

"We don't have to worry about Pat Parker. I don't subscribe to the 'auteur' theory. She's just the director. She does what I tell her to do. What *we* tell her to do. So far she knows nothing, but if she doesn't like it, she can walk."

"And Latham?" Melissa wanted to cover all the angles. In moviemaking it was vital to understand where the ultimate power lay. She could hardly control her excitement. A beautiful idea was forming in her mind. Could Emma Guinness be thinking it, too?

"Latham will give me carte blanche. My control at Cosmos is total. He's promised me that." Emma waved an expansive hand in the air for emphasis.

"So we're going to make a very steamy movie," whispered Melissa. Her pink tongue darted out to moisten already damp lips.

"Oh, yes, we are," agreed Emma. "A very sexy, very *realistic* movie."

Melissa had been given the opening. She had hardly needed it.

"In a couple of my shows," she said, "when the chemistry has been right, I've found that a closed set can do wonders for a love scene. It helps if you can really let go—keep the acting to a minimum, if you know what I mean."

"I know *exactly* what you mean. Keep the acting to the *bare* minimum," Emma laughed.

"I wonder if Tony could be persuaded . . ." said Melissa wickedly, the lewd images already dancing in her mind.

"I feel absolutely certain that he could, if it's put to him in the right way . . ." Emma's X-rated thoughts were steaming up her brain. "Of course, Pat Parker would have to direct the scene, wouldn't she? There'd probably be fireworks!" The glee positively creamed from Emma's words.

"Yeah, she'd go wild, wouldn't she?" agreed Melissa, delighted. "But if we sort of insisted on it, and didn't back down. If we stuck together and issued ultimatums and things, then everyone would have to fall into line . . ." Melissa twiddled her fingers in her hair like the willful child she was.

"Pr*ecisely*." Emma Guinness leaned back in her chair. Her voice was thick with satisfaction.

They were singing in harmony. They were joined to each other at the hip. They were glued to each other by the intensity of their hatred for Tony Valentino, and by the force of their weird lust for him. It was an unholy alliance. It was an invincible one.

"Have you by any chance got a copy of your revised script? I'd like to take a look at it tonight."

Melissa Wayne was a throbbing beacon of perverse desire. Lust bubbled in her blood. Loathing foamed in her soul.

Emma picked up the blue-covered script from her desk. She held it out toward Melissa. "Take a look at page one," she said.

Emma Guinness was taking the meeting. She sat behind the vast desk and peered around the room like a scientist eying a cage of experimental rats. Her audience had the expectant, hang-dog appearance of Hollywood hotshots in the presence of someone hotter than themselves. They smiled a lot, shifted about, and behind their nervous eyes you could see them dreaming up clever things to say. The executive producer, fat, blond, and forty, was clearly a candidate for gallstones. The two junior production execs in identical Montana-type brown leather jackets, 501's, and boots, seemed thin and worried as well they might be with bank repo orders threatening on the serious cars they couldn't quite afford. The scriptwriter was desperate, and with excellent reason. He was facing the firing squad. The producer, pulled into the project both because he had an on-lot deal with the old Cosmos and because he had a mahogany-brown nose, was tuning up.

"I'd just like to say—on behalf of us all—that Mr. Latham has made a brilliantly original choice in hiring you to run the studio. I'm a great admirer of your new magazine, and I just know that wonderful times are ahead for Cosmos. It's a thrill to be part of them." He pulled out a large handkerchief and wiped sweat from his greasy brow. Had it been enough? Was his producer deal safe? He hadn't had a sniff at a hit in five years. He was about as expendable as it was possible to get.

Emma nodded curtly. "We're here to discuss the *Malibu* script," she said in a way that made it sound like an all-purpose rebuke.

She picked it up from the desk between thumb and forefinger as if it were contaminated. Then she dropped it. It fell, and lay there among the pencils and telephones, half-open, half-closed. "I think you should all know that I'm rewriting it."

Everyone looked at everyone else. Power went to heads in Hollywood. Delusions were always grandiose. The fawning subservience of inferiors and the inventiveness of their flattery unhinged even the most stable, and there were few enough of those in town. However, it usually took a week or two to happen. The Guinness chick, having pulled the job from the hat against odds that were far greater than astronomical, had apparently succumbed to Tinsel Town's occupational disease with earth-shattering speed. Now, she thought she could write a script. Clearly, she was a frustrated "serious" writer. A lot of people who ended up running magazines were. Starved of a Nobel, the intellectual manqué had her sights on a screenwriting Oscar. They all groaned inside. This was a textbook example of how movie stinkers got born.

"Major rewrites?" tried the jumpy scribbler who'd done the first draft.

"Not so *very* major," said Emma. The writer brightened visibly. His credit might still be safe.

"What I've basically done is strengthened the sex. We're lucky enough to have Melissa in this movie, and you don't hire a Streisand unless she gets to sing."

Tweedle Dum and Tweedle Dee, the nervous young Turks, laughed obsequiously to show that they'd got the joke. Melissa's love scenes were the stuff of legend. They were what her box office was all about. Then there were those rumors—the ones about her liking to do it for *real*.

"Is that wise?" tried the producer. "I mean, the sex has been understated in this summer's movies, and they've done great."

Emma laughed her nastiest laugh.

"Well, you have vast experience, Mr. . . . Mr. . . ." She petered out, rudely insinuating that she had forgotten the man's name. "And we must all listen to what you say, but at the new Cosmos we are going to *try* to escape the old thinking. That was why Dick hired me. The safest thing to do, supposedly, is to copy the movies that worked last year. We are going to try to live a little more dangerously, and with a little more imagination. I happen to think that *Malibu* needs hot sex. It's a movie about obsession and about love. Love and sex go together, you know. You ought to try it sometime."

The producer was eager to show that Yes was his middle name. He did a 180-degree handbrake turn.

"Yeah, Emma, you're right. *9½ Weeks* might not have hit big domestic, but it was hot as hell on video, did a hundred million overseas, and made Basinger an international star. They're making a sequel. And *Sea of Love* did gangbuster business. In an age of look-don't-touch sex, I think the public wants sensuality. No nasty diseases from watching it. I'm game, up to and including . . . if you know what I mean. Is Valentino?"

"Valentino will do whatever it takes," said Emma, drifting away into the reverie called "revenge."

She had never forgotten, nor would she ever forget, the things he'd once said to her. This was the payoff from the pact she'd signed with the devil. Her new life was running clockwork smooth. Murder and blackmail had been swapped for a studio, and ultimate power over those she hated. It was the perfect deal, and it had taken steel nerves of a strength they didn't know about in Hollywood, where they were supposed to have invented the things. These losers in her office had no idea what she was allowed to do. The poor fools thought that Latham was the boss-man. How could they know that she owned Latham, far more surely than if she had married him? A single phone call and he would be booked on a murder one. She could do it right now. She could pick up the phone on her desk and say to the cops, "Latham did it." They had only to take his fingerprints, and it would be Hello, San Quentin. Later, she'd make him give her money, and all the other things. Right now she had what she wanted—people to play with, and power over the boy who had done her wrong, and over the woman who loved him.

"I get the feeling that you'll be taking a day-by-day interest in this show," said the producer carefully.

"You feel right," snapped Emma. "Pat Parker reports to me. Everyone does, okay? Of course, we will respect *all* Melissa

Wayne's opinions. She's the engine on this thing. It's her vehicle. She gets what she wants when she wants it. Understood? If there are any problems, anytime, day or night, somebody contacts me. I can't emphasize enough how badly I will feel if anybody upsets Melissa."

She peered around the room for nonexistent dissent. She knew she was encouraging breach of the usual chain of command, and that it was totally unorthodox. But that didn't matter. These idiots thought the name of the game was to make mere money. They hadn't a clue that it was called "revenge."

"Send her in," said Emma. She took a deep breath. This was going to be fun, but it was going to be dangerous fun. Pat Parker was her own size. She felt like putting her ankle boots up on the desk as a power play, so she did. What a pity she never smoked. For the first time in her life she saw the point of cigars.

"Listen, Emma, what the hell's going on around here? I've just heard from some gofer that you're rewriting the script. Why wasn't I told?"

Pat came in at the run and shooting from the hip. She was furious. Her words splattered like bullets into the armor-plated shield of the Guinness aura.

"Yeah, I did some rewriting. You know how it is. Nobody can write out here. On this side of the Mississippi, words are things you use on telephones."

"Don't be clever. Explain why I was out of the loop."

"Heavens, Pat, you're so *direct*. This isn't a John Wayne movie. Calm down, for goodness' sake."

"I'm not calm. Why the hell should I be? The studio boss rewrites the script and holds a script conference without me, and I get to hear about it on the grapevine. It's incredibly unprofessional . . . at the very least."

She towered over the Guinness desk, her cheeks red, her eyes flashing.

"Ah, yes, we movie old-timers must remain professional at all costs, mustn't we? As a veteran studio chief, I salute your concern as an experienced director." The sarcasm didn't last long on her mean lips. Emma's eyes narrowed. "Actually, I didn't tell you because I thought you might object, and I wanted to sound out the others first, the ones who've actually made a movie before. I know it doesn't count for much, but I thought I'd pick what passes for their brains."

"The rumor is you want to make a porno flick," said Pat, cutting through the bullshit to the bottom line.

"Pat! Pat! Do me a favor, will you? I mean, *really*. Please don't underestimate me. It's true that I've made the movie more sensual. It needed that. And I've made some changes to emphasize the obsessional aspect of Tony's feelings for Melissa . . . but that's it. I don't think you should be overreacting like this. Why don't you sit down and relax?"

Pat didn't want to sit down. She wanted to find out what was going down. Something was. From the moment the bombshell had been dropped that Emma had gotten the Cosmos job, Pat's antennae had been twitching like crazy. She had seen the vicious side of the English girl, and she knew that Emma hated Tony, and disliked her. Now she was taking a personal interest in *Malibu* to the extent that she was actually fiddling around with the script. She must have a billion more important things to do in her new job. The whole thing was deeply sinister. She was hotting up the sex —between Tony Valentino and the nympho star he'd been involved with while Pat's relationship with him had been on hiatus. Pat couldn't avoid the bizarre feeling that this was personal, that the entire movie, the script, the casting, the weird choice of Emma to run Cosmos, were all part of a plot to drive her mad. Of course, she also realized that was impossible. The movie would cost twenty million bucks minimum. Nobody would risk that kind of cash to work off private grudges. Anyway, this was Latham's show. He was first and foremost a businessman. Although he had reason to hate her, he had seemed to love her, and the fact that he had kept her on the picture was a powerful indicator of the respect he felt for her. Then there was Latham and Tony. Tony had saved Latham's life. That would count for something when the chips were down, if it ever got that far.

Despite all that, Pat knew she was going to be baited. It had started already. The script changes were part of it. Later it could get worse. But she was in a tricky position. How did you object to something as nebulous as love scenes without sounding like some souped-up Jerry Falwell? She needed to know where she stood.

"Just how strong are the new scenes?" she said.

Emma smiled. She'd been waiting for that one.

"Let's just say that nobody is going to ask 'Where's the beef?' " She paused. "Of course, it may be that you won't feel up to directing them, Pat. That's what I was worried about. That's part of the reason you were momentarily 'out of the loop,' or whatever it was you felt out of. I mean, given that you . . . and Tony . . . and Tony . . . and Melissa . . ." She stopped. She tapped with her pencil on the leather of the desk. "I had hoped," she continued, "that we'd all be able to rise above personal differences and difficulties, but if there are going to be problems, I think we should confront them now."

"Listen, I can handle personalities," barked Pat. "What I want to know is who's directing this movie. Me or you?"

"You or I," said Emma, congenitally unable to ignore bad grammar. "You're the director, Pat. But you direct my script." There was steel in her words.

"And what happens when we disagree?"

"It's Frank Sinatra time. We do it my way."

Pat was furious. Her voice quivered as she spoke.

"Listen, Emma, I'm not a grip or a gofer on this show. I'm the director. Okay, so I'm not the most experienced person in the world and I believe in teamwork and all that stuff, but I'm not going to be your servant on this thing. I have artistic control or I walk, understand? So can the Harry Cohn line and start learning a little civility. You're a woman, remember, not Genghis fucking Khan."

Emma's eyes narrowed.

"Let's get one thing straight," she snarled. "This is a new-style studio, but I'm going to run it the old-fashioned way, as a medieval kingdom, and you can like it or you can lump it. I'm sure," she sneered, "that there are studios all over town just dying to pick up a box-office legend like you. Be my guest. Give them a try. Go across the street. It'll take you a couple of years to find an agent, let alone a job."

Pat jumped up. That was it. She was history. The movie wasn't worth it. She'd nearly betrayed Alabama to do it. Now she was being manipulated by a psychopath. Okay, she had wanted it desperately. She still did. But there were limits. They had been reached. As far as she was concerned, it was over.

"You go, Tony goes," said Emma Guinness.

Pat stopped in her tracks, but her mind whirred on. At the very last minute, the Guinness bitch had raised the stakes. Tony was apparently tied to her deal. In her mind she could see his stricken face. Pat might want this movie, but Tony would sacrifice his life for it. Pat knew that. So, apparently, did Emma. If she walked out of the door, she would not only be destroying her own embryonic movie career, she would be callously aborting Tony's. She loved him. Hell, she wanted to marry him. Could she stamp on his dreams to satisfy her self-respect? What would he think of her if she did that? What would he feel about her if she didn't? Carrots and sticks filled her head. She grabbed at her one lifeline. It was time to bring Latham into the equation. He had wanted her on this movie. He had made a deal and he hadn't broken it, despite her diatribe against him at the Getty. They had an unwritten contract, signed by bodies in the oldest agreement of all. She wasn't particularly proud of it, but she didn't regret it. Especially now.

Yes, Latham was her trump card. The moment had arrived. There was no question. This was the time to play it.

Pat walked back to the desk. She sat down, folded her arms in her lap, and said quietly, "I think we should discuss what you have just said with Dick Latham."

"Do you?" said Emma Guinness. "So do I."

Her face was wreathed in a horrible smile that turned Pat's stomach. It wasn't the response she'd expected. She'd imagined that Emma had been indulging in a personal power trip and that the mere mention of the Latham name would bring her to heel. It hadn't had that effect. Apparently Emma knew something that Pat didn't.

Emma pushed a button on the intercom.

"Get me Latham," she said, and the absence of the prefix "Mr." was the most worrying development of all.

Latham's voice came over the intercom quickly. Too quickly. Usually, he would have kept her waiting for a minute or two behind the secretary wall.

"Yes, Emma?" His voice sounded strange.

"Listen, Dick, I've got Pat in my office. I just wanted to get something clarified, and she's listening in right now. Do I have complete control of this thing—hire and fire, everything? Can I replace Tony and Pat and deal with any legal problems along the line, all on my own say-so? Can you confirm it so that she can hear?"

She beamed across the desk. She wasn't asking a question. She was giving a demonstration.

"I hope that won't be necessary, Emma," said Dick Latham in a distant voice. "I hope Pat will see things your way, but yes, you have complete control. Cosmos is your baby. Whatever you decide will have my complete support. My votes are your votes. You have my word on that."

"Thank you, Dick." She flicked a switch and cut him off without bothering to say good-bye.

She leered at Pat, her eyes gleaming with pleasure at the demonstration of her awesome power.

"So, Pat Parker, it's make-your-mind-up time," she said.

It was. Pat tried to understand the extraordinary conversation she'd just heard. Latham had come across like a Guinness lapdog. It was the most bizarre thing she'd ever witnessed. What on earth had happened to him? But there wasn't time for that sort of speculation. The fact was that her trump had been effortlessly trumped. It was down to her. It was down to this. Could she destroy Tony's dream for a matter of her own personal principle? The answer was quite simple. No. She couldn't. She loved him too much. He wanted too much. There was only one thing to be done with her pride. She must swallow it, even if it choked her.

"I'll direct on your terms," she said.

SEVENTEEN

Pat buried her head in the towel and shifted around in the sand as she tried to get comfortable in the ninety-degree heat. She'd felt like Zuma, and boy had she gotten it. This wasn't the sophisticated dunes of Broad Beach or the semiprivate sands of the Colony. This was Togetherness, Love, and the Beach Boys in a Coppertone plastic paradise of hard young bodies and the dreams of teenage queens. All around, beachland throbbed. Bats whacked against rubber balls, Frisbees skimmed the hot sand, and rock blared from ghetto blasters as the Angelenos enjoyed their escape from the sticky city. Beside her, Tony Valentino screwed up his eyes as he read the script. From time to time Pat noticed him wince.

"What do you think?"

"It's a great part. Could be a neat movie. It's just the sex bits. They're porno. Hard, not soft."

"We can tone them down. Words mean nothing in a visual medium," said Pat with a bravado she didn't feel. She agreed with Tony. *Malibu* was a fascinating study in obsession. The characters were the plot. It explored the neurosis called "love" in a spellbinding way. But the sex was true blue. For years Hollywood had been flirting with the idea of hard core with name stars, and the best that it had managed was the watered-down *9½ Weeks*. Well, *Malibu* was straight up and there was little or nothing Pat could do about it. The day before she had surrendered to Emma Guinness, and a foot or two away, his bronzed body slicked with oil in the bright sun, was the gorgeous reason. The fact that her gut instinct told her the movie would make him a star was both the good and the bad news. The question on her mind was this. How the hell would she be able to direct the sex scenes that Emma had dreamed up?

"But how much *can* you change if Latham told you both that Emma has total control?" said Tony. "I wonder how the hell she conned him. It's funny, I thought the guy was tough. I thought he was brutal, but wise. But he's a fool, and a weak one. Guinness has hung him out to dry."

He was puzzled. Latham had surprised him. It seemed as if he'd undergone a dramatic character change. It was difficult to explain.

"It's not going to be easy to handle this," said Tony.

"I expect Melissa will find it easy enough to handle."

Pat wanted to bite off her tongue. She hadn't meant to say that, but she had a lot on her mind. They were back together again. The past, however, didn't vanish overnight. They hadn't discussed Melissa Wayne, but Pat and the rest of Hollywood knew they'd had an affair. How had it ended? Hell, *had* it ended? There were unanswered questions and now the script called for on-screen reincarnation of the off-screen lust. If he had been the boy next door, Tony and she would have spent the rest of their lives talking about it, *communicating*, sharing their feelings in the way that was universally supposed to be healthy. But Tony had never lived next door to anybody. He came from some Spockian planet. The normal rules didn't apply to him. It was a reason to love him.

"How will *you* handle it?" He threw her remark right back at her. If they were to survive the Guinness/Wayne assault, it would have to be together. If they were divided at this early stage, they would fall fast.

"I'm a big girl," said Pat, feeling like a little one. "It's only acting. I'm not a popcorn muncher from Peoria who thinks it's real. Kissing someone for twenty-six takes before breakfast isn't fun. It's work."

"Kissing isn't the problem," said Tony, throwing the script down onto the sand to the envious glances of half a dozen Valley girls. "Emma is. Melissa is."

"You worried she'll try her famous let's-forget-the-acting routine?"

He didn't answer. He remembered the Wayne body draped over the bed while he used it for his angry pleasure. He had been in control then. He wasn't now. This wasn't his show, and, despite her title, it wasn't Pat's either. The movie belonged to the only two women in the world who had reason to hate him.

Pat sat up. "I've got a great idea." She laughed. "Actresses always want to direct. Melissa and I could swap. That way you'd get to do all those dirty things with *me*."

He smiled at her gallant attempt to lighten up. He touched her shoulder, letting his finger rest on the oiled skin, tracing a *P* on the firm flesh.

"We ought to be working," he said. "I should be learning lines. You should be scouting locations. What the hell are we doing on the goddamn beach?"

"I love you," she said.

"I love you back."

"You send my love back?"

It was their joke. She rolled over to be closer to him. She could smell him, and he smelled so masculine, as if his body contained all the strength in the world. She wanted to lick it, to taste the saltiness of him. She did.

"Hey, this is a public beach."

"There's no rule against eating," said Pat, her voice soft and silky.

"Oh, yes there is," he said. A few feet away a trio of tanned teenagers were giggling at them.

Pat stared up at the brilliant sun. It was the lull before the storm. Yes, she should be working, but work would be her life for the next year, and there would be no fun in it, only blood, toil, sweat, and tears. She had come here with Tony today because in her heart she knew it would be their last togetherness. Soon they would be on the set, buffeted by storms and the raging sea and all the perils of the celluloid deep. They might not survive it. At least they would be able to look back to this day, and remember when life had been simple—suntan oil, hot dogs, cold Cokes—with the low surf rasping at the beach and kids all around who didn't know the meaning of care. She smiled to herself. They were the director and the star of a major studio movie. There wasn't a person on the sand who wouldn't have traded places with them. Yet she envied *them*, their simplicity, their freedom, the security of their tomorrows. The dice man, as usual, was dealing out his paradoxes and his oxymorons. The failures were happy. The successful were miserable in the prison of their fame. Why not, then, try to fail? Why, then, try to succeed? There was no sense in the conundrum. Life, as always, hoarded its mysteries and defied those who sought to understand it.

"I wonder if Alabama can see us now, and King," she said, and her voice caught in her throat as she remembered them.

"Alabama'll be too busy sampling the cold Mexican in heaven," Tony laughed.

But it seemed that he was wrong. The portable cellular telephone was ringing in Pat's Mark Cross tote bag, and when she picked it up the voice on the line was quite clear.

"Pat Parker? This is Pete Withers. I'm an attorney at Withers, Salisbury, Caldwell, and Carruthers. I wanted to talk to you about Mr. Ben Alabama's will."

"His *will?*" said Pat.

"Yes, it seems that he has appointed you the sole beneficiary of his estate, and the curator of his entire photographic legacy. I think we should meet as soon as possible," said the man called Withers.

Pat's mouth was wide open, but she managed to make it work.

"I think we should," she said.

Tommy Havers paced up and down on the carpet of Latham's study.

"I don't think Mary Grossman is up to the job at *New Celebrity*," he said. "Maybe we should try to poach Tina Brown from *Vanity Fair*, or get Emma Soames to come over from London. We'll be okay for an issue or two, but then it'll start to unravel."

Dick Latham waved away the worries as if they were of no account. Havers looked at him, astounded. This was his *baby*. The magazine had topped their conversations for the last year and a half.

"What have the police got on the Alabama arson thing?" he asked abruptly.

Havers shifted gears. He appeared distracted. A sixth sense told him that his boss was losing it. That mattered. If the business started to slide, *he* would be blamed for it.

"Oh, I don't know. Let me think . . . oh yes, the police say it was premeditated. They've got the prints of the suspect. And they think he was driving some high-end sports car. There were tire marks on the gravel. They've got casts. They seem to think it was a Porsche."

"One or two of those in L.A. County," said Latham.

"Only one guy's prints on the gas can, though," said Havers.

He was impatient. He wanted to get on. There were important things on the agenda, like Cosmos and the behavior of the volatile Emma Guinness in the preproduction of its first vital movie.

"They can hardly fingerprint everyone with a Porsche, can they?" said Latham. He didn't sound very sure about that.

"Hardly," agreed Havers. "I wonder if Alabama was really a target or whether it was just some well-heeled fruitcake who likes to start fires."

"I'll buy the nut theory," said Latham. "It's safe to do that in California."

"Speaking of which," said Havers. "Emma Guinness has got them all bobbing like corks over at Cosmos. She's spent her first five days rewriting the *Malibu* script, for God's sake, as if there wasn't anything more important to do. Turned it into an haute-porn skin flick, by all accounts. The only good news is that Wayne's thrilled. Maybe that's a clever move. Parker and Valentino aren't exactly Fellini and Cruise. If the movie opens, it'll be because of Melissa."

"How are Parker and Valentino taking it? I mean, you know, they're an item."

"Who cares?" said Havers. "Let 'em walk if they don't like it. They need the movie. The movie doesn't need them."

"As Alabama's heir, Pat Parker doesn't need anybody," said Latham shortly. She had become rich overnight. People like Havers underestimated the power of serious money. Those like Latham, who had it, didn't.

"No, she's staying put. Her guy's got stars in his eyes, and she's hot for him. And Cosmos is putting up twenty million to finance her directing debut. That's a lot of Alabama prints on the block at Sotheby's and Christie's. She's not going anywhere . . . unless she gets pushed."

Havers sounded hopeful. He didn't know much about the making of movies but, like the business pro he was, he was learning fast. People were telling him things. The cognoscenti agreed that if the movie was to have a chance in hell, the clever move would be to ditch the unknowns.

"Don't underestimate her, Tommy," said Latham. His voice was gentler now. "She's tough, and she has more talent than you think. Valentino, too. He's got what it takes."

"Yeah, and he saved your life." Havers, the perennial servant, sensed a new weakness in his usually masterful master. It encouraged him to live dangerously.

"That's not the point," snapped Latham. "The guy can act. He's got the X factor. I'm surprised you can't see it, but then it's not exactly a profit-and-loss statement, so I suppose you can't be expected to. Tony's an original. He doesn't give a damn about other people, and he's motivated. When people cross him, they get to see the terror of his ways. In fact," mused Dick Latham, "he rather reminds me of myself."

Emma Guinness erupted onto the tangled chaos of the set like a hurricane hammering into the Gulf Coast. Secretaries, personal assistants, and junior studio executives flew about in her wake. They scribbled as they half walked, half ran, trying desperately to pick up the pearls she was unloading before the swine.

"I want the studio lease deal with Universal tied up tight as a bondage freak, okay? Tell the lawyers they're history if there's an 'out.' Somebody write it, I'll sign it, if anybody *can* write these days. I know the telephone murdered word ability. Maybe the fax'll kiss it to life."

"What's the news on the Malibu site?" dared a lowly assistant.

"Shit, I don't know. They just buried the old fart who kyboshed it. The least we can do is stick a sound stage over his grave. Beats rosemary's for remembrance. But that's a Latham thing. Depends on whether or not he's got the nuts for a fight."

The underlings exchanged glances as they scurried along. Guinness was flying high indeed if she could afford shots at the boss of bosses. How soon would it be before flight turned into a free fall? Not long, was the collective prayer.

"I don't want there to be *any* problems with the studio space. We're trying to make a sodding movie here, and I don't want any pissing around. Understood?"

They got the message, but only just. The plummy Guinness vowels and the odd British usage posed problems for Southern California shorthand on the run.

Emma jumped over the wires that ran like varicose veins across the floor, dodged the boom microphones and the camera tracks for the dolly shots, sped past the wardrobe people and the makeup crowd. She headed for the middle of the set, toward the vast double bed. When she reached it, she stopped.

"Christ!" she said. "These are nylon sheets."

"No, they're not *actually* nylon, they're a combination . . ."

"Lose them," barked Emma, cutting off the assistant executive producer as if he were corn in a field. "When I say Pratesi," she thundered, "I *mean* it. And when I say fired I mean that too."

They cowered around her. There was no resistance. It wasn't just the money and the mortgages, the mistresses and the Maseratis. It was more than that. She had hire-and-fire ability for sure, but she had power over people because, ultimately, she was so bright, and so vicious and so utterly convinced she was right. To stand up to her was to be humiliated. She was a masochist's dream, a sadist's worst nightmare. Compared to Emma Guinness, Elm Street's Freddy Kreuger was a friendly old man.

A couple of grips stripped the bed.

"For God's sake, wash your horrid hands before you put the Pratesis on," she grumbled at the gofers. "I don't want my star catching communicable diseases."

Even the surly union members took it, and they weren't in the taking business. On any other set that remark would have closed down the picture.

"Where's Melissa?"

"I'm right here," said a voice from behind her. Melissa Wayne was indeed there. She was undressed to kill. The outsize Ralph Lauren Polo dressing gown was half-undone. Her naked breasts poked provocatively from it. She wore plain white cotton bikini briefs, and nothing else at all but a look of steamy expectation.

"How clever of you, Emma," she pouted, "to run a love scene with the opening credits."

"Well, you look just *wonderful*, Melissa. If I was a fella I'd be in love. Listen, I think I'm in love anyway."

Emma smiled a greasy smile at her secret ally. Sex objects weren't fussy about the gender or the species of their compliments sources. Animals would do. Plants at a push.

"Well, thank you, ma'am," simpered Melissa. "And where, I wonder, is my lover of the morning?" she added.

"Thanking God for his good luck?" joked Emma.

"I'm not so sure." Melissa smiled. The conspirators laughed. In a few moments, when the cameras began to roll, a start would be made on the dish of revenge.

"Okay," said Pat Parker. "We'd better go through this."

She had arrived unnoticed, and it was clear that she wasn't in small-talking mood. She looked pale, short of sleep, and her let's-get-on-with-it manner didn't hide the anxiety that wrapped her like an aura.

"I think," said Melissa, "that we ought to wait for the other half of the love unit. Otherwise, you'll only have to repeat yourself."

Her words were innocent. Her tone wasn't. The "love unit" was invested with the most lascivious connotations.

"Somebody go tell Valentino he's late," barked Emma.

"Late for love," giggled Melissa.

They stood in silence as a minion went to fetch the star. Then Tony was threading his way across the set in a dark red silk dressing gown.

"Hi," he said to no one in particular, tossing his head in the air with a nonchalance Pat knew he didn't feel.

"Well, good *morning*, Tony," purred Melissa. The catlike sound was leopard rather than Siamese.

Pat started talking fast.

"Okay, as you know from the script, this is an under-the-credits shot. The idea is to set the scene for the movie's sensual/obsessional themes. We want the audience to know there's going to be lots more where this came from. Isn't that right, Emma?"

"Oh, yes, that's right. Lots, lots more."

Pat winced at the delight in Emma's voice. "Of course, the usual view is that you introduce the characters before you have them make love, on the principle that sex between strangers is either dull, pornography, or both. However, on *this* occasion Emma's script calls for the ignoring of that particular convention. Ours," she added sarcastically, "not to reason why."

"Ours but to do and die . . . until we drop." Melissa Wayne laughed, demonstrating a surprising knowledge of Tennyson's poem.

"So you start on the floor, and we pan across the room before hitting some close-ups. Then Tony picks Melissa up, walks across to the bed, and then there's the bed bit."

Pat was aware that her bare description hardly did the scene its full erotic justice. She couldn't bring herself to go into more detail.

The silence was expectant. They wanted more direction. They were waiting for her to spell it out.

"The script is quite explicit. I know you've all read it. So perhaps I can leave the mechanics up to you two, and concentrate on the photography and the lighting. Obviously, if there's anything that needs to be changed, I can help with that as we go along," said Pat defensively.

"I like to be directed all the way. I find it helpful. When I'm fucking in public, I need feedback," said Melissa, definitely.

"We're *not* fucking. We're acting," said Tony, angrily.

"Sometimes I get confused between the two," said Melissa, totally unfazed by his irritation. A nearby cameraman suppressed a laugh.

"It was a *façon de parler*," said Emma. "That's French for a manner of speaking." She smiled a superior smile. Melissa smiled back at her.

Melissa and she were singing in unison. It was turning out far better than she had dreamed it could be. Both Pat and Tony looked furious, miserable, and, best of all, totally impotent.

"Is it direction you're after, or a congratulatory running commentary?" Pat sneered at Melissa.

"If you can't handle the one, the other will do," said Melissa wickedly.

"Let's get the hell on with it," said Tony.

"Isn't he romantic?" Melissa giggled. "Thank God I'm a pro."

"You said it," growled Pat.

"Do we need all these people around?" said Emma. She didn't want Melissa to be inhibited.

"No, don't worry, it's fine. I'm not ashamed of my body. If they're going to see it on Main Street, why shouldn't the guys here? We'll save the closed sets for later when it gets a bit more intense."

As if to emphasize her point, she threw back her shoulders and dropped the terrycloth robe on the floor. Her breasts stood there, pointing straight out at the eyes that ate them, in the way the breasts were supposed to do, but never did. It was like a party trick—clever, unexpected, and performed with panache.

Pat couldn't help watching them. Emma gazed in open admiration at the twin weapons of the war that she and the star were waging.

Tony took a deep breath. In the past he had used Melissa Wayne as mercilessly as she would have used him, if she'd been able to get away with it. He didn't feel guilty. She was diamond tough, and the bars of Hollywood were full of beaten-down guys with angel faces who'd been broken on the wheel of her capricious lust. Body dancing with Melissa Wayne was a cardinal terror for all but the very brave. He'd not only survived it, he'd enjoyed it, and best of all had been watching the biter bitten. Now the roles were reversed. She was the one with the power. Only by giving up his dream could he deprive her of it. But still he had feelings, and the seminaked Melissa Wayne had stirred them up as she had intended.

No man could remain neutral in the presence of her beauty. The script called for their lovemaking. Across the short space that divided them, he could all but smell her sex. He would have to lose himself in the role as he always did. To seem to love it, he would have to live it. To feel it, he would have to be it. It was his method. It was what he would do now. Pat Parker would have to be banished from his mind. Emma Guinness must disappear. Then there would be only the heat of bodies beneath the hot lights, and the intensity that made his acting so much more real than dull reality.

He, too, looked at the breasts on which Pat and Emma focused.

"It's rude to stare," said Melissa flirtatiously.

Pat walked across the set. "I want you to start here," she lied. "There are three camera angles. Directly above, left oblique, right oblique. We start from above, and that should be Tony on top, naked butt please, with Melissa's legs intertwined in his. Forget the soundtrack, that's heavy classical or some shit. You're kissing passionately, openmouthed with lots of tongue action for the side cameras to catch. I want mouth moisture, lots of it. If you want, that can be artificial. Somebody sponge down Tony's back for the sweat."

"Don't worry, I'll make him sweat. I've done it before," said Melissa.

Pat groaned inside. "*Please* try to remember we're making a movie here," she said sharply.

"I *have* made the odd one or two before," said Melissa, "which is more than can be said about you."

Tony slipped the dressing gown off his shoulders, letting it hang around his belt. A production assistant sponged his back. Pat signaled for lights. The floods came on, bathing the set in instant heat. Pat and Emma retreated to the relative darkness at the edge of the set, leaving the two "lovers" alone.

"I'm looking forward to this," whispered Melissa. "And to the next time."

She sat down on the floor and watched him. He would be new to doing this in public. However good he was, and she sensed he would be very good, it would not be easy for him. He reached for the knot of his belt, and he stared away into space as he undid it. He flung the robe away out of camera. He was naked. Melissa's eyes feasted on her target. It would be her barometer. She had one purpose in this scene, one single purpose in life. She had to excite it, make it firm, make it strong, make it want her as she already wanted it. She focused in on her objective, willing it to be, to become, to live and to love her, and her hands reached for the elastic of her panties. Convention dictated that she keep them on, that her costar's body be draped carefully over her to hide the fact that she was wearing them. But that wasn't the Wayne way. Real was real, and fake was fake, and flesh must touch if hearts were to beat faster. It was the surefire way to turn the box-office cash flow from a trickle to a raging river. It had worked before. It would work again.

She pushed her panties down her legs and kicked them free. She lay back on the floor, her legs tantalizing inches apart, the perfect triangle of blond pubic hairs framing delicate lips of pink.

"Okay, Tony, get into position, please." Pat's voice was strained as she tried desperately to be businesslike.

He lowered himself onto her, and she thrust up to meet him. The warmth of her downy hair pushed gratefully against his still sleeping flesh. He shuddered at the tender touch of her as he was supposed to. She reached up, putting her arms around his neck, and drew him in toward her, capturing him in the closeness trap where minds deferred to bodies and the will was weak. The scent of her wrapped him. She was so soft and yielding, so firm in her purpose. The cameras were not yet rolling and already she was making love to him, warming him up, preparing him for what was to come.

"Action!" shouted Pat Parker, and Melissa Wayne's lips rose up to feast from his.

Pat began to sweat. She could feel the wetness beneath her arms, and it wasn't the arc lights that were causing it. It was what they were bathing. On one level this was just a kiss. It was neither the first nor the last of a billion such celluloid lip meetings, and it should have had about as much significance as an arms control chat in Geneva. Except that this was Tony, and that was Melissa, and the only thing parting the bits of them that rubbed together was skin. Pat looked away. She looked back. She fought back the clammy nausea that gripped her. It had hardly started, and she herself had called for "action." Now all she wanted to do was to scream "Cut." She tried to calm down. She was the director. She had to think like a lens. She did it all the time in photography. Usually it was second nature to her. It wasn't now. She fought to be objective. Was the kiss too long, too deep, too open, too closed? Hell, it was perfect. It was perfect hell. The on-camera lovers meant it. Tony was eating Melissa. She was devouring him. They were as close as two pages of a scented letter in an envelope, and it was as welcome to Pat Parker as a tooth in a pumpkin pie.

It was Melissa who came up for air.

"How are we doing?" she murmured through soaking, bruised lips.

Melissa smiled across at Pat. She pouted up at Tony, his face inches from hers. All her plans were working. God, it was wonderful. Tony was entering into the spirit of the love scene as she had hoped he would, and the damage was all over the face of the director. The mouth action was the hors d'oeuvre, but it hadn't existed in isolation. The lower half of her body had been wriggling and writhing with snakelike sensuality. Already it was having its inevitable effect on the flesh and blood of the boy she hated to love. For now it was invisible. Soon it wouldn't be. In a few minutes they would all know that he wanted her. They would be able to see his lust. Pat Parker would have to watch the undeniable evidence of his desire.

How were they doing? Melissa had asked.

"Fine," mumbled Pat. "Are you okay, Tony?" she said, aware that it was a ridiculous question. She desperately needed some warm response from him. "I'm suffering for my art"; "I still love you"; "The cow's got bad breath"—any or all of those would have been music to her ears.

"Maybe we should get on with the scene," he answered coldly, after a long pause. He hated being brought back from the super-reality of his illusion. That was why the stage was so wonderful. There, he was on his own in his private make-believe world. The critics came before and after, never during the performance. But he could sense Pat's pain. It filled the set. He should care about it, but he couldn't because this was work. This was his art. The only thing that mattered was that it be good. Anything else was a distraction. In the story he was a lover obsessed with a legend. That meant for now, for these brief moments, he *was* that person. He wanted to get back to Melissa's body. He wanted to drown in the juices of Melissa's love. The fact that he despised her in real life was a dangerous, art-crippling thought. As such, he fought to banish it from his mind.

Pat heard what he said. She understood him well enough to read between the lines. She knew what he was thinking, and it hurt like hell. But there was no going back. There was only one thing she could possibly do, and so she did it.

"Okay, let's go to take two," she said.

"What a *terrific* idea," said Emma Guinness from somewhere behind her back.

Pat Parker stormed into the Winnebago, slamming the door behind her. Tony, sitting at the dressing table, wiping makeup from his face, spun around.

"You fuck rat," she shouted. "You were making love to her."

"Don't give me that shit, I was acting . . ."

"Acting. You weren't acting. I could *see* you weren't acting. Jesus, you had a . . . everyone could see it. I mean, Tony, really . . ."

He jumped up. "I was acting, damn it. Don't do this, Pat. Don't do this to me. Don't do this to yourself. You're playing into their hands. Emma wants it. Melissa wants it. Don't give it to them on a plate."

"It's you. Hell, it's *you*, Tony. Don't lie to me. She was turning you on out there. Admit it. Go on, admit it."

"It doesn't mean anything, Pat. It was nothing." He knew he wasn't giving her the answer she wanted, and he couldn't, because her accusation was true. He was human. It was blood that ran in his veins, not water. Nobody could have carried off a scene with Melissa Wayne and remained sexually neutral. Yes, she had turned him on. She understood a man's wiring. She had a map of the male circuitry. And that was good. So did the Melissa in the movie. It was why his fictional character had fallen for her. The scene had been real because both actors had wanted to make it real. That was the way he operated. If Pat didn't understand that about him, she understood nothing.

Neither sweet reason nor sweet charity, however, were the emotions playing stage front in Pat Parker's mind.

"It might mean nothing to you, but it means one hell of a lot to me," shouted Pat, her voice breaking. Her eyes were misty. She didn't want to cry, yet tears were close. The heat from the coupling couple had warmed the set. Okay, so it was wild footage and it would be great cinema, but it had tied Pat's stomach in knots. She hadn't had to direct, as threatened. All she'd had to do was watch, and it had been the worst ten minutes of her life so far. In vain she tried to cut herself off from reality, and to retreat into some private world of dissociation, but she hadn't pulled it off. She wasn't an introvert. She was all up front. She always had been and she always would be. Her feelings lived neither in her head nor her heart, but on her sleeve. Well, here they were—the disgust, the jealousy, the anger, and the terrible, horrible pain.

"Pat, please, try to understand . . . you know how it is, we're trying to do something big here, something important. This movie can be totally original. You've got to rise above the pettiness—you've got to."

"Don't tell me what I've got to do. I'm telling you what *you've* got to do. You've got to get the hell out of my life, forever, okay? And I mean it. I don't love you anymore. I don't even like you anymore, because you're a cheap, hustling, egotistical sex maniac. You can't love anybody because you're too in love with yourself."

"Pat, listen. Listen . . ."

But Pat wasn't in a listening mood. What she wanted was action, and not some steamy kiss. Her wild eyes searched the room. She was looking for a weapon, a missile, anything that would escalate this ridiculous word-fest to something genuinely painful. But Tony's dressing room was as bare as his soul, as sparse as his emotions. Then she saw the Sony Sports Walkman. It sat on the chair beside him. He didn't listen to music on it. He listened to himself, saying the godforsaken lines that were the only things he cared about. She bent down, scooped it up, and backed away from him. The wire was wound around it.

"Pat!"

"You fucking *bastard!*" she screamed. She whirled it around her head until it twirled in the air above her like a bright yellow bomb. He didn't duck. He wouldn't would he? Too much bloody dignity. His one concession to self-defense was to raise a halfhearted arm. It didn't stop her. She let fly. The plastic sound machine snaked through the air and whacked into his arm. Then it unhitched itself from the black lead that had held it, and sailed on to catch him a glancing blow on the side of his head above his ear. It didn't stop. It flew toward the dressing table, and made direct contact with the framed photograph that sat there, smashing it to smithereens. The girl in the picture didn't look surprised by the fate that had overtaken her. Maria Valentino was smiling a warm, open smile, full of love and tenderness, through the broken glass that now swathed her. Her beautiful face stared across the years through the devastation and seemed to be talking directly to Pat. "Don't hurt my Tony," said the deep blue eyes. "He's difficult to understand, but you must try to understand him. He's good, and he needs you. You need each other."

Pat's hand flew to her mouth.

"Oh, Tony! Oh, Tony, I'm so sorry."

He walked to the table. His eyes filled with tears. He picked up the wounded portrait, clearing away the broken glass with his fingers, and he stared into the eyes of the mother he loved so desperately. Her picture was torn, down at the bottom, near the soft hands that had so often comforted him; that had rubbed his back to send him to sleep as a child; that had bathed his wounds and held him close when he needed the love he could accept from no one else. A tear squeezed out, a tear for the memories and all the love that had gone unspoken until the dread night when it was too late. Now, there was just his mother's picture, and out there, somewhere in the still heavens, her spirit was watching over him as it always had.

He turned to Pat, and his face was full of sorrow. He wasn't angry. On his grief-savaged face were all the regrets of all the children through eternal time. Why, when you loved so much, were the words so difficult to say? Why, when it was too late, was it so easy and so painful to feel? There were no answers to the past, only ill-learned lessons for the future, but in the present there were the tears of regret that streamed down the cheeks of Tony Valentino. His shoulders crumpled. He sat down hard in the chair, and he buried his head in his hands. From between them came the sound of his sobs.

For a brief moment Pat stared at him in wide-eyed shock. It was a moment of total revelation. She was looking through a window into Tony's soul. Now at last she knew what it was she wanted. She wanted this, the quivering heart of him wrapped in the beautiful, heartless package that was all he would allow the silly world to see. On the table lay the photograph of the only person he had genuinely loved, and Pat knew with a terrible certainty that she wanted to be her replacement more than she wanted life itself. Light-years ago, Pat had been angry with him. Now she adored him with a greater intensity than she had dreamed possible. She knelt down beside him, and she held him tight in her arms as his mother would have held him. She drew him close, to squeeze out the sorrow, and her fingers reached up to caress his neck, to give comfort, to say sorry.

"I love you, Tony," she whispered. "Oh, my God, I love you so much."

* * *

"I need to talk to you."

Melissa Wayne climbed into the passenger seat of the studio golf cart and stared straight ahead. The fact that she didn't look at Tony as she spoke made two points at once. She was going to say something that was difficult to say, and she was going to say something important.

Tony Valentino took a deep breath. Off the set he didn't want to have anything to do with Melissa Wayne. She was big trouble, and any interaction at all could disturb the vital on-camera chemistry he was working so hard to get right.

"Okay," he said, without enthusiasm. "I'm going over to business affairs. Want to come for the ride?"

"I want to do it for real," said Melissa. Bushes were not things she beat about. Still, she didn't look at him.

Tony swallowed hard. He'd wondered when this was coming. He knew exactly what she meant.

"What do you mean?" he said.

"I mean on the set, making love, for real. It's the best way. It's the only way. I've done it before. It works."

She talked fast, as if afraid he'd interrupt her.

"You're joking," he said.

Now she turned toward him. He leaned over the wheel and faced her.

"No, Tony. I'm not joking. You know that. I'm serious. It's vital for the movie. It'll give it total believability. Trust me. There's no problem. We've done it before . . . and it was fun." She allowed herself a provocative half smile. Fun was what it hadn't been. It had been wild, painful, ridiculously intense, but it had never been fun. Time and again he had treated her like a slut in an alley, a shuddering, juddering stand-up trick, five bucks' worth at the most in the poor part of town. To be used like that had been a first for the movie star—a delicious, humiliating first that must and would be paid for with Tony Valentino's peace of mind.

"You're crazy," he said, and the disgust was in his voice. The old anger was building, overriding the delicate politics of the shoot. Melissa Wayne might be a famous actress, but at heart she was a two-bit nympho.

"I'm not crazy," said Melissa Wayne evenly. "I'm the star."

"Drop dead, Melissa," he said.

For a long time she looked at him, and her face ran the gamut of emotions from initial shock, through irritation, to a frighteningly self-confident calm.

"I wonder," she said at last, "just who will end up getting dropped."

"Congratulations, Tony. I saw the dailies last night. Your scene with Melissa was a blast."

Emma Guinness stood up as Tony Valentino stalked into her office. He sat down in the chair opposite her before she had a chance to offer it to him. He made no reference to her pseudocompliment. Instead, he slid his eyes up and down the cream silk coat and skirt she wore, and his expression said he'd like to throw up over it. Emma's most senior personal assistant had delivered the summons to the meeting. There had been no way to avoid the one-on-one, but he didn't have to like it.

"Which brings me to the little problem that has arisen."

She sat down again, smoothing the skirt over her fat thighs.

"It seems," she said, a smirk on her lips, "that our star is not happy. By 'our star' I mean, of course, Melissa."

Tony stared at her aggressively. He'd guessed it. Melissa had gone whining to Emma. Had she told the truth? Or had she invented some other complaint? The latter, most likely. She could hardly have gone bleating to Emma that her costar wouldn't screw her on the set. He said nothing.

"It seems that her initial enthusiasm for you has waned, if you will forgive my British understatement," said Emma carefully. "She's produced a long list of grievances ranging from . . ."—she peered down at her desk seemingly to consult some list—". . . from 'lack of professionalism,' whatever that means, to . . . to 'bad breath.' " She laughed heartily. "I guess after the kissing scene yesterday she is in a position to know about *that*, although judging from her performance, it didn't seem to put her off."

The twin spots of anger sprang up on Tony's cheeks as they were supposed to. He was a vain man, and he didn't like being made fun of. In all his life he had never been accused of anything as deeply wounding as having halitosis. It didn't matter that it wasn't true. It was the cruel falsity of the accusation that enraged him. Body odor, dandruff, greasy skin, dirty ears were things that other people had, not Tony Valentino. He didn't mind being thought a bastard, cold and aloof, mean and uncaring. They went with the turf of obsessional ambition. Supermen suffered those afflictions. Only nerds, however, had bad breath. He wouldn't deny it. That was beneath his dignity. So he glowered in silence, and he waited for the other things that he knew were coming.

"I suppose I owe it to you to let you know what else she said. It's a real litany of grievances, I'm afraid, and the bottom line is that she's badly upset. Let's see, oh, I don't know, 'ignorance of fundamental movie techniques, bad acting, lack of consideration for colleagues, unfortunate personal habits, hygiene'—that's apparently *apart* from the breath problem—and, last but not least, she said you embarrassed her dreadfully by getting . . . sort of . . . excited . . . during the lovemaking. She says that's happened before with amateurs and that it always makes her 'sick to her stomach,' yes, that was the actual expression she used."

"She wanted me to screw her for real on the set. You've heard the rumors. She has a reputation for it," Tony exploded. "I told her to forget it, and now she's come to you with all these lies."

"Ah!" said Emma Guinness, with the wisdom of the sage. "So *that*'s it, is it?" She managed to insinuate that she half believed Tony, but that there was room for doubt. "Argue your case," said her eyes.

"No way," said Valentino's. The "I don't have to explain myself to you or to anyone" was written all over his face.

"Tony, I'm not quite sure that you appreciate the situation in which I find myself," said Emma Guinness in the tones of a kindly schoolmistress addressing a dull student. "I'm trying to run a studio here, make a movie, an important one, a *vital* one. Cosmos is new. I'm new. We're both going to be judged on how this show turns out. If it's a stinker, nobody in town will want to bring their people and their scripts to us. We'll be the Mickey Mouse outfit of the minute. It'll take years to rebuild the studio's reputation . . ." She paused as if she had a lot further to go.

"So?" said Valentino rudely.

Emma smiled indulgently. *God*, she loathed him. He'd learned nothing. She had more power than the Almighty, and still he patronized her. Heavens, she wanted him. Right now she wanted to rip off his blue jeans and eat him till she was full. She wanted to drown in his wonderful breath, and experience firsthand the state of his personal hygiene. Dirty, clean, and everything in between, she wanted to taste and enjoy him, until the itch that plagued her was so well and truly scratched it would never trouble her again.

"So, as I said, I've got big problems. You know how things

work. The nearest thing to a guarantee that a picture will open is the star. That's Melissa, not you, I'm afraid. She's serious box office, and she's not happy. If she walks, we're gone. Everybody knows everything in this town. They'll be talking 'on the-set' problems. The movie could become a bomb before it ever gets made. I can't allow that to happen."

"You want me to screw her?"

Tony stuck his jaw out as he dared her to come clean. If she admitted it, at least she'd be honest. She'd also be a greasy, brown-nosed bottom dweller who was prepared to sacrifice every last principle of professionalism to the demands of turning a buck. And, not least, she'd be making a movie without Tony Valentino. Method acting had its limits.

"I'm not saying that," said Emma cunningly, as she wiggled out of his trap. "I couldn't, could I? But I'm asking you to have a little sympathy for the dilemma in which I find myself. Melissa's the star. She's unhappy with you. You're the unknown. You get the drift?"

"You're going to fire me because some slut tells you lies?"

"Oh, Tony, Tony, life isn't so black and white," laughed the wryly philosophical Emma. "I haven't said that . . . yet."

The "yet" came as a whiplash, and it brought Tony Valentino up short. He had retained a naïve belief in the power of truth, that right triumphed in the end over wrong. Of course, he remembered times it hadn't happened, but on the whole it did. Suddenly, it looked as if this was going to be yet another example of the exception proving the rule. His career was at stake, the shot at stardom that was as vital to him as the air he breathed and the food he ate. He was under no illusions. If they broke his contract and forced him from the film, he was finished. He knew that. Emma knew that.

"Frankly, Tony, the business people here are worried. They worry a lot about you. They worry about Pat. I can handle them, of course. They belong to me, these people, but I can't ignore what they say entirely. And it's not just the marketers and the distribution people, it's the guys at Latham Enterprises, too. Tommy Havers rings me three times a week. He wants you fired, Tony. He thinks that's the safest thing to do, and safety is all he cares about. I spend more time than I have available to spend fighting for your job in this movie, and now Melissa comes howling out of the woodwork, screaming for your blood. What do I get from you in return? I get scowls, and bad tempers, and scarcely veiled dislike. Does that sound like a fair deal to you? What would you do in my position?"

Emma sat back and watched her missiles fall on the enemy position. They were deadly accurate. It would soften him up a bit for the next assault. Emma ladled on the powerful imagery. She was his champion, fighting off the dragons to save his life, her brave sword arm seared by the flames of the filth. It should twang the heartstrings. Bullshit so often did.

"I can see you might have problems," said Tony with minimal generosity. "They don't sound quite as serious as mine."

Emma laughed to show she appreciated his scrawny olive branch. "Other people's problems seldom do," she said. She tapped a pencil on the table. She always did that before she escalated the nastiness.

"I was wondering, in view of everything, if you might find yourself able to meet Melissa halfway, if indeed it is possible to get a little bit pregnant." Again, she laughed to camouflage what she was asking. "It seemed the love scene was going so well, and that . . . to say the very least . . . you were not repulsed by it. Perhaps you could find it in your heart to indulge her, assuming, of course, that your version of her real grievance is true."

"Do you honestly think that I could do that to Pat?" snarled Tony. The disgust was back in his voice.

"Would Pat be happy to see your career go up in smoke?" said Emma.

Tony said nothing. It would certainly be a price that Pat would pay. The question was could *he* pay it. After all, *he* knew that he despised Melissa Wayne. Making love to her had about as much emotional significance for him as brushing his teeth. His problem was his pride. He couldn't stand being manipulated into doing something he didn't want to do. But on the other hand, could he live with the death of his dreams? What did you do without them? What could life mean when they were gone? When he finally got around to dying, at least he wanted to be alive.

"Because it *would* destroy your career," Emma continued. "You do *know* that, don't you? Gossip circulates like blood in Hollywood. They'll have you down as a temperamental no-talent asshole who was a giant-size pain in the butt on the set. 'He believed his own PR,' they'll say. 'He did a cheesecake spread in some magazine and thought he knew how to act. He had the good fortune to get to play opposite Melissa Wayne, who never met a man she didn't like, and he managed to turn off the turn-on queen.' Tony, you won't just be gone, you'll be gone like you'd never been."

"Yeah," said Tony Valentino. It was a time-stretching word. Hell, he needed time to think. This was all too fast. He had to talk to Pat. He had to talk again to Melissa. Something had to be done to stave off the Emma Guinness disaster scenario. Every word of her dire prediction was true. He believed it implicitly. He had one chance. This one. If he didn't take it, the only noise he would hear for the rest of his life would be the sound of doors slamming in his face. Could he do what he was being asked to do? He'd done it before. For *pleasure!* But he'd be destroying his relationship with Pat, and he'd be signing a deal with the devil that would undermine his self-respect forever. On the other hand, how would self-respect survive among the undead where he would be spending his zombie future? His marked card would probably extend to Broadway, off-Broadway, up to and beyond repertory in the Styx. He might have to give up acting altogether. He recoiled from the thought. Melissa Wayne's body formed in his mind. He could see its curves, smell its alluring smells, hear the wet noises it made when it was excited. Then the vision faded, to be replaced by Pat Parker's accusing eye, large in the viewfinder, as he betrayed her in public.

He shifted from side to side on the chair.

"Yeah, what?" said Emma. She leaned forward, gauging him, sizing him up. When was the correct moment to strike? Now? Milliseconds later? Life was timing. You had to read it right.

"You could order Melissa to back off," he said. Not for one second did he think that was a remote possibility.

Emma smiled the smile of the almost-victor. She was so nearly where she wanted to be, and still Tony Valentino had no idea of her real destination.

"I'm not sure that Melissa is the sort of person who takes orders," said Emma. Inside she was smiling. Every word of Melissa's golf-cart ultimatum had been discussed and planned by the conspirators. Melissa's goal had been Tony Valentino in flagrante delicto on screen. Emma's was slightly different.

Tony felt the cloud of gloom descend, blotting out false hope. It was true. Melissa had the ultimate power. He was being asked to sacrifice his career or his pride. Either way he would lose.

"Of course, as you say, it *would* make all sorts of difficulties for Pat," mused Emma, as if thinking aloud. "I wonder, I just wonder, if we might be able to work something out . . ."

He said nothing. He just stared at her. There was a creepy feeling at the base of his spine.

"I guess if I *really* put myself on the line, I could save you from this. I don't know . . . I could try."

She looked down at her pudgy fingers. She looked up slyly at him. "I could read the riot act to Melissa. Play hardball. Call her bluff. If I say you stay, and dare her to walk, she might not. She'd damage her own reputation if she did. Not fatally, of course, but she'd lose brownie points. And I could hang in tough with Havers, Latham, the people at Enterprises, and the turds in the basement at Cosmos. I could say, 'He stays or I go,' and see how it plays. Of course, they might get rid of *me*. I'm hardly indispensable around here. Studio bosses in this town have the life expectancy of hibiscus flowers. But I *could* try it. I *could*."

She looked out to the Hollywood Hills, a dreamy expression on her face as she went through the motions of considering the self-sacrifice.

"Of course, if I *did*," Emma continued, "I'd expect a little something in return. If not necessarily your friendship, at least your gratitude. We'd have to work very closely together to minimize the damage, and I'd have to count on your absolute support and your total loyalty. We'd have to be a team, you and I, and nobody would need to know about that. In fact it would be much better if they didn't. It would be our little secret, between you and me. I think it would even be better if Pat didn't know about it . . . or Melissa."

She looked up to see how she was doing. Had he caught the drift? Did she need to spell it out more clearly?

"What *exactly* do you mean?" said Tony Valentino. He had an overpowering sense of déjà vu. He'd been here before—in the auditorium at the Juilliard all those light-years ago. Suddenly, he could see it. It was a gigantic conspiracy. This thing in front of him had created this moment. He had imagined that he'd been running his own life, that Pat had been running hers, that Latham was in charge, that events were random. But he had been wrong. All the time, *she* had been in control. They were flies caught in the net of the web that she, the spider woman, had spun. Emma had never forgiven him for the humiliation she had suffered at his hands. Now she wanted revenge. The *New Celebrity* spread, the role in the movie, Emma's job as studio boss, the hiring of the impossibly sexual Melissa Wayne, the choice of Pat as director—all had been carefully planned. All along there had been only one objective, only one goal, only one target. Him. To save himself, he was being asked to give himself to her. It was his only way out.

Emma Guinness smiled.

"Let's just say," she drawled, "that if I put myself on the line for you, I would expect us to get to know each other very well indeed."

"What did you *say?*" said Pat, her eyes glinting with fury.

"I told her the only person she'd get to fuck her would be herself."

Pat smiled a wintry smile. She would have signed away her soul to have been there. She had never wanted to kill before. She did now. And not just Emma Guinness. There was Melissa Wayne, too.

"And the Melissa business?" she snarled.

"We didn't go into it. I think she got my message."

Pat laughed a bitter laugh.

"So it's over."

"Yeah, I guess. Either we jump, or we're pushed."

They looked at each other, and the love they were both learning to feel took the edge off the anger and the disappointment. This was where someone was supposed to say, "You know, I'm glad." But neither of them was saying it, because neither was thinking it. Disaster had struck. Denying it wouldn't help. Tony had done the good thing, the right thing, the decent thing, and it had cost him the thing he wanted most, his movie career. Pat, too, was desolate, both for him and for herself. Her one chance at directing was history, and all because of the evil of two women.

She threaded her hand into his.

"We've got each other," she said. "We wouldn't have us if you'd done what they wanted you to do."

He smiled a strange smile that almost looked like tenderness. Pat wanted him to do it again.

"Say something to me," she said.

"What?"

"Think!"

He laughed.

"I love you?"

"No!"

"I love you."

"Right second time. You've got to practice," she joked, nuzzling into him as the irritation began to fade in the reality of their new togetherness. There was a bond between them now. It was deeper than it had ever been, strengthened by the disasters they had faced, and all the future ones they would survive.

"What are we going to do, Tony?" she said. In the closeness it seemed safe to talk about the uncertainty of their future, of his future.

"Well, you'll be up to your eyeballs sorting out Alabama's estate. That has to be a job for at least ten people."

"At least we'll have all the money we could ever want."

"I'm an actor, Pat. I have to act."

It was a gentle rebuke, but already the problems were surfacing. Their love was going to be tested.

"What will you do?"

"Oh, I don't know, knock on doors, beg, plead, act somehow."

"In L.A.?" It would be where Pat was, where Alabama's estate was. But it wouldn't be where the stage jobs were. She knew that. So did he.

"In New York, I'd imagine."

She took a deep breath. It was happening already. Their ambitions would separate them physically. How long would it be before the spiritual bond weakened? Whatever the logic, in his soul Tony would blame her for this. If she hadn't existed, if *they* hadn't existed, Tony could be riding to glory by now. At the stage doors of the icy city he would remember that as the rejections piled up, and the dreams dissolved, leaving only the empty obsession behind. If Tony had traveled light, he'd still be swimming. She was the emotional baggage that had sunk him. Damn it! She wasn't going to lose him like this. Not again. There had to be a way out. How could she smash through the evil and the darkness to the light? Emma Guinness floated across her mind, a simpering, billowing target of taffeta and lace, and the bloody mist of Pat's loathing wafted like a veil before her eyes.

"Tony, we've got to *do* something. We could sue, I don't know, go to the press, anything. We can't just sit here and let them do this to us."

"Forget it," said Tony. "It's gone. Sue Cosmos? You'd need a billion dollars just to get someone to file the complaint. The media'd love it, and the joke'd be on us."

Pat walked over to him. She knelt down.

"Tony, I'm not going to let them break us up. I'm not going to let *us* blow this. I'm not. I'm not. Help me." There were tears in her eyes. She rested both hands on his knees. He covered them with his, and he tried to smile at her.

"I could sell insurance, and we could have two-point-five kids," he said. It was the best he could do.

She smiled determinedly through her misery. Her mind tumbled over itself in search of the elusive solution.

"I'd try Latham," said Tony bitterly. "I saved the asshole's life. But you heard him on the phone. He's given Cosmos to Guinness as her personal toy. I'm for sure not begging to that son of a bitch."

Pat froze as he spoke, and immediately she knew what she would do. Tony couldn't ask Dick Latham to save him. She could. After all, she had asked him for something before.

EIGHTEEN

Dick Latham strode along the beach as if getting to the far end of it would solve the problems of his life. He spoke fast, and Pat Parker had to strain to hear him as his words blew away on the desert wind.

"Don't even ask me, Pat. I had it all yesterday. Faxes, telexes, my telephone occupied all day. Emma is crazed. I don't know what Tony said to her or did to her, but she's a basket case. She wants him dead, obliterated, wiped off the face of the earth. Firing him from the movie is just an appetizer as far as she's concerned. You're a target by proxy. You're gone, too. She's adamant, and I can't change her mind. I've tried, and I can't."

He strode on, his guilty eyes avoiding Pat's suspicious ones.

"That's bullshit, Dick," exploded Pat, "and you know it. You invented Emma Guinness like some Frankenstein monster. You made her. You're responsible. You can blow her away. You owe it to the world to do that. Cosmos is your toy train set. Fire her, not us. She was a crazy choice anyway. Everyone thinks that."

"Don't tell me how to run my business!" He looked at her now. She had touched a raw nerve. Nobody told Dick Latham he'd made bad choices. Not anybody.

"I'm sorry, Dick, but I'm just so angry and so sad, not for me but for Tony. You know the story. Melissa wanted him to screw her for real on the set, and then Emma wanted body visiting rights for reining in Melissa. If you believe that, and it's true, you can't let them get away with it. It's not . . . it's not . . ." She paused. She was going to say *right*, but with the Dick Lathams of this world that wouldn't be powerful enough. "It's not professional," she spat out at last.

Latham walked on. He didn't answer her right away. He couldn't tell her that Emma owned him. There was no way even to intimate that he was a blackmail target because he was a murder suspect. Of course Pat was right. She always was. Emma was a psychopath of the most dangerous and violent kind, and she held his beating heart in the palm of her hand. The game she was playing on the set of *Malibu* wasn't just unprofessional or immoral. It was downright evil. He knew all about Tony's obsession. He'd had obsessions of his own. He knew, too, that if he didn't intervene, Valentino's life would be over. But it was Tony's life, or his. Someday there would be a way to deal with Emma Guinness. At the top of the money pile there always was. But it would take precious time, and planning, and the careful covering of tracks. Right now, he was under the gun. Emma was insisting on his written endorsement of her firepower. That, or else. He had to give her what she wanted.

"Pat, this isn't personal. This is business. I have to choose between my studio boss and the unknown director and star of *one* movie. It has to be you and Tony that go. If I fire Emma after a few days on the job, I'll pick up a reputation as a man who can't make up his mind, and a guy whose word can't be trusted. That's death in this town. In any town." He winced as he thought of it. That much was true.

"Is your reputation so important, Dick? Isn't there anything else in your life, like decency and morality, and goodness?"

Her voice was sad, accusing, as she felt her hopes slipping away from her.

He was strangely subdued when he answered her. "There was once, a long time ago," he said. "In Paris there was someone who was decency and morality and all the stuff you talk about, but I lost her. Then there was nothing but making money and building . . . building the company because it was the only thing I had that couldn't hurt me. There was no peace of mind after that, no relaxation, no enjoyment, because everything was strictly business. It was profit, not pleasure. The bottom line, not happiness. If I couldn't turn a profit on a person or a thing, I simply threw it away. Then there was you. You were different. You made me feel different. I thought I had a chance with you, Pat, but you always loved Tony." There was no accusation in his voice, just a world-weary sadness for what might have been.

"And now you're throwing me away, and Tony?"

"I guess I am."

"Don't do it, Dick. Try to do the right thing just this once."

"I can't. It's out of my control."

She was silent, angry, and miserable, but still she walked beside him on the beach.

"What are you going to do about Cosmos?" she said suddenly. "Now that Alabama's dead, are you going to try to build it in the hills after all?"

His pace slowed. "You'd fight me if I did, wouldn't you? As Alabama's heiress."

"Yes, I would. For the right reasons, *and* for the wrong ones. I'd fight you until I burned in hell."

He laughed a bitter laugh. "And you'd win," he said, "like Alabama won. I respected him, you know. I respect you."

He turned toward her, and there was longing in his eyes, longing for the sort of girl who reminded him so much of the love he'd lost. But he had to tear his eyes away. He could never have her, not after what he was about to do to her and to Tony.

"Will I have to fight you?" she said.

He paused.

"No, you won't. I *can* give you that. I'll build Cosmos in Palm Desert, just to show you I can do a decent thing."

The mini-surge of relief was lost in the flood tide of Pat's general disappointment. How could this man *be* like this? What did he mean—"I *can* give you that"? Her next words came out direct from her instinct.

"Dick . . . is there some problem . . . I mean between you and Emma?"

"What do you mean?" he shot back at her quickly, too quickly.

"I don't really know what I mean. It's just that she seems to have so much influence over you, and nobody else does . . . it's weird, because she's so wicked and you have so much power."

"When you're responsible for a company the size of mine, power is an illusion," he offered. "The business decisions make themselves."

Pat had reached the end of the line. There was nothing left. He still wanted her. That she knew. But he didn't want her enough. There was something else that he wanted, perhaps needed, more. He said it was business success. She didn't buy that. Beneath the surface, things weren't as they seemed.

She stopped and he slowed, but he kept going. Both knew it was the parting of the ways. Both knew that each shared at least some regret.

"Good-bye, Dick," she said.

"Good luck, Pat," he replied.

She took a deep breath as she watched him walk on.

In the fireproof vault of the Bank of America in Century City, the temperature was precisely seventy degrees. It had been seventy degrees for ten years now, and it always would be. Pat sat at the long table and sighed at the enormity of the task ahead of her. The entire room had been rented by Alabama, and the steel shelves had been built especially to house the collection of his lifetime's work. Here, the beauty was safe from the world; from the fire that had consumed his poor, dear body; from the mudslides in the hills; from burglars, vandals, and earthquakes. Now it was Pat's responsibility. She had to decide what to do with it. The possibilities were endless—traveling exhibitions; a permanent, revolving exhibit at some gallery in L.A. or Malibu; the sale of some or all of the work to finance the environmental causes that Alabama had loved. She couldn't begin to make a decision on what to do until she had seen exactly what was there. That meant weeks, if not months, going through the prints and the negatives; putting some order into the chaotic cataloguing system; sorting through the photographs that were a bittersweet essay on her old friend's life.

In front of her were ten hatboxes. All of them were stuffed with pictures. No wonder he had stopped. The photographic desert of his later years was more than compensated for by the unbridled fertility of his earlier ones.

She flipped the lid from one of the boxes and began to work her way through the images. These were personal photographs, Alabama's snaps, if the extraordinary originality of the composition, lighting, and point of view could be described by such a word. He had made his name as a landscape and portrait artist, but his street reportage was the equal of that of Brassaï, Lartigue, and Cartier-Bresson. No wonder the French photographers sprang to mind. Because this was Paris, Paris in the sixties, Paris at the time Alabama had taken the famous photograph of the young Dick Latham.

The relaxed faces of the boulevardiers sprang to life across the years. Man Ray kissed his wife Juliette by the banks of the Seine. Jean-Paul Sartre held hands with Simone de Beauvoir in a flower market. André Malraux and Teilhard de Chardin sat, talking earnestly, at a roadside café. Some of the faces Pat recognized instantly. With others she had to turn the prints over to see Alabama's scrawled inscriptions on the back. "Man Ray and Pat Booth looking at his prints. 1966." "Juliette, furious, May 1965." "Brigitte Bardot and Roger Vadim at La Coupole, Summer '64."

Pat sighed. This was fun. She was losing herself in the past in a wonderful escape from the pain of the present. The gaiety of the sixties was alive on the shiny surface of the prints, and she could picture her dear friend, stoked up on absinthe or Kir Royale, crouching behind the camera as he spied on the friends who would have loved him.

She picked up the photograph, and quite suddenly her world turned. Goose bumps sprang from her skin. Electric fingers probed her spine. The print swam before her eyes. Her breath caught in her throat, and shock squeezed at her neck as the flood of adrenaline welled up inside her.

Dick Latham stared at her from the distant past, but it was not Dick Latham that she was looking at. It was the girl by his side. Pat recognized her instantly. Not for one single second did she doubt who it was. The girl beside Dick Latham, smiling out at the world with a calm, self-confident loveliness, was the girl that Latham had loved. But she was also somebody else. She was the girl in the broken photograph in the trailer of Tony Valentino. She was his mother . . . and she was pregnant.

Pat's trembling fingers turned the print over. Alabama's handwriting was quite certain.

"Dick Latham and Eva Ventura," it read, "with their baby, Paris 1965."

Pat's mind was on fire. She turned the print over once again as the pieces of the puzzle slotted into place. Ventura. Ventura. Pregnant with Dick Latham's child.

Her hand shot out to the telephone on the table in front of her. Please, God, let him be in. She punched the number. Tony's voice answered.

There was no time to say hello.

"Was your mother ever called Ventura?" she shouted into the mouthpiece.

"Yes, why? She changed her name to Valentino so my father couldn't find her."

"Stay where you are! Don't move! I'm coming over," screamed Pat as she banged the telephone down.

Dear God! It was true.

Tony Valentino was Dick Latham's son.

Pat erupted into the room. She held the print in front of her, brandishing it like the ticket to heaven it was.

Tony jumped up.

"What the hell's happening . . . ?"

"Tony, omigod, Tony, look, look . . ." The excitement was all over her face.

She couldn't get it into words. There was too much to say and nowhere to start. What was the most important part? That he'd found a father? That his father was a billionaire? That his father was the sole owner of Cosmos Studios? On the helter-skelter drive from Century City she had sorted out some vague priorities. Now, confronted with the reality of Tony, all she could do was thrust the photograph into his bemused face.

He looked at it and a wave of tenderness broke across his face as he recognized his mother.

"Where did you *get* this?"

Pat fought back the excitement and the exasperation. The most important thing that had ever happened to Tony Valentino was happening right now, and he hadn't gotten to the point.

"*Look* at it, Tony, look at it!"

Once again Tony looked at the picture. He looked at his mother. He looked at the bulge in her belly that she was wearing like a badge of honor. And then he looked at Dick Latham. Still, he didn't speak, but his face was changing. The bloom and the excitement of early spring, of light, bright summer, faded through a fast fall to the depths of dead winter. Pat watched the extraordinary barometer that was his expression, and she knew she had to help him understand the importance of what she had discovered.

"Tony, turn the photograph over. Alabama took it. Look what he's written on the back." He did so in a dream, a cold, bleak dream.

Pat decided. He was in shock. His brain had gotten there, but this discovery of his father was so strong, so vast, he was unable to think and to act on the information.

Her voice was patient now, as quiet and careful as was possible when your world had changed.

"Tony, it says 'with their child.' 'With *their* child.' It's your mother and Dick Latham, with their child in Paris, in the year you were born. It's Alabama's writing. He never made mistakes. Not with his precious pictures. Don't you see? Dick Latham is your *father*. You're his son."

She wanted to reach out and touch him, but she was too fascinated by what would be the wonder of his reaction as the truth sank in at last.

He looked up from the photograph. He looked at her, and his face was curled up with a bitterness she had never seen before.

"I know," he said simply.

"You *WHAT?*"

"I know," he repeated. "I know Dick Latham's my father."

Pat's mouth was wide open. So were her eyes. She closed both as she spoke. It was she who didn't understand.

"You've always known?"

"Yes."

"But, but . . . why . . ." The words drifted away into silence. Her hands tried to do the talking. Her whole face attempted to display her disbelief.

"Why didn't I tell everyone? I'll tell you. Because I never wanted to give the bastard the pleasure of knowing he had a son." His face was brutal. The words were spitballs of scarcely suppressed rage.

Pat was coming back from the no-man's-land of numbness. There were so many questions. Which first?

But Tony was talking.

"That prick walked out on my mother. He got her pregnant, and he left her without a penny, with nowhere to live, with nowhere to go, with nobody to love her. He wrecked her life, because he's a callous, vicious, mean-spirited *bastard*. And the only thing in the world that I've got over him is that I know who he is, and he doesn't know who I am. He's never had a child. Now he's older, he probably wants one. Hell, he's picked up all the other toys along the way." Tony's fists were white. His teeth were bared. He was beginning to shake. "The only thing I regret is that I didn't let him drown. I wish I'd *drowned* him."

"No!" Pat almost shouted her denial. It wasn't like that. He had it wrong. Alabama had told her the story. So had Dick Latham. And the versions had agreed.

"What do you mean, no? What the hell do you know about it?"

"I know what Dick told me. I know what Alabama told me. Dick didn't leave your mother. She walked out on *him*. He tried to find her. She disappeared. Okay, he behaved badly and she found out, but he worshiped her. He wanted to marry her. It's why he's never been able to love anyone else. It's why he's so horrible to women."

The vehemence of her words reached him.

"What?" he said at last, doubt creeping in around the corners of the hatred.

"It's true. You trust me, don't you? I wouldn't lie to you. I love you, Tony. Latham behaved really badly to Alabama in Paris, and your mother was Alabama's friend. Then Latham was unfaithful, and so she left him. Alabama says she was the ultimate free spirit, a real child of the sixties. She wasn't impressed by all his money and his class. When he was mean and low, she just went away, and she took his baby with her. She took you with her, Tony."

"But she couldn't have done that—I mean, she had nothing. We never had anything. There were times when there wasn't enough food, and it was cold, and all those apartments and always moving . . ."

"She was proud, Tony, and she was free. Christ, can't you understand that? Where the hell do you think *you* got all that stuff from? You're constructed of it. You'd have done exactly what she did. You don't take anything from anybody. You'd die in the gutter rather than ask for help. Look at you. You're doing it now."

"I'm not," he said, and never in all the time she had known him had Pat heard him sound less convincing.

"Oh, yes, you are." She laughed as she spoke, because it was funny that he could even *think* of denying it.

"He could have found her if he'd tried. If he'd really wanted to."

"Tony, she *changed her name.* You said it yourself. She went on the run, and you ran with her. The point is she didn't want him to find her. She didn't want the millions and the houses and the neat little schools with their neat little uniforms, and all the WASP shit, and the cotillions and the cradle-to-grave security that sucks those people dry of all their feelings, and desire, and possibility. She didn't want that for you. She wanted to bring you up herself, with all her wisdom and love, and it didn't matter that it was hard and uncomfortable, because it was honest and good and right, and because it made you into what you are."

"What did it make me into?"

"The man I love," said Pat simply, and she walked over to him now and held both his hands. She lifted them up to her mouth, and he didn't resist as she kissed them. But his eyes were still haunted. It was hard to give up the hatred that had sustained you.

It was hard to acknowledge that the assumptions on which you had built your life were wrong. Inside, Tony was in turmoil. Dick Latham had been the devil of his existence. At first he had been a shadowy figure of evil, and then, through Pat and Alabama, he had taken human form. It had been difficult to deal with him as mortal man, but there had been a strange poetry in using him as he loathed him, in holding the vast secret so close to his hating heart. Then there had been the time in the sea cave, when his blood had overridden the cold command of his intellect and he had risked his life to save the man who had been so indifferent to the baby he had been. Day after day he had watched Latham, and recoiled in disgust at the similarities he shared with him, the gestures, the aloofness, the callous ambition, the need to win. They had even wanted the same woman. They had even *had* the same woman, and Tony had felt a weird ambivalence about that too, as he had seen Pat drawn to both of them by the siren call of the genes. But what now? If hatred was based on illusion, what was left to be felt?

"What should I do?" he said, when he meant, What should I feel?

"We've got to go and see Dick," said Pat. "We've got to tell him." She had never in her life felt so strongly about anything. She squeezed his hands for emphasis. "He's got to know. It'll change his life. It can change yours. He's your father, damn it. What do you think will happen to Emma Guinness now?"

The smile broke through the gaunt features, like a weak sun over hard snow.

"Yeah," he said at last, and his smile broadened. "He can throw Emma Guinness back in the shit she came from. What the hell else are fathers for?"

Dick Latham buried his head in his hands, and the sound of his sobbing filled the room. He had never cried before, but it was all so overwhelming, there could only be tears. They poured through the fingers that covered his face, and they washed him clean. It was the moment of his rebirth. He had a son. The lost had been found. The empty had been filled.

Tony Valentino stood beside his father and he was determined to hide his own emotion as Dick Latham succumbed to his. He hadn't known what he would feel at this moment, but he hadn't expected this. The incredible strength of his father's reaction proved everything that Pat had said. He had loved, all right. He had worshiped. He had adored. It was more than blood that tied them together. It was the love of his mother. What would come next? Where would the brand-new relationship lead? Already he was aware of a ridiculous sense of competition. Who would handle the scene best? Who would steal it? Jeez! He smiled through watery eyes at his cold ability to introspect at such a time. But at least he hadn't thought of the reunion as visual software for some future stage performance.

Dick Latham's shoulders heaved with the strength of his feelings. Tony could feel their intensity. There needed to be touching, but neither of them were any good at that. Despite himself, Tony's hand reached out and laid itself against the immaculate cashmere of his father's blazer. There it stayed, exerting no pressure, in an ambivalent gesture that fell short of commitment, yet was clear in its desire to comfort. Through the emotion that wracked him, Dick Latham recognized it. His hand closed over his son's, and at last he looked up at the man to whom he had given life, at the son who had saved his own.

"I can't believe it," he said, but he did. The photograph on the desk before him said it all, but it was his heart that was certain. There was no reasonable doubt, because he didn't feel any. He knew, and, now that he knew, there was a sense in which he had always known. Why had he, the cold lover of women, the hater of men, been drawn to the prickly boy with the daggers in his eyes? Because of Tony's obsession. It hung around him and Dick Latham had recognized the aura whose colors were the same as his. They had shared dark dreams of greatness; they had shared the body of the woman who had brought them together; and in their rivalry there had been the mutual respect of those who were more similar than perhaps they would have liked to be. Why else had Latham believed in the novice actor? Why else had he put him in his movie against all sense? And why, in the caves of Santa Cruz, had the boy who pretended to despise him risked his life to save him?

The sudden lump in Tony's throat stopped the sentences that were trying to form. He swallowed, but it didn't go away, and the mist in his eyes was denser now, the pressure of his fingers stronger on the shoulder of his father. There was no script for this. The writer was the heart, and words were a language it had never learned. In his mind, the thoughts tumbled over themselves. He was glad, but he was sorry. He felt warm, but there was resentment, too. Why should he be pleased to have found the man his beloved mother had spent a lifetime trying to escape? Yet, how could anyone not be moved by the moment when flesh met blood?

"I'm . . . sorry . . . that Mom wasn't here for this," he said at last, as a large tear made its escape from the corner of his eye. It scurried free, and rolled down his cheek, giving away the secret of his feelings, as tears were supposed to do.

"She changed her name," said Latham. "So I would never find her. If only you could ever know how much I loved her."

He buried his head again, and his tears came harder now as grief crept to the center of his stage, elbowing out shock and joy and hope for the future. He would never see Eva again. All the years he had hoped for that, and time had dulled the pain, but not the memory. That had remained, shrouded in glory at the altar of his heart, irreplaceable, always to be worshiped. Now she was dead, and he could never say sorry. How many times had he rehearsed the speech that would never be spoken? But she had left her legacy. Before him stood the son he had last seen in the body he'd loved. There, before him, was Alabama's evidence of his vivid memory. Here, beside him, was the living proof, the living product of the only happiness he had ever known.

Tony was being asked to forgive. He felt it strongly.

"I thought you deserted her," he said. "I didn't know she left you." He was still trying to get it straight in his mind. The earth was round, not flat. It took some believing, some getting used to.

"Yes, she left me, because I was a bastard who deserved to be left . . ." He paused. He had to know. "Did she ever talk about me? Did she ever say she loved me?"

Latham looked up. Hope bathed his face.

Slowly, Tony nodded. He wasn't certain that it was the truth, but deep down he knew it had to be. His mother's reaction had been too extreme, for too long, her silence too quiet. In this life lack of faith, the cruelty of youth, were not so rare, perhaps not so heinous. But Latham's lapse from grace had changed his mother's life, and uprooted his. Until the day of her death it had affected her. Yes, she had loved him—been obsessed by him anyway, and that was the strongest love of all.

He was aware that he was issuing absolution, and strangely touched that it should be so desperately needed. In the early days, fathers existed to look after you. But the early days had gone. In the latter years, fathers were for looking after. Had those days already arrived?

Latham stood up. The future would not be easy, but God, it would be so wonderful. He was alone no longer. He had an heir, a tough, straight, resourceful son. Perhaps it was better like this. Tony had been spared the weed-killer of Latham's overbearing personality. He had not been stunted by the emotional poison of power-seeking and moneymaking. He had been raised by an angel in poverty and physical insecurity, and he had learned strength and resilience in the hard-knocks university of life on the road. Now they stood shoulder to shoulder as equals, joined by the accident of birth, but not hampered by it. No garbage would be dished out, no shit taken. Hypocrisy could relax in this father-and-son relationship, and the innocent love of the gullible child would never founder on the disappointed rocks of grown-up judgment.

On an impulse he reached forward and hugged the man who was his child. All the warmth he had was in the embrace, and Tony, wrapped in his father's arms, felt his own respond. The spigot of tears turned with his world as he joined with the father who had made him. He began to sob, letting it all go at last. As his tears splashed down onto Dick Latham's shoulders, he was lost in an incredible joy.

It was a war council. Pat Parker sat on the edge of her chair. Tony, on red alert, sat on the corner of his father's desk. Behind it, Dick Latham was finishing the unbelievable story of Emma Guinness's blackmail.

"So you see, there was nothing I could do except the right thing, and I was too weak to do that. Whatever happened, I was going to be ruined. I was going to jail. Your careers seemed a small price to pay for avoiding that. Now, of course, it's different. I'll stand up to her, whatever the cost. She might destroy me, but I'll take her down too, and you'll be safe . . ."

He seemed happy that it had come to this. Dick Latham was about to do a fine thing. He was about to make a sacrifice, for the son he had found and the girl that his son loved. It felt extraordinarily good. Was the cliché really true? Was Schweitzer at Lambarene *really* more content than Donald Trump?

"No!" said Tony and Pat in unison. They looked at each other, and smiled at the synchronicity of their unrehearsed reaction. They had heard the story, and their minds were still whirling at the extraordinary invention of the wickedness, but at gut level they recoiled from Dick Latham's solution. Pat tried to keep her thoughts on course, to hold back the forces of incredible hatred that threatened to derail them. In her mind's eye, she could see the flames of the fire that Emma had set, see it racing down the mountain to devour the man she had admired and respected more than any other on earth. It seemed impossible that there could be a more terrible crime than that, but Emma had constructed one. She had compounded it. She had added blackmail to her disgusting, devilish stew and used casual murder as an instrument of revenge. That it was the action of a madwoman didn't lessen the crime. It was the callousness that made it so evil. Emma had no reason to hate Alabama. She had hardly known him. He had never crossed her. Yet, to avenge a personal slight, she had rubbed him out as if he were no more important than a chalk scribble on a child's blackboard. It was as forgivable as genocide. It demanded and would receive thunderbolt retribution. The only questions were when and how.

"She tape-recorded your conversation that night at La Scala," said Pat. She was thinking out loud.

"Yes, she must have wired herself for sound like in some James Bond movie."

"You could do the same," said Pat slowly.

"What do you mean?"

But Tony had gotten there.

"Yes, that's it. When you tell her you're not going to fire us from the movie; when you stand up to her and call her bluff, you could be tape-recording her reaction."

"Tapes aren't admissible evidence," said the lawyer in Dick Latham, but already he loved the idea. Emma's La Scala recording wouldn't have been admissible either, but its psychological effect on him had been devastating. Together with the other evidence, it would have given the cops the motivation to nail him to the wall. Emma Guinness was clearly unhinged. When he confronted her, she would rant and rave like a Billingsgate fishwife, as she painted her dark threats. What's more, he could arrange for Havers to be in the next room, with maybe a notary public, a cop, hell, a whole worship of bishops as witnesses. If it was handled correctly, he would be off the hook and Emma would be impaled on it.

"You're right," he said at last. "It's a wonderful idea. I guess I need a voice-activated recording device or something. I probably haven't got an employee who isn't wearing one." He laughed, but not at the thought of his wall-to-wall minions being wired for sound. He laughed because he was happy; because he was no longer alone; because he had a son.

And Pat laughed too, because she had just learned about revenge and the beauty of it; and because soon, so soon, the fiend who had burned Alabama and tried to destroy both her and Tony would be getting hers at last.

Tony laughed loudest, because he was allowed to be in love again; because the hideous girl in the hideous clothes would never again sit like a monkey on his back; because he had a father; and because now the world would get a chance to see the brilliant art he longed to show it.

It was coming together. They all knew that. They were close to an end that would also be a glorious beginning.

Emma sat across from Dick Latham where, a few hours before, Pat Parker had sat. The self-confidence oozed from her. She sat in the chair the way Victoria Brougham would have sat in it; legs wide apart, arms draped casually over its wings, her head lolling easily against its back.

"So it's 'Good-bye, Tony' and 'Good-bye, Pat,' and the only thing left to say is 'Good riddance.' "

"No, you're wrong," said Dick Latham with counterfeit innocence. "There's one more thing left to be said."

Emma smiled. She liked guessing games. She was rather good at them. She thought she might try "Congratulations." Someone like Dick Latham wouldn't be much more imaginative than that.

"Good-bye, Emma!" said Dick Latham, before she could answer him.

She laughed. "What do you mean?"

"I mean that's what's left to be said—'Good-bye, Emma.' "

Emma's laugh wasn't so relaxed now.

"Meaning?" she said, waiting for the explanation of what was clearly a ponderous Latham joke.

"Meaning," said Latham, "you're fired."

"What?"

"Fired, sacked, out of a job, out on the street. You're finished, Emma Guinness. I can't answer for the Third World, but in the first two you're history."

Her small eyes got smaller. Surely he wasn't going to take her on. Surely he wasn't fool enough to doubt her resolve. Maybe it was just a dealer's ploy to test her. Yes, that would be it. He'd try standing up to her, and then fold like a pack of cards the moment she didn't back down. How *pathetic!* Sometimes the powerful behaved like children. They held out their knuckles and they wanted them to be rapped so that they could find out where their limits lay. Oh, well, if bib-and-tuckered Dick wanted strict nanny Emma, then that was what he would get. With knobs on.

"Listen, Latham," she snapped. "I didn't burn that old fart Alabama because I liked setting fires. I did it so that you could take the rap for it. I can finger you for his murder and you know it. The can I stuck up there is locked up where you can't get at it, and when I call the cops and play them that tape, they'll want your prints, billionaire, and they'll want to know what the tires of your Porsche look like. And you won't even have time to change them, honey, 'cause unless you get very wise very fast, I'm going to give them a call right now."

"And tell them what?"

Emma looked at him like she might a beach bum. She'd never thought of Latham as being thick before, but why not? Most people were, and making megabucks didn't require intelligence, just creativity, the two being totally different things.

She put on her I'm-trying-to-say-it-as-simply-as-I-can tone and, in true English fashion, she raised her voice as if talking to a foreigner. "I'll tell them that you murdered Alabama, Dick," she said.

"But I didn't. You did."

She shook her head from side to side. Good Lord, wasn't Alzheimer's supposed to be a gradual process? "*I* know that, dear," she said in a voice dripping with patronization. "*You* know that. But the clever bit is that the *cops* won't know it."

"Oh, yes they will."

Emma opened her mouth to blast him out of his complacent idiocy. At that precise moment, he drew back the blue blazer that reminded her so much of Lord's in June.

The words died in her throat. The vision seared into her eyes. A recorder was strapped across his chest. A smile of triumph was plastered across his face.

Emma Guinness was dimly aware of a door opening at the back of the room. She was in shock, but she knew what had happened. She had walked straight into an ambush, and she would pay for her mistake with her life. In front of her was the tape recorder. Behind her, there would be witnesses.

She heard herself speak. Her own voice seemed to come from light-years away, but she had to have the answer to one question.

"Why?" she said.

"Because Tony Valentino is my son," said Dick Latham.

Emma Guinness stood on the edge of the cliff and looked down to the rocks below. Her party was over. It was time to call it a day. The pretty balloons drifted over her head among the black clouds of doom, and the bright sun laughed at the misery she would feel if feeling was possible. Even the surf sounded strange inside her head. It whooshed and crashed, but it carried a weird echo, and the gulls that soared on the Santa Ana wind were like swooping bats in the twilight of her life. Malibu mocked her. It was straight and light, so clean, crisp, and monumental as the mighty mountains met the sea in a place shorn of care and short on sorrow. Here she stood, in contrast, beaten and alone, as far from all the things she wanted as from the state of grace she would never know. The wind picked up the hem of her short skirt, the one that strangled her fulsome thighs and ringed her ample waist like a hangman's noose. Was she dressed to be killed? Who knew? Who, any longer, cared?

The surfers were riding the waves out there—sun-bleached brains directing sun-faded boards to the sun-drenched beach. How she envied them their hard bodies and their soft minds. She was hovering at the gates of hell, full to the brim with hatred and despair, while on the ocean humans like her asked only for a white-topped curler to carry them in, thought only of Coke and pizza and Mary-Lou as they planned their open jeep ride home. She took a deep breath as she blotted out the peace of Malibu. It was time for her own demons. Her head twisted from side to side, as the Wagner played. Tony Valentino was Dick Latham's son. His heir. The man who would one day own the billions. He was safe from her. He always would be. He was safe to love and be loved by Pat Parker; safe to soar above the world in the firmament of fame; safe to savor every one of the dreams he had dared to dream. His obsession was satisfied. Hers was doomed.

She laughed now, at the joke that had been her life, and the bitterness cackled in the sound. They had let her go, because they had suspected that it might end like this—suspected it and wanted it. Well, it was the least she could do. At the very end she would do something for others. Her last act would be her first generous one.

She took a step nearer to the edge, and peered down into the abyss. A hundred feet below, the rocks looked so clean. Would it hurt? Nothing could hurt more than the hurt now. Would she bump on the cliffs on the way down, breaking things, before the final oblivion? It was a thought. She ought technically to have forward momentum. Mmmm. That would entail a run before takeoff. She looked back over her shoulder across the steam-ironed lawn. Yes, that would do the trick. She walked back twenty paces toward the house. Was this the long jump or the high jump? On school sports days she had been lousy at both. She crouched down, like you did at the start of a race, and she stuck out her jaw to intimidate the competitors who weren't there. Inside her head she was waiting for the gun. But *she* was the starter, and the finisher, the producer, director, the star.

And she was also the audience. As she launched herself forward, she realized just how ridiculous she must look, especially from above. The gulls would see her short, squat frame as it tore across the lawn to the cliff edge. They would be catching the piston action of her pumping legs, watching her straggly hair floating in the warm wind, wondering at her heaving breasts as they bounced up and down on the journey to destruction. She was almost there now, and already there was no turning back. She braced herself for takeoff, the sadness gone as she immersed herself in the business of orchestrating her death. She would sail like a bird to Paradise. Arms outstretched, she would swallow dive from the cliff, dumpy and awkward no longer as she flew toward destiny. For one brief moment in time she would soar on the wings of angels in the light and wind, and then it would be over and there would be no more pain and hatred, only perfect peace.

But she hadn't factored the garden hose into her equation. Green and surreptitious, it was a snake in the grass at the edge of the bluff. Emma's speeding ankle caught it. The top half of her body rushed on. The lower half slowed dramatically. But it was too late to try again. It was far too late for that. The cliffside launch, however, was not to be a serene occasion. Instead of a graceful descent to a stylish death, Emma Guinness was doomed to go out like the sack of potatoes she had always so closely resembled.

Headfirst, tumbling over herself in an uncontrolled jumble of flailing limbs, Emma Guinness shot from the cliff. Upside down,

327 downside up, she cartwheeled through space, and the surfers
328 below turned to watch as they heard her final comment on the life
329 she'd loathed.

330 Emma's last will and testament shivered on the Santa Ana wind.

331 "Fuuuuuuuuuuuuuuuuuck!" she screamed.

EPILOGUE

The moon licked the long beach, casting silver shadows on the surf. High in the sky the stars shone in the cloudless sky, and beneath their feet the sand was cold and damp as they walked to nowhere. The mountains, massive and dark above the deserted highway, glowed in the twilight, and the rush of waves, loud on soft, serenaded the love of the lovers.

"Every time I walk here, I think of us and how we started," said Pat, slipping her hand into Tony's. She sighed against the salt breeze, in love with Malibu and the ocean and the caramel sand, in love with the man it had given her.

"It's like the edge of the world here,isn't it?" he answered. "It's so near to infinite space. You feel you're part of the universe. That day, when I came here, when you wanted to take my photograph, I needed that feeling. I was so sad, so beaten, but the beach gave me perspective. Life, death meet here. I was dying, then there was you."

"Oh, Tony." She squeezed his hand, because he so seldom said things like that.

He turned to face her, and the moonbeams illuminated a face that was already alight with love.

He stopped. She moved closer to him, and he opened his arms to take her in. There on the beach she clung to him, merging with him as life and death merged, and she wanted to stay where she was forever. There could be no happiness like this. On the sands of Malibu, her Paradise had been found, lost, and found again at last.

"I don't hate anymore," he said suddenly, as if some dark screen had been lifted from his eyes and he could see once again. "I don't hate Dick. God, there's even a part of me that loves him. I don't even hate poor Emma."

She looked up at him through misty tears of adoration. "The beach cleansed the world of her, didn't it?" she said. Pat couldn't forgive. Emma's broken body on the rocks of Point Dume had been perfect justice.

"She'd have been driven crazy by the movie's success, wouldn't she? I mean, an Oscar nomination for the picture, for you, for me. And Allison replacing Melissa. The chances of that happening were as small as finding a lost grain of sand on this beach." Tony shook his head in disbelief.

Pat laughed. "It wasn't luck," she said. "It was a little thing called talent. The world will know that the next time it happens, and the next, and the time after that . . ."

"I thought I was supposed to be the one with the ego," he said, smiling down at her. "So do I get to be the star of the next Pat Parker production?"

"No *way!*" said Pat. She had been waiting for the right time to tell him. It was now, and the moonlit Malibu beach was the perfect place. "Either he does . . . or she does." She stood back from him. She laid her hand on the flat of her stomach.

"Pat?" The question exploded from him.

"Yes," she said.

His eyes were on fire with wonder, with amazement, with delight. And he bent down, and she reached up, and his lips closed over hers, and they joined forever in the child they would share.